Published by Joseph W. Bebo
(An imprint of JWB Books Publishing)

Joseph W. Bebo
PO Box 762
Hudson, MA, 01749
Email: joewbebobooks@gmail.com

Editor: James Oliveri
Interior and Cover Design: Elyse Zielinski

Library of Congress Cataloging in –Publication Data
Joseph W. Bebo
Lamp of the Gods /Joseph Bebo – First Edition

ISBN: 978-0-9819724-6-6
1.   Techo-Thriller; Science-Fiction
Printed and bound in the United States of America

Lamp
of the
Gods

Joseph W. Bebo

Maybe nothing ever happens once and is finished,
but like ripples in a pool moves endlessly forever in time.
- Henry Thomas Peeble

Prologue

World Press News Bulletin

WPI sources have informed the bureau that Dr. Benjamin Teller, director and chief scientist for the Peeble deep-space telescope has mysteriously disappeared. Dr. Teller, who was last seen at a reception at the Boston Museum of Science, was in the final stages of building a giant telescope that would allow man to look into the farthest reaches of space, the very edge of our galaxy, as if it were right next door. Actually a massive collection of huge mirrors and telescopes of a special design and configuration invented by Dr. Teller, placed at strategic places throughout our solar system and beyond, the giant inter-galactic probe promised to usher in a whole new realm of possibilities for man's understanding of the universe.

Plagued by massive budget overruns and considerable delay due to the complex nature of the project and its use of still experimental components, it has been one of the government's biggest space efforts since JFK's pledge to land a man on the moon in the early 1960s. The project is a joint effort of several universities and corporations under the direction of StellarScope, Dr. Teller's company. When it is operational it will have the ability to view the planets of any star in our galaxy.

Much of the controversy over the project, besides its staggering cost, is the concern, although slight, that this project like many others might be usurped for military purposes. Although a telescope is not a weapon, the new technology involved has immense implications for further advancement in many technological areas. Dr. Teller is one of the few people in the country who understands this technology, so his disappearance has caused great concern.

At this point in time, there is no indication of foul play, although the authorities have little information to go on. Teller is known as a bit of an eccentric, and often wanders alone in the woods to ponder the imponderable, but he has never been known to disappear for more than a few days at a time, and has always, until now, left word of his whereabouts. All attempts to contact him have failed.

Sources at StellarScope continue to insist that the new telescope will be operational on time, but our own sources tell us that there are key components of the giant galactic telescope that are missing. The government has a lot at stake in the effort, and could face difficulties in the mid-term elections if the project fails. All efforts are being made to locate the missing scientist.

J. Banks

Chapter 1

Josh took a sip of his lukewarm coffee as he contemplated the last few years of his half-formed life. Single, in his late twenties, with a good job and a shiny new BMW, he should have been on top of the world. Instead, he had turned prematurely cynical and jaded, living in a city he didn't like at a job that kept him caged in a web of conspiracy, corruption and crime, a sordid business that filled his days and nights with the nastier side of human nature.

Joshua Banks, Josh as his friends called him, worked for a small but upcoming news agency based in Manhattan that had recently branched out into Boston and Philadelphia, and planned to open other branches on the east coast. Josh was one of the agency's best investigative reporters and had come to Boston with his boss to get the new office going.

Born with an eye for the news, Josh was brought up near Burlington, Vermont, which he thought was the biggest city in the world growing up, and it was, compared to most of the other towns in the state. Even the capital was not much more than four corners and a building with a cupola. Growing up as an only child, Josh had spent many hours by himself, most of it in his back yard hitting rocks into the field next to his house with his well-chipped baseball bat or throwing and kicking balls against some backstop.

Someone watching might have felt sorry for the apparently lonely boy – though he had plenty of friends at school - but Josh never felt alone. He was always accompanied by his thoughts, mostly about how things worked or why people acted the way they did. He had a knack for getting to the bottom of things. He just turned it around in his mind until he had it figured it out. First looking at it one way then another, magnifying each detail then pushing it out to get the bigger picture, rotating everything 180 degrees to get a different perspective. From every angle, from close and far, he would probe a situation until he owned it. He would often only realize that hours had passed when his mother called him in for dinner and it was getting too dark to see the ball or rocks he batted into the tall grass like baseballs.

After earning a degree in journalism at Boston University, where his natural analytical mind and prodigious memory stood him in good stead, he accepted a position in a news firm in New York City. He thought it would be exciting and fun, and it was at first. But after three years of objectifying everybody and everything, hunting every headline for a potential scam, scandal or conspiracy - finding intrigue and wrongdoing everywhere even in the most innocuous of stories - he started to become jaded. Everything seemed to lose its luster. Luckily his outstanding performance and growing reputation landed him a position in a more reputable news organization. Even though it wasn't the nightly news, it gave him plenty of scope and responsibility, and allowed him to pick his own stories, at least most of the time. But you couldn't do this job for long without turning sour on human motives and integrity in general.

If it wasn't for his boss, Frank Sullivan, he probably would have quit long ago. Josh had started to doubt his own motives. It was Frank who brought home to him exactly what it was he was doing. He was a beacon, a lamp in the darkness, shedding light on the real intent behind the words and actions of men in power. He was a watchdog, a bulwark against those who would rob and cheat the people they were pledged to serve. Without men like him and Frank, the weak would be at the mercy of the strong, and the blind at the mercy of those who should be leading them. Theirs was a just cause even if the day to day reality was sordid and sad. At least that's what Josh tried to convince himself of when things got tough. A transfer to Boston was a godsend, though it would be hard work. Most of his New York friends thought of Beantown as little more than a village by the sea and his favorite Red Sox a second-rate team. And they never let him hear the end of it. To Josh, however, Boston was like home, not a big pressure-cooker like Manhattan.

Now here he was, in a near empty, temporary office on the second floor of a building in some town called Wakefield, sitting on a single chair at a lone desk plucking on the keyboard of the only computer in the room. Before him was a single whiteboard on which was scrawled a collection of as yet unrelated facts and figures. His screen was filled with stacks of windows, all viewing a different web site or news page, all somehow related to the story of the missing Dr. Teller. His boss didn't have to tell him that this was probably the biggest story of the decade. He was already on the investigative trail when Frank called him from the road.

"Hi Josh," he had said, over his cell phone while driving down 93 into Boston. "You hear the latest news about Teller? There's speculation he was having an affair. I wonder if he's gone and run off with his secretary."

"I doubt it," answered Josh. "I hear he was almost obsessively dedicated to his work. It was almost a religion to him if you read any of his writings. You should see the tapes of his interviews. He sounds like some kind of prophet. No, I doubt he would just walk away from it for a fling with his secretary, not now after it's all but completed."

"I wonder. Maybe something's happened to him. Maybe he drove off a cliff somewhere in the mountains. Perhaps foul play. You've got to find out what's going on there."

"I'm on it, Frank. I've been checking every lead. I know all there is to know about this guy Teller and his project. I've been following his work closely for the past two years. What they're doing is totally incredible, makes landing a man on the moon a kindergarten game. It's not only the cost that's astounding, the science is amazingly complex. Teller's one of the few who really understands it. You should see some of the pictures they've published. Even with a small fraction of the final capabilities they're beyond belief. They'll be able to take pictures of a planet in orbit around a distant star as if they were floating a hundred feet above it. They'll be able to zoom right down on the planets of the most distance stars in our galaxy just like they had a satellite camera stationed above it. Some are even saying they could use the telescope to look back in time."

"I know, that's all well and good, but I'd like to know what's going on behind the scenes, especially now Teller's missing."

"Don't worry. Your favorite reporter is nosing around as we speak. I'm curious myself."

"Good, call me later tonight and let me know what you come up with. I'm on my way into town to check out a new location for the office, down in Back Bay."

"Great, we'll be close to Fenway."

After hanging up the phone, Josh went back to his investigations.

He had been working on the usual crop of crackpot conspiracy theories when the Teller story broke. The latest one involved a supposedly secret time-travel club, believers swearing you could go back in time if you could afford the exorbitant fee. Others believed the world was ending on the end of the year, in a month and eighteen days. Well, maybe that's not such a bad thing, Josh thought to himself. The human race probably could use a good old biblical cleansing. Now this Teller mystery, was it foul play?

Josh already knew a lot about the missing scientist. How the forty-four year old astrophysicist had PhD's from MIT and Stanford. How he invented and built the mirrors and controllers, as well as the madly complex software to drive the system and take advantage of the very structure of the universe itself. How he had studied with the brilliant but controversial and erratic Dr. Henry Thomas Peeble, for whom he had named his telescope. How his young wife died in an automobile accident and how he had risen from the depths of his grief and despair to resume his work, building the greatest marvel of modern science since Galileo's telescope.

Teller's mentor, Doctor Peeble, whose theories on stellar mechanics were only now being verified, had a weird side. Some of his theories bordered on the fantastical. It was Peeble who said the secret of life lies in the vast distances of the universe. If you look out far enough, he said, you will find your beginnings. It was also Peeble along with a Cal Tech scientist named Kip Thorn, back in the late eighties, who said time travel was possible, which may account for the latest underground rumors. It was Teller's work with Peeble during his graduate days at MIT that prompted him to develop ways to probe deeper and deeper into space. After contributing to the Hubble Telescope in the nineties, he went on to found his own company, StellarScope, to revolutionize the art of photography in deep space, something already carried to amazing lengths in the current stage of ocular telescopes and high-definition 3-D imagery. Teller's achievement promised to carry those advances to the next level and beyond.

Josh knew that the scientist had last been seen at a promotional dinner in Boston, where he had spoken about the possibilities now opened to mankind with the implementation of his invention. There had been many gainsayers along the way. Some said it was impossible, just a hoax, a scam to bamboozle the government out of billions of dollars. Some feared exactly what Dr. Teller and his teacher Peeble had promised, afraid of what they would find and see. Some felt that there were much more pressing and important things to spend the money on, like reducing hunger and poverty, or sending a manned flight to Mars. Whatever your bent, there was something for everyone to object to in the Peeble Deep Space Telescope, any one of which might account for Teller's disappearance.

Then there were his rather peculiar habits. He had a reputation for erratic behavior. It had occurred to Josh more than once that it was strange they would put so much responsibility on a person that seemed so unstable, and yet there was no denying the man was brilliant. He was not only able to build the advanced contraption but understood its highly complicated theoretical underpinnings, based on string theory and quantum physics.

Josh looked at his white board, where he had thrown ideas up like garbage against a wall, to see what would stick and what would slide down to the floor, without judgment of their merit. It was just a sort of brainstorming exercise he did, where he wrote whatever jumped into his mind. It worked better with a team of people throwing out ideas, but Josh had developed the technique through years of practice to the point where he could do a decent job on his own. He hoped it covered the range of possible reasons for the doctor's disappearance, and maybe even some of the less probable ones.

With all the people who would like to see the project fail, it was natural to consider kidnapping as a possible theory. Many of the ideas thrown up on the board were the names of organizations or persons, from fringe groups to religious sects, including the government itself, who might want to see the scientist out of the way. Then there were the huge sums of money involved, which might lead to motives of theft or embezzlement, and the involvement of organized crime. All these possibilities and more had to be analyzed, weighed, and investigated, including a little scribble in the corner of the board that read, 'abducted by aliens', a conclusion sure to be favored by the conspiracy theorists.

Josh browsed the different on-line news agencies, both public and private, some he had access to through his professional affiliations, looking for anything concerning the case of the missing Doctor Teller that might help. Speculation was rampant, fueled by the ever hungry conspiracy mongers. Such rumors had haunted the project since its inception, despite prodigious sums spent on publicity to counter it. One theory was the project was really a front for a top secret government plot to spy on every human being on the planet. There were many others, including a rumor that the government was really building a time-machine.

It was well after seven pm before Josh looked up and realized that it was too dark to see the white board, well after most of the other offices had closed up for the day to start their weekends early.

Josh rubbed his eyes, which were almost always red and sore - probably because of the long hours he spent hunched over his computer screen - and decided to call it a night. He could think while he drove home to his rented house in the western suburbs of the city.

As he drove, he couldn't help ponder the mystery of his own life. With the festive holiday season approaching, his own happiness seemed as elusive as ever and far more worrying to him than the disappearance of a missing scientist, no matter how distinguished. Life would go on as usual regardless of what may have happened to Dr. Benjamin Teller. It was probably some crooked scam or sordid love affair. It was all the same to Josh. He would be alone and depressed like he always was this time of year.

He could call home any time and make plans to stop by and see his mom, even stay in his old room, but the thought only made him want to eat acid. He could probably use one of the countless dating services to meet someone. God knows he'd had enough dates and superficial affairs since his move to New York to last him a lifetime.

Although he wasn't new to the Boston area, he had been away almost nine years since graduating from BU, and didn't know anybody in town, having lost touch with most of his college acquaintances. Living out in the suburbs didn't help, but he had found a nice house to rent for cheap in a quiet neighborhood that reminded him of his home in Vermont, complete with a vacant field next door, perfect for batting rocks.

Eventually his mind came back to the question at hand. What has happened to the Dr. Benjamin Teller? He had already tried to contact Teller's company, but had only gotten an answering machine. He had not yet received a return call, not surprising given the situation and the adverse publicity involved, just when the big project was going operational. He had contacted his office back in New York asking for assistance, but given it was after five on a Friday evening the chances of hearing anything before Monday morning were slim. Anyway, StellarScope's headquarters was only a few miles away from his place, along 495. He was much better placed than his employer to make things happen.

On the spur of the moment, instead of taking the exit to his rented house in the suburbs, he continued up the highway toward the StellarScope headquarters building. While he drove, he listened to the news, which, of course, had to do with the missing Dr. Teller. There was yet no word as to his whereabouts, or whether or not foul play was involved, but recent investigations had turned up the fact that the Peeble Telescope project might not be as close to completion as advertised. There were rumors, some quite persistent, that the project had been sabotaged or otherwise severely damaged in some way, perhaps by the very inventor himself.

From the information gathered so far it was hard not to consider the whole thing a case of a disgruntled genius unable to work with his government overseers and other stakeholders. It wouldn't be the first time, and Dr. Benjamin Teller had a reputation of being difficult to work with. Maybe one too many differences of opinion led to his quitting and running off, perhaps throwing a monkey-wrench or two into the works to gum things up on the way out. The fact that the much touted Peeble Telescope might not be operational as planned could have a distinct connection to Teller's disappearance. Can't miss another scoop like that, Josh reminded himself, stung that someone else had discovered the delay in the project, although it wasn't surprising given the sequence of events and knowledge of the project's difficulties, which were many.

"Another Atlas shrugs?" wondered Josh aloud as he drove. No wonder no one was talking at StellarScope.

Chapter 2

Josh drove slowly past the entrance to the StellaScope headquarters, past a row of long, low buildings and well-manicured yawns. He continued on through the industrial park until he came to a shopping mall. At the nearest end of the shopping center there was an English Pub, its red and blue sign hunched between Macy's and Jordan Marsh. Josh headed in the general direction and found a parking space a fair distance from the entrance.

Despite the hour – it was after eleven – and the seeming out of the way location of the place – at the far end of the mall away from the bright lights and bigger store entrances – the pub was mobbed. There were at least thirty people standing in the reception area between the bar and the doorway waiting for a table or booth. Josh made his way discreetly to the men's room and refreshed himself. On his way back from the rest room, he noticed a rather plain looking, moon-faced woman, with dark hair, sitting alone at the end of the bar. She was a little plump for Josh's taste but had a pleasant smile and an attractive face. She seemed to be watching the crowd with a shy, wary look, as if she were trying not to be noticed, when all the time no one in the room seemed to pay her the least attention, including the bartender, whose eye she had been trying to attract for several minutes.

"Hi," said Josh walking up to her. "Can I help? You seem to be having trouble getting the bar-keep's attention."

"Yes, hi," she replied, distractedly. "He seems to be ignoring me."

"It is rather busy. He's got his hands full. They get kind of snobby when they have a captive audience like this. Oh, here he comes," said Josh as the bartender came toward them. "Hi there, can we get a couple over here?" He yelled over the noise and stuck his arm in front of the guy next to him, who was almost nudging the young woman off her bar stool. He had a fist full of twenties. The bar tender trotted right over.

He ordered their drinks, a vodka gimlet for himself and a daiquiri for the lady.

"Hi, I'm Josh," he said, extending his hand and introducing himself.

"Maria," replied the woman. "Maria Cavello. Thanks, I thought I'd never get a drink."

"Yeah, bit of a mob scene. And I thought I'd stop in and have a nice quiet drink. Who'd of known this place would be so busy."

"Oh, it's always like this on a Friday night. They all come from the office buildings down the street to let off steam."

"You work around here?" Josh asked, shouldering his way between the woman and the guy sitting next to her, who was all elbows and quite inebriated. They were at the very edge of the bar, next to the rest rooms. The crowd at the door was larger and more boisterous than ever. They had to put their heads close together and talk loudly to be heard over the din.

"Not any more. I was laid off today."

"Oh, I'm sorry to hear that. Are things that bad here?"

"No, just the sorry company I work for. You're not from around here I take it."

Josh had already fabricated a cover story, finding it easier to elicit information by not advertising his line of work.

"No, I just moved here from New York City." That was the last true statement he would utter for the rest of the evening. He told her he was a computer programmer and just got into town. Said he was looking for work and came to Boston to be closer to his mom.

Josh found he did much better with women when he lied than when he was just being himself. As himself he was tongue-tied and awkward. Impersonating someone else, he was witty and suave. He had long ago learned the secret of getting women - lie. The only problem was how to remember the web of fibs one lays down. Josh was already unsure of himself, but he plunged on anyway, hoping to find out something useful.

"That's very nice of you," she said. "I mean to take care of your mom. That's rare these days. Most people are just out for themselves, the rest of the world be damned."

"Oh, there are still few of us left out there," replied Josh, the cynical investigative reporter, who hadn't called his mom in months. "What about you? What did you do before they so rudely fired you?"

"I was a glorified executive secretary at a place called StellarScope. You may have heard of them. They're the ones building the Peeble Telescope."

"Oh, yeah, that space probe thing. Cool. That must be very interesting."

"I wouldn't know. I didn't have anything to do with that project. I work, I mean I used to work in the HR department, mostly coordinating travel arrangements. These people fly all over the world."

The mention of StellarScope almost made him choke on his drink. He recovered from his surprise quickly, thanking his lucky stars, or whatever instincts brought him to this place.

"Well, don't worry. I'm sure something will turn up. You must have quite an impressive resume. Then there's always unemployment."

"Oh, I'm not worried about that. I've got a little money put away. I may even retire. No, it's just the way they did it, treated me like trash after fourteen years. They couldn't have asked for a more dedicated person than me. It's just not fair."

"Is the company having financial difficulties?" he asked, feigning perfect ignorance.

"Don't you read the papers? Haven't you heard the news?"

"I've been kind of busy lately," Josh continued. "So the company's having financial problems. These things always seem to cost more money than expected."

"It's not so much that. The project's just so big it's swallowing up the whole company. They're under so much pressure, everyone's under so much strain." She stopped suddenly and looked at him. "I really shouldn't be talking about it. We're not supposed to talk about it to anyone."

"But they fired you, haven't they? That kind of negates your obligations, doesn't it?"

"Not if I want to get my severance package. I signed a paper. I'm not supposed to divulge any proprietary information."

"You can tell me what was in the news I've been missing, can't you? Now you've got me curious."

"I suppose," she replied, looking around the room.

Josh followed her gaze, which rested on the people crowding the bar and the doorway, but he could see no one watching them, although the dark interior of the pub where the tables were was invisible to him.

"You've heard of Dr. Benjamin Teller haven't you?"

"I'm afraid not," said Josh feigning ignorance again. "Who's he?"

"You do live under a rock. Nobody but the most famous scientist in the world. He's the one that invented the Peeble Telescope."

"Oh," said Josh pretending to be ignorant. "Like I said, not exactly my area of interest."

She looked at him hard, as if she doubted that anyone could be this obtuse.

"Well, he's world famous and he's disappeared, clean up and vanished."

"Whoa there, now that is interesting. Does anyone know what happened to him?"

"No, he wouldn't be missing if anyone knew where he was, but there's plenty of speculation."

"And the company fired you because of that?"

"No, at least I don't think so. I'm not exactly sure why they fired me. I've been there fourteen years and got along well with all my bosses. Everything was fine up until today, then without warning, they laid me off, said they no longer had work for me, but I know that can't be true. I know there's a big shake up in the Peeble project, with Teller missing and all, but we were told everything was fine, business as usual. Then today..."

Her words trailed off. Josh waited for her to continue. When she didn't, he began to probe.

"So what was it like to work there, what's its name?"

"StellarScope? It was a great place to work until today. I guess it was really too good to be true. Like I said, I wasn't involved in the project, but I know some of the people who were, mostly a tight-lipped bunch who all sit together at lunch. Real snobs if you ask me, not so much as a hello from most of them. But my friend Ellen is nice. She works for one of the VPs on the project. She even got to work with Teller every now and then. I met him once. He stopped by my desk and asked me to do some travel research for him, but I ended up having to ask someone else who knew more to do it. Anyway, he's a strange sort of guy. He'll play softball with you one day and walk by you as if you don't exist the next. I'm not surprised something happened."

"What happened?"

She looked around the room again nervously. The crowd standing by the door had finally thinned out, though the bar was still mobbed with noisy, boisterous people, mostly men, standing three deep and all clamoring for drinks at the same time.

"Let's see if we can get a table," suggested Josh. "Maybe we can get a little something to eat. Want to join me? I think they're still serving food." It was a little after midnight.

"I really shouldn't. I really hadn't meant to stay this long. I should be going."

"Are you sure? You're the first real person I've had a chance to meet since I've been in town. I sure would enjoy the company."

"OK, why not. Maybe we can help find you a job."

"Now you're talking." He led her past the receptionist who nodded politely and found a booth. As they settled in and checked the menu, they continued their conversation.

"So what happened?" he asked, after a waitress came by and got their order of spicy potato skins and nachos.

"I guess it won't hurt to tell you. It's in the news."

"What's in the news?"

"About the telescope being sabotaged."

"Sabotaged!" he whispered loudly. "You mean someone broke it?"

"Shh, not so loud. It's not so much a telescope as a large array of telescopes and mirrors spread through space. The mirrors and telescopes have to be very precisely placed in order to work. That's what Teller did, design the programs and mathematics to make it all function. I don't know much about it but Ellen was a real whizz in math. She could practically explain how the whole thing operated. Now that I think of it, Ellen knew there was a problem. She said how crazy it was to have so much riding on a blithering idiot like Dr. Teller, a real absent-minded professor she called him. Couldn't do his laundry without messing it up. Now he's gone they can't get the thing to work."

"Do you think your absent-minded professor broke it, or left some key thing out when he left? You know, like spoiled grapes. If he can't have it, nobody can?"

"I suppose. I wouldn't put it past him."

"Could somebody have kidnapped him, someone who didn't want the project to succeed for one reason or another?"

"Now you sound like one of those security guys, but it's funny you should ask that. I was questioned by the FBI a few days before I was laid off even though I have practically nothing to do with it. I'm in a completely separate part of the company."

"Sure sounds like things are going sour there. Good thing you're out of it."

"I guess so, but it sure doesn't feel that way."

"Well, that explains it then. They fired you because things are going bad and the company's in trouble. I wouldn't take it personal."

"Then why was I the only one handed a pink slip? I didn't see anyone else get fired, just me."

"I'm sure there will be others. After all, they must have spent millions on the project. Then to have it fail, that can't be good."

"No, I guess not, but I would have felt a lot better if someone had just given me an explanation. One minute everything was fine, then the next I'm asked to come into an office where my boss and the VP of HR are sitting. Then without explanation I'm told I'm to collect my belongings and escorted out of the building. It was downright humiliating."

"I'm sorry," said Josh in sympathy. "Here's to new opportunities." He raised his glass and tried to smile, but his new friend had worked herself into quite a funk.

"I'm sorry," she said. "I don't feel much like celebrating. It's late. I'd better be going."

With that she stood up abruptly and a little unsteadily, and grabbed her coat.

"Let me walk you to your car," Josh offered, a little under the influence as well. He was wondering if he'd be able to find his way home in the fog that had enveloped his brain as well as the night.

It was surprisingly mild for this time of year, not much below fifty-five, the result of an unusually warm spell of weather that had lasted since the middle of the month, after snow in November. They were experiencing strange weather patterns, which taken together with severe tornado activity where they usually didn't occur late in the summer, added to the end-of-the-world speculation then gaining momentum.

"Nice night, you don't even need a coat," observed Josh. "Where you parked?"

"Over here," she replied, as she pointed to her car at the far edge of the huge, now almost empty parking lot. "There were no closer spaces when I got here earlier this evening." Her car looked tiny in the distance.

"Let me give you a ride to your car."

"No, that's all right, the walk will do me good."

He walked next to her toward the distant vehicle, looking her over as he did. Nice legs beneath the long skirt; pretty eyes and no make-up; not a bad figure under a frumpy, too large, grey flannel sweater. Still, he decided, she wasn't quite his type.

"Want to come over to my place?" he asked, almost by habit.

She didn't answer for a minute.

"I haven't had an offer like that in awhile."

"I'm surprised," he said, just as naturally. "I think you're quite attractive. I bet you get offers like that all the time." Just because she wasn't his type, that didn't mean he couldn't hit on her, especially since she might know something.

"Not exactly. I don't get out much."

"I bet you were dedicated to your job. They're cads for firing you."

"My sentiments exactly. I didn't even get to say good-bye to my friends. It will look like I did something bad, maybe even illegal, to get fired like that. I mean the thought of it."

"Can I have your number?" he asked, when they reached the car.

"Sure, I think I have a piece of paper and a pen in there somewhere."

He stood by the door as she searched in the car for a pen and paper.

"Here," she said, scribbling her name and number on the paper and handing it to him. Just at that moment, the lights of a van that had been parked nearby flashed on and the engine rumbled to life. As they stood and watched, it screeched out of its parking place and headed right toward them. Instinctively, Josh pushed his new acquaintance over into the passenger seat and jumped behind the wheel. The van screeched to a halt right where he had been standing.

"The keys!" he said loudly. "Give me the keys."

She rummaged wildly in her pocketbook, pulling out a heavy keychain ringed with keys and silver charms just as the side-panel door of the van slid open and two large men jumped out. Josh jammed the key into the ignition and twisted the starter, slamming his foot on the gas pedal at the same time. The little vehicle lurched out of the reach of the first man as the second leaped on the hood.

Slowly, the second-hand Ford lumbered to second gear, then third, as the van gave chase. The man on the hood skidded off as the car bounced over a curb and plowed through a low hedge going forty. The van was gaining on them, not bothering to pick up the guy who had tumbled off onto the pavement.

Josh had his foot pressed to the floor, but the old car hardly seemed to be gaining speed, while the van sped after them like it was turbo-charged.

"Who's that?" he whispered through clenched teeth as he tried to maneuver the car down a twisting road not meant for over twenty-five mph, between the impressive entrances and walkways of the industrial park. "What are they after?"

"I don't know. This is all too bizarre. I can't believe this is happening," said his terrified passenger.

"Well, they must be after something. Is there something you're not telling me?"

"No, honest. I don't know what's going on."

As she said this the van bumped their rear fender.

"Jesus!" yelled Josh, slamming his foot down on the pedal, willing the car to go faster. The van bumped them again, harder, almost making him skid off the road.

"Up here," yelled his companion. "Turn here, now, sharp."

Josh turned the wheel hard to the right as he slammed on the brakes, spinning the car almost too far. They swerved around the corner just missing a signpost by inches. The auxiliary road, which Josh hadn't even seen when he turned, led in back of the buildings they had just sped by and gave them a few moments before the van could turn and follow. They had a couple building lengths between them. Maybe that would be enough. The van, which still had its lights off, was gradually reducing the distance between them.

"Here, between these buildings," she shouted, as Josh slammed on the brakes and skidded around another sharp right. The car bounced over the curb, scraping metal and chrome in the process.

"Sorry," he said lamely, realizing the damage he must be doing to her vehicle.

"Don't worry about it. Just get us out of here," she yelled. The van had overrun the turn and had backed up. It was now bounding down the small road after them.

They were in a maze of buildings and parking lots, interspersed with roads and sidewalks going in every direction. After a few sharp turns and short runs, they were soon out of sight of the van heading down a small back alleyway.

"There, cut across here," said the woman, pointing to what looked like the entrance to an underground parking garage. He yanked the wheel in that direction, speeding between two stone walls and down a slanting ramp. Turning past a row of thick pillars, he headed for the far end of the dark empty space, taking a quick glance in the rearview mirror. He did not see anyone following. Backing into a dark corner, he eased the car between the wall and another vehicle that had been parked there overnight.

"I think we lost them," he said quietly, as if the people chasing them in the van might hear him.

"You think so?" she whispered. "I don't think it's safe to stay here. They may figure out where we are."

"Yeah, I know. Got any ideas?"

"The other end of this garage is near the entrance to highway. Maybe we can get out that way without being seen."

Josh peered into the darkness. There was no one in sight. Slowly, he inched out of his hiding place and drove toward the far exit. Just as they were nearing the ramp up to the street, a pair of headlights swung into view at the other end of the garage. They heard an engine being gunned and the squeal of tires. Josh pushed his foot to the floor. The car shot up and out of the garage like it had been fired from a canon, landing on the pavement amidst sparks and the sound of scraping metal.

"There!" she pointed, where a gaggle of green signs announced the entrance to the highway. He headed for the one that would take them back toward his house, running a series of red-lights in the process.

There was a lot of activity at the intersection, the highway cluttered with busy weekend traffic from the city, but somehow Josh managed to dodge and swerve and avoid any collision. Once on the freeway, he drove over the speed limit, weaving in and out of traffic, often glancing nervously in the rearview mirror for signs of a pursuing vehicle. Maria Cavello, the ex-travel coordinator from StellarScope, sat half-backward peering intently out the rear window.

"I can't see them. I don't think they saw what ramp we took. The way you blew through those lights like that with all those cars coming, I didn't think we were going to make it."

"Neither did I. Now what's going on?" asked Josh, still not sure they had gotten away.

"I don't know, honest."

"I wonder if this has anything to do with your company and Teller."

"I didn't have anything to do with him or his project. I just coordinated their travel arrangements once in awhile."

It was some time before Josh began to relax. He was almost home before he remembered he'd left his car at the pub.

"We've got to call the police."

As soon as he said this, however, and played out the likely scenarios in his mind, he realized that none of them were very good. His job was to get the news not make it.

"Maybe it was just a couple of kids trying to roust us," she said.

"Those guys didn't look like kids. More like goons. You sure you've told me everything? You didn't recognize those two or the van? You don't know who might be after you?"

"What makes you think they were after me?"

"They were sitting there watching your car. Why would they be doing that?"

"I don't know, but they certainly weren't after me! That's crazy."

While they were talking Josh reached his house. He turned onto his street and immediately pulled into the driveway behind the house.

"Where are we?" she asked, as if aware for the first time of her surroundings.

"My house. If what I think is true, your place may not be safe tonight."

"Nice," she said, on getting out of her car and surveying the building in the moonlight. "Kind of cute. You own it?"

"Thanks. No, I'm just renting. I'm still getting settled. Haven't really fixed it up like I want it yet, but it'll do for now. Once I get a job. I'm not sure I'll be able to keep it."

Josh decided to maintain his false identity as a computer programmer looking for work. It wouldn't do for her to know he lied to her and it certainly wouldn't help if she learned that he was an investigative reporter looking into her company.

He let them in and turned on the living room light.

"Let's go into the kitchen. I'll brew up some coffee. We can try to figure out what to do."

"Are you going to call the police?"

"I'm not sure what to tell them. I'm not too sure what happened. Maybe they only wanted directions."

"Then why did they chase us?"

"I don't know. Maybe they were miffed we drove off. Maybe someone wanted to serve you papers."

"No one's serving me papers."

As much as he wanted to rationalize the whole thing away as some harmless misunderstanding, the more he thought about it the more sinister it seemed and the more he was certain it had something to do with StellarScope. Maybe he was getting paranoid with all the conspiracy theories he'd been digesting, but his instincts as far as a story was concerned were pretty sharp. These well-honed instincts were now telling him something was afoot and he was in the middle of it.

He wondered who was after them - if that was indeed what was happening - and if they would figure out that it was his BMW sitting in the parking lot at the pub. If so, would they be able to trace it to his house? He had only been in the area a few weeks but being the fastidious jerk that he was, he had already registered the car in Massachusetts and put in a change of address at the post office. That had been two weeks ago. His new registration would lead them right to his place. He walked to the living room and turned out the light. Sneaking a peek through the curtains at the street, he saw that it was empty.

"Is everything all right?" his guest asked, as he returned to the kitchen. The coffee had finished perking. He poured her a cup.

"Fine, I'm trying to conserve electricity until I see what the bills are like or until I get a job, whichever comes first. I hope it's the latter."

"I'm sure you'll find something with your skills. Software engineers with experience in the aerospace and medical fields are in demand. I know a couple people who may be able to help you."

"Thanks. That would be great."

"So what are you going to do?"

"I need to get my car back. It's brand new."

"It may not be safe. They could be there watching it, waiting. They're probably still driving around looking for us."

She laughed when she said this, as if the image tickled her.

Josh again considered calling the police, but knew he'd have to confess his true identity. It wouldn't do to lie to the cops. They tended to frown on that sort of thing if they found out and Josh didn't know how long he could carry on the masquerade.

"I think we should call the police," she said finally, after they had sat staring at each other, as if reading his thoughts. They were both confused and exhausted after a long day and a stressful evening.

"Ok, you're right. You might be in danger. We can get them to go back and get my car."

He was about to dial 911 when there was a knock on the door.

Chapter 3

Josh sat in the back of a white van next to Maria Cavello, on a small seat just big enough for the two of them. The interior of the vehicle was covered in soft grey upholstery, but was otherwise bare. Two men sat in the front separated from Josh and Maria by a panel of the same material, with a small wire-mesh window in the middle of it. He couldn't tell where they were going.

He had peered through the front curtains when the knock came, to try and see who it might be at his door at this hour of the night. He could just make out two men, one in a dark suit, the other in a light white jacket, jeans and tennis shoes. They didn't look like the police. They looked like the men in the van.

Josh ran into the kitchen.

"They're here. Quick, out the back door."

He threw her coat to her and ran to the rear of the house and the door to the backyard. The knocking at the front increased in intensity and a voice called out through the door. "Mister Banks. We know you and Miss Cavello are in there. We need to talk to you, sir. Please open the door. Mister Banks…"

They ran out into the cool night, throwing their coats over their shoulders as they ran. Josh dug in his pockets for the keys. To his dismay, there were two men standing by Maria's car. They started toward him.

"Hold it, sir," said the first one. "We need to talk to you and Miss Cavello."

"Who the hell are you?" yelled Josh, agitated and scared. He didn't like being rousted out of his house.

"We'll explain all that after you come with us," said the second man.

"We aren't going anywhere. I'm calling the police."

"I'm afraid we can't let you do that," said the first one, slapping Josh's cell phone from his hands. There was a brief scuffle as the man tried to grab his wrists and Josh swatted his hands away. When the two men from the front came back, however, Josh realized he was outnumbered four to one. He put his hands up and surrendered. They were then bundled into the back of the van and driven away. Josh assumed the other two were following behind in another car, perhaps even in Maria's old Ford.

"Where do you think they're taking us?" she asked Josh.

"I don't know. Did you recognize any of them?"

"No, but I know the type."

"What type is that?"

"Security geeks. Think they're such big-shots 'cause they have a badge and can search your purse."

"You mean security personnel? From StellarScope?"

"I wouldn't be surprised."

"What do they want? This is kidnapping!" He yelled it again, loudly so the men in front could hear. They ignored him.

He turned back to Maria.

"I think they're the same ones who were chasing us earlier. They must have followed us somehow. Maybe they found my car and traced it here, I don't know, but that's the only thing that makes sense. It's got to be connected with your work. Someone doesn't want us to talk."

Their speculation was interrupted as the van slowed and jerked over a short incline, and then descended a long ramp into what sounded like a tunnel. Soon they stopped. A moment later the side door slid open to show their four abductors standing in a semi-circle around it. There was no place to run.

They were in a large, virtually empty, underground parking garage. One of the men motioned toward a metal door with 'No Admittance' painted across it.

"What's this all about?" asked Josh. "I know my rights. You just can't take people off the streets like this. It's kidnapping. Are you kidnapping us? Is that what's going on here?"

"We haven't threatened or harmed you in any way," said the man in the suit. "You and Miss Cavello have come of your own free will."

"That's not true," Josh said.

"You weren't forced. You decided it was smarter to come along without causing a fuss. Why take a chance on someone getting hurt. And we wouldn't want that, would we?"

"This is kidnapping. I demand you let us go immediately."

"We'll do better than that. We'll see you home safely. Once you oblige me and come with us. Even though Miss Cavello has left the company, that doesn't negate our obligation to protect her from harm, from those who might try to use her against the corporation, someone like the press, for example."

"What do you mean the press?" asked Maria, who had recognized the garage as an area of her office building reserved for security personnel.

"Oh, didn't Mister Banks tell you? He's a journalist, an investigative reporter assigned to the StellarScope story, isn't that right, sir?"

"I thought you said you were a software engineer looking for work? You were lying to me the whole time?" She looked both hurt and surprised.

"You might as well come with us, Mister Banks," said the tall man in the suit. "There no way out of here as you can see, and it's much warmer and more comfortable inside where we can sit down and have a nice hot cup of coffee."

The mention of coffee gave Josh pause. It must have been almost four AM. He was cold and tired, and his companion looked like she was ready to drop. Tears peek out of the corner of her eyes. Josh didn't know if it was because of their predicament or because he had lied to her. The thought that he had hurt her bothered him more than he would have imagined, since he hardly knew the woman. He didn't have many alternatives. Maybe if he just went along, it would all be over soon. Then he could go to the cops and press charges. He started listing them in his head as he and Maria followed their abductors through the metal door and into StellarScope corporate headquarters.

In a way, things couldn't have worked out better. Here he was being led into the very building that he had wanted to gain entrance to for an interview. The bad news was that he was the one being interviewed. The only thing he had going for him was that they knew he was from the press. Unless they were total crazies they wouldn't risk harming a journalist. It was a slim assumption to go on, but it gave him the hope he needed to face the situation.

He was led into a small conference room with no windows, furnished with a single table and four chairs. There was no phone or clock. A table next to the wall held a logbook and note paper with a number of pencils and pens in plastic cups. Josh sat at one of the chairs and waited. He assumed Maria Cavello had been taken to another similar room.

Before long a man he had not seen before walked in. He had on a dark, crumpled suit and a faded gold watch that he must have found in K-mart. Looking more like an overworked bookkeeper than a security chief, he had that hard glint in his eye that told otherwise.

"I'm sorry we had to bring you here like this, Mister Banks. Those security guys can get a little heavy-handed, but this is a matter of national security after all."

"National security? I thought the feds handled that," observed Josh.

"Well yes, if it gets to that level, but we try to take care of these things ourselves. Unless further action is called for we don't call in the federal boys. Hopefully that won't be necessary."

"I'm calling my lawyer the first chance I get. By my count you've broken about a dozen laws, starting with kidnapping."

"I assure you no laws have been broken, Mister Banks, at least none that you can prove. As a matter of fact, you're lucky we haven't decided to press charges ourselves. Taking Miss Cavello's car, luring her into your house with lies, I wouldn't be so quick to yell kidnapper if I were you, Mister Banks."

Josh tried to speak, but nothing came out. It wasn't that his tongue was tied or his throat constricted, his brain just went blank for a moment and he couldn't form any words.

"Trying to turn the tables on me like that won't work," he said finally, as his wits tumbled back to him. "Maria will collaborate my story."

"I wouldn't be too sure of that, Mister Banks. I wouldn't be too sure of that at all."

"What happened to Dr. Teller? Why has he disappeared?"

"I'm asking the questions here. Why did you lure Miss Cavello to your house?"

"Is that why the telescope's not operational?" Josh figured now that he was here, he might as well get his money's worth.

"That's no concern of yours. You have more serious things to answer to, like attempted rape."

"Rape!" yelled Josh, his voice edged with anger and fear. "You can't pull that on me. You're in big trouble and I'll tell you what that trouble is. You're trying to cover up. Teller's flown the coop. Those military boys tried to steal his invention, use it for their own purposes, whatever the hell that is, and he took the secret with him and disappeared. Now you're left holding a bunch of empty commitments you can't keep. How's that for a story."

"I'm afraid the only story here is yours and it's a very sorry story indeed." With that he got up and left the room.

Josh sat and stewed for another twenty minutes before two men in security uniforms came and escorted him out of the building. He emerged in another parking area at the side of the office complex where two police cars were waiting for him, lights flashing

"What's this?" yelled Josh, as he was handcuffed and put into the back of a squad car. Instead of answering him, they read him his rights.

He tried to explain to the officer driving him to the station that he hadn't done anything, that he was the victim of a kidnapping and that it all had to do with the disappearance of Dr. Benjamin Teller and the sabotage of the Peeble telescope.

"What about the girl you tried to rape?" said the cop, looking back at him with an angry expression through the rearview mirror.

"That's a lie. I didn't try to rape anyone."

"Well, I just got through talking to that young woman and that's not what she said."

"They must have scared her into lying. Look, I was walking her to her car and this van pulled up. These two men jumped out and we drove off. They chased us through the parking lot. They must have followed us to my house. They kidnapped us, four of them. Those two guys who led me out are in on it. It's all a conspiracy."

"Tell it to the judge," said the cop.

Josh was booked, fingerprinted and kept in a cell until his arraignment early the next morning, where he was released on his own recognizance – because of his journalistic status – and told not to come within 200 yards of Miss Cavello or StellarScope corporate headquarters. He arrived back at his house at 11am, famished and exhausted. After a shower and a quick breakfast, he called his boss's cell phone.

"Jesus, Josh!" Frank exclaimed when Josh spoke. "What the hell are you doing? You're supposed to write the news, not be it. Your name's plastered all over the papers. Abduction! Attempted rape! Are you crazy?"

"Frank, wait a minute. It wasn't like that at all."

"Oh, what was it like? 'A representative from World News Affiliates in New York City on assignment in Boston was arrested early this morning for seducing and kidnapping an employee of StellarScope Corporation in an attempt to get information concerning the company's recent disclosure. Mister Banks, an investigative reporter with World News for the past four years, was later charged with rape when it was found out he had tried to force himself on the distraught victim after hijacking her car and taking her to his house.' It goes on but I think you get the drift."

"Frank, you know me. It's all a fabricated lie to cover up what really happened. I'm on to something. The company goons followed us out of the club. I met her in a bar. She had just been fired for no apparent reason from the company, had a lot to say. I walked her to her car and got her number. A van with a couple of heavies showed up. I got spooked, jumped in her car and drove off. They chased us! I lost them and took her to my place. They must have followed or traced me from the plates of my car. I left it at the place I met her. Her name's Maria Cavello. She seemed nice enough and on the level. They must have gotten to her somehow, gotten her to lie."

There was silence on the other end of the line as his boss digested Josh's story.

"That's quite a tale," he said finally. "Too bad you won't be able to tell it."

"What? Why, don't tell me you're pulling me off the story."

"It's not me. The board of directors just got through meeting. They called me from New York. You've been suspended for ethics violations without pay until this thing is settled."

Josh was stunned. "Frank, that's not fair. I've spent most of my savings relocating here so I could help you set up the office. What am I supposed to do now?"

"It's only temporary. You've got a couple more paychecks coming. You've got some vacation pay coming, right?"

"Frank, how can you do this to me? After all we've done together. I'm on to something I tell you. You know I'm the best journalist you've got."

"There's nothing I can do, Josh. It's only temporary, until things get worked out. In the meantime, get a good lawyer."

"Frank!" said Josh, finally at a loss for words.

"Look Josh, if you get something solid let me know, but it will have to be completely unofficial, on your own. I'd be careful if I were you. You're in a lot of trouble."

Josh shut his cell phone with a snap. He couldn't believe his ears. Not only had he been arrested for kidnapping and attempted rape, he had lost his job. He couldn't leave the state and he couldn't work. Worst of all, he had again become the news.

He tried to sleep, but despite his complete lack of it found it impossible even to lie down. He was upset at his dismissal and nervous

30

about his impending prosecution. He had only been released on his own recognizance due to his journalistic affiliations. Now that he was no longer a journalist, he wondered how long it would be before they picked him up and incarcerated him. He needed a lawyer, but with his meager funds he'd be lucky to afford a burnt-out ambulance chaser.

He had taken a cab back to the shopping center earlier that day to get his car, but it had been towed. No one knew why. It took quite some time for Josh to track it down and even more time and money to retrieve it.

After a brief nap later that day, he went over all he had been able to gather about the missing scientist, Dr. Teller, and his company. Based on this information, he went back to the web and surfed some more, filling in details and missing pieces until he felt he had the complete picture up to the most recent events. Then he added his own data, things he had picked up on his intelligence gathering operation, his talks with Maria and what he was able to learn during his time with their security people.

While he was on the Internet, Josh used the phone number he had obtained the previous evening – it seemed like years ago – to look up Maria Cavello's address. Against his better judgment, he had decided to stake out her place. He knew it was a risk, especially with the restraining order and charges hanging over him, but he had to take the chance. He was desperate for information, and just might learn something. He'd take his camera with its telephoto lens and his small recorder, just in case.

He got directions to her front door using MapQuest. For good measure, he used the satellite-view to look down on her apartment. This gave him a bird's-eye perspective. Using this he was able to get the lay of the land and perform a thorough reconnaissance of the place before he got there. He found the best spot to park and observe her apartment, and located possible escape routes to the highway, and so on. He felt like he had already been there long before he got in his BMW and drove to the place.

Earlier that day after talking to his boss, he had gone to a payphone and tried to call Maria, the woman he had met the night before, the woman he had tried to help - admittedly after lying to her - the same one now pressing rape charges against him. Her answering machine picked up after five rings but he didn't leave a message, fearing that would be used as evidence for the prosecution. He expected the police to show up at any minute. He had the unsettling impression that there was someone listening at the other end, someone who was not Maria Cavello.

Now he was parked beneath a tree down the street and across from her apartment where he could observe the place unnoticed. He settled down for an evening of surveillance. It was just turning dark, not quite five pm this time of year. Unseasonably warm, there was still no snow in sight, much to the dismay of the local skiers.

He sipped the coffee he had brought and opened the sausage with onion and pepper sandwich he had picked up at a greasy sub-shop on the way. He was tired but hoped that paranoia and anger would be all the adrenaline he'd need to keep him awake. His eyes were already heavy and his neck hurt. His head felt like it weighed a hundred pounds. After eating the sub, he took a couple Advil and washed it down with the remains of his lukewarm coffee. It was the last thing he remembered doing.

Chapter 4

Josh awoke with a start and sat up not quite sure at first where he was. A huge wave of panic almost overwhelmed him. The scene in front of him added to his sense of alarm.

It was a bright day. Josh's shirt was plastered to his chest with sweat as the sun burned through the car's windows heating it like a microwave. Two police cars had just rushed up the street in front of him from different directions, their sirens blaring and lights flashing. They both screeched to a stop in front of Maria Cavello's apartment building. Four uniformed policemen jumped out of the cars with their pistols drawn.

Josh shrank back in his seat trying to will himself invisible and wondered if they were after him. After all, he was breaking the law, being well within the 200 yard limit of his restraining order. They didn't appear to be interested in him, however, as they rushed into the building. He could hear more sirens approaching in the distance.

Easing his car out of its spot beneath the tree, he made a U-turn and headed back up the street in the opposite direction, making a left at the lights to head toward the highway. Looking in his rearview mirror to make sure he wasn't being followed, he almost jumped out of his skin. Right behind him, following much too close, was a black and white. Josh almost panicked, but instead of slamming on his brakes - an action sure to cause him to be rear-ended - he managed to keep the car on the road and moving at a steady pace. Much to his relief, they soon flipped on their lights and passed, accelerating down the road. Breathing a silent prayer of thanksgiving, he headed up the highway back to his house.

As he drove, he wondered what had happened back at Maria Cavello's apartment. He had a sinking feeling that it was bad and had something to do with him. That feeling was confirmed when he arrived back home and found two squad cars parked in front of his house. He turned down a side street and circled back in the direction he came. He kept on driving as he tried to put things together. His heart was pounding and his palms were sweaty. His mouth tasted like he'd been chewing dusty cardboard. Luckily, he wasn't spotted.

For the tenth time that morning he rubbed his eyes strenuously. He needed a cup of coffee and a newspaper, but was afraid of going any place in town for fear of being spotted by the police. Whatever had happened, the cops were looking for him and that couldn't be a good thing.

He soon found himself in the country, on a small road that meandered past farmsteads, fallow fields, and barren trees. At a spot where four of these small roads met at a ragged intersection, was a combination service station - convenience store. Josh pulled into the parking area and went in.

A young girl behind the counter was stacking and arranging things. The radio played a country song with some guy singing how he wished he could bring back the past and do it all over again, only this time get it right with his woman. Josh felt like he had no yesterdays, at least not where love was concerned. Josh had no woman. Now he wished he had someone to talk to, someone to confide with. He didn't know what way to turn, or what to do. He felt totally alone.

He bought a coffee and Danish, along with a newspaper, and slid into one of the booths along the wall. He needed to catch up on things and try to think. The coffee was wonderful and almost made him feel human again. The Danish tasted stale. His throat was so dry and constricted with worry he could hardly swallow, but he forced it down anyway, figuring he needed some kind of nutrition.

He had scanned a couple of local papers while he stood by the counter, and had read the Boston paper carefully, but there was nothing related to him or Maria Cavello's apartment. As he sat there sipping his coffee, listening to heartbroken cowboys and girls singing their blues away, he tried to figure out what was going on.

StellarScope had somehow gotten Maria to accuse him of rape in the hopes of discrediting him, which had worked big time. All in an attempted cover-up for some sort of internal company intrigue, perhaps even the murder of Dr. Teller. Had they gone even further and silenced Maria Cavello as well? Maybe she knew more than she had admitted. Or maybe she got cold feet, unless this was all just some sort of bizarre coincidence. That was the only reasonable explanation he could come up with for the morning's events.

He decided to call his boss, but was afraid to use his cell phone. He had already turned it off, worried they might be able to use it to triangulate his location. He doubted the local cops would have bothered with that at this point though, unless they thought him somehow involved. If someone wanted to find him that bad they could do it.

"Do you have a payphone around here?" he asked the sales clerk on the way out.

"Yeah, on the other side of the building, next to the air pump."

"Do you have change for a couple dollars? My cell phone's dead and I need to make a few calls."

"Sure, no problem. Hardly anyone uses that old payphone any more. They were thinking of taking it out. People would be lost without their cell phones."

"Ain't that the truth. Thanks," he said, pocketing his quarters and walking out of the building and across the lot to the phone booth.

He put in the required amount of change and dialed his boss's number.

"Hi, Frank. It's Josh. You got a second?"

"Josh!" His name exploded in his ear like a cherry bomb. "Where the hell are you? I've been trying to call you all morning."

"My phone's dead," he lied. "I'm out trying to find out what's going on with StellarScope and clear my name. Why, what's happened?"

"The cops are looking for you, is what's happened. There was a murder last night."

"What? Who? Where?" stammered Josh.

"Yeah and who's on first. This is no joke, Josh. Where were you last night?"

"Look, Frank, this all has to do with that company. There's something going on and it looks like it's taken a turn south. Did they kill Maria Cavello?"

"I don't know. We're waiting to get more information later today, but you're wanted for questioning in relation to it. I hope you have a good alibi or a good lawyer, or both."

"Believe me, I have neither. I was hoping I had a friend."

"Look, Josh, this is out of my league. I can't help you. What do you expect me to do? The police were here this morning asking questions. We can't have the agency implicated in any of this. They're ready to call me back to New York as it is. This has jeopardized all their plans. I have my own career to think about. I don't mean to be blunt, but I warned you about some of those tactics of yours. You really push the envelope sometimes."

"I never heard you complain when I brought you all those breaking stories. You've even said I was a big part of that Pulitzer you got."

"That was before you decided to drug and seduce young women to get a lead."

"Like you've never taken a girl home for a story."

"No, Josh, fortunately I haven't. Maybe that's why I have a wife and family."

"And I don't. Is that what you're trying to say? I don't see any reason why I should live by your moral standards, whether for a lead or not. Since when have you become a prude? Anyway, it wasn't like that. I told you what happened."

"Morality has nothing to do with it. It's the story. You've put the agency in an awkward position, compromised our integrity, at least as far as this piece of news is concerned. You've become superfluous. You've become a bigger piece of news than the story you were supposed to be covering. You've broken the number one rule of reporting. The best thing for you to do now is turn yourself in."

"I need a lawyer, Frank. The least they can do is get me a lawyer."

"I've already talked to the front office about that. They think it'd be a conflict of interest, since you're being investigated by the company's legal department for ethics violations. They can't have the same people investigating you and representing you in a criminal case. They've advised me to tell you to get your own independent council."

"I don't have a lawyer. Do you know anyone?"

"Not really. My guy doesn't handle criminal cases. I've already asked him. He gave me a name of a good lawyer in New York who you might call."

"New York? I need someone local, someone who knows their way around this court system. I need somebody here if I'm going to give myself up."

There was a pause on the other end of the line. Soon another voice came on the phone.

"Hello, Mister Banks. Why don't you listen to your friend here and give yourself up. We only want to ask you a few questions."

Josh slammed the receiver down so hard he was afraid he might have broken the phone. Knowing the agency wasn't going to back him, after all the years he'd worked there and all the stories he'd brought in for them, was bad enough. But the fact that the cops had been listening in and had gotten to Frank completely unnerved him for a moment. Now, on what might be one of the biggest stories of the new century - scandal and misdeeds on a highly visible, multi-billion dollar international space project - they were letting him go, as a scapegoat, to be devoured by the piranhas.

It wasn't until he had turned to head back to his car that he noticed the trooper. He had pulled up behind Josh's vehicle and was looking in the side windows.

"Can I help you, officer?" he said, coming up and unlocking the driver-side door.

"Nice car. I've always wanted to get me one of these. How much she go for, if you don't mind me asking?"

"I got a good deal. My brother's a dealer," lied Josh. "I may have a card in here somewhere."

"Oh, that's all right. I'm sure it's way out of my reach," said the trooper, giving the car another appreciative once over before going into the store. "Have a nice day now."

Josh got back in his car, breathing shallowly and pulled out onto the road. Luckily, not everyone in uniform was looking for him that day, but that could change at any moment, especially if he really was wanted in connection with a homicide.

Back on the highway, he found an ATM machine and took out $500. He had to take the chance they were not yet monitoring his bank account. He used his credit card to get $1000 more. Then he found a small motel on a strip-mall at the other end of 128, on the North Shore, under an assumed name.

He was on his way to a nearby sub shop to grab a pizza when his cell phone rang. He had forgotten to turn it off again after using it to get his boss's number. He didn't recognize the caller. He answered it with not a little trepidation. Who could be calling him now, he wondered

"Hello, Josh? This is Maria Cavello." He almost swallowed his tongue, making it all but impossible to answer. "Josh, I need to talk to you. Something awful has happened."

"You're telling me. What's this about a rape? What's the big idea of lying like that?"

"I'm sorry, I had no choice. They had my son. I had to do what they said. They must have gotten my friend Ellen to take him from school. She was the only one he'd of gone with. She's picked him up for me before once in awhile. She didn't know they were going to use him against me like that, even before I met you. They thought I knew something from their travel itineraries, but I swear I didn't know a thing. They didn't have to take Robby."

"Calm down. Where are you? Are you all right? My boss told me something about a murder."

"Yes, it's terrible. I just can't believe it. They killed Ellen."

"Who killed her? Where?" Josh said, trying frantically to keep up with events. Things were moving faster than he could follow.

"The same ones who chased us. They tricked her into take Robby and when she tried to help him, they killed her. She brought him back to me last night. She was staying in my apartment while I took him to my mom's on the North End. They must have killed her while I was away. Now they're looking for me. You've got to help me."

"Why don't you go to the police?"

"'Cause I think they may be in on it."

Josh hesitated trying to digest this last little bit of information, remembering how quickly the police had come to do StellarScope's bidding.

"OK," he said finally. "Where are you? I'm in a bit of trouble myself thanks to your little lie. It appears they think I may have killed your friend. I wouldn't be surprised if they're trying to pin the whole thing on me." He didn't tell her he'd been sitting in front of her apartment building fast asleep during the night.

"Are you at a pay phone?" he asked.

"No, my mom's."

"OK, I'm going to call you back in a few minutes. I don't want to talk any longer on my cell. They may be able to trace it. I've got to ditch this car in the meantime or change the plates or something. OK?"

"OK, only make sure you call me back. Here's the number."

"No, I've got it here on my phone. Stand by. I'll call you back in a few minutes. And Maria…"

"Yes?"

"Thanks for calling."

"Thanks for helping."

Josh hung up. He had an urge to throw his phone out the window. Instead, he shut it off and found the nearest payphone at a service station a short way off the highway. Before making his call, he borrowed a screwdriver from the mechanic and removed his Massachusetts plates, replacing them with his old New York ones, which he still had in the trunk. Then he went to the pay phone and dialed Maria back, getting directions to her mother's house in the North End, though he wasn't exactly sure what he was going to do when he got there.

He had thought to take his computer with him on his failed stakeout, but it was low on batteries and there were no public Wi-Fi hotspots in the area. Not entirely trusting Maria's directions and not being able to Google it, he bought a roadmap of the city and verified the route.

On the way to Maria's mother's house he thought about his own mother in Vermont. His father had died five years before. One of the reasons Josh was an only child and had spent much of his spare time by himself was because his parents were rather old by the time he was born. His father was in his mid-fifties, his mother forty-five when Josh was only ten. They were loving parents but had trouble keeping up with a rambunctious, inquisitive boy, especially when he reached puberty. His father was in his mid-sixties when Josh graduated from high-school and pushing seventy when his son was in college. His premature death at sixty-eight when Josh was only twenty-three shook his world to its foundations. He couldn't work for weeks. It didn't help his sense of guilt that he hadn't called or written to his mother for months and hardly ever visited.

A few years back, he had used MapQuest to get a satellite view of his family home. He put in the name of his hometown, which produced a satellite picture of Lake Champlain and part of the Vermont shoreline, as if seen from several thousand feet in the air. He clicked the mouse on a magnify icon and the picture became the recognizable outline of the city of Burlington, Vermont. A few more clicks and he could see the university and buildings on the main street of the city. He scrolled the map to the right to display Route 89, coming up from White River Junction. With a few more clicks of the mouse and a little left and right scrolling, he was soon above his family's house looking down as if he was suspended a mere hundred feet above the ground.

There was the familiar fenced-in backyard with its shed. There was the field next door where he had hammered rocks like baseballs in a home run derby for hours at a time. There was his father's pickup in the front yard.

He stopped for a moment and took a second look. His father had been dead almost a year by this time. One of the first things they had done was put the truck up for sale. It sold in a few weeks for almost $5000, despite being nearly ten years old. People who knew his dad and how well he kept his vehicles had a bidding war over it. In any case, it hadn't sat in the driveway since a few weeks after his death. He realized instantly that the image must have been several months old. It seemed his childhood home didn't rate much updating, but the sight of his father's truck sitting there as if he were still inside watching the game on TV stunned Josh and brought tears to his eyes. After a moment's reflection he was bawling like a baby. He just hadn't expected it. The sight had brought back a flood of memories and associations. For some reason, he was thinking about that experience now as he drove down Route 93 toward Boston's North End. He wished he could bring his father back as easily as he had zoomed down on their family home with his computer. There was so much he wanted to say.

Chapter 5

The lights and traffic of the city were a startling change from the quiet roads and towns in which he had spent the last forty-eight hours. Except for the night in the car and a catnap in his motel room, he hadn't had a full night's rest in at least as long.

Using Maria's directions, he followed the highway as it entered the city to the exit he had memorized. This led him to an intersection where he joined a mass of pedestrians and traffic all jostling to get through several rows of stop lights as six lanes rapidly became two.

Finding the address, he parked his car in what he hoped was a legal spot and ran the three flights up to the apartment number he had gotten from Maria over the phone. He was winded and breathing hard by the time he reached her floor.

When he knocked, which he had to do several times, each one a little louder than the previous rap, a small old lady with her coarse gray hair cut rather short, poked her head out warily and asked Josh what he wanted.

"I'm here to see Maria," he answered. "We just talked over the phone."

She gave him a thorough up and down and shut the door abruptly in his face. A moment later, Maria opened it and invited him in.

"Sorry about my mom. She's a little upset by this whole thing."

"I don't blame her. So am I."

"Come in. Mom, this is Josh, the guy I told you about."

"Humph," snorted the old woman. "Sounds to me like he's the cause of all your trouble. The sooner he leaves the better." She walked into another room without any more comment.

"Don't mind her. She's old, and *doesn't have any manners!*" These last words Maria said loudly, yelling them into the next room so her mother would hear.

"This is Robby," she said, pointing to a child of about six or seven sitting on the couch watching cartoons.

"Hi, Robby. Nice to meet you," said Josh. The child looked up for an instant but otherwise ignored him, engrossed in the living drawings of a cat being pummeled by two nasty little rodents.

"Thanks for coming," said Maria, after Josh had taken off his coat. They were sitting at the kitchen table, which was just off the living room where Robby sat watching TV. She had put on a pot of coffee.

They would need it. "I didn't know what to do. This is all so terrible. One day everything is fine, just going about my normal life. Then next thing you know I'm in the middle of this nightmare. I can't believe all this is happening, all because I talked to a guy in a bar."

"I think there was something going on before you met me. Like you mentioned earlier on the phone, probably something to do with you being fired in the first place. You must have seen or heard something even though you weren't aware of it."

"What? I didn't have anything to do with their project."

"Maybe not, but you must have seen something. Maybe it has something to do with their travel plans. Can you think of anything that might be significant?"

"No, I told you I don't know anything."

"Maybe if I took a look."

"You'd have to get on my computer somehow."

They were silent for a moment as she tried to think of what it might be that had caused them to come after her. Then she remembered something.

"Ellen brought this last night when she brought Robby back," she said, pulling a heavy black leather satchel from beneath the table. "She said the company told her that I asked them to have her pick Robby up for me while I was working late on some special project for them. When she found out that they were using Robby to pressure me into lying about you, it really ticked her off. She knew they were slimy but had no idea they would stoop to something like that. Who knows what they would have done with him. The things they said when they grabbed us really scared me. They said I'd never see him again...alive."

She shuddered visibly at the thought and went on.

"Just to make sure they wouldn't try coming after Robby and me again, Ellen took a few things from her boss's office. There's a batch of papers and reports in this bag, a whole bunch of stuff. I haven't looked at it all, but there are some pretty incriminating documents there. No wonder they killed her."

Josh watched in amazement as she emptied the contents of the heavy satchel onto the table, stacking papers and printouts, along with notebooks and loose-leaf binders in a pile. After leafing through a few emails and memoranda on the top of the stack he looked up at Maria with a whistle.

"This stuff is dynamite. Those memos there describe a problem with the telescope. I'm no scientist but it sounds like Teller screwed things up before he left. You're right. I believe they'd do anything to get this material back. We need to get this to the proper authorities, and fast. I don't think it's safe here. If they're after you, as I'm sure they are after what you've told me, it's only a matter of time before they trace you here. We've got to go. Once we get to a safe place, I can call my old boss and see if he can figure out how to bring us in safely. I wonder if there's anything about us in here," he said, ruffling through the papers.

"I don't know. I haven't looked through half of it. Where can we go?"

"As far away from here as possible," said Josh, taking the map he had purchased earlier out of his back pocket.

For some reason, he didn't feel safe going back to the motel room he had on the North Shore. It seemed too close to the city and too easy to cut off. He decided they'd be safer in the middle of the state, halfway between New York and Boston.

A short time later they were in his car heading west on the Mass Turnpike. He hoped the New York plates would throw the police off the track and give him the time he needed to get out of town undetected. Now, as he passed through several tollbooths, each with a contingent of grey and blues parked next to them, he was having second thoughts and held his breath at each stop. On a whim, he had removed Maria's plates from her second-hand Ford before they left. Perhaps a third set of plates might come in handy. It was either this or steal some, and he wasn't quite ready for that yet.

As they drove down the Pike toward the western part of the state, Maria pulled one document after another from the satchel. Each one contained information more startling and disturbing than the last.

"This is a status summary from the project manager to the CEO, dated after Dr. Teller's disappearance. It explains the most recent findings of their investigative team. Listen to this. 'All the deep space platforms have been constructed as specified, as have the mirror components and auxiliary scopes. The servo-mechanisms that move the telescopes and adjust the mirrors are also in place. However, the software that controls the positioning and the electronics to display it visually have not been tested in a live setting.' That testing was to take place on the sixth but was postponed when Dr. Teller disappeared."

"What else does it say?" asked Josh, eyes focused on the road while his mind concentrated on Maria's words.

She read a bit further in silence while her son lay on the backseat fast asleep.

"Sounds like it was all implemented backwards."

"What? What do you mean, backwards?"

"Instead of pointing outward at the distant stars, the telescope is directed back at earth. It's backwards. At least, that's what I think it says here." She read the remainder of the document out loud and then several others that seemed to be relevant. When she was through they sat in silence.

It was almost midnight by this time and the traffic, which had been heavy when they started out from Boston, had thinned to almost nothing as they reached the outskirts of Springfield, Massachusetts. They were both exhausted from lack of sleep. Josh pulled into the first vacant motel they found on the outskirts of town where they rented a room as husband and wife, niceties forgone in the desire to finally rest in a soft bed with a pillow. Maria and Robby slept in one single bed while he had the other. Josh fell asleep immediately, in spite of the thoughts whirling around in his mind.

The next morning, while they sat in the room sipping coffee and munching on donuts compliments of the motel's continental breakfast deal, Josh looked over key memos and documents from the satchel left to them by the late Ellen Primrose. What Maria had stated the previous night appeared to be correct. For some reason, instead of pointing out to space the telescope was programmed to look back at earth, hardly the outcome envisioned by its planners. Obviously, Teller had sabotaged it at the last minute for some reason. They began hunting through the remaining pile of papers for that reason.

"Look at this," said Maria, interrupting the silence. "It's a letter from the Secretary of Defense. It says that due to the potential military use of the telescope the President has authorized him to direct the final stages of the project. It complains about the government's failure to obtain timely information about the status of the work and management's inability or refusal to comply with the government's standard documentation requirements concerning a project of this importance and magnitude. This seems to confirm what you were saying about Teller's unorthodox management methods."

"Yes, and that could be the motive for Teller leaving and sabotaging the whole thing. They were interfering, trying to take it over."

"You don't think he had planned to dupe them all along, do you? Like the whole thing was one big joke?"

"I don't know," replied Josh. "But if so, it was the biggest prank in history."

"Why would he do such a thing?"

"The only thing I can think of is he didn't want the government to get their hands on it. He suspected something like that would happen. Perhaps they had ordered the changes so they could spy on everyone. The conspiracy theorists were right. But Teller was ready for them. He had been planning this all along. It's just a guess, but it will do for now. We have to get this information to someone we can trust. I'll call my boss. This is the evidence we need to get people to believe our story. The company is covering up for the fiasco and is willing to kill people to keep it secret. This is the break we've been waiting for."

He waited until after midnight to call Frank Sullivan, his ex-boss, hoping to find him alone. Frank answered after the fourth ring, just before his answering machine clicked on. He had felt bad after his last conversation with Josh and believed the company should have done more to help him. He had felt his own career slipping away with his junior partner's so hadn't been as supportive as he felt afterward he should have been.

"Josh!" he said on recognizing his friend's voice. "I was hoping you'd call."

"Have any little eavesdroppers there in bed with you?" Josh replied sarcastically, still smarting from his friend's treachery.

"I'm sorry, Josh. I didn't have much choice. They were waiting for you to call. They had warrants to search the premises for any information regarding you. Our whole operation out here has been screwed up and that's putting it mildly."

"I know. I'm about to change all that. What would you say if I have hard evidence, documents and printouts, along with witnesses, proving that Dr. Teller left the Peeble Telescope for parts unknown, sabotaging the whole thing in the process, after the Department of Defense tried to take over his work. I can't tell you any more over the phone, but the murder of Ellen Primrose...."

"How did you get her name?" asked a surprised Frank Sullivan. "The police haven't released any names yet, just the fact a murder took place late last night and that the murdered woman worked for StellarScope."

"Well, it's all connected and I have the documents to prove it."

"How'd you get them?"

"I can't tell you any more now. I'm at a payphone. Your line may be bugged. We need to find a safe place to meet and a safe way to communicate. Anyone involved could be in danger. The stakes are high and these guys will stop at nothing to cover their asses. Call me at this number in fifteen minutes. We can make arrangements when you call back. Find a payphone or a phone you know is clean. They may be tracing this call as we speak. Call me in fifteen. Bye."

Before he could hang up, Frank yelled into the speaker. "Wait, Josh! Why so soon? Why can't we wait until morning? I don't want to go traipsing out at this hour of the night looking for a pay phone. I'll get mugged."

"You'll get worse than that if they're tapping your line. They may be outside of your door at this very moment. I hate to drag you into this, but you're the only one we can turn to, the only one in a position to do something about this whole thing, but we have to move fast. You're in danger now that you know what's going on. I'd get out of there as fast as you can. Call me in fifteen. Bye."

With that he hung up and went back to the room to wait. Maria and her little boy were asleep on the far bed. He lay down on the nearest one, stretching out his hands and resting them behind his head. Needing to rest, he forced himself to keep his eyes opened so he wouldn't miss his friend's call. Finding it difficult to stay awake, he wondered if it was possible to fall asleep with your eyes open.

He thought about all that had happened. It seemed to fit. The papers Maria had gotten proved everything - project sabotaged by eccentric scientist; government's defense department involved; billions of dollars wasted on a telescope that didn't work. Josh thought for a moment. The telescope looked back at earth. That's just as the conspiracy mongers had been saying all along. That it was going to be used to spy on every single person on the globe? That sure as heck appeared to be what was going on. Maybe Teller found out how his invention was being perverted and ran away in disgust. Or even more likely, perhaps he had been put out of the way or otherwise eliminated.

Josh tossed this thought back and forth in his mind like a light feathery bird, until it was time for Frank to call him back. He went out into the cold night and walked down the row of dark rooms to the far end of the building where the phone was located. A yellow light marked its existence. He hoped it was the light at the end of the tunnel he found himself in and not a locomotive coming at him from the opposite direction.

Chapter 6

Josh spent a good deal of the next morning at a used car dealer just off the highway, trading in his BMW and swapping his New York plates with Maria's. He hoped they weren't as hot as his and that the flipping of plates back and forth between cars would throw off the authorities. It just might give them the time they needed to get their story to press.

On the way back from the dealer, Josh stopped to buy breakfast for Maria and Robbie. While there he picked up a paper at a nearby kiosk and almost dropped the food. His name and picture were on the front page of the daily news along with Maria's and her boy's. Not only was Josh the prime suspect in the murder of thirty-three year old Ellen Primrose, but he was also wanted for questioning in the death of seventy-seven year old Rose Cavello, Maria's mother. There was also an amber alert out for the boy. He glanced up from the paper and looked around the parking area. No one seemed to have noticed him yet. His stomach did back-flips as he drove back to the room.

"I talked to my boss last night," he said on entering. "He agrees. The best thing to do is publish the damaging information. That way the story will be out and they won't be after you anymore. At least that's the hope. Then you can clear me."

"What about the fact I know what happened to Ellen? They know I know they killed her. I'm a material witness."

"Once the authorities know what's going on, I'm sure they'll work out some sort of witness protection deal for you and Robby."

"Great, just what I need."

"You have any better ideas? We can't keep running like this. I have to clear myself. They think I murdered your friend and raped you. Maybe we can try to change our appearance a little. No sense making it easy for them. We can cut your hair, get me a pair of glasses. I can remove my mustache. We might turn little Robby into a little Joanie."

"Not on your life," she said laughing.

"I'm glad you haven't lost your sense of humor."

"You almost have to laugh. The whole thing's just so ridiculous. If it wasn't for what happened to Ellen." Her smile turned into a frown. Tears welled up in her eyes.

"What's happening to me isn't so funny either," said Josh, not feeling sorry for her. "Nether is what you told the police about me."

"I told you, I didn't have a choice," she replied, a slight edge in her voice.

"I know. I'm sorry. I probably would have done the same thing in your place. By the way, there's an amber alert out on Robby. They think I kidnapped you and your boy."

"That's ridiculous. All they have to do is talk to Mom."

Josh didn't say anything but knew he had to tell her about her mother. He figured sooner was better than later, but still he hesitated.

"Every busybody and their neighbor will be looking for Robby now. We have to change appearances. They still think we're driving the BMW. That gives us some time. Maria, I'm afraid your mother's been killed. They're trying to pin it on me, along with you friend's murder."

"What? Mom? No, it must be a mistake. She didn't do anything."

"I'm sorry, Maria. No one is safe around us, including your son, not until we get this bag of information to the media where it can be made public."

"No, no, it can't be. Not mom. She was only seventy-seven. No..."

She started sobbing uncontrollably. Soon the boy was crying as well. Josh was afraid they would attract attention.

"Maria, there will be plenty of time to mourn your mom once the truth of her murder is known and the people responsible are punished. Until then, you've got to keep it together for your boy's sake. We have to get through this."

He put his arm around her shoulder and pulled her close, so her head was resting on his chest, which was soon wet with her tears.

"Your little boy needs you. I need you. We need to change identities, especially Robbie's. His and our lives depend on our actions. The next few hours are critical, OK?"

She seemed to stiffen with resolve and shook her head, as if to shake the tears away like seawater.

"OK, I'm OK. They killed her 'cause she wouldn't talk. She was a tough old lady. I'd hate to be the guy who did it when Uncle Louie finds out." Still, Josh could tell she had taken the news hard. It would be some time before Maria was her old carefree self again.

Josh didn't ask about Uncle Louie. They left the keys in the room and discreetly left the motel. He had paid in advance with cash. Finding a Wal-Mart, he soon had a pair of scissors and black-framed glasses, and a blond wig for Robbie. After cutting and dying her hair in a gas station restroom, Maria bought a number of dresses and blouses for her new daughter. Josh looked like another person in his new specs, without the facial hair he'd become accustomed to.

As arranged previously the night before, he stopped at the payphone he had used and waited. It rang a few minutes later.

"It's the Feds," said Frank, as soon as Josh put the receiver to his ear. "They're on to you. They came to my house last night after I talked to you. They must have had my phone bugged."

"The Feds? Why are they involved in this? I thought this was a local case. Isn't this out of their jurisdiction?"

"I guess not."

"Did you tell them what I told you about the murder and cover-up? I think somebody from StellarScope may have killed Maria's mother last night."

"I can't talk long. This isn't a good spot. The Feds are after you and I don't think it has anything to do with homicide. They didn't seem interested in your whereabouts on the nights of the murders, just the top secret papers your friend's supposedly stolen. They seem to think you're some kind of national threat."

"What? That's ridiculous. What the hell's going on?" With that the line went dead. He hung up the phone and hurried back to his car. Getting in, he sped off without explanation.

He hadn't gone two blocks when he heard what sounded like a hundred sirens converging on the area. A helicopter appeared overhead circling over the highway, but luckily they weren't spotted, the police attention diverted by someone driving a dark BMW.

With the federal government after him with their unlimited resources and technology, he wouldn't have a ghost of a chance. He should have known they would get involved with anything having to do with the telescope project. Now that he thought of it, he was surprised they hadn't shown up earlier. The rumor mongers had been right all along.

After leaving the Springfield area they meandered aimlessly in a northeasterly direction while Josh tried to decide where to go. Part of him wanted to head north toward Vermont and home, but he knew that they would surely be waiting for him there. Another part of him felt he should go to New York City where his agency was and there were five million people to hide among. But basically he didn't know where to go or what to do, so he drove about as if on a sightseeing tour with no destination in mind. While they drove, Maria looked through the satchel of documents.

"I think I found something that explains why they would want to kill Ellen," she said after a while. "It's in one of the loose-leaf notebooks we hadn't looked at. It's another set of books. There's no name on it, but it looks like someone was siphoning off millions of dollars from the Teller project."

"That would explain the budget overruns they've been experiencing for the last two years. I wonder if Teller was the one doing it. That would explain his disappearance."

"I don't know, but I've been looking through every scrap of paper in the box to try and find out who's involved."

"You'd make a good investigative reporter, if you ever want a job."

"I may take you up on that."

"Boy, this is dynamite. Wait 'til the press gets a load of this. 'Top executives steal millions from American tax payers'. We've got to figure out how to get it to my agency. Whatever we do we can't keep driving around like this."

"Where are we going to go?" she asked plaintively, vocalizing Josh's thoughts precisely.

"I don't know, but we'll have to think of something. I don't think they can trace us here as long as we don't use the phones or credit cards, but we may have been recognized despite our disguises. I'm not sure how long we can go with your plates. They've probably already figured out we might be using those as well as my old ones from New York. They probably know we bought another car. Frank is being watched, so he can't help us. I don't really know anyone else in the area."

"Why don't we give ourselves up to the police?" she asked reasonably. "We have the proof of what they're trying to do. We can go to the government for protection."

"How do we know someone in the government's not involved in the embezzlement or the cover-up? You said yourself you thought the cops were in on it. With this much money involved any number of people could be mixed up in it. Who knows how high it goes. No, we have to get this material to someone in the media who we can trust to make it public in a credible way.

"Where can we go? Are you sure it's not better to sit tight, find a place and hide out?"

"I don't know. If it's a federal agency like the FBI that's after us, we might have some time before they focus all their resources on us, but once the NSA gets involved, forget it. They may already know where we are. They could be closing in as we speak. The best thing is to keep moving, or at least that's what they say. The problem is we'll be even more vulnerable out in the open. I wish I knew where we could go until we can get help."

"I know, my step-brother, Jeremy. My mother re-married when my dad died. I was just a kid, four years old. I guess it was pretty hard on Mom being a widow with a child and all. She remarried not long afterward, just after my fifth birthday. My stepfather had a kid my age. We grew up together. God, I hated him. What a little brat he was, always crying and complaining when he didn't get the most attention or the biggest share of something. He was so selfish he wanted everything I had. He even used to open up all my Christmas presents. He's not so bad now, but he's still a jerk sometimes. He lives in southern New Hampshire. Not that far from here, up 140. I'll show you."

Getting the roadmap from the car, she outlined the route, east back up Route 2 a short way, then along US 140 toward Keene, New Hampshire, not more than an hour and a half away.

As Josh headed the car in that direction, he wondered if he was going toward the resolution of his problems or just digging himself a deeper hole. He suspected that he'd know soon enough.

Chapter 7

It was dark by the time they reached the town where Maria's brother lived. She directed him up a side street to the top of a steep hill to his simple domicile.

"I haven't been here in years," she said, getting out of the car. "Jeremy hasn't seen Robby since he was two years old."

"Are you sure your brother will help us? It doesn't sound like you two got along that well."

"Oh, he'll help us. At least he won't throw us out. He loves the kid and he hates the government big time."

"Great, I hope you're right."

Maria took the lead with Robby at her side and knocked on the front door of the small white house. It was somewhat like the one Josh had rented, a rectangular, two-story building with a short, tiled front entrance and a screened side porch. But this one was in need of a paint job, with boarded porch windows and junk strewn across the yard. A large man with a pale complexion and curly brown hair opened the door. His fat stomach protruded beneath an armless undershirt, which also exposed a swath of long brown chest hair. He blinked dumbly at the woman standing at the doorway facing him.

"Jeremy, it's Maria. I've got Robby. We've come to see you. Have you heard about Mom?"

"Yes," he blinked. "Come on in. What happened? They said you were kidnapped." He hadn't seen Josh at first, but as Maria and Robby went up the short flight of steps to enter the house, he noticed Josh standing in the shadows. "Who's this?" he said in alarm.

"That's Josh. He's helping us. I haven't been kidnapped. It's all part of a cover-up. We think the same people who made up the story about my kidnapping killed mom."

"I'm so sorry," said Jeremy, who turned out to be not such a bad guy after all. He led them into the kitchen where he made them the first home-cooked meal they'd had since their ordeal began three days ago. Besides being a good cook, Jeremy was a computer geek who hosted his own web site. After dinner they retired to his den in the basement where he showed them the wall of servers and network hubs that comprised his computer service business. Besides having his own website, he hosted a number of commercial and personal sites for various customers.

"It's not much, but it pays the mortgage," he explained, as they sat on a sofa before an array of computers and disk drives. In spite of the urgency of their problem and the notoriety associated with the murders, Josh had to wait for half an hour before he could explain what had happened to them, while Jeremy described each piece of equipment in the room.

"Whoa," Jeremy said on hearing their story. He scratched his ample belly and burped. "That's some tale. Like out of a movie, man. You think mom's murder has something to do with Teller and his telescope?"

"We've got the documents to prove it," replied his sister.

"Gee, that's pretty heavy, man," said Jeremy forgetting all about his computers for a minute. "But why kill mom? What did she have to do with it?"

"She saw the papers," said Maria. "She could overhear us talking. She knew what was going on and where we were going, but wouldn't tell them, so they killed her."

"What are you going to do?" her half-brother asked.

"Tell Uncle Louie."

Jeremy said nothing, but shook his head up and down and gave her a knowing look.

"So you think Teller sabotaged the telescope before the government could use it to spy on everyone?" he asked Josh. "That's really a shame what they did to it, man. That thing was supposed to be really something."

"Either that or they killed him before it was completed, to get him out of the way. Maybe he found out they were pilfering the till."

"I doubt they killed him. That Teller guy was a real smart dude. He would have been steps ahead of them."

"I'm glad you have such faith in him. I really didn't know the guy."

"Neither did I, but I've read everything he's ever written. I've been following this project since it was a subject in his PhD Thesis at MIT where he worked with Professor Peeble. Now there was a misunderstood genius if there ever was one. He disappeared too after those small-minded pricks at MIT tried to malign him and steal his work. He was into some really esoteric stuff, man, time travel, multiple dimensions. Anyway, these government dudes are bad news, real hard-noses. They're not liable to talk first and shoot later, if you know what I mean."

"We've got to get this material published," said Josh.

"I can put it on my web site. I've got followers all over the world, man."

"I don't think that would work. For one thing, you're an underground, anti-establishment site. Only the fridge groups and crackpots, no offense, will see it. And even fewer of them would give a crap. No, we need a reputable news agency to release to. Someone who will stand behind the story and people will believe."

"Like the one that fired you when you tried to drop the story in their lap?"

"Yeah, something like that."

Jeremy laughed sarcastically, clearly offended by Josh's offhand remark.

"Why don't you drive to New York and give it to them then?" he said.

"Because I don't think we'd get that far."

"OK, I'll help. First thing I want you to do is get rid of your car. Move it somewhere away from here. They may get around to connecting me to Maria eventually, but I don't want some dumb cop to stumble on your illegally parked vehicle and find you here. Please move it."

With Jeremy following they drove the car to the train station and left it there with the plates removed. They then went back to Jeremy's house to sleep for the night. Even though Josh had to sleep on the couch, while Jeremy and his step-sister and nephew slept upstairs, it was the first good night's rest he'd had in days. Heaven knows he'd need it.

Josh woke up the next morning to the smell of bacon and eggs with French toast, compliments of their host.

"That smells great," he said, pulling a chair to the table. Maria and Robby were not yet up. "It's nice of you to help us out. You should know that two people who have helped us have died, one of them your stepmom."

"I know. I'm glad to help. I'll be even happier if we nail those creeps who killed Rose. She was a nice lady. I knew the government was behind this. We were right. It's all just a cover for their spy cameras."

"I was wondering about that. It doesn't make sense they would use a billion dollar telescope to spy on people when they've got hundreds of satellites orbiting the planet. They can spy on just about whoever they want whenever they want."

"Maybe so, but I understand this thing would be far beyond anything they have. At least that's what they're saying on the street. They say it can look right through buildings like an x-ray."

"Yeah and they're also saying you can buy tickets on a time-machine."

"It's true. I've talked to someone who knows someone whose brother's been on one. With the world ending, people want to travel back in time so they can have a few more decades to live instead of days."

"Please, Jeremy. You don't believe that bunk do you? The world's not going to end and time travel is theoretically impossible. Einstein proved that."

"Well, Peeble thought differently. He found another solution to Einstein's equations. Ever hear of wormholes? He supposedly had the evidence to prove his theory, but no one believed him and it was lost. Some say his student, Teller, learned it from him before Peeble disappeared. Maybe he's gone into hiding to build it. Or maybe he was building it all along and used it to go to another time. Anyway, how do you know the world's not going to end?"

"I don't, but neither do I believe all the sensational tripe being put out by these fringe papers and websites by so-called experts about some cataclysmic event the government's trying to keep secret."

"How can you be so sure? Some say it's the Peeble Telescope that discovered it. That's why many scientists without the aid of such equipment debunk the story. They can't see it yet. But it's coming and it's coming fast."

"There's absolutely no evidence for such an event, no comets or meteors. Those so called prophecies are just a bunch of bunk to sell cheap newspapers. They've been saying the world's going to end for a thousand years, yet it's still here, alive and kicking. No, I just don't buy it, that or time travel. I mean really, Jeremy, and you're an engineer."

"What does that have to do with it? So was Peeble. He was a renowned astrophysicist. How about L. Ron Hubbard? No, just because we're scientists, doesn't mean we don't believe in higher powers."

Josh contemplated the overweight computer geek as he sipped his coffee. Maria and Robby came into the kitchen a short time later.

"So, can we transmit the material over the net using Jeremy's computers?" she asked without preamble.

"Someone's been thinking while she's been sleeping," said her half-brother. "Josh here doesn't think we have enough credibility to publish it ourselves. What about it, want to try uploading it to your company's computers in New York?"

"I hadn't thought of that. Can you do it?"

"If you give me an IP address or a URL I can, or an email address. I'd have to scan some of the material into the computer. Of course, the feds will trace it right to our door. Oh, I'd say in about ten seconds."

"Maybe we can find another location, somewhere we can upload the data but not give ourselves away."

"That makes things a lot more difficult. Maybe I can find another network to bounce it off, use a proxy account or something. We have to find a hot spot that's not secured. I'd need to do a bit of work to prepare for something like that. It's pretty risky, even if I do manage to hide our identity. They may be surrounding us already."

"You're getting paranoid with all that conspiracy theory hogwash you read," said Maria.

Josh was lost in thought for the remainder of breakfast, after which Maria watched TV with Robby while the two men went to the basement to scan some of the material they had obtained from StellarScope. As they worked, Josh noticed some of the ads on Jeremy's web site.

"You advertise for the time travel club on you website? Isn't that a rip off?"

"I don't know, man. Like I said, some people swear it's true."

"Where do the ads come from?"

"Don't know. They started appearing a month ago, came over the net. I get a monthly fee for running them. Not much but I don't have to do much. Just display it. I checked out their site once out of curiosity. Nothing but a notice saying it will be available soon and offering a preview if you go to the center. I think it's out in the central part of Massachusetts somewhere."

"Sounds like a scam to me .You underground guys don't have many scruples, do you?"

"Hey, it's probably just as much on the level as most of the ads you see on TV. And what about political ads, they're just as far fetched."

Josh couldn't disagree, though he considered this time travel business just about as far out there as you could get. Then he had a thought.

"You say these ads started turning up about a month ago. Isn't that when Teller disappeared? I wonder if he's behind it. You said yourself his mentor had a theory about time travel."

"Yeah, I've been wondering the same thing myself."

"How would you get in touch with Teller if you wanted to find him?" Josh asked.

"Put an ad in the paper."

"An ad, you mean like a want ad?"

"An ad, man, like in the Personals. You know, lonely computer geek seeking soul mate, send photo to PO Box so and so."

"How would that work?"

"Put it in a few of the big newspapers. People do it all the time. If he's looking for contacts, he'll be looking in the personal ads. Maybe he's already put one in there himself. Maybe these time travel ads are messages. Of course, it'd have to be in code. Something that's only meaningful to him and the other person. Something, you know, personal."

"Hmm, you said you know a lot about him. Think we could cook up some sort of personal ad?"

"I don't know, maybe. I'll give it some thought. In the meantime, let's go through this material and organize what you want to upload so I can scan it."

They went through the satchel of documents and printouts, which they emptied in a pile on a card table. Much of it was emails and memos from the VP of engineering to the CEO regarding the status of the Peeble Deep Space Telescope project. Some of it was letters to and from the Secretary of Defense discussing the potential military use of the telescope. Then there was the incriminating second set of books. Selecting key pages from the pile, Josh handed them to Jeremy for scanning into the computer. Once they had the papers scanned, Josh edited them into a single Word document, adding a commentary and comments concerning the key pieces of evidence and how they fit together. He also provided a number of scenarios describing the likely train of events, including the probable fate of the missing scientist.

While he was doing this, Jeremy prepared a number of laptops for their nocturnal mission. As they worked, Maria's step-brother talked.

"The government's got things sewed up so tight you can't take a crap without them knowing it. Your banking records, your credit cards, your ATM, your cell phone, you can't scratch your ass without them knowing about it. They can watch you from the sky, intercept your conversations, listen in on your most intimate secrets. They can read your mind, man. They have your health records and the records of your entire family from the time you were born. They know everything there is to know about you."

"That's nice," said Josh, not sharing his host's paranoia. "Have you come up with an idea of how to contact Teller?"

"You mean your ad?"

"Yeah."

"Sure. We need a couple things. First of all, a name or nickname from the past that will catch his eye. Something that will freeze him in his tracks, make him take notice and alert him that someone is trying to contact him. Something no one else like the authorities will notice."

"Tall order."

"The more intimate knowledge we have of our target the better chance we have of finding him. Second, we need a way for him to contact us. Phone numbers are out. PO boxes are also a problem. Someone can easily stake one out. The best thing is to have a secret meeting place, some spot known only to Teller. Some place of special significance to him that we can check out ahead of time. Finally, we need a message. It doesn't have to make sense, at least not in a normal logical way, but it should have some meaning for the recipient. Something to tip him off it's for him."

"So what have you got?" asked Josh, estimating the diminishing odds of ever locating Teller this way. "It sounds pretty near impossible."

"Not really. I've got a few ideas," said Jeremy with confidence. "Teller's teacher and mentor was Henry Thomas Peeble. His nickname was Chic. Not too many people know that. It will make a good name to sign the ad with. Peeble was into time travel, so we could use something about time and traveling in the body of the message. We can use Teller's name in the body of the message as well, but use it in a way not associated with a name. It will be one more piece of the puzzle leading him to conclude it's a coded message for him. The place is a little more difficult. Teller's wife died about ten years ago. It almost destroyed him. He went on a hiatus, stopped working for almost two years. Peeble also disappeared around that time, so two of the most important people in Teller's life were gone at the same time. Perhaps he's trying to go back in time, to be with his beloved, who knows. Anyway, she's buried in the Meadow Glenn Cemetery in Newton. That can be the meeting place."

He handed Josh a slip of paper with some writing on it.

'Ardent time traveler seeking Fortune-Teller for hire. Meet me at the beloved's Meadow – chic'

"Hmm, clever. Look's good to me. Let's try it. How would we rendezvous with him?"

"That's the hard part. We have to run the ad for a couple of weeks. That will cost some serious change. Then we'd have to stake the place out, you know, visit it every day for a couple of weeks or so."

"Yikes!"

"You got a better idea. Maybe we could give him your phone number or your address? As a matter of fact, you can tell him the exact place and time you want to meet, so everyone else will know. Not to mention the fact that he may not see the ad in time. Or something may happen and you won't be able to keep the appointment. No, this is the best method of trying to contact him. It gives us the most flexibility and the most allowance for the unforeseeable."

"OK, can I take this?" Josh asked, folding the slip of paper. "I'll see if I can arrange to place it in a few papers."

"Sure, I'd try the Boston Globe and New York Times for starters."

The cryptic message would not mean much to most people, but might attract the attention of the missing scientist, especially with the nickname of his mentor. That is if he read either paper. It was a long shot but no longer than the one he had just spent the last few days following.

Still wondering if the time travel ads Jeremy was running on his web page had anything to do with the missing scientist he asked him a question.

"What about the money you get for running the ad, how does that come?"

"I get a check every month in the mail, a money order actually."

"Does it show where the money orders come from?"

"It must. I think I have one here from this month," he said, rummaging around in the top draw of his desk. "Yeah, here it is. It says, 'Post Office, Town of Pelham. I think that's in Massachusetts, near the Quabbin Reservoir, due south-east of here about fifty or sixty miles."

"Hmm, I might have to check that out," said Josh.

Chapter 8

Later that night, they took Jeremy's Jeep Cherokee and headed out to a quiet rest stop along the throughway. Like most of the rest areas along the main highways of New Hampshire and Vermont, it was furnished with a public Wi-Fi network.

It was a crisp cold night, the temperature suddenly starting to feel like winter after the long warm spell. What did they call it, an early Arctic vortex? The results of a shrinking polar ice cap, but hardly the end of the world like some viewed the unusual weather conditions and rapid transitions from season to season. The sky was sprinkled with myriad stars while a quarter-moon hung low in the sky. A long line of dark grey clouds that dotted the horizon to the north promised precipitation. They were going to attempt uploading the material they had scanned earlier with Josh's commentary. Hopefully, it would find its way to his ex-employer's headquarter computers. The question was would anyone know what to do with it. Josh planned to follow up with a phone call to his department head to help ensure that they did. He wanted desperately to call his ex-boss, but didn't know if Frank was being watched or not. His phones were definitely bugged and Josh had to assume he was being watched as well. No, Josh was on his own.

They parked behind a small building in an area reserved for trucks, a few of which were parked further on. The rest stop sat on a small knoll, which overlooked the town where the highway began its torturous route through the foothills of the White Mountains and ski country.

"This is as good a spot as any," said Jeremy. "We've got a good strong signal here and no interference. This will do just fine."

"What if somebody comes?" asked Maria, voicing Josh's own concern. She had insisted on coming and bringing her six year-old son along. Josh agreed, wanting to keep them near for his own security, although he wasn't sure it was a good idea. There was still an Amber Alert out on the boy. Whatever happened, it was probably better that they all stayed together. Robby wasn't old enough to know what was going on. To him it was one big adventure, except that he was beginning to worry about Christmas and whether Santa Claus would know where to find him.

""No one will bother us here," said Jeremy. "OK, I've got us connected to the worldwide web. Give me that address."

Josh read it off his business card.

"We'll try the email address first. If that works, we can attach the document you created to the email. That would be the easiest way. Otherwise, I'll try to spam their SMTP server, which will be a bear from out here over an unsecure network. Anyway, their security system would probably squash it."

"Then let's hope this works," Josh said. "What if someone intercepts it?"

"I've encrypted it, just in case. No one will be able to read it until we phone in the key. Of course, the feds would have no problem with it. Those NSA boys could decipher this simple code in a couple seconds, but somebody else, a casual hacker or the staties would have a problem. It's not much, but it's better than no encryption at all. We can phone the key in later, when you call to tell whoever we're sending this to what it is. Here we go."

He jabbed his finger on a key and a little 'Send in Progress' status bar appeared on the screen, showing the message had gone out. The icon stayed up for some time. Then a message box appeared with the words 'Estimated time to upload….20 minutes'.

"Twenty minutes!" yelled Josh in dismay. "It's going to take that long?"

"Hey, man, my wireless modem's only so fast. You've got a lot of documents concatenated together there, with figures and graphs. I've even compressed it, but it's still going to take a while. That's just an estimate anyway, based on normal times when the network is busy. This time of night, out here, we're practically the only ones on it. It won't take that long. Don't worry."

Jeremy was right and after about ten minutes another message box appeared saying 'Send Complete'. He hit the button to close down the connection but nothing happened. He tapped it several times, all to no effect. He went to the task bar and tried stopping the process manually, but still the computer ignored him. He checked the network management console, which indicated the connection was still open and active. He picked up the computer and shook it, then tried the exit buttons again, but nothing happened. The computer was completely ignoring him.

"What's wrong?" asked Josh, noticing Jeremy's annoyance.

"I don't know. The application's not closing like it's supposed to. I can't stop the process."

He pressed the power button and kept his finger down on it for several seconds. When nothing happened he kept the button down for a prolonged period, but still the machine did not shut off. The screen remained on showing the laptop's desktop and the message box.

"Crap!" yelled Jeremy, slamming down the computer top. "We've been spiked."

"What do you mean, spiked? What's wrong?" Josh asked again, now totally alarmed.

"Someone's deciphered our message and traced our transmission to this computer. From that they can triangulate in on us. They've found us. They've sent some kind of virus back up the network so I can't shut down my machine. It's acting like a LoJack unit homing in on our transmission. I can't shut it down. They must have been close by, waiting for us to transmit. We've got to go."

As if to punctuate his statements, they heard a loud whirling sound and saw lights approaching from the south. The lights seemed to be suspended in air. It had started to snow.

"What's that?" asked Maria, pointing in the direction of the lights.

"A helicopter!" yelled her half-brother in alarm. "They've found us."

With that he whipped the laptop out the window and turned on the ignition, spinning the Jeep from a dead stop to forty miles per hour. Peeling out of the rest stop, he sped down the highway, the helicopter now following right behind not more than a hundred feet in the air. Turning off the first exit, they saw two state police cars on the opposite side of the highway, going at top speed back toward the rest stop they had just left.

Jeremy instinctively headed toward the mountains, hoping to hide from the helicopter in the deeper wooded ravines beside the river, but at this time of year with the trees bare of leaves, it was a hopeless gamble. Yet the tall pines did offer some concealment as they raced toward the hills.

The snow began to fall in earnest and the wind to blow, hampering their vision as they sped up the road. The helicopter was closer now, not much above the tree tops. It followed the road after them, up one knoll and down another, around outcroppings and rocky hillsides. At one point it hovered right in front of them blocking the highway. Jeremy turned at the last minute down a small country lane already partially covered with snow. The jeep swerved as he drove, the rear end skidding to this side and that. Despite his bulk and a continuous string of swear words, he kept them on the road and moving away from the copter, which swayed in the air by the intersection at a right angle to the river. It then flew up and away and circled back sharply after them, as they slalomed back and forth down the road, following the river as it twisted across a small valley. It was back on their tail now, not thirty feet above them.

"We're not going to get away like this," Josh observed.

"I know. They've probably radioed ahead by now. I've tried to stay on the back roads, but sooner or later we're going to bump into a roadblock."

"What's that up ahead?"

Josh pointed straight ahead and to the right. In the feint light thrown off by two forlorn street lamps, a house appeared to be suspended over the river.

"A covered bridge," said Jeremy. "I've picnicked out here."

"Go for it. I have an idea."

"I got you, buddy," Jeremy yelled. "There are some trailers and farms back there," he said, pointing to the left at a road, which intersected the one they were on at the bridge. "Cut back across there about half a mile. I'm sure with the kid and all you'll be able to get some help. I doubt anyone up here knows about the trouble back in Boston. You'll be OK. You guys ready?"

As they came to the bridge, Jeremy slammed on the brakes. The helicopter flew by with a loud whoosh as he turned the jeep sharply to the right, almost skidding off the road. Again he got it under control, although at one point it looked as if they would smash through the covered bridge into the river. After swerving back and forth halfway across the structure, Jeremy slid the car to a stop.

"Now!" yelled Josh, grabbing Robby while Maria snatched the satchel of documents. They had their coats on, but it seemed insufficient protection from the wind and snow, which was now blowing like a blizzard.

"You'll be OK," yelled Jeremy, as he pulled the door shut and sped off. "Head across the road and up the hill."

"I hope so," said Maria, still doubtful about the whole thing, especially with the storm and a six-year old child to contend with, but her step-brother had already accelerated across the bridge. Hanging a hard right, he raced back up the other side of the river in the opposite direction, on the snow covered road. Any other vehicle would have had a problem, but Jeremy's had been built for just such conditions, and sped up the slick, slushy, white-topped road with relative ease. Its tires seemed to cling to the ground. The helicopter, which had stopped and hovered over the hard-covered bridge for a moment, took off after the jeep like a hawk going for a jack-rabbit.

When the coast was clear, Josh and Maria headed back across the bridge, Josh carrying the boy while Maria carted the bag of documents.

Cautiously, he peered out into the dark, silent night. Only the snow moved, fluttering down sideways now in soundless ranks of white. It covered everything with a blanket of wet powder. Part of him wanted to stay under the cover of the bridge, but he knew that others would be following right behind the copter. Time was of the essence. Without further hesitation, he led them across the highway and up the road approaching them, which came from the west to form a small intersection where two street lamps stood alone.

The snow stung their eyes. Josh carried the boy, who had fallen asleep in his arms as they walked, his head covered with the hood of his parka, itself white with snow. Maria wore a long thick coat with black sneakers and jeans. Not exactly the attire for hiking up a country road in a blizzard. Josh wore no coat at all, still in his clothes from three days ago, a heavy sweater and a pair of brown khaki slacks. Or was it four days? He had lost track.

There was nothing in front of them but empty road and the snow as the three tired and cold fugitives walked up the ice-covered track. The bitter wind blew at them with growing fury out of the darkness. Maria began to complain when Josh held up his hand.

"Wait! What was that?" he said. "There it is again - dogs."

They walked further up the dark road toward the sound. Soon they saw a light and behind it a low, squat log cabin. As they got closer they could hear several dogs barking, the sounds coming from the rear of the cabin.

"Sounds like a kennel or something. Maybe we can get help. Here's what we'll say."

Josh explained their cover - three motorist lost on the road after their car spun out on the bridge. He planned on dissuading whoever lived there from calling for help until the morning, using the storm and the child as an excuse to wait until then. Hopefully the storm would be over by that time and they could continue on their way without assistance.

The winter, which had held off for most of December had hit the northeast with a vengeance and was now making up for lost time. Josh

66

doubted whether anyone but a rescue team would be able to make it out in the present conditions.

He wondered how Jeremy had made out. He gave him better chances than the poor fools in the helicopter, whoever they were. Feds? Staties? He wished he had more information. He hadn't even been aware a northeaster was coming. Now he was a beggar out in the cold, without a car, without a home, without a friend.

The house was set back from the road. They approached with caution, Josh in the lead. Maria and Robbie, who had woken up by now, held back behind him. They walked along a long dirt drive where a truck and a smaller foreign car were parked. As they got closer to the house the dogs barked louder, so that now there was a virtual chorus of howls and yelps emanating from the rear of the building, a small, square, single-story structure made of logs.

Josh approached the concrete stoop at the side of the house and climbed the four steps to the door. A small lamp hung above the entranceway. Josh knocked. There was no answer. He knocked a second time and the door opened.

A short, thin man peeked out. He had dark skin and long hair that hung down to his shoulders, still black despite his sixty-two years.

"What do you want?" he said, looking at Josh.

"Can you help us? Our car's broken down up the road back there somewhere. I'm afraid we're lost and there's quite a blizzard blowing. We have a child with us."

"Oh," said the man, straightening up and looking over Josh's shoulder at Maria and her boy.

"Come in," he said after a short pause. "You might as well get out of the cold."

They entered a tiny but warm kitchen. The room was filled with the aroma of something baking in the oven. Their host motioned for them to come around the corner to the main room of the house.

The inside of the cabin was sided with finished pine. A fire burned in a large stone hearth. Assorted hunting implements – various knives, two hunting bows and a rifle - hung above the mantle and along the wall, together with animal furs and a pair of snowshoes. The head of a twelve-point buck adorned the opposite wall, the flames reflecting in the dead deer's eyes. The ceiling was high and pointed with a loft above the mounted trophy, reached by a ladder nailed to the wall. A skylight, now dark, gaped in the steep ceiling where a fan also hung. A bearskin rug sprawled across the wooden floor. Another carpet with what looked like an Indian design sat under a rough, wooden table in the dining area.

"You have an accident?" asked the man. "Is everyone OK?" He was short and slight with a dark complexion. He could have been a jockey, but this guy raised dogs not horses.

"No. Nothing serious," said Josh. "Just skidded off the road back by the bridge, slid into a ditch. We're all OK, just a little stressed out being out in the middle of nowhere with this snow storm kicking up like this. I couldn't get it out of the rut, car wouldn't budge. Then the motor gave out. I'm off the road enough where it's not a hazard. With my luck they'll probably tow it. That is if they can get a truck out here. It's pretty bad out there."

"Yeah, the radio says we got a big northeaster coming in. If it stalls like they say it might, we could be in for quite a storm."

"That's why I was hoping we might be able to stay here for the night. Wait for this thing to blow over."

The man remained silent and looked the three of them over.

"I don't know," he said slowly. "As you can see, I don't have much room. I don't have people here, never. Especially folks I don't know. I'll call the sheriff. Maybe he can help you."

He went back to the kitchen with Josh and grabbed the phone off the wall.

"Wait," said Josh. "We don't want to cause you any trouble. I doubt the sheriff can get out here anyway. I was in a jeep and could hardly drive in this storm. I couldn't see six-inches in front of my face. Look." He went to the kitchen where there was a big picture window and peered out. His host cut the overhead light and joined him. The snow was blowing sideways and had already begun piling up on the ground and drifting in small white piles on the fence and vehicles.

"Wow," said Robby, who had followed the men into the kitchen. This was his first blizzard and the large window and wild scene outside looked like a big hi-def TV screen.

"It's pretty bad, but the Sheriff has some all-terrain vehicles. He can make it or know someone who can. They're prepared for this type of thing."

"That may be," countered Josh, "but I'd rather not risk my wife and boy out in that type of weather. I don't care who it's with or what they're driving."

"Well, you can't stay here," said the little man, just as vehemently, closing the blinds and blocking out the snowy scene.

"Do you own a kennel?" asked Maria, changing the subject, as the dogs howled in the night against the wind. "I'm Maria. This is my husband Josh, and this is our son Robby. Sorry we haven't introduced ourselves earlier. We've had such a trying evening. Robby here has had quite a scare. To tell you the truth, I don't know what would have happened to us if we hadn't heard your dogs and seen your light." She stopped and started to cry. "We didn't mean any harm. But my husband's right, we can't go back out there again until morning. Please, can we just stay until morning? We won't be any trouble. We can sleep on the floor. We'll be out of your hair first thing tomorrow no matter what."

"Nice to meet you all," said the man, taking his eyes reluctantly off Josh, who was staring back angrily. He introduced himself as Dan Little-Wolf. "But I'm sorry, you can't stay here."

Josh started to object again when there was a knock on the door.

Chapter 9

Josh was having trouble adjusting to the scene around him, still not believing the events of the past few hours. It all seemed like a vivid bizarre dream.

None of them had seen or heard anyone approach, and were all startled at the sound of the knock. Josh and Maria, along with Robby, moved to the living area while Dan Little-Wolf answered the door in the kitchen, sticking his head out cautiously much as he had with Josh.

"Yes, can I help you?" he asked, facing a deputy dressed in winter gear. Another sheriff's deputy, equally garbed, stood behind him. Next to him was a man in a long, black dress coat and tie, as if he was going to a formal dinner engagement.

"We're looking for a couple of terrorists," announced the deputy. "They were trying to sabotage key government installations using transmitters in the area. The state police got their accomplice up the road, over by Herring's Junction, but the other two got away. They've got secret government documents. They also have a child with them. We're concerned about his safety. He could be in danger. They're wanted in connection with a couple murders as well. Have you seen anyone like that tonight?"

Dan was silent for a moment, as if thinking. Then he said, "No, Ruddy. The dogs were barking about a half-hour back, but that could have been the storm or a jackrabbit. I haven't seen anybody."

"Well, please call this number if you do," said the deputy, a local boy, and handed Dan his card. "It's a good night to have sled-dogs, eh, Mister Little-Wolf."

"Even I wouldn't take my dogs out on a night like this," said Dan through the half-closed door. "Hope you boys make it back OK." With that he slammed it shut.

"Damn white men," he said angrily. "Who was that with them? Government sticking their nose into everybody's business. What do they want you for?" He eyed the satchel of papers and notebooks still hanging on Maria's shoulder.

Josh was sure they were going to be handed over to the police, but just the opposite had happened. It appeared Dan Little-Wolf, half Micmac Indian, half French Canadian, didn't much care for the US government.

70

"Nothing," said Josh, thinking fast, hoping his host's anti-government leaning would be to their advantage. "We just have some material they don't want to see made public, something that will bust their homeland spying scheme wide open. Can you help us?"

"What's this about a murder?"

Maria answered, explaining what had happened to her friend and her mother. "They're trying to blame it on Josh here," she finished.

Dan Little-Wolf took a few moments to reply. "I don't know. They're no fools. They'll be back by morning with the staties when they don't find you. There's no place out here for you to hide. Where you going?"

The only place Josh could think of when asked was the location of the post office where the money orders for Jeremy's time-travel ads had been sent from.

"We're trying to get to here," he said, pointing to the center of his roadmap, to a little spot called Pelham, Massachusetts, located next to a large blue smudge labeled Quabbin Reservoir. South by south-west as the crow flew.

Their reluctant host turned out to be a guardian angel. He made them comfortable and gave them something to eat while they made plans.

"That's quite a trek, especially in this weather," said Dan, after hearing what Josh had in mind.

Josh didn't know if their attempt at uploading the information concerning the graft and cover-up at StellarScope had worked or not. In any case, he certainly hadn't had a chance to follow up with the key to the encryption scheme. While the NSA may have been able to decrypt the message without it, it was doubtful his news agency could. They wouldn't even know what it was.

"They traced us while we were trying to upload the evidence to my news agency in New York," observed Josh. "We barely got away. I don't know if the message got through or not. Or if they were able to decrypt it."

The revelation that Josh was a newspaper man from New York City did not especially endear him to Dan Little-Wolf, but the fact that the FBI was after him – as evident by the stiff in the suit – impressed him to no end. Dan sometimes got downright violent where the federal government was concerned, though he got along with the local boys well enough.

"My dogs could take us there," he said matter-of-factly. "Is that where you aim to send off your message?"

"What?" Josh said, momentarily confused. "Dogs? Where?"

"Where you want to go on the map there? My sled dogs could take us there."

"That's over fifty miles. With a child?"

"The woman and boy can ride in the sled. We could bundle them up with furs and blankets. It will be like a sleigh-ride. We can't stay here. We should be gone before morning."

Josh loathed the thought of going out into the blizzard with Maria and her young son. They were exhausted and not yet recovered from their recent ordeal.

"What about me?" he asked. "Where am I supposed to ride?"

"You'll have to run behind," replied Dan to Josh's dismay. "Have you ever used snowshoes?"

"I've done some cross-country and downhill as a kid. It's been awhile. Never been on snowshoes, though. Exactly how are you planning on doing this? We certainly can't stay out in the open the whole way. We'll have to have a place to stop and rest, right?"

"More than one," said Dan. "A trip like this, in this weather, could take a couple of days. But don't worry. I have a whole network of friends who can help us, all working to resist big brother."

Before Josh could object further, Dan took command, as if he had trained and practiced for this type of emergency all his life.

"You folks have a few hours to rest yet before it's time to go. We'll let the snow build up a bit more. From what I can tell the storm won't let up for hours if it ever does. I think it's going to stall for a couple of days and dump a mountain of the white stuff on us. I wouldn't be surprised if it doesn't stop everything, including the search for you people, but it will be nothing for the dogs."

"Why are you doing this?" asked Maria. "You don't even know us."

"Like I said, you're helping the cause. Someone's got to stand up to big government else they'll think they can walk all over everybody, like they've been doing to my people since you came here to steal our land."

Josh had heard it all before from angry Native American activists, but now from this small, dark man who was helping them, the words had new meaning. Now he felt like a downtrodden red man himself, one of the last of a few proud remnants of a dwindling race, fighting for their lives against the all-powerful government.

Dan went about readying the supplies and equipment they would need for the journey, and contacting a few of his friends along the route via his ham radio. Josh was too preoccupied with what they were about to do to get any real rest. He laid next to Maria and her boy in the small loft above the living room and tried to let sleep overtake him, but thoughts, worries and alternative plans bombarded his brain instead, making it impossible.

It seemed Dan was right. They didn't have much choice. It was only a matter of time before, by process of elimination, the police returned to check the area out in more detail, with many more men. While they might be safe until the storm abated, they would certainly be trapped and helpless when it did. The storm might actually be their only hope of escape. Or it might be their death, another small voice whispered to him. He went back and forth like this all night until Dan poked his head over the entrance to the loft.

"It's time to go. I've got the dogs ready and all the gear packed. Breakfast is cooking. You folks better get up and start getting ready. We have a long day ahead of us."

As Maria and the boy took their turn in the bathroom, Dan went over the day's route with Josh.

"The blizzard's still going strong. There's already a foot of snow on the ground and there'll be another six inches before daylight. Visibility is practically zero. It's a little before midnight. There's just enough darkness remaining to get out of the area without being noticed. I doubt we'll see much activity on the road except for the snowplows, and even they may have difficulty in this storm. It's a complete white-out. The drifts on the back roads are already three feet high, but we're not going that way. As soon as I can I'm going to head through the forest trails. In the summer you can hike for miles through here. That way we can travel most of the day. We'll head southwest and stop to rest at this point here," he said, pointing vaguely to a spot on the map in the northern part of Massachusetts, toward the middle of the state.

Dan had packed the sled with supplies and built a comfortable bed of fur and coverlets for the occupants. He would ride on the back rungs and drive the team of eight dogs and their lead, which were harnessed and arrayed in pairs. Josh tried out Dan's snowshoes in the front yard while their host made last minute preparations, after closing up his house. The snow continued to come down sideways, blown by a fierce wind from the northeast. It drifted in high mounds against the fence and parked cars, which were now almost buried.

Once Maria was settled in the sled, which Dan had pulled out onto the snow-covered drive, with Robby comfortably between her legs, they started off. There were still a few hours of darkness left, the unseen moon hanging somewhere to the west, the sun still beneath the horizon in the east. Not that it would cast much light on this wet, heavy, cloud-filled day. Now Josh found himself rambling behind a team of sled dogs in a raging blizzard.

He was keeping up well enough, but was soon winded and drenched in sweat. At first it was comforting to be blanketed by the snow's soft cocoon of whiteness, which enveloped them like down. After awhile, however, it became a driving, freezing obstacle that threatened to engulf him, tugging at his feet, making it hard to move forward. Although the snowshoes kept him from sinking knee deep in the snow, they were awkward to walk in. Each step took extra concentration and energy. After several hours, the exertion was starting to get to him. Falling further and further behind, he stumbled on blindly following the path of the sled, which was now out of sight. At one point he slipped and fell. Getting back up took all his energy. He called out but there was no reply. For a moment he thought they had left him behind.

"You having trouble keeping up?" asked a figure coming out of the darkness dressed in black with a red flannel hat. It was Dan Little-Wolf.

"Boy, I'm glad to see you," said Josh on recognizing their guide. "I need to rest. I'm not too good with these shoes. How far did you say we have to go?"

"Sixty miles, and we'll never make it like this."

It was getting light as the two men got back to the sled, which was resting by what used to be the main route south. It was now a mass of shifting, blowing snow without definition, except for a half-buried fence and a few half-covered telephone poles, their wires whipping in the wind. The dogs sat in a row, seeming impervious to the cold.

"It's getting light," said Dan Little-Wolf. "We need to get off the main drag. There's a side road up here that leads to the trails. They won't be doing patrols out here, if they're doing any at all. Then again, with you being an enemy of the state, who knows what they'll do. I think it'll be OK if we let you drive the team for awhile. It'll be straight going with little to worry about. My lead dog, Samson, will do all the work. All you have to do is stand on the back, push once in a while up the hills and hold-on on the way down. Once we get onto the steeper parts, I'll lead the team and you can push from behind. We'll see what it's like, but I think I can manage on the shoes better than you can."

"I'm sure I'll get the hang of it once I get used to them. I can pull my own weight."

"I know you will, and when it's your time to do so, you will run behind as best you can. For now you can ride."

He gave Josh a few more instructions and told him what to yell to get the dogs to stop and go. After testing the commands a few times, they were off, Josh riding on the rails at the back of the sled while Dan glided effortlessly behind on a pair of snowshoes. Soon they left the roads altogether and moved along snow-carpeted hiking trails.

They made good time and by morning, which looked much like the evening except a little brighter, they were in a wooded area interspersed with broad, picturesque meadows that would have been considered a beautiful winter landscape if it were not for the urgency of their plight.

Robby, who slept most of the time due to the gentle motion of the sled on the soft snow, seemed to be doing fine. He was swathed in furs and blankets, and when he was awake, was fascinated with the novelty of being pulled by a team of huskies. Maria kept him otherwise occupied as they rode silently through the woods.

Josh took his turn running behind the sled in the snowshoes, which he was starting to get the knack of. Still, the going was tough. At one point Dan had to lead the dogs by their bridles to get them up the steeper part of the trail, while Josh pushed from behind. Now Josh was on the shoes again, trudging through the deep snow that had fallen all that morning. The sled was somewhere ahead of him, lost in the stinging pellets of white that made it impossible to see more than a few feet ahead. He was walking through a wooded area following the path of the sled when he passed two large pine trees and an old wall made of field rocks, into a short clearing. At the end of the clearing was the vague outline of a narrow country lane where Dan had stopped the sled. He was peering warily from left to right.

"It's all clear. My friends live up the road here. They're expecting us."

With that, he brought the dogs and sled out onto the unplowed road. Before long they came to a mailbox that was almost buried in snow. At the opposite end of a long, half-plowed driveway, which snaked through a wide, empty field, was an oddly-shaped, two-story house. The living area was built over the garage, while the right side of the house faced the road. The rear of the building was at ground level, while the front door and porch were perched almost twenty feet in the air as the land fell away to a river that ran to the left of the house, just visible through the bare limbs of the trees that lined it. Dan reigned in his dogs at the end of the drive next to the comfortable looking dwelling. Smoke curled invitingly from a double-sized chimney.

"Where are we?" asked Josh, struggling up to Dan, who was unhitching the dogs. Maria and Robby were extricating themselves from the bundles of fur and blankets, the boy rubbing the cobwebs from his eyes.

"This is my friends, Gladys' and Archie's place. I told them we'd be stopping by and that we're on a mission to screw the man."

As they talked, a large man, who looked like a husky himself, came out of the house and stood staring at them from the front porch. He had a long, frizzy blond beard and unkempt hair of the same color, and wore overalls with suspenders and a red flannel undershirt. Slowly, still staring at the newcomers, he descended the stairway that led from the second level porch. A couple of large dogs were barking from behind the house, which set off a chorus of yelps and howls from Dan's Huskies.

"Shut up there, Shasa. You too, Hesha. Keep quiet, Samson. You should know better." Dan's dogs obeyed him instantly and stopped their whimpering. The man at the porch yelled even louder down at his two shepherds, which also brought instantaneous silence.

"Hi, Arch," said Dan, climbing up the stairs with his knapsack. Josh, Maria and Robby brought up the rear. "Thanks for shoveling the stairs. I'd like you to meet the friends I told you about."

"Hi," said the wild-looking man, eyeing his guests suspiciously. "You won't need them stairs to get up here if this snow don't let up. I better bring in the dogs. Don't want to leave them out here with your pack of wolves. They might eat them."

"Naw, not in one sitting. I fed them today anyway."

They both laughed, as their host invited everyone in out of the storm.

"Quite a blizzard out here, eh."

"Yeah," said Dan stepping into a spacious living room with pine-paneled walls much like he had in his log cabin. "Finally. I've been waiting for a storm like this."

A large stone fireplace took up most of the opposite wall, where even more hunting implements and trophies hung than in Dan's lodge. Two huge bear skin rugs covered the wood floor. Archie, their host, went through an entrance into the kitchen, where he opened a rear door and called down to his dogs. Moments later two large German shepherds came bounding into the house like stampeding buffalo, but stopped short of the living area on a stern look from their master. He left Dan to make introductions.

"Josh, Maria, this is Gladys."

"Hi, kids," said an overweight woman in maroon sweatpants and matching pullover. Her hair was long and tangled as if she hadn't combed it in days, and already prematurely grey. "Nice to meet you. Who's this little guy?" She glanced behind Maria where Robby tried vainly to hide.

"This is Robby, my boy," answered Maria. "Say hi to the nice lady, Robby."

"I hope you folks don't mind dogs. They won't bite, but they'll slobber all over you if you let them."

"No, not at all," replied Josh looking over at Maria and Robby who were already petting the big dogs. The dogs, in turn, smelled them and wagged their tails in unison.

"They love company, especially kids," said Gladys. "Our nephew Andy loves them."

"How's the hunting?" asked Dan, sitting down on a sofa couch, which was next to the entrance facing the large fireplace. Two large men in tight fitting shorts wrestled each other on the TV, which sat in the corner.

"Not that good. It's been too dry. Now with the snowfall things will be better. That is if it ever stops. Too bad the season's almost over."

"Archie hunts with a bow. Just like my ancestors. He killed both of those bears on the floor there with his bow and arrows. Ain't that right, Arch?"

"I'm sure your ancestors were a lot better at it than I am, but I do OK. That brown one there almost took me with him. You folks like venison?" he asked his three visitors.

"Not sure," said Maria. "I've never had it."

"I have. When I was a kid," volunteered Josh, remembering when his dad and uncle used to go hunting in the mountains of upstate Vermont. "Taste kind of gamey if it's not cooked right."

"Gladys cooks up a mean venison steak. Maybe if you're around long enough, we can get you some."

"That'll be nice, Arch, but we kind of got to move on. We need to get Mister Banks here to Quabbin. We only plan on staying a few hours, just enough to rest the dogs and get a few winks. Do you mind? We need some sleep, and a supper before we take off again would be nice. We can stay in the garage. We've got bags."

"You'll do no such thing," said Gladys, who was known at the gun club as Mrs. Pollock. "Maria and Robbie can stay in our room downstairs. Joshua can sleep up here on the couch. Arch and I will be in the den on the first floor. Dan, you can stay in your usual room."

"That will be fine. We'll be leaving at midnight when the moon is high. I noticed you don't have any lights up. Where's your tree? I thought you'd have it up by now. Christmas is only a week away."

"Ain't putting up a tree this year," growled Archie. "Why bother, with the world coming to an end."

"Not much use doing anything any more," added Gladys. "The Lord has had it with us humans. It's been written. The day of judgment is coming."

"That may be so," countered Dan. "But you might as well keep on living until the last moment, like a warrior. Be brave and die young."

"Not all of us are warriors," observed Gladys, retreating into the kitchen to make her guests something to eat.

"Hey, I know him," said Archie, who had been looking at Josh as if he were trying to remember something. "He's the one wanted for kidnapping and murder!"

When their host mentioned murder his demeanor turned hostile. His dogs picked up on their master's vibes, and started growling at the tall stranger. Their tails stopped wagging simultaneously. Josh noticed the big guns sitting over the mantel, as well as the high-powered hunting bows and steel-tipped arrows. Dan looked on with a questioning expression, not quite sure his new acquaintance's previous explanation had been adequate. Josh started feeling uncomfortable.

Chapter 10

They were now on their way again, but for a moment Josh wasn't sure if he'd be going anywhere.

He had stood there unable to utter a sound in his defense, waiting for Maria to come to his aid, but she seemed not to be following the conversation as she watched TV with Robby. Finally, when she said nothing, he spoke up.

"I didn't kill anyone. The people after us are the killers. They killed Maria's friend after she brought us these papers. They tried to get her to kidnap Maria's kid but she refused so they killed her. She was at Maria's apartment when it happened. Isn't that right Maria?" She nodded, but didn't take her eyes off the TV and the big men in tights. "They made her lie to the police about me to ruin my credibility so I couldn't harm them. They killed her mother too when she wouldn't tell them where we were. Maria?"

"I don't know who killed my mother," she said, finally tearing her eyes from the television, where a half-naked man lay unconscious on the canvas. "But I know Josh didn't do it. He was with me when it happened. What he's saying is true. He's not a murderer and we're not kidnapped."

"Then why don't you give yourselves up and clear your name if that's the case?" said their host, who still didn't quite believe Josh's story despite Maria's collaboration.

"Because the government's in on it," said Josh. "They're not interested in the murders. They're probably involved and covering up as well. There's a huge amount of money involved, billions. Part of covering it up involves eliminating any incriminating evidence and that includes the three of us."

"So what are you planning to do?" asked Archie. "Why you going to Quabbin? What's there?"

"I'm not sure. I've got no place better to go. We tried to transmit our material over the Internet but I'm not sure it worked. That's how our accomplice got caught, her brother, Jeremy Gereau."

"Hey, I know him," said Archie. "His web site is real cool. He's a real righteous dude." He looked at Maria with new-found respect. "He's your brother? He got caught?"

"Yes, my step-brother," responded Maria.

Josh continued. "That's what the deputy said who came to Dan's door. Jeremy showed me an address from his web site. He was displaying these time-travel ads on his web page. It's just a hunch but I think they may have something to do with the Peeble Telescope and the missing scientist, which is the story I was working on when all this happened. Jeremy thought the government was trying to take over the project to spy on people."

"Well, ain't that just like the man," said Archie in indignation.

"Jeremy said something about a decryption key. He was going to phone it in. They can use it to decipher the message we sent earlier, but we were chased and separated so I don't have it. I'm not even sure the message was sent successfully."

"And you don't know the key?" asked Dan. "He didn't leave it with you?"

"No. Everything happened so fast we didn't even have a chance to talk. One minute we were sitting in the rest stop sending out the message over his laptop on a Wi-Fi network, the next we were being chased down the highway by a helicopter. We jumped out under a bridge. They must have caught him after we left and met Dan. Dan's been a life-saver. He offered to help after he heard what it was all about. He's a real patriot."

"Hear that, Dan? He's calling you a patriot." They both laughed loudly. "Dan here would just as soon see the whole country go down in flames."

"The world's going to end," said Gladys, coming back into the room with a tray of sandwiches and various dressings. "It's supposed to end on the last day of the year. It's all been ordained, you know. I saw a show on TV that told how there's a comet coming that no one even knew about, and it's on a collision course with earth, but our government doesn't want the public to know about it, because there's nothing they can do. They showed all sorts of evidence, but for every scientist who says it's true, the comet is coming, there's another one who says it isn't. Or that it would be close but no closer than other comets that have flown through our solar system. But with all the other signs, the strange weather and astrological events, I believe it's going to happen, you wait and see. Then only the righteous will survive to carry on the human race. It's been foretold. The signs are everywhere."

Everyone stopped and stared at the slightly deranged sounding woman. Of course, they had all heard the rumors, which had persisted for years. Now that time had passed, those rumors had only grown louder. Josh for one, didn't believe it, nor had anyone in his circle of acquaintances or associates. However, many did, including Gladys and Archie. Dan didn't seem to care either way, and was hoping the ancient texts predicting the end only applied to white people.

"This weather sure has been strange," Archie volunteered, not dismissing the predictions out of hand. "No spring or fall, unseasonably warm winter, then bam, this raging non-stop blizzard. Not to mention the hurricanes out west in Chicago. How weird is that, eh? The animals have been acting strange as well. It's almost like there's some kind of migration going on. No game where you'd expect it or always seen them, and herds of animals where you've never seen them before. Something's up."

"Animals can sense that sort of thing," said Dan. "My dogs have been acting funny."

"Then maybe none of it matters," said Josh. "But right now I feel our lives are in jeopardy. Just in case it doesn't all end in a dozen or so days, I'd like to see if I can't end this nightmare I'm in and get my life back to normal."

Gladys went into the kitchen to feed the dogs, while Dan went out to do the same for his. Josh could hear them all barking with anticipation, as he greedily ate his ham and cheese sandwich on white bread. While they were eating, Maria noticed something Robby was playing with.

"What's this, sweetie?" she asked, lifting the small, wrinkled, grease-stained piece of paper from his hands. "It's got something written on it, with your name, Josh."

Josh took it from her hand and held it up to the light.

"Hmm, just a meaningless phrase, 'I get hungry drinking milk'. I wonder what that could mean." He thought for a minute but in his tired state couldn't think straight. He had almost given up when it came to him.

"Wait a minute. I wonder if this is the decryption key? That's the only thing that makes sense. He must have written it on a piece of paper and left it on the table, and Robby picked it up and put it in his pocket. Or maybe Jeremy stuck it there, whatever. We'll give it a try."

"Look's like it's your lucky day," said Archie.

"Now if I could only get to a phone," replied Josh.

"Not from here, I'm afraid," said their host. "You're not calling out from here."

"No, I know. They're sure to be monitoring the news agency. They could trace the call. I wouldn't want that, though whoever's eavesdropping has probably already decoded our message by now. The important thing is the newspapers get it and publish it so the whole world knows the truth. Then maybe it will be safe for us to turn ourselves in."

Even though it was still light at the time and wouldn't be dark for a few hours, they had all gone off to their designated spots and tried to catch a few hours of shut-eye. Josh closed the blinds and shut the drapes to make the room where he slept on the couch as dark as possible. Gladys brought him a pillow and blanket.

"Come on, Thor," she said to one of the dogs that was getting too interested in Josh as he tried to ready his bed. "I'll put them in the garage so they don't bother you. Get some rest. Knowing Dan, he'll have you going all night. We'll wake you a little before midnight."

"Thanks, you folks have been so kind. I don't know how to repay you."

"The world's going to end. Do God's work and he'll do right by you. Be with God," she said, leaving Josh alone in the darkened room, where he was soon asleep. It seemed he had only just lain down when Dan woke him.

"It's time to go if we want to get there by noon," he said.

It was pitch dark outside, the moon and stars blocked by the dark grey clouds, which continued to spew forth their cold white particles of icy condensation. At least another foot or two had fallen since they stopped six hours earlier. Without ceremony, they had readied the sled for the next stage of their journey. The dogs seemed raring to go.

The snow made a strange misshapen landscape as it covered fences and automobiles like mounds of white flowing lava. Nothing was recognizable. Sign posts and fence posts were totally engulfed, telephone poles and trees only a fraction of their normal size. Everything was hushed as if covered with a blanket of cotton.

"I'll have to steer us out of here," Dan informed them. "You'll have to follow with the shoes, Josh. It's too deep for skis."

"When's it going to stop snowing?" asked Maria, joining them at the sled. She had on an oversized parka that Gladys had given her.

"By the looks of it never and that suits me fine," replied Dan, going to his lead dog to talk to it as usual before starting out.

Their hosts had come out to see them off. Archie, in just his overalls and red flannel undershirt, seemed impervious to the wind and

82

cold. A Russian-style fur hat with the ear-flaps down was his only acknowledgement to the elements. Gladys wore a light blue parka like the one she had given Maria, and ear-muffs with a scarf.

"Here, I thought you might like this for the road," she said, handing Dan a red thermal-lined bag. "There's some sandwiches in there, trail-mix and a few other things. It ain't much, but it will taste good on the road. There's a thermos of coffee too. Keep that by your side, dear. It'll keep you warm."

She gave the food and coffee to Maria once she had settled in the sled with Robby between her legs. Dan took up his place behind her, driving the dog team, while Josh stood ready behind. With the few hours rest and some food, he felt he'd do better keeping up on this part of the journey.

"Be with God," said Gladys. "We are all on the brink of Armageddon. Only your actions can save you."

They started out much as they had the night before from Dan's house. Soon the warm lights of Gladys' and Archie's place were no longer visible through the tree limbs and blowing snow.

That had been over an hour ago. Josh concentrated on his breathing and balance, and tried to expend as little energy as possible. Despite the relentless, driving snow he felt good. They couldn't have had a better means of transportation, and the storm promised to keep all but the hardiest search parties grounded for the duration.

Of course, it all seemed hopeless, now that he thought about it. What, after all, did he hope to accomplish once he got to the little town in the middle of Massachusetts. So the fees for the time travel ads on Jeremy's web site came from there. What did that prove? What possible connection could that have with the missing Dr. Benjamin Teller and his telescope? More than likely none, he reasoned. No, his best hope of contacting Teller was the ad Jeremy had suggested he put in the Personals. He still had the piece of paper with the cryptic message written on it. He resolved then and there, as he jogged behind the dogsled in the snow, to put the ad in the papers the first chance he got.

The first thing they had to do, sometime before daylight, was find a payphone, preferably one in an out of the way spot. Some place where Josh could call in the encryption key to his news agency unobserved, in the hope they had gotten the material and hadn't deleted it. Once he explained what it was he had sent them, it only awaited the key to make it publishable. Finding a payphone in the four-foot snow drifts, however, could prove difficult and would only get harder as the blizzard, which showed no signs of abating, raged on. The weather report they heard on the TV before they left Archie's and Gladys's house showed the big Nor' Easter stalled just off the coast of Gloucester. Some were predicting a repeat of the Blizzard of '78, which dumped as much as seven feet of snow in some places and stranded motorists across the state. That was a few years before Josh or Maria's birth, so it all meant little to them, except that there would be plenty of white stuff for the sled. It had already snowed more than thirty-two hours.

About 4:00 am they found a small convenience store. Because of the early hour and the storm the place was as deserted as an outpost in Greenland. High drifts blocked the entrance, piled wind-blown against the front windows. The phone actually had a booth, which someone had thought to shut, so it was empty of snow. A long, thin path, half re-covered, snaked from a small parking lot where someone had also attempted to plow, to the front of the booth, the remaining three-sides of which were all but covered.

Dan and Josh worked their way through the high drifts from the back of the store, where they hid the dogs and the sled, to the phone booth.

Shutting himself in, momentarily out of the wind but not the cold, which permeated the metal box like icy fingers, Josh made his call, using the change he had gotten from Archie and Gladys just for this purpose. Dan stood close by watching the road.

His fingers were so cold he almost dropped the coins, and had trouble dialing the number. After seven rings he got a recording.

"Damn," he swore. "It's too early. It's a recording."

"Give them your message and hang up. It's bound to be traced," urged Dan.

Josh dialed the extension of the VP of his department, his boss Frank Sullivan's boss, the same one they had sent the email with its attachment to. Josh hoped that Frank had talked to him about the situation and that the VP would be sensitive to any information related to it. At the beep, he gave his name and said he had very important information concerning the Peeble Telescope project and the missing Dr. Teller, as well as possible corruption in the defense Department – a phrase sure to catch his boss's attention – which he had sent yesterday evening. Here is the key you need to read it."

"I get hungry drinking milk."

He repeated the phrase and hung up. He had given them all the information they needed. Now they had the key as well. They were smart enough to put it all together. The ball was in their court. He was banking that they would know what to do with the information now that they had it.

"Let's go," said Dan when he was through. "We've got to keep moving."

Dan let him drive the team for awhile, now that it was getting light and the way ahead lay along straight, flat country roads, impassible to all but tracked vehicles, but easy for the dog-sled to follow. Only the top halves of the telephone poles were still visible in the high, plowed drifts along the roadsides.

The storm ebbed and flowed but continued unabated. It would appear to wane at times, only to pick up again with added fury. The wind seemed confused, as if not quite sure where it was coming from, first blowing from the northeast, then the west, then directly from the south. The snow swirled around them in endless eddies, twisted by the schizoid gusts, so that it was impossible to tell which of it was from the ground and what from the sky.

They had left the Jaffrey area in New Hampshire early in the morning over twenty-four hours before, and had stayed at Archie's and Gladys's house just across the border in Massachusetts for a little over six hours. They had marched south from there for another five hours and were now approaching the town of Athol, to the northeast of their destination, which was the village of Pelham on the western side of the long finger of water known as Qaubbin Reservoir.

"We're in South Royalston," said Dan, who had run ahead on the snowshoes and now came back to halt the team. "Athol's dead ahead. I think we should get off the road, head a little southeastward to skirt the village. We can cut back below the town and follow 66 west from there. There's a trail along here if I remember right. I used to race down here a few years ago, around the reservoir."

"Are we going to stop and rest soon?" asked Maria. "Robby's tired and so am I."

"Me too," said Josh. "I don't think I can go much further if I have to walk in those shoes again."

"Don't worry," said Dan, giving his lead dog a treat and pulling the team to its feet. "I have some friends who live in South Athol. We can stay there. They know we're coming."

85

They had not gone ten feet when Dan held up his hand to stop them again.

"What's that?" he said, looking straight ahead down the road into the swirling misted grayness of the blizzard.

Barely visible in the whiteout was a vague form with flashing lights moving up the highway in their direction. The dull thud of an engine laboring under a great strain gradually emerged over the sound of the wind.

"It's a snow plow. We have to get off the road."

He looked around frantically, but there was no place to go. The sides of the road were piled high with six-foot banks of hard encrusted snow where the plows had fought their losing battle with the elements. Now they were making one last attempt to keep the roads open before giving up. Unfortunately, Dan and his dogs were right in the way.

The large truck was moving fast, blowing snow up in front of it like a mini-cyclone. Dan grabbed his lead dog and tried to pull him and the team after him up the lowest of the snow banks as the truck whooshed by raising even more whirling gusts. Directly behind it was an all-terrain state police vehicle with red and blue flashing lights. They pulled up and skidded to a halt next to the sled before anyone had a chance to move. Another state police vehicle, which had been following a short distance behind, pulled up as well. The troopers got out with their guns drawn.

"We've been looking for you," said the first officer, as he approached Josh with his revolver pointed at his head.

Chapter 11

Dan and Josh had been handcuffed and placed in the back of the squad car, while Maria and her son were put in the larger all-terrain vehicle. The trooper in the passenger seat read them their rights as the car turned around and headed back up the highway toward the town of Athol.

"Since when is it against the law to ride a dog sled?" Dan had asked, indignantly. "What's this all about?" Josh didn't say a word. He suspected their most recent phone call had been all that was needed to track them down.

"You and your dog sled are abetting a fugitive who's wanted for kidnapping and murder back in Boston. There's been an Amber Alert out on that boy for almost a week now."

"That's bull," said Dan vehemently. Josh only hoped his lawyer would be as aggressive. "I've been with the boy and woman he's supposed to have kidnapped. Ask them if they've been abducted!"

"There'll be plenty of time to tell your story when we get to town. The FBI wants to talk to Mister Banks." With that Dan had fallen silent, realizing the less he said the better. Josh's heart sank through the seat to the bottom of the car to be dragged along the road behind them.

Now he was sitting in a holding cell in the state police barracks just outside of town. He had been there alone for almost two hours, when he heard doors clang open down the hallway and steps coming his way. They echoed off the polished floor and hard stone walls of the small cellblock, which appeared to be empty except for Josh. He wasn't sure where they had taken Dan or Maria.

"Hello, Mister Banks," said a man in a dark expensive suit. He looked like the same one who had come to the door of Dan's cabin. "We've been looking for you."

"So I've been told," said Josh. "I haven't kidnapped or killed anybody, but I can tell you who has."

"Whoa, slow down there. There's plenty of time for that. Anyway, that's not why I wanted to talk to you. Miss Cavello has told us how you tried to help her. As a matter of fact, Miss Cavello has told us quite a bit, some of it hard to believe, I'm afraid."

"It's all true. It's all a cover-up by that company building the Peeble Telescope, and they'll stop at nothing, but then I guess you already know that since the government is in the company's pocket."

They were alone in the room, a small corridor surrounded on three sides by four rectangular cages, the holding cells for prisoners before they were taken to the county jail or prison. A locked door led out to the station itself.

"Suppose you tell me what happened, from the beginning."

Josh hesitated.

"It will be on the evening news if all goes well," he informed the FBI man.

"That's what I'm afraid of. That could cause more harm than good."

"For who?" said Josh with a smirk.

"Contrary to what you may believe, Mister Banks, I'm on your side. Tell me what happened."

Agent Tom Hagen had been following this case ever since the scientist for the much publicized Peeble Telescope had disappeared. Years on the job investigating corporate crime and the agency itself had given him a unique perspective and a nose for digging up facts other people wanted buried. He knew of the rumors that the government was trying to convert the telescope to military purposes and was secretly pumping billions of dollars into the project, which was now behind schedule and in financial trouble. He had been asked to look into just such allegations, yet when he tried to do so he was blocked every step of the way by his counterpart in the Defense Department. It was looking more and more like a conspiracy, especially when put together with what the fugitive news correspondent and his girlfriend were telling him. When Josh finished his story, bringing it up to the present moment, Tom Hagen mopped his wide forehead.

"That's quite a story," he said, as if he was having trouble believing it. "There's no record of you being picked up that night by StellarScope security. The police report for that evening says nothing of it, except that they arrested you in the town of Marlborough after receiving a complaint from the woman, who now denies it."

"It's a big town. That's where their facility is. The police could be part of the cover-up, especially with the amount of money involved."

"Ellen Primrose could have been murdered by anyone after Maria left her," said the FBI agent. "Just like her mother. Violent crime is on the increase, it seems, with the end of the year coming. It could all be a big coincidence. What makes you so sure this StellarScope company is involved?"

"Who else had a motive to murder these people? No, it had to be them. Why don't you believe us? It's so damn obvious."

"I've looked over the documents you had. The information you went through so much trouble to publicize may be embarrassing for the company, especially considering the financial problems they're having right now, but hardly a motive for murder."

"That's what we thought at first, but there's another set of books in there proving theft on a grand scale. There are also memos from the Secretary of Defense implicating him in the affair. If news of this got out some very important men could go to jail for a very long time. People have been known to kill for a lot less. You just haven't looked close enough. It's all spelled out in the documents I uploaded to my news agency. If all goes well they'll be putting it on the air as we speak. It's definitely no happenstance that the Primrose woman was murdered immediately after helping us. And what about Maria's mom? No, it's too much of a coincidence to be rationalized away. These people must be as arrogant and cock-sure as a bunch of Gestapo thugs to think they can get away with this."

"Hmm, I get your point," said the lawman, as if he hadn't already reached the same conclusion. "You think the government is involved?"

"The feds didn't seem interested in any kidnapping or murder," said Josh, finishing up his story. "Just the documents."

Tom half-believed the fast-talking newsman, but wasn't going to let him know it, and the last thing he was going to do was let him go and add to the speculation already rampant in the media.

"Regardless of what's in those documents the police still think you're the murderer. So you see we have quite a dilemma here. We'll have to put you all in front of a judge back in Boston and let him sort it out. That is if this snow ever lets up."

Tom left his prisoner stammering in protest. The FBI man's agency had taken over the case from the state boys after the Cavello boy was reported kidnapped. The NSA had been monitoring Josh's news agency on behalf of someone in the Bureau. It had been the NSA who had intercepted their uploaded message and sent the helicopter after them. Tom was trying to connect the pieces and find out who in the FBI was pulling the strings.

The helicopter went down shortly after Josh and Maria left Jeremy's car in the covered bridge, killing one person on board. Maria's step-brother had been apprehended a short time later trying to get back across the river to the main road. Tom's superiors in Internal Affairs were enraged over the loss of the helicopter and man, both of which belonged to the Bureau, and sent Tom to investigate and take over the case. They were in no mood to tolerate shenanigans in one of their departments. When it came to the NSA, however, all bets were off. Anybody could be pulling their strings, and trying to find out who it was would be next to impossible.

For now Tom had other things to worry about. The first thing he did was contact his boss in Washington, who ordered him to take the prisoner, along with Maria and the boy, back to Boston to a federal judge. The next thing he did was check the latest weather forecast. The huge low still hung off the coast, whirling wind and moisture down from the northeast in shrouds of cloud and precipitation. It had already snowed more than forty-eight hours non-stop. If it kept up like this much longer, the roads would be completely shut down. The state and local police had been rescuing stranded motorists for the last twenty-four hours. All highways except a small stretch of the Mass Turnpike and 128 had been closed since 10:00 pm the previous evening. Only specially equipped vehicles or skidoos were moving, along with an occasional dog sled or two.

Tom figured his two prisoners were either telling him the truth or great liars. He had to admit, the material in the box was potentially very damaging to the company. If what Josh claimed was true, it might very well prove to be a motive for the murder of the Primrose woman and Maria's mother. It was obvious Maria and her son had not been kidnapped. The prisoner's and the girl's story appeared to coincide in all important details. Their testimony together with the evidence, which the experts back at the lab would be able to examine thoroughly, seemed to indicate that not only were top officials in the company stealing millions of dollars, but someone high in the government might be involved as well. If that were the case, they could have someone in the Bureau on their payroll.

He grabbed another cup of coffee and sat at an empty desk to write up his report. He had learned nothing from the dogsledder, except that he had a healthy contempt for the government. If he had wanted, he could have booked him on aiding and abetting a fugitive - and given the man's sarcastic and rude manner he had a good mind to - but after further reflection he didn't think it fair to the dogs, so he had charged him with a misdemeanor and ordered him let go. He'd have his day in court with a local judge. The sooner the man was out of his hair the better. They knew where to find Mister Dan 'Little-Wolf' Peters if they needed to.

He got on the radio and made plans to have the prisoner moved the next morning, along with Maria and her child, but was told whatever arrangements he made, they'd have to wait until the storm ended. There was no way they would be able to go anywhere by rail or road until then.

It was now well past six pm. It had been snowing for nearly three days straight. The town was closed up like a bank vault. If Tom wanted to have dinner he'd have to catch it and cook it himself. He went to the lone vending machine by the entrance to the barracks and perused the meager selection, finally settling on a ham and cheese sandwich, even though it was something he rarely ate. He was hoping it would settle his stomach, but searching his wallet he found he didn't even have enough for that.

"Four-fifty!" he swore, slamming the machine with his palm. "Anyone got a couple of dollars I can borrow until I can get to an ATM?" he yelled over his shoulder.

A couple of guys in gray uniforms looked up from their desks, but otherwise pretended not to hear or understand what he said and went back to whatever they were doing without answering.

Tom put on his coat and went outside in search of something to eat. He found a small convenience store, which was the only place opened in town. The streets were only partially cleared, the plows slowly losing ground to the storm. A lone stoplight swung in the wind, casting first red, then yellow, then green shades of illumination over the empty intersection. Street-lamps and telephone poles stood half covered by the huge snow banks that lined the roads. There was an ATM next to the store, which he used to get some cash, with which he purchased a sandwich and some chips.

"Surprised you're opened," he said to the sleepy clerk.

"I wouldn't be here except I'm stranded. They closed the roads out of town. I'm staying in the back. Might as well keep the store open. They have to pay me time-and-a-half. This is the best Christmas I could have asked for."

"Good for you," said Tom. "I know I appreciate that you're open. Have a nice evening."

Tom went back across the street to the police station, where he planned to spend the night in one of the cells. Some Christmas, he muttered to himself, though if he was lucky he still might be home in time for the holiday. When he found himself alone, he took out his phone and called his wife Alice in D.C.

"Hey, Hon," he said, when his wife picked up the phone.

"Hi, Honey. Where are you? Andrew asked me if you'd be home for Christmas."

"Tell him I'll try like heck. With any luck, if this storm let's up, I might be able to make it back by Christmas Day. We'll see. I have to accompany a prisoner back to Boston. Then I should be able to slip back to DC and spend a few days with you and Andy."

"That would be great. I can't believe they've got you out in this weather. The whole city's closed down. They haven't seen anything like it in a hundred years."

"I know, but it's got to end sometime. Say hi to Andrew. I'll try and call Christmas Eve."

He felt instantly depressed when he disconnected the phone. Sleeping in a cell didn't help his frame of mind either.

Tom spent most of the next day trying to arrange transportation, but the snow was still falling and the roads were still closed. The only things moving were large, multi-terrain vehicles or tractors that could make their way through the four and five foot snow and even deeper drifts that blocked the route back to Boston. But these weren't suited to transporting prisoners, let alone a woman and small boy. For a brief moment Tom thought of the short, dark man with the dogsled, but put the thought out of his head. He'd have to wait until the storm died down if he wanted to go anywhere. He had both lunch and dinner in the corner convenience store, chatting with the stranded clerk and half a dozen locals who lived within walking distance. A lot of people were out and about that day, mostly from curiosity, having never seen that much snow before. Frustrated at the elements and his lack of a home-cooked meal, Tom spent another night in a cell. When the prisoner insisted on talking well into the night, trying to convince him to let him go, Tom went back into the office and slept on a bench.

That night, a little after 9:00 pm, after more than seventy-eight hours, it finally stopped precipitating. The next morning, with the help of the Sheriff and the staties, agent Hagen was able to commandeer two vehicles for the trip to Boston. Still, because there was a child involved, he hesitated to order the move until he was sure the roads would be clear.

Later that afternoon, after an army of snowplows and graders had completely plowed and sanded the highway, Tom decided to make the attempt. The child would stay with the sheriff, whose three kids would keep Robby company for any number of snow days. After cuffing Josh, Tom escorted him and Maria to the first of the vehicles, a large, all-terrain van with heavy-duty chassis and a high-powered engine. They sat in back, while the FBI agent was in the front seat next to the driver, who was a trooper in uniform. A large dump-truck filled with sand and salt led the way. A squad car with lights flashing took up the rear. No one expected any trouble, except maybe with the snow.

"It finally stopped snowing," observed Maria to no one in particular as the small caravan started out. It was 2:30 pm, yet little light was being thrown by the sun as thick gray clouds continued to dominate the horizon.

"I don't know," said Tom looking up. "Look's like it wants to start up again. We'd better get a move on."

Josh had resigned himself to his incarceration as well as the ride back to Boston. His message had been transmitted. The FBI, at least this guy, seemed to believe him and was on the right track. All they had to do was present the evidence to the judge and everything would be all right. Then he thought about the power the StellarScope company must wield if they could control the local police. If some organization or person from the government was involved with the embezzlement and the cover-up, who's to say who else they may have power over. This Tom Hagen character might not be able to help him if the judge, say, was in their pocket. Despite his mixed feelings there wasn't much he could do in any case but go along.

They were heading back east along the main highway, which would soon join Route 2 going to Boston. The wind blew the snow off the high white banks lining the road directly into their windshield, making the visibility almost as bad as when the blizzard was raging. They had to use the tail lights of the massive truck they were following as a guide, as it plowed the way, moving at a tortoise-like fifteen miles an hour. After only twenty-minutes out, the plow stopped dead.

"What's the matter?" asked Tom, as the driver of the lead truck came back to consult with him.

"Some kind of obstruction in the road. I'm not sure we can get by. I'll have to take a closer look. You'd better come with me."

The men in the trailing vehicle had gotten out and pulled on their fur jackets and gloves. They wore state police uniforms with high leather boots. Tom pulled on a heavy, fur-trimmed jacket he had gotten in the Air Force when he was stationed in Greenland. At least there was one good thing about being sent to that god-forsaken, barren land. It made this three day blow seem like a walk in the park.

"Wait here," he said to Josh and Maria, although neither of them had the slightest intention of getting out of the warm, dry vehicle.

No sooner had Tom stepped out of the van then he heard the heavy whine of several revved-up engines. At that moment five snowmobiles came rushing up the road behind them. At first Tom thought it was a race of some kind, a bunch of avid skidooers taking advantage of the newly fallen snow. But as the five snowmobiles got closer it was apparent they had something else in mind. Several of the men had rifles strapped over their shoulder or across their backs. They began to slow down as they got closer to the police vehicles with their flashing lights. Before any of Tom's team had a chance to react, they were surrounded by helmeted armed men on skidoos.

"Don't move!" ordered the apparent leader of the group, flipping the rifle off his shoulder and pointing it at the men standing by the caravan. Others rounded up the troopers who were up in front of the truck examining the log and snow barrier that had been erected to impede their progress.

"What's going on here?" asked Tom, stepping forward.

"I said don't move!" yelled the man, taking a step toward Tom and pointing the rifle at his head. His men did likewise, pointing their guns at the other men in his convoy.

Tom stopped and held up his hands. "Don't do anything rash now. What do you boys want?"

The men surrounding them all had their visors down and were dressed in full-body, fur-lined jump suits against the cold. Some had their thick hoods up over their helmets.

Instead of answering, the man, who was short and thin, even beneath his bulky outfit, walked past Tom to the door of the van and opened it.

"Would you mind coming with us?" he said, motioning to Josh.

Josh had watched the whole thing develop like a slow-moving dream, hoping that whoever was holding up the convoy wouldn't notice him or Maria. Now it turned out it was him they were after. He didn't know who they were and had no intention of leaving the warm confines of the vehicle.

"No," he said, defiantly. "I'm not going anywhere. Who the hell are you, anyway?"

"We're your friends. I don't think you'd like where they're taking you."

"I know where they're taking me, which is more than I can say for your intentions."

"You're in danger as long as you stay with these people."

At this point Tom stepped in, despite a man standing in front of him with a rifle blocking the way.

"Wait a minute, here. No one's in danger. That is until you gun-toting vigilantes showed up."

"They think you know where Teller is," said the small man to Josh, ignoring the FBI agent altogether. "That's who they want, not you. They're taking you in to grill you about your knowledge of his whereabouts and they're not about to believe you don't know. They'd torture you to get what they want."

"That's simply not true," said Tom again, as if he were in court trying to argue a tough case with the judge. "We're taking both of these people to see a federal judge to hear evidence regarding several felony charges that need to be reviewed. Once things have been cleared up, Mister Banks here will be free to go. I don't know what you're talking about with this Teller business, but I assure you we're not after him."

"You might not be, but some of your superiors may differ."

"How do you know all this?" asked Josh, still not inclined to go with the hooded band of terrorists, for that's what they seemed like to him.

"Just say we have better sources than you. We need to find Teller before they do."

"But I don't know where he is," said Josh honestly.

"That may be, but you have information that could be helpful. We're not about to let you be taken. I'm afraid you'll have to come with us." He pointed his gun at Josh and told him to get out of the car. Josh complied and stood next to the vehicle. Maria started to get out as well but the man with the gun motioned her back inside and ordered Josh uncuffed.

"You can stay here. Go back with these people. Tell the judge what happened and clear this man's name. Then there'll be no reason for anyone to be after him, and that includes you." He looked pointedly at Tom as he said these words. Then he motioned Josh onto the back of his snowmobile.

"Where are you taking me?" asked Josh nervously, as they revved up their engines and circled away in the opposite direction.

"Where you were headed in the first place," said his enigmatic kidnapper.

Chapter 12

They sped down the road at fifty miles an hour, Josh hanging on the back of the skidoo for dear life. Soon they turned off the highway and headed across a barren field into the woods, along broad, rolling trails back toward the reservoir to the vicinity of South Athol.

Josh's mind was a jumble of emotions, none of them good. He had descended into a numbing limbo where all thought and feeling were suspended, not much more than an animal clinging to the present moment.

Being incarcerated and manacled was bad enough. Now he was being abducted by a band of masked ski-mobilers with guns. He tried asking where they were taking him, but the buzz of the engines and the blowing wind made it impossible to communicate even if the man had wanted to listen to him.

After about an hour of moving through snow-covered fields, wooded trails and country roads, they arrived at a small farm house nestled amidst a thick stand of pine. Most other distinguishing landmarks and markers were covered in snow, making the landscape look barren and slightly grotesque, with everything shortened. Any tracks they may have left were instantly obliterated by the wind.

The front porch of the house - a simple square, two-story building - was nearly covered in high drifts. A deep, tunnel-like path led through the snow to the house. A barn stood across the road, which was now all but invisible. It was red and looked new, and lodged several head of cattle.

Only two of the skidoos stopped at the farmhouse, the other three continuing up the road. The passenger of the second ski-mobile jumped on the one Josh had been riding, while he and the driver went into the house, entering through the tunnel of snow into the kitchen area.

His abductor, who still wore his ski helmet visor down and had his rifle in his right hand, turned on the lights. Even though he held the gun casually, with one hand, holding it by the top and middle, as if not particularly concerned or on his guard, the weapon caused Josh no little amount of worry.

"What's this all about? How long are you going to keep me?" he asked.

Instead of answering, the man took off his helmet.

"Dan!" Josh exclaimed, recognizing his friend, this time without his dogs. "How did you...? What are you..? Where are ...?" he tried to ask, but couldn't quite form the question.

"Relax, Josh. Why don't you sit down. Did they feed you in that stinking jail?"

"They gave us lunch. That FBI agent wasn't really a bad guy."

"You haven't met the bad cop yet. It's all a game. They were using you to get to Teller."

"But like I told you, I don't know where Teller is."

"Yeah, but you were looking for him. You have an idea how to locate him."

"What are you going to do when you find him?" asked Josh, not quite trusting his new friend's motives. After all, they had met under rather peculiar circumstances.

"Keep those government bastards from getting their hands on him and stealing his invention."

"How'd you manage all this?"

"Like I said, there's a whole network of us, an underground railroad, so to speak." The two other men came in at that moment.

"This is the Bolin brothers, Jess and Roy. They're helping me out. Thanks for hiding the skidoos, boys."

"No problem," answered the older and bigger of the two, as they took off their snowsuits and put more wood in the stove.

"Boy, that's some wind," observed the younger of the two, slightly smaller than his brother, but better muscled with dark eyes partially covered by a long strand of black hair. "Can't hardly see with all that snow blowing. Have you ever seen a snowstorm like this?"

"Yeah," replied Dan. "Back in '78. At least there won't be a lot of people moving around. That windblown snow will cover our tracks just as good as if it had kept snowing."

"Yeah, you've told us," the oldest Bolin responded, "about a hundred times."

"This is Josh," said Dan introducing him to his two accomplices. "He's one of them nosey newspaper guys. You know the ones, always stirring up trouble on the nightly news, hounding some crooked politician or flea-bag official on the take."

"Why, thanks, Dan," laughed Josh. "I haven't been paid a compliment like that since my last raise."

"How are the dogs?" Dan asked Roy Bolin.

"They're fine. I've got them behind the barn," answered the younger Bolin brother.

"I hope they're well out of sight. After what we've pulled off, the cops will have everything they've got out looking for us."

"They won't be able to do much in this weather," said Jess Bolin. "I don't care who they are. There won't be anyone coming or going until the wind lets up."

"Then we don't have much time," replied Dan. "We're not the only ones who have snowmobiles. Roy, why don't you cook us up something to eat. Josh, you still want to go to Pelham?"

"I guess so," answered Josh, scratching his head, as Roy banged pans in the cabinets until he withdrew a skillet to his liking, hefting it like a billy-club. "I can't think of anywhere better to go. Might as well stick to my plan. I can phone in my ad for Teller from there."

"OK, my sister lives in Pelham. We can go there." Dan drew out a map. Roy pulled a couple of steaks out of the fridge and opened a can of green beans. Josh's mouth started to water.

"We're here," observed Dan, opening the map and pointing to the middle of the state, at the top of a large body of water labeled Quabbin. "We need to drop down here to the midpoint of the western shore. My sister's place is right here. We can start tonight when it gets dark. We'll take the dogs. One of us can ride this time. It will be a lot more comfortable."

"Won't the skidoos be a lot quicker?" asked Jess, who was helping his brother set the table. "What are you guy's drinking?" he added.

"I'll have a beer," replied Dan.

"I'll have the same," said Josh. He figured it would help him sleep a couple of hours until it was time to leave. It didn't sound like he'd be getting much rest after that.

Dan continued, "They're looking for snowmobiles. The engines will attract attention. The dogs are pretty much silent. No one will hear them. We could walk right by somebody in this snow and no one would know. They can go places the heavy machines can't. No, the dogs will be much better."

They ate what Josh thought was one of the best meals he could remember, a top restaurant caliber steak enhanced by the beer and the fact that he hadn't eaten anything more substantial than sandwiches and McMuffins for several days. He helped himself to a heaping helping of string beans and potatoes.

"Why don't you try to get some rest," Dan said to Josh after he finished a piece of apple pie that Roy pulled out of the fridge. "You can use the room in the corner upstairs. One of the boys will show you."

"Thanks," said Josh. "I just might do that."

While Josh napped in the quiet farmhouse, the wind, which had been blowing in fifty-mile per hour gusts, began to slowly die down. By the time Josh was awake and finishing his midnight breakfast of eggs, bacon, and toast, it had stopped altogether. When he stepped outside he could see stars twinkling brightly in the clear cold sky for the first time in days.

With Josh seated comfortably in the sled, Dan thanked his hosts, Jess and Roy, and 'mushed' his dog team out of the yard with a wave and a yell. Unlike the ski-mobile, the sled moved silently through the glistening snow, allowing the travelers to talk as they sped along gliding over the soft-packed, snow-covered landscape.

"The wind's stopped," observed Dan. "That'll mean they'll probably start sending out search parties, if they haven't already done so. We'll have to stay off the roads."

"You think they'll have the trails covered?"

"I doubt it, not until morning. No, we'll be fine until then. They're looking for skidoos not dogs."

"You think that FBI guy figured out it was you?"

"I don't know," said Dan. "But it hardly matters. Like I said, we'll be at our destination before daylight. We've got nothing to worry about until then. I doubt they'll be able to get more than a handful of men to track us."

"Now that the storm's cleared, they'll be able to get help out from Boston," reasoned Josh. "They've probably already got planes or helicopters searching for us. We wouldn't be too hard to spot in this snow from the air, especially when the moon comes up."

"If it makes you feel any better you can get out and walk."

"No, that's all right, I'll shut up," said Josh, settling down in his warm, comfortable seat of fur and blankets.

After a moment Dan asked something that had been on his mind for quite awhile, ever since he became involved with Josh's situation.

"You really think the government wants the telescope for spying, or do you think something else is going on?"

"What do you mean?"

"You said they've got enough satellites up there looking down on us to spy on every man, woman, and child on the globe. Why would they need this big elaborate telescope to do it? Maybe there's something else going on."

"Like what?" asked Josh, curious where Dan was going.

"Well, you said yourself this guy's teacher was into time-travel. Maybe Teller built a time-travel machine."

"That's ridiculous."

"I'm not so sure. I know a little bit about astronomy. It was one of my hobbies as a kid. In the service I worked in listening stations in Viet Nam, monitoring transmissions over satellite, and kept up my reading on my own afterward. There's a theory that black holes may provide a means of time travel."

"I thought time travel was theoretically impossible."

"Perhaps not. There's a giant black hole, millions and millions of miles in diameter at the center of our galaxy. Some say that these singularities, as they call them, these tears in the fabric of space, lead to worm-holes that can transport you to the opposite ends of the universe. That is if you could somehow survive the tremendous pressure of the gravitational pull. Some even say they can transport you through time. I'm not a mathematician, so I can't follow it entirely, but there are mathematical equations, solutions to Einstein's equations that supposedly can prove all this."

Josh was silent as he heard Dan out. He had no idea his Micmac friend had such knowledge or interest in astronomy. He hardly seemed to know about the Peeble Telescope when Josh had first mentioned it. His only motivation for helping them had seemed to be his bitterness toward the government.

"I hadn't thought about that," answered Josh. "I just thought that since Teller's mentor had once written a book about time-travel, Teller might be using these ads as a way of communicating secretly to his friends that he was OK and free. It's a long shot I admit, but it was the only lead I had. Now it seems so tenuous, I can't believe I even considered it in the first place."

"Well, I think you're instincts are right on. Didn't you say you had a nose for news?"

"I said that?" said Josh, laughing. "Lately I seem to have a knack for getting in the news instead of finding it."

"What if the time machine is real and it's the only way we can save ourselves when it all ends on the end of the year?"

Any credibility Dan may have had evaporated into the cold, star-filled night.

"You really don't believe the world's going to end, do you?" Josh asked.

"Like Gladys said, it's been foretold. All the signs seem to be there for anyone to see. Even my dogs seem to know something's up. It's only the human race that's blind to the ways of the Great Spirit."

Josh tried to get his mind around the possibilities, but failed. His imagination and knowledge of astronomy just weren't up to it.

"I doubt this time-travel ad is on the level, or has anything to do with the missing scientist. It's probably just a hoax. I think I have another way to try and get in touch with Teller." Josh explained Jeremy's idea of leaving a craftily-worded message for Teller in the newspaper personal ads.

"That might work," said Dan. "We can try it when we get to my sister's place."

Josh hoped he could reconstruct the message Jeremy had concocted from memory, as the scrap of paper on which it was written had been confiscated along with the rest of his possessions when they had been apprehended by the police.

They made good time moving through the snow. It had turned warm, almost balmy as they traveled down the west shore of the reservoir, along back roads and fields in the area of New Salem. Keeping well west of Route 202, Dan soon veered to the east to avoid the town of Amherst. It was an area he knew well from his dog racing days. After almost two hours, they pulled into a long, curving, snow-filled drive on the edge of the reservoir near the small village of Pelham.

"This is my sister's place," Dan announced, steering the team between a rambling two-story house and a ramshackle barn. Both looked like they had been deserted for years. The vague shape of a road continued down behind the house where other equally dilapidated, snow-covered buildings appeared barely visible in the darkness. Scattered among the buildings were strange piles of snow, which covered a collection of discarded old junk cars, trucks and farm equipment.

"Look's like the place is deserted," observed Josh, pulling himself out of the sled and stretching.

"They like it that way, less maintenance."

The only sign of life was smoke curling out of a chimney pipe. The front porch was completely full of chopped wood and offered no form of entry. The stairs to the second floor deck and rear door of the house were half gone, the top portion held on with boards and a few nails. What looked like a rear entrance at ground level was covered with dead bushes and snowdrifts.

Dan unhitched the dogs and led them down in back to a long, low building that looked like a chicken coop. Josh went to help him.

"My sister Lilli and her husband sell junk metal and old cars, and things. Their land goes on for miles back here. They're pretty self-sufficient, grow their own vegetables in the spring and summer. Hunt their own meat. Raise a few chickens and pigs. This is my family home, where we grew up. Lilli took over the farm when my folks got too old to work it, but it's been hard for them with four kids. Lost most of their cows back in 2008. Pretty near lost the place, but I was able to help out a little. They're just squeaking by."

"I hope we don't cause them any inconvenience. I hate to get them involved in all this."

"They already are. My brother-in-law was with me when I grabbed you. They're believers in the cause."

"And what cause is that?" asked Josh as they trudged back to the house.

"The cause of freedom from government interference in every little aspect of our lives; freedom from taxation to pay for taking care of those who don't want to do an honest day's work; freedom from getting involved in every other country's business; freedom from the whole rat race that's called modern civilization."

Josh didn't want to offend his friend, especially when he still had a high-powered rifle slung over his shoulder, but he found it hard not to object. He certainly wasn't a radical like these people all seemed to be.

"The government's a necessary evil," he said in response. "Not everyone can live out in the wild like you and your friends. I for instance, would probably not last four days before I succumbed to cold and hunger. The government enforces the laws so people can go to work and earn a living. It provides a safety net for those who are temporarily unemployed or hurt on the job, for people who get old. And we'll all get old one day. You can't turn back the clock, Dan. As much as we'd all like to, we can't go back in time."

As they reached the house, the unreachable door on the second story opened and a pretty girl with dark hair and eyes peeked out.

"Is that you, Dan? Who's that you got with you? I've asked John to shovel a path to the back door, but he's too lazy. Been sitting watching sports on the satellite dish for two days now. That is when he wasn't off gallivanting with you. At least it's finally stopped snowing."

"Hi, Lillian," said her brother looking up and smiling. "If the snow was a little higher we could get up there."

"You might try the front. You can use the snow bank to get to the roof of the porch and come in through the front window. That's what we do."

"OK, we'll give it a try."

They went around front and helped each other up a huge bank that half-covered the front of the porch, on to its roof, to the second story window. Dan's sister was there waiting to help them in. She looked at Josh with some misgiving.

"Lilli, this is Josh," said Dan, as they descended a staircase to the kitchen. "He's going to help us find that missing telescope scientist before the government does."

"Hi, Josh, nice to meet you. You're just in time for breakfast." She was short and athletic-looking in a pair of jeans and flannel shirt, which she wore out. She had long black hair, which she had tied in braids, and long-lashed brown eyes. Josh thought her the prettiest girl he had seen in a long time. Too bad she was married.

"Where's that lazy husband of yours?" asked Dan, half in jest.

"He'll be down soon. He stayed out late last night with the boys."

"Well, I haven't slept much either."

"Yeah, but you're a wolf." They both laughed. A few minutes later her husband, a large man with a wide, black beard and a sour demeanor, came down. Josh recognized him as the intimidating one from the day before.

They talked about the assault on the police convoy and the possible repercussions. Now that the weather had cleared and the search had picked up, everyone was on edge.

"He can't stay here," said John, Dan's brother-in-law. "It's too risky. We've got kids. There's no room anyway. Why'd you come here?"

"'Cause he thinks the missing scientist the government's looking for is out here. No telling what will happen if they find him first. I thought you said you'd help us."

"Yeah, I did, else you wouldn't even have him in the first place, but I didn't say he could stay here. It's almost Christmas for Christ's sake."

104

"Exactly," said Lilli, jumping in. "It's Christmas. We're not going to throw my brother and his friend out in the cold during Christmas."

"Where's he going to stay then?" asked her husband unhappily.

"We can stay down back in your work-shed," volunteered Dan, not wanting to cause an argument. God knew his sister and brother-in-law argued enough on their own. "You've got a stove and a bunk in there. The kids use it to camp out. It'll only be for a day or two. We'll be fine."

"What if the cops come snooping?" said Lilli's husband, still not happy with the situation.

"I doubt they'll wander in back there with all the snow," said Dan, trying to sooth his brother-in-law's concerns. "If someone comes by, tell them you've got relatives staying for the holiday."

After awhile, John agreed, although he still obviously wasn't happy with the idea. After breakfast, where they were joined by John's four rather boisterous boys, all elated to see their Uncle Dan, their father and uncle went out to ready the shed so that Dan and Josh could get a few hours of much needed rest. The four boys - thirteen, ten, eight and five - went with them to give them pointers on how to make the place comfortable for camping. While they were away Josh had a chance to talk to Lilli alone.

"So, how long have you known my brother?" she asked, as she sipped her coffee. It was finally fully light outside, the warm sun already beginning to melt the snow on the roof.

"Not long, only a few days really. He helped us out of a jam. I and the girl I was with were being chased by some goons from the company she worked for. I was investigating the disappearance of Dr. Teller, their head scientist, and the possible difficulties the company was having. They chased us through the streets and came to my house. They took us back to their offices. Somehow they got the girl to say I kidnapped and tried to rape her. They took her little boy. Then they ended up killing the woman who helped her get him back. The girl's name is Maria and her little boy is Robbie. They must be back in Athol, unless they've been taken to Boston already. It's all rather incredible."

"I'll say. That's terrible. And my brother helped you?"

"Yes. He saved our lives. The FBI got involved, probably because of the alleged kidnapping. They said we stole some top secret papers, but all we had were internal memos regarding the company's own investigation into the status of the project after Teller's disappearance. It may have been confidential and embarrassing, but hardly information critical to the security of the country. There was also some evidence they were cooking the books, robbing the company and the U.S. tax payers of millions. Anyway, they were obviously trying to cover up the whole thing. The feds got involved and tracked us down as we were transmitting all this information to my news agency for publication. They chased us with a helicopter, if you can believe it. Maria and I got away during the chase. We were about to freeze to death in the blizzard when we heard your brother's dogs barking and stumbled onto his place. He hid us when the police came and brought us here. I don't know what we would have done without him."

"Isn't that just like Dan to stick his neck out for strangers."

"He's quite a guy."

Lilli was silent for a while, and stared into her coffee cup, which she held suspended in front of her, her elbows on the table.

"So how long have you lived here?" asked Josh, trying to get the conversation going again.

"All my life," she answered. "Dan and I were born here. The place used to be a lot nicer then. My mother inherited the land from her father, who was quite a prosperous farmer back in the early part of the century, after the First World War. Our parents ran it for years after he died. We had a lot of livestock back then, even a few horses, but they take a lot of work. The land goes on for miles in back. Things were good until my folks got older and it got harder for them to do the work. We had hands, and Dan helped some, but he went off to the war in '65. He never liked farming anyway. He never came back when the war was over."

"He was in the Marines, right?" Josh asked, remembering Dan saying something about it.

"Yeah, he was a radioman of some sort. He doesn't talk about it much. He saw a lot of people die, not only his own men, not only soldiers, but women and children too. It messed him up pretty bad. He was always a sensitive kid."

"Yeah, the Vietnamese War messed up a lot of people's lives. War does that."

"Especially unnecessary war."

"Especially unnecessary war, but one man's unnecessary war is another man's just cause. There *is* such a thing as a just war, but I don't want to argue about that now. That was over fifty years ago."

"It's like yesterday to Dan. He still has flashbacks. Did he tell you about his kid?"

"No, Dan has a kid? He never mentioned it, though he's not exactly the talkative type when it comes to himself. Was he married? What happened?"

"Yeah, he was married, had a six-year old boy. Same name as you, Josh. Maybe that's why he latched on to you."

"I remind him of his son?"

"No, but you have the same name. Name's mean a lot in our culture. To you it's a coincidence, but to Dan, the fact that you and his boy have the same name has meaning. Maybe he thinks you will take him back to his son."

"What happened?"

"Dan and Beverly got married soon after he returned from the service. He went to college compliments of the government, and learned how to program computers. They got married after he got his first job at a local computer company. Things were going well. Then one day she left him. He came home from work, and Beverly and the kid were gone. No letter, nothing. He was frantic, called everybody, but no one knew where she went. Then he went to cash a check only to find their joint bank account had been cleaned out. She took everything! Can you believe it? It was all quite a shock. Dan's lawyer called a few days later to tell him he should hire another attorney, as he would be representing Dan's wife. She was suing for a divorce. Of course, the fact that she had all his money made it difficult for my brother to find a good lawyer. She got sole custody. I don't think he's ever recovered from that."

As she said this, Dan and her husband came into the room.

"The shed's all set up," said Dan's brother-in-law, looking back and forth at the two of them. "Kind of cozy aren't you? What are you two up to?"

"Nothing. I was just telling Josh here about the farm."

"Josh? Why don't you call him sweetheart. I'm out of the house ten minutes and you're telling some stranger our life story. Ain't you got some work to do?"

"John, don't be like that," said Lillie, embarrassed at her husband's jealous outburst. She knew it wasn't so much jealously as an excuse to abuse and belittle her. "I apologize for my rude husband. He wasn't taught any manners."

"Aw, screw you," said John, putting on his hat and stepping back outside.

"You two will be fine in the shed," she said. "No one goes back there, not this time of year. John's always burning wood in the stove to keep it warm so he can work, so the smoke won't attract any attention."

"Thanks," said Josh. He felt slightly embarrassed for her. He had been sitting rather close to her when her husband came in, and was enjoying her company. Unlike Maria, who was on the plump side and not exactly his type, Lilli was as lithe as a dancer, despite having four hefty boys. Not for the first time that day, Josh found himself regretting that she was already married. Still, he didn't feel they had been flirting and resented her husband's remarks at her expense. "I'm sure we'll be comfortable."

He felt like he hadn't gotten a good night's sleep in days, and couldn't remember when he had been in a real comfortable bed – his own. He wasn't exactly looking forward to sleeping in a shed, but when he finally followed Dan back to get a few hours rest, he was pleasantly surprised.

The long, low building housed most of John's tools, various power saws and drills, and some farm implements. The floor was made of wood planks and covered with sawdust. The walls were also bare wood planking, on which hung more tools and implements of various kinds, some for working on cars, others for working on the land. The place was well-built and sturdy, however, and warm, with a wood stove in the middle of the room throwing out considerable heat. At the far end of the shed, which was clear of tools and sawdust, were a round wooden table and some chairs, one of which was a rocker. A small bunk-bed stood against the wall. A reading lamp sat on the table, along with an ashtray full of butts.

Since Josh was the only one being searched for, at least as far as anyone knew, he would be staying in the shed alone, while Dan stayed in the house, which suited Josh fine. He fell asleep as soon as his head hit the pillow on the lower of the two bunk-beds, still feeling the motion of the sled as he drifted off.

Chapter 13

Woken by a jerk on the arm, Josh peered up at his friend Dan Little-Wolf.

"Hey, there, it's almost one. You wanted me to wake you."

"Oh, thanks," said Josh, once he realized who it was and that he was not on the back of a sled racing through the Yukon. "I wanted to try and contact my old boss at the news agency, see if he can help us with that ad. It's going to cost a few bucks. Does your sister own a computer?"

"I doubt it. They're lucky to have a TV. You'll have to use the library in town. Come up to the house. Lilli made a sandwich for you."

"That's some sister you got there."

"Yeah, she's all right."

Before Dan and Josh could head back up to the house, Lilli came down carrying a basket with the food.

"John's getting paranoid. They've got your picture and name on the TV and radio. There's a big manhunt out for you and the men in skidoos who took you. He doesn't want you in the house. He says the sooner you go the better."

"That's going to make it hard to walk around town," Josh realized out loud. "I wonder what picture they've got of me."

"It look's like a recent one from when you were last in custody," said Dan's sister. "You'll be easy to recognize."

'Damn," swore Josh, fear welling up in his mind like a backed-up drain.

John came in a few minutes later.

"Did she tell you the news?" he asked on coming into the shed, stomping the snow from his black rubber boots. "He's hot as hell. They've got the whole state out looking for him. You've gotta go."

"What did you expect when you helped me break him out?" said Dan, visibly annoyed. "They'd just forget about it?"

"I thought it was just a local thing. I didn't know the feds were involved."

"Well, now you do. This doesn't change a thing. We'll stick to the plan. I'll take care of everything, don't worry. When have I ever let you down?"

"You've helped us out a lot, Dan, and we appreciate it. That's why I agreed to come along in the first place, but I have four kids to think of. It's too dangerous to keep him here."

"This is the safest place to keep him," replied Dan.

"Look, I don't want to cause any trouble," said Josh. "John here is right, the longer I stay here the more dangerous it is for everyone involved."

"Where you going to go?" asked Dan in concern.

"I'll try to place the ad in a couple of major newspapers. I'll set a meeting place and head there. There's no sense sitting around here. John's right, I need to go. You folks have been a big help with the food and bed, but now it's time to leave."

"Where are you going to get the money for the ads?" asked Dan. "You said yourself it'd cost a fortune to place prominent ads in the Personals of two major city newspapers for a week or so."

"I don't know. That's why I wanted to contact my associate."

"At least let me help you with that," offered Dan. "I'll pay for the ads. You tell me what to put in them and I'll do the rest."

"Do you think they suspect you?" Dan's sister asked. "They did take you in when they arrested Josh remember. Maybe you were recognized."

"I doubt it. Even Josh didn't know me. They may figure it out by a process of elimination. That is if they're really smart, but it might take them awhile. Even if they did, they might not be able to trace me here right away. Not many people know your maiden name. It would take some footwork to track me here to you, but it's possible, eventually."

"You never can tell with these federal guys," said John, still worried. "They're pretty sharp. They found you once."

"You're right," agreed Josh again. "It's probably best I keep on the move and don't involve you folks any more than I already have."

"You're helping us all," said Dan, as if Josh had just given them a million dollars.

John and Lilli went back to the house, while Dan and the fugitive remained in the shed eating their sandwiches. As they ate, Josh tried to reconstruct the personal ad as he had heard it from Jeremy.

"OK, Teller's mentor's nickname was Chic, so we'll sign it with that. Then we'll mention Teller's name and something about time travel in the body of the message, along with the meeting place, which is the cemetery where his dead wife is buried. Something like Meadow Lane or Meadow Brook. So let's see."

He took a thick pencil John used to mark wood and a scrap of tissue paper and began to write.

'Ardent time traveler seeking Teller at the Meadows – Chic'

He repeated the phrase a few times.

"No, that's not quite it. 'Ardent time traveler seeking Fortune-Teller for hire. Meet me at the beloved's meadow – chic'. That's better," he said satisfied he had the basic idea. "It may not be exactly what Jeremy said, but it's close enough."

Dan was looking at the message, lost in thought.

"Hmm, I get it. You've got his name and his teacher's nickname. That will attract his attention. The time travel reference will tip him off it's a coded message, and you have the meeting place. Might work, if he reads the paper. The only thing I see missing is when. How will he know when to meet you?"

"We were going to stake out the place for a week or so, while the ad ran."

"Hmm, that's not too convenient. Why don't you just give him a date, like a week from today?"

Josh thought for awhile. "That might make it too easy for some uninvited person to join us. Might as well put a big sign up, here we are. No, no dates."

He stopped for a moment, leaning over the table lost in thought.

"I've got it!" said Josh, straightening up and brightening perceptibly. "I remember one of the pieces they did on Teller when he disappeared mentioned his wife's death and how it almost destroyed him. The whole point of the piece was how he battled back to become one of the most important men of the century. But what struck me most about the piece was the fact that she had died on the day before New Years. A tough bit of luck if there ever was one. What's the date today?"

"The twenty-third," replied Dan. "Christmas is in a couple of days."

Josh added the phrase 'on our beloved's last day', to what he had already written.

"There, that should do it. It's a long shot, but what have I got to lose."

"'So you're going to use the date of his wife's death, New Year's Eve day, as the meeting date. That might work, but it doesn't give you much time. You only have a week or so."

"Then we don't have any time to lose," said Josh.

They both laughed as they put on their coats and left the shed.

Lilli agreed to let Dan borrow the family station-wagon for the mission. It was the least she could do after he had given them money so their kids could have a decent Christmas this year. What had promised to be a sad, penniless holiday turned out to be the best one yet. Her brother was very good to them. She hoped he and his friend made it out of this OK.

Josh joined Dan, donning a baseball cap and sun glasses, as he went into town to make the calls to place the ads in the Boston Globe and New York Times, after Dan cashed a check at the local bank. When it came time, Dan read what Josh had written on the scrap of tissue paper, over the phone to the advertising rep at the newspapers.

'Ardent time traveler seeking Fortune-Teller for hire; meet me at the meadows on our beloved's last day– Chic'.

After Dan had placed the ads, they headed back to his sister's house.

"We can leave tonight, use the dogs to get to the general area. Then you're on your own," said Dan as they drove along the snow-encrusted street. The sun continued to shine, the thermometer above fifty degrees Fahrenheit. The melting snow was threatening to cause major flooding in some areas if the thaw happened too rapidly. In the meantime, there was still enough of it on the back trails for the sled.

"Dan, you've already helped me enough," said Josh. "I can't ask you to do any more."

"You haven't asked me, I've volunteered. After what I went through in Nam I have a different perspective on things. I can't waste my life. There were too many wasted lives left back there in the jungle. Each day has to mean something. I have a feeling that what we're doing will mean a lot to a lot of people."

"Maybe," said Josh. "But right now the only one I'm worrying about is me."

"Hopefully your friend Maria has cleared your name by now. So it should be cool."

"Yeah, except for the part where I escaped at gunpoint. We're both in trouble if they find us."

"It may not matter," Dan said.

"Why?" said Josh.

"Because the world may end in a week."

"Don't tell me you still believe that."

"I don't know. It's not only the ancient books of the Cathars that say so. There are American Indian myths about the end of the world that can also be interpreted to correspond to this being the time. What about the comet?"

"First of all, I've done a little research into this. It's all based on the flimsiest of evidence, unverifiable except by a very small body of experts with the necessary equipment, and those few who are talking don't agree on a thing. There aren't any models to simulate the path of this so-called unknown comet, and half the experts don't agree it exists. The dozen or so models scientists have been able to slap together give a wide range of possible trajectories, something like 500 million miles. Only a few of them have the comet passing within fifty-two million miles of earth, and only one has it coming within 250,000 miles of us. Granted, even that close of an encounter with a comet could have serious consequences for our planet, but nothing like the end of the world. Many of these so called experts are crackpots with no credibility. They've spent their whole careers building up these ridiculous fabrications so they can dupe the gullible into buying their books and filling their lecture halls. Just like the nuts who talk about time travel."

"I've done some of my own research, and there's more than one model that predicts a collision given the probability of error of three or five percent. This is the closest anything like this has come to earth in thousands of years. And this thing is coming from nowhere. No one knew it existed until Peeble's student, Teller found it."

"Oh, you know that for a fact, do you?"

"Who else? And it's not only some glory-seeking scientists who are saying this. The bible itself speaks of the time of the four blood-moons as being a time of great cataclysm. I wouldn't be so smug if I were you. And as for time travel, I wouldn't mention you think his teacher's theories are a bunch of hogwash when you meet Teller." Dan laughed. "The world's got to end sometime, why not tomorrow or next week?"

Josh had to admit, anything could happen. There had been reports in the news just as recently as last month of an unusual surge of sunspot activity and solar flares, representing huge gaseous storms on the sun. If one of these flared up enough, it could wipe out the solar system in a heartbeat, not to mention the earth. Not a few people believed it was going to happen. There was no shortage of end of the world scenarios floating around, and even though such predictions had come and gone for centuries, the current batch seemed to have more credence than previous ones. There wasn't exactly mass hysteria yet, but people all over the world were on edge. Attendance at religious services had increased significantly over the past few months, as had admissions to mental institutions around the world. It wasn't just the animals that were acting strange.

"I guess anything's possible," said Josh finally. "But it's just as likely to be a hundred million years or a quarter of a billion years from now. These things happen in such huge cosmic timescales."

"These things are happening all the time. Do you have any idea how violent the universe is? Whole stars are exploding every second, billions of them. At some point it just happens. The ancients knew more than you may think."

"We have thousands of years on them, millenniums of learning and discovery. We know much more now. The universe is no longer the superstitious, mysterious thing it once was. Much has been explained."

"And much still remains mystery," said Josh's friend. "In a lot of ways we know less about our own world now than our elders did. My people understood the earth, the ways of its plants and wildlife. All that knowledge has been lost."

"Not quite, not as long as you remember."

"I don't know when the earth is going to end," said Dan. "But if and when it does, I'll sing my death-song. Otherwise I'll keep on trucking."

"My sentiments exactly," said Josh, as they reached Dan's sister's house.

"How'd it go," asked Lilli, as they entered the cluttered upstairs family area.

"Mission accomplished," replied her brother. "We sent off the message. Now I'm going to take Josh to the meeting place. If we're lucky, he'll find the missing scientist and get to the bottom of the whole thing. Then he can write the story and win his Pulitzer."

Lilli looked dubious but smiled pleasantly at Josh anyway, a smile that made Josh's eyes water.

"Where's John?" asked Dan, noticing his brother-in-law was not home.

"He took the kids into town to see a movie. It's one of their Christmas gifts. I think it's another Harry Potter movie. Can you believe it? That actor must be thirty years old by now."

"At least," said Josh taking up the joke. "I thought the last one was supposed to be the final movie."

"Yeah, and the one before that," laughed Lilli. "But it's such a cash cow I guess they just can't stop making them."

"Lil, can you fix us a little something to eat?" asked Dan. "I'd like to hitch up the dogs and get going as soon as it's dark and there's still some snow on the ground. We can get up to Archie's place before dawn and then figure out how to get Josh back to Boston."

"Sure. Will American chop suey be OK?"

"Great," said Josh and Dan in unison.

Just then they heard several cars drive up. They thought it was the fire department at first, because of the flashing red lights, but became even more alarmed when the loud throbbing sound of a helicopter could be heard hovering over the house.

"What the …" Dan started to say. Then there was a knock on the back door.

"Open up, this is the FBI. We have a warrant for the arrest of Josh Banks and Dan Peters. We know they're in there, Misses Cole. Please open the door."

Lilli went to the second-floor deck, opened the door with the missing stairs and called down.

"That door don't work. You'll have to come through the front."

Two men in FBI jackets stood looking up at her. They were backed up by a half dozen oversized and nervous looking state troopers. She noticed her husband standing by one of the police cars looking on sheepishly.

"What's this all about, officer?" she called down.

"Your brother's under arrest for aiding and abetting a fugitive. The man with him is wanted for espionage, kidnapping and murder."

He waved the warrants and looked past her at Dan and Josh who had come to the door.

"It's OK, Lilli," Dan said, stepping forward. "She doesn't know anything about this. We're coming. Just let us put on our coats. I'm sure this can all be straightened out."

"Read them their rights," the agent in charge told the uniformed officer standing next to him when Dan and Josh climbed out the front window and down from the roof of the porch. His sister joined them. "Don't worry, Missus Cole," said the agent. "Your husband explained everything. He and the children are safe. Your brother's friend is an escaped felon wanted for terrorist activities back in Boston. Your husband recognized him from the news reports and turned him in. I'm afraid your brother is in a lot of trouble as well." With that he got in his car and backed it out of the drive.

As they drove off, Josh, in the back of the squad car and handcuffed, spoke up.

"I'm sure this is some mistake. Maria Cavello and her son Robbie have already collaborated my story. Talk to agent Tom Hagen. He can tell you who the real murderers are. There were no top secret papers, only incriminating evidence that will put the real criminals away. Where's agent Hagen?"

"He's been reassigned," said the FBI man sitting in the front seat next to the driver. "In any case, we have our orders directly from headquarters in Washington. This is no longer Hagan's operation."

"What about Maria and Robbie? Are they all right? Where are they?" asked Josh, his concern rising.

The FBI agent didn't answer, which made Josh even more nervous. Not only did he genuinely care for the woman and her boy, she was the only thing standing between him and a murder rap.

When the police had left and John Cole returned from his parent's house where he had left the four boys, he had a terrible argument with his wife Lilli. John Cole would spend the next several nights in the shed wondering what was going to become of his marriage.

Chapter 14

For the second time in a week, Josh was photographed and fingerprinted, and put in a cell in the Amherst state police barracks. This time no one came to talk to him, although he did get a meal around 5:30 that evening. Not long after that, he was informed they were taking him back to Boston.

The agent in charge, Fred Stanley, wasn't wasting any time, and he certainly wasn't going to wait for that stiff from internal affairs, Tom Hagen, to stick his big nose in. He'd escort the prisoner back to Boston – God help anyone who tried to take him – and fly him back to DC himself. They'd be back at Quantico by ten that evening. Imagine his chagrin when he was forced to wait over a week due to a paperwork snafu at the local administrative level, missing Christmas with his family altogether.

While in jail, Josh missed much of the mass hysteria that seemed to grip the country with the coming of the New Year. For some reason, the general public was giving greater credence to the current batch of dire predictions about the end of the world, made more strident by the absurd advertisements for the time-travel club, which offered an escape from the inescapable - in the past.

No one answered Josh's repeated questions as to the whereabouts of Maria Cavello or her son, and no one would tell him exactly what the charges were.

"What am I being charged with?" he asked the head agent as he got into the backseat of the vehicle finally taking him to Boston. "Where's agent Hagen? He knows all about it."

"You're in a heap of trouble, Mister Banks. I'm not at liberty to discuss the details of the case with you. You'll find out soon enough when you stand in front of a federal judge and prosecutor. If you have anything to tell us, I'll be glad to take your confession. You still have kidnapping, murder and espionage charges against you. Then there's the little matter of your escape, at gunpoint, from federal custody. I'm afraid you are still very much in trouble, Mister Banks. Agent Hagen let you escape. That just made things worse for you. You will not escape a second time."

"I had nothing to do with that. They made me go with them. Tom was there. He saw how it went down, ask him. I was an innocent victim of kidnapping myself."

"You can tell it all to the judge in Washington".

"Washington?" yelled Josh.

"I'd advise you to calm down, or I'll stick a gag in your mouth and cover your head with a canvas sack."

Josh was going to object some more, but decided to save his breath, which was a lot easier to do without a gunny-sack over his head.

Fred Stanley was tired and hungry and under a lot of pressure to find the missing scientist and see that his project was completed. His superiors had impressed him with the importance of the outcome. He remained silent for the rest of the two hour trip to Boston.

The snow was still deep in places, although the highway itself was bare of it. Josh had fallen asleep in the back of the van, not having gotten much rest the previous forty-eight hours. When he woke, they were already in downtown Boston. It was about seven-thirty by the Custom's House Tower Clock on State Street. As they got closer to downtown and the Federal building, the number of people in the streets increased.

As they had entered the city they had been surprised by the amount of traffic, even for a Friday night. Everyone was honking their horns. There was a festive spirit in the air, but it had nothing to do with New Years Eve, which was still a day off. While Josh had been on the run and incarcerated he had not been able to keep up with the latest Internet buzz, something he would normally have done. That buzz was telling people to come to Boston for the biggest - and last – end-of-the-world New Years party ever.

Many people, like Agent Stanley for instance, refused to believe the world was coming to an end, but many couldn't discount the persistent rumors and troubling signs. Some chose church, some wild abandon, and some didn't get out of bed, but no matter who or where you were, it was hard to escape the possibility that the world could end in the next forty-eight hours.

People stood on street corners with signs haranguing passersby with one version of the apocalypse or another, while crowds of vandals roamed the streets stealing and smashing everything in sight. Before long a throng of rowdy youths looking for trouble had surged into the street from the Commons where they were initially congregated, spilling onto roadways and alleys. Many held hands or walked arm in arm. Many carried bottles of liquor or weapons.

Unbeknownst to Agent Stanley and his two vehicle convoy, inmates from the Charles Street Jail had recently been freed after the prison was ransacked by a mob of armed crazies who screamed, "The world is ending! Free the downtrodden! The world is ending!" They beat anyone in sight that tried to stop them. The police were out in force trying to protect shopkeepers and their stores from roving bands of shoplifters intent on having a taste of the good life after a lifetime of deprivation. Street people were taking over homes. Old scores were being settled and new ones were being born. Even normal people were on edge. The abnormal were going over that edge.

"What the hell?" exclaimed Stanley, as he contemplated the crowd of people standing in the street in front of him. Some, obviously drunk, either with alcohol or violence, started rocking cars back and forth and battering sign posts with their fists.

"Look's like some kind of riot," observed his driver. The radio crackled with a call reporting the escape of a dozen inmates from the Charles Street facilities. "People are going nuts."

"Yeah, they think the world's ending, and for some of them it just might," said Stanley ominously, as the convoy proceeded slower and slower until it finally crawled to a halt because of the crowd.

"I don't see why you guys are so surprised," said Josh, finally finding his vocal chords again, though a little nervous at the size of the mob that had materialized out of nowhere around them. "This is what happens when one of their teams wins the Series or Stanley Cup or the Super Bowl. They go crazy. People can't take too much emotion, either good or bad. Some of them have to let it out."

"You'd better get us the hell out of here," yelled Stanley to his driver as they sat dead in traffic.

Suddenly, Josh had an idea. Perhaps the crowd could be his friend. After all, they had broken prisoners out of the Charles Street jail, why not out of a police car?

As people looked in the cars that sat stalled in their midst, Josh raised his cuffed hands in a pleading gesture, making sure to make eye contact so that whoever saw him would be less likely to defer responsibility for helping him to another.

"Hey!" a person in the crowd yelled. "The pigs have someone. The world's coming to an end and the pigs are still arresting people. Set him free," he yelled loudly, repeating it like a chant over and over again as he started banging on the roof of the car. "Set him free."

Soon others joined in and were shouting in unison and banging the flats of their hands on the sides and hood of the car.

"Damn it," yelled Stanley, pulling out his service revolver and starting to open the door.

"Sir, I don't think... I wouldn't do that if I were you," said the uniformed driver. His warning fell on deaf ears.

Whether it was lack of sleep that affected his judgment or just a short-fuse, agent Fred Stanley threw open the door and shoved his way out of the vehicle with the intent of shooting his gun into the air a few times to clear the crowd away.

It was then that Josh noticed some people in the mob were carrying weapons of their own, mostly pipes and bats. He suspected there were guns in that crowd as well, and began to regret his foolish attempt at escape. As these thoughts passed through his mind, he watched the FBI agent step out of the van with his revolver pointed high. He never got a chance to fire it.

Someone in the crowd knocked the gun out of his hand, while another grabbed him around the arms. In an instant, they had him wrestled to the ground, while others leaned into the van and pulled out the terrified driver. The same was happening to the other vehicle in the convoy. The occupants fled for their lives as Josh saw their transportation being tipped over behind him. A brick flew through the side window almost hitting Josh in the head. Instead, it grazed his knee and landed on the floor. The next thing he knew, he was being pulled out of the van and passed through the crowd like a rocker in a marsh pit, as they chanted, "Set him Free. Set him free."

Stanley had removed Josh's leg shackles before he put him in the vehicle, but he still had the handcuffs on. Just before Josh was whisked away by the sea of people, someone in the crowd handed him the heavy keychain that had been hanging on Stanley's belt. As their eyes met in a silent thank-you-your-welcome, Josh was pulled away by the mob, which continued to jostle the FBI man back and forth between them like a pinball.

Josh clutched the keys as he made his way to the edge of the throng. Once free of the rioters, he headed for the park area along the Charles River, moving west on the south bank toward Brighton. The whole area was mobbed with people, as if waiting for the Fourth of July fireworks.

Josh had a vague idea of the location of the cemetery where he was to meet Teller from seeing the place when Jeremy Google-mapped it. All he really knew was that it was somewhere in Newton. He figured he'd head in that general direction so he would be in the area on the appointed day. His first task, however, was to remove the cuffs.

There were crowds of people everywhere, all along the Charles River parkway from downtown out to Brighton and beyond. Cambridge across the river was awash in lights and sounds. Someone had released a series of pyrotechnics that lit the sky with colored splashes of light and the air with loud echoing booms. The intersections were choked with unruly young people, threatening store owners and gas station attendants with the loss of their livelihoods. One of them discharged a rifle somewhere within earshot of Josh, as he crouched beneath a large, florescent Coca-Cola sign and used the lights from the billboard to find the key to the cuffs. After some time and almost giving up, he found a small, thin silver key that fit the lock, and the cuffs snapped open, much to Josh's relief. There were sirens blaring all over the city.

Still hoping to elude both the crowds and the police, he moved in a general southerly course toward Brookline. People were running in all directions, some carrying armloads of goods, few of them with receipts. Large bands roved the streets all but sweeping Josh along with them in their frantic swirls of humanity.

Trying to avoid the larger thoroughfares like Commonwealth and Harvard Street, he made his way in the direction of Brookline. From there he would continue south to hit Cleveland circle and the beginning of Route 9 in Newton. He'd have a whole day to locate the cemetery. Hopefully, Teller would have read the papers and seen the ad. Becoming curious, he would go to the meeting place at the appointed time. That is if he was still anywhere near the area. If not, Josh might have to revert to plan B and stake out the place for a few days in the hope that the missing scientist might still show up. It was more than a long shot, but Josh never worried about the odds when he was determined to do something.

As he walked he was bombarded with questions of his own devising. Where were Maria and agent Hagen? Had she testified and cleared him? If so, why were they still after him for kidnapping and murder? If she hadn't, what had happened to her? What about the box of evidence. Where was that? Did Hagen still have it? If he did, why didn't this other agent know about it? It seemed that at a minimum people in the agency weren't talking to each other. Or worse, they were working at cross purposes. Why were they going to take him to FBI headquarters in Washington? Josh had the sneaking suspicion that perhaps Dan and the conspiracy theorist were right, the cover-up went right up to top officials in the government and this agent Stanley was working for them. Whatever the situation, Josh didn't have much choice but to try and escape. As long as he was free he had a chance of clearing himself, finding the missing scientist, and blowing this story wide open.

At some point during his trek, he came across a newspaper dispenser, which had been broken open, glass and papers strewn all over the dirty, wet street. Picking up one of the news-rags that still had more or less all its pages, he skimmed through it quickly beneath an electric sign from a Laundromat. There was no mention of StellarScope or the documents he had released to his news agency. For some reason, they had decided not to publish them, much to Josh's disappointment.

He was now in Brookline, in a little better area of town, where the crowds were thinner. There were still more people out on the streets than usual, but no longer large gatherings at the intersections.

Josh was emotionally drained and disoriented. He needed to find shelter for the night, and a warm place to rest. Up ahead, on a wide street with a parking strip in the middle, he spotted a house of worship. It was a low, brown stone building with a large, round stained-glass window. Next to the window was a bell tower with a flat roof and a cross on top. Instinctively, Josh made his way toward the structure. The warm colored light spilling out of the church's windows seemed very inviting to him in his present state of mind.

Like many, Josh hadn't attended church since he was a kid when his parents used to take him to mass every Sunday. He didn't like it then, and as soon as he was on his own he stopped going all together. The last time he had been in a church was when his father died, for the funeral, which was held in the same place of worship he had gone to all his life. It had brought back memories that mingled with those of his dad and only added to his grief. He was thinking of his father and what he would have thought of his son's current predicament when he opened the large, wooden front door and walked in.

There were two double-rows of pews on each side of a wide center aisle leading to a slightly elevated and unostentatious alter. The building was packed, every seat taken, with people standing in the back, filling the entire area between the door and the rear of the pews. Josh, momentarily taken aback by the number of people, slid sideways toward the right where there was enough space to stand unobtrusively.

122

A rotund, rather cheery-looking man with red cheeks and glasses, who reminded Josh of his long dead grandfather, was talking about the final judgment and the end of days.

Josh was about to leave when someone sitting right in front of him, an elderly lady, suddenly got up and left. When no one rushed to take the spot, he slid into the seat to rest. He had been walking for a couple of hours since fleeing from his captors. His feet hurt and his legs ached. He wasn't used to hoofing it, although walking in the snow shoes had built up his stamina a little. He needed to rest and think.

The first thing he had to do was to find somewhere to stay for the night. Perhaps this was as good a place as any. No one would notice or mind a down on his luck, undernourished man with long sandy hair, who'd fallen asleep during a dull sermon. He had all day tomorrow to find the cemetery, if he could remember the actual name of the place. There couldn't be that many 'Meadow' something cemeteries in Newton. At least he hoped not. He could ask at the church for that matter. They would know. Maybe he could even find a soup kitchen and have breakfast. Yes, Josh had come down a long way since that fateful conversation with the ex-employee of StellarScope. He closed his eyes and wished he could go back and do it all over again. This time he would do things differently.

Across town from the Brookline Episcopal Church where Josh sat and if not exactly prayed, contemplated his universe, agent Fred Stanley spoke through his cell phone.

Things had happened so quickly back at the caravan that he had been taken by surprise, and the situation quickly got out of hand. If his partner had worked with him instead of trying to stop him, things might have turned out better, but Fred had recovered quickly, grabbing the gun that had been knocked to the ground. Granted he had been manhandled, but when his tormenters saw the large round hole of his service revolver pointing at their heads, they had backed off with haste. The other men in his group also quickly gained control of the situation. No one was crazy enough to mess with six armed men brandishing their weapons. That did not, however, keep the mob from tipping over the two vehicles and setting them on fire.

His small force made their way to the Federal building on foot, while Fred tried to contact various officials on his cell, most of whom were on emergency duty in one part of the city or another, or home with their families.

Once in the Federal building he went to the FBI offices and contacted his superiors, who were less than pleased at yet another agent's failure to bring in a suspect for questioning. Instead of making excuses, Fred asked for a direct line to his counterpart in the NSA. He didn't want to waste any time in throwing up a net to re-catch his escaped prisoner.

"Hi, Jake, it's Fred Stanley. Yeah, I'm here in Boston. I need you to re-establish all those taps and surveillance resources you had on that Banks fellow. You know, the one who stole secret papers from the Peeble project. He's escaped again. Yeah, well, he had some help. They're having major riots up here in Boston and we got caught in the middle of one. Oh, down there too, eh? Well, some of these people are just using that as an excuse. Come the first of the year a lot of them will be feeling pretty stupid. If they're not in jail or dead. We'll do what we can. Oh, yeah, you too."

Fred had forgotten it was almost New Years.

"So you got the list, right," he continued, "his cell, bank card number, credit card? Good, what about his old boss, the guy he used to work with? Where's he? In the City? Good, that will keep him out of my hair. What about that woman, Maria Cavello? Put a tap on her too. And anyone else involved with him or his family. We kept his friend, Dan Peters. Calls himself 'Little-Wolf'. I'll give him a little wolf. We've still got him in custody back in Amherst. I'll have him brought here and lean on him a little, see if he can tell us anything more. Also Bank's folks, we've got all their bio info on record in the agency's computers if you need it. You have access, right? Dale will give you what you need. I'd also like some of your satellite resources and someone to work with me. Well, he got away on foot. I'll need something in the area by tomorrow morning. I don't know, I'll start from where he left us, drop a fifty-mile grid around it and work outward until I get more data. Then maybe we can focus the search better. I'm going to try and get Dale to authorize a helicopter to help with the hunt."

When he was through, he phoned the state police barracks in Amherst and ordered them to send the prisoner Dan Little-Wolf Peters to Boston under armed escort. To his surprise the familiar voice of Tom Hagen answered the call.

"Is that you, Stanley? I understand you have my prisoner."

"First of all he's not your prisoner. You've been superseded. I'm taking over and you know it. You were informed when I was. If you have a problem call Quantico. You internal affairs guys never should have gotten involved."

"I've tried talking to your boss. Dale's got a rag up his ass and won't answer my calls."

"That's 'cause you're an internal affairs dick. When you took that assignment you became the fall guy. Now you're non-gratis at the bureau."

"I may be a dick to you, but I'm not dumb. There's something wrong about this whole thing."

"You would say that, after losing your man."

"When the tip came in to the state police in Amherst from that informant, the first thing they did was call me. I'm the local agent on the case. We had just put out an alert through the area. I was working directly with the local boys. I knew it was only a matter of time until he was spotted. There aren't many places he could go without being recognized from his photo on the news. How did Quantico hear about it so quick?"

"The Staties obviously called us."

"Why would they do that? Why would they take the time to call Washington about a local event when they've got the agent in charge right here on the spot? Anyway, I'm at the barracks and there's no record of anyone calling DC. No, they were bugging my phones. As soon as I got the call they were tipped off. I was taken off the case before I even had a chance to call it in."

"Which you didn't do."

"No, I didn't. I was too busy following the real leads."

"Well, partner, you've been taken off the case. Why don't you just go back to that little wife of yours in DC."

"Leave my wife out of this," said Tom, raising his voice slightly. "Why were they bugging my phones, even before the escape? What's going on, Fred?"

"What's going on is you screwed up. I'm not surprised they were watching you. You made a lot of enemies putting your own men behind bars."

"Crooks and dirty cops are not my own men. As a matter of fact, the dirty cops are worse than crooks because they do their dirty work under the guise of helping folks. Instead of doing good they're really preying on people."

"Ah, get off your high horse, you dumb shmuck. You're no better than the rest of us. You're a screw-up. Now hang up the phone and have them send that prisoner to me in Boston."

"Why, what do you need him for? You've got the person you want. What do you want Little-Wolf for? Why are you guys so interested in Banks anyway? The Cavello woman cleared him of kidnapping. He has an alibi for at least one of the murders."

"Where was he during the first one?" asked Stanley, not convinced of anything Hagen was saying.

"I don't know, but his story checks out. Maria Cavello confirmed everything he told us. What motive would he have had to kill a complete stranger, who just happened to be connected to the company the Cavello woman worked for? And what about those documents we have? It's all in my report. There's the motive if you want one."

"I've seen your report. Nice job of obfuscation."

"The agency's interest in this guy makes no sense. They should be investigating that StellarScope company. And what about his story? How come his news agency hasn't published those documents? I would have thought they'd make the front page, but I haven't heard a thing about it. It's like it's being covered up, and you're a part of it."

"Screw you, Hagen."

"You may not realize it Fred, but they're up to something. It could go all the way to the Defense Department."

"I'm sure it does. That's why they're after this guy in the first place. It has to do with state secrets and our national defense."

"It's a telescope for Christ's sake. They're stealing millions and fooling everyone, that's what's going on. You're being duped."

"Send me that prisoner, Hagen, or I'll have you brought in with him."

"Good luck," said Tom, slamming the phone down.

Chapter 15

Josh woke with someone gently shaking his shoulder.

"Excuse me, son? Hello, my boy. You can't stay here. You'll have to leave."

"I'm sorry, Father," said Josh, blinking away the sleep and looking up into the face of the pastor, who had recently been giving his sermon to a full house. Now only a few old women sat in the pews praying or sitting with rosaries in their hands.

"We're getting ready for a special early morning service," said the priest. "If you are not going to participate, you will have to leave."

"Certainly, Father. I came in last night to find peace. I'm afraid I've had rather a bad time and fell asleep. I'll leave immediately. Oh, by the way, if you have some time afterward, I'd like to talk to you if I could. I need some assistance."

"The parish kitchen opens at 8:00 am. It's in the basement. You can wait down by the back door until then if you wish, or join our service. There's a shelter down the street if you need a place to sleep. I can give you a name to ask for."

"Thank you, Father, but that won't be necessary. I'm only in town for a short time."

Josh slipped seamlessly into a new false identity, made up on the spur of the moment to elicit the sympathy and aid of the elderly cleric.

"My boy died a few months ago. I'm from out of town. My wife and I are divorced, haven't seen them in several years. She didn't even tell me. All I have is the name of the cemetery."

"And what is that, my son?"

"Meadow something; Meadow Grove or Meadow Brook. It's in Newton I believe. Would you know where that is?"

"Yes, I think so. I'll tell you what. We're short-staffed today and need a hand in the kitchen. If you want to volunteer and help out, I'll see you get a good hot meal and draw you a map. Why don't you wait downstairs. My assistant will let you in. We can talk when I'm finished up here."

Josh thanked the churchman and went out and around to the back of the building, where the entrance to the basement facilities were located. A sign advertised both the soup kitchen and a free clinic on Mondays. Josh knocked and asked for the name the pastor had given him. It had begun to rain, a cold heavy downpour that soaked him in moments.

"Hi," he said, when a matronly woman answered the door, her hair gray, her eyes hazel-blue. "I've come to volunteer. Father Peters told me to talk to you."

"Yes, come on in out of the rain. You're a little early. We don't open for another couple hours yet, but I'm sure we can find something for you to do until then."

She ushered Josh into a long corridor to the back of the building where there were piles of cans and boxes that needed to be brought to the kitchen.

"The other volunteers won't be here for another hour yet," said the old lady. "But if you want to, you can start moving these into the pantry and unpacking them. I'll show you where. Can I get you anything, a cup of coffee maybe? You can eat a half hour before we open."

"Coffee would be great," he said, taking off his coat. "Do you have a restroom I could use?"

"Certainly. Straight down this corridor on your left."

On the way to the restroom, Josh passed a payphone. He had been thinking about his mother before he fell asleep in the pew. She must be worried by all the news reports about him. In spite of the fact the Feds might have a trace on his mother's phone he stopped and dialed her number.

I'd like to place a collect call," he said, when the operator came on the line. "My name is Josh."

After waiting a few moments, his mom's voice came on the line.

"Hello, Josh, is that you?" she asked in an anxious voice.

"Yeah, Mom. I can't talk long, but I wanted you to know I'm OK."

"What happened? What's all this about? I'm reading the most terrible things about you in the news."

"I know. None of it's true. I'm on a big story and there are some very important people who don't want it to get out. I don't want you to get involved. I just wanted you to know I'm OK and I'm going to straighten this whole thing out. So don't worry. I've got to go. I love you. Bye."

"Josh," she said, trying frantically to form some words to keep him on the line. Her heart broke into a thousand pieces when she realized he had hung up. The main thing was that he was all right and hadn't done any of those terrible things they said about him. She had faith that he would prevail. When Josh put his mind to something, no matter how hard it was and how long it took, he always succeeded. Whatever he was up against this time, though, seemed especially dangerous. She said a silent prayer and asked her late husband Earl to keep a special eye out for their boy.

Josh's nap in the church had invigorated him and the hour and a half of opening cartons and stacking food went by fast. He was happy to have a place to hide and something to occupy himself with for a few hours. The hot breakfast of ham and eggs, with toast and jam and hot coffee positively rejuvenated him. After breakfast he stood behind a big vat of hot oatmeal and ladled it into bowls for hungry people.

Josh was surprised at the number of homeless who came in, and not just drunks and derelicts off the street, but whole families of otherwise normal-looking human beings, children as well as women. Most looked at the ground in embarrassment at finding themselves in such a predicament, but every now and then someone - mostly a woman or a child - would look up and smile, and say thank you. Josh asked himself why he hadn't done this sooner.

During a lull between breakfast and lunch, while they switched the vats of oatmeal for chicken soup, the volunteer next to him, a retired music teacher from the neighborhood, struck up a conversation.

"More than usual this morning. If the crowds keep up like this, we won't have enough food. The donations this year were the smallest I've seen."

"Yeah, things are bad, have been for a long time. We've been at ten percent unemployment over the past four years now and it's not getting any better. We did a number of pieces on it last year."

"Oh, you a writer?" asked the man with interest.

"Sort of. I, eh, I'm an editor for Business Week," replied Josh, realizing he had said too much and pulling the name out of his hat. It was one of the many magazines he read.

"Oh, and what brings you to this neck of the woods and our little soup kitchen?"

This is what he got for lying. Now he would have to tread carefully if he didn't want to blow his story. The odds were high that this Good Samaritan would talk to the priest sooner or later.

"Eh, I'm here on personal business, nothing to do with the job. Family matters."

"Oh, I hope it's nothing serious," said the man with concern.

"I'd rather not talk about it," replied Josh, hoping he wasn't being rude, but the less he said the less chance of being caught in a web of lies.

"I understand," said the friendly volunteer. "Father Peters can be very understanding and helpful. I know he helped me when my wife died."

"Yes, I plan to talk to him later. I'm sorry to hear about your wife."

"Thanks. It was very hard. I can't help feeling it was all my fault. I was in a bad car accident coming home from work one evening, in the hospital for almost two weeks, a month in rehab. It really affected her. I recovered fine, but a little while after my recovery she was diagnosed with cancer. We didn't even know she was sick. She was so worried about me she didn't pay attention to her own health. She had developed diabetes. She must have had some kind of symptoms but ignored them because she was so focused on helping me get better. The cancer, which started in her pancreas, must have been caused by the diabetes and her failure to detect or control it. It spread to her liver and kidneys before we knew what was happening. She was pretty sick by then. She fought to the end though, bless her soul. Awful way to go."

"I'm sorry," said Josh again, ashamed at the pitiful story he had concocted for the priest about being here to see his dead son's gravesite. He resolved more than ever not to tell the lie to the poor man, who had just bared his soul to him. Luckily, a second wave of hungry people soon came in and made it too busy to talk.

"Where are all these people coming from? Is this usual?" Josh asked, after two more hours of dishing out soup,

"No," said his fellow volunteer. "I think there are a lot of people like you, here from out of town with nowhere to go. This end of the world scare has got people spooked. A lot of folks, those on the edge, you know, with mental or emotional problems, they're coming out of the woodwork, congregating in the cities, mixing with those already homeless on the streets. It doesn't help that someone advertised a big end-of-the-world party with free booze and sex. They're having them in several cities, even though the authorities have refused to grant permits and threatened to arrest participants."

"Well, if last night was any example, the authorities have their hands full. What I saw was a full-blown riot There were people out in the streets everywhere, from the Commons to Kenmore, all the way

130

past Brighton and over in Cambridge. Even out here there were crowds. They think the world's going to end. I never would have believed the mass hysteria if I hadn't seen it myself."

"I heard the governor has declared martial law and issued a curfew for the greater Boston area. The demonstrators are promising more disturbances tonight if their demands aren't meant. They want everyone released from prison and all stores and retailers to open their doors so people can take what they want so their last hours on earth will be happy. It's crazy. Do you have a place to go tonight?"

"Ah, not exactly. I was hoping to stay with friends, but I can't get hold of anybody. I was caught in the riot last night by a gang of toughs. They took my phone and wallet, my watch as well. I lost my suitcase with all my clothes when my taxi driver ran off. I'm in pretty sad shape. I'll be glad when all this nonsense is over and things get back to normal."

"Yeah, some people will be feeling pretty foolish come Wednesday."

The lunch line had finally ended. They had served breakfast and dinner to over 700 people, with only a short break in between. Josh was exhausted as he ate his own lunch of turkey and dressing, with mashed potatoes and gravy. It was a soup kitchen holiday dinner, but it tasted like a grand feast to Josh.

After eating he was hit with an overwhelming urge to sleep, as if the short naps of the last few days had never been. He could hardly keep his red, heavy eyes open as he sought out the parish priest. He found him in the kitchen washing pans.

"Oh, there you are," said the priest as he splashed water on a sudsy sponge. "Martha told me you volunteered. She says you've been here all day. Thank you."

"My pleasure. I figured it was the least I could do for falling asleep in your church."

"Oh, don't apologize. It happens all the time. I don't want to encourage that sort of thing but my sermons do tend to be on the boring side."

"Well, you had a full house last night."

"It's been like that all week. People are honestly concerned that the world might end."

"So I guess I'd better find my boy's gravestone. If the world's going to end that's where I want to be. You said you knew where the cemetery was?"

"Yes. I believe the place you're looking for is the Meadow Glenn Cemetery. It's off Route 9 in Newton. I'll write out the directions for you."

"That would be great, Father. I was wondering, I need a place to rest for a few hours. I'm exhausted. Could you give me the name of that shelter?"

"Why don't you stay here. We have a cot in the back. The staff uses it occasionally when they have to stay over. Once the kitchen's closed down, it's quite quiet down here. You can close the drapes. I'll leave the door unlocked. Please flip the latch when you leave."

"I'll only be a few hours, until this rain lets up. It's really coming down."

"Yes, I'm afraid with the snow covering the drains it will cause some bad flooding if it keeps up like this. I'll have another full house today just with all the folks coming in to get out of the rain."

"Break a leg, Father," quipped Josh. "I'm sorry, I didn't mean any disrespect."

"That's quite all right, my boy. That's a very appropriate saying for an old ham like me."

They both laughed, as Josh helped the priest dry the pans and hang them up before closing down the kitchen.

There were still a few hours of daylight left. Josh planned to sleep most of these away and then head for the cemetery following Father Peter's directions. However, the rain promised to put a monkey-wrench in that scheme if it didn't stop soon. Unless, that is, he planned to float to the cemetery.

He had just shut off the light in the kitchen hall and settled into the small back room where a cot was set up next to a cluttered desk, when there was a knock on the rectory door. The rectory was behind the church, right next to the basement room where Josh had just lain down. The knock disturbed him, especially when it was repeated a second time with more force. He vaguely became aware of a light flashing in the alley. Without thinking, he jumped up from the cot and ran through the kitchen and adjoining dining area to the rear of the basement, which faced the street-front. A door with a frosted window led up a short flight of stairs to another door leading out to a landing a few steps below the street. He emerged a second later a short way down from the church's front entrance.

There were police cars parked in front of the building with their lights flashing. Several uniformed men stood by in their rain gear. A crowd was already beginning to gather in the street. The rain was coming down in buckets, churning up the deep piles of dirty, soot-covered snow, and causing torrents of water to run down the sides of the streets. If the end of the world was coming, thought Josh, it was probably going to be a flood by the looks of it.

No one noticed him as he hurried up the street, a borrowed black slicker pulled over his head to shield him from the rain and the eyes of the police. As uncomfortable as the pelting raindrops were, they gave him some cover from whoever was looking for him, and would make him virtually invisible. Unbeknownst to Josh, the heavy dense clouds in this part of the northeast made the millions of dollars of satellites they had pointed at Boston virtually useless as well. They'd have to find their man the old-fashioned way.

As Josh headed in the direction of Cleveland Circle and Route 9, Fred Stanley searched the premises of the church, despite the objections of its occupant. They found nothing. The call picked up on the line of Mrs. Margaret Banks of Burlington, Vermont, had been traced to this small parish church in Brookline, Massachusetts. Stanley had been informed exactly 101 seconds after the call was made. The FBI isn't one of the NSA's best customers for nothing.

Unfortunately, the escapee had fled moments before they arrived. Either he was tipped off or he had good instincts. Even more regrettable was the fact that their satellite resources, along with the helicopter were next to useless in the present weather conditions. He phoned for a canine unit as he instructed his men to fan out and canvas the area

"Stop any single, white male who looks the least bit like the picture and hold him until I can question him," he ordered. "He couldn't have gone that far".

While he was waiting for a dog, his phone rang. It was his man in the NSA.

"Hi, Stanley here, what's up? I know, this weather is tailor made for eluding detection. When do you think your satellites will be able to see? No let up in sight, eh. Cripes, that's going to mess things up. There's already a flood up here. Yeah, where's Noah when you need him," he laughed.

"I've got a bird, but if this keeps up, it will not be able to go up. The conditions are terrible. Yeah, I've got a house to house going. We only missed him by minutes. He must have been tipped off somehow.

Yeah, maybe the priest. You got what? An ad? In both papers? Hmm, in the evening ones too? So, what's the connection? From where? Yeah, that's where we caught him, Pelham. What time? Yeah, I'm writing it down. That's quite a coincidence if you ask me. What's it say again? Eh-hum, yep, OK, I got it. Do you know what it means? Teller? Well let me know what your boys come up with. In the meantime, I have a dog coming. We'll track him the good old fashion-way."

Chapter 16

Josh hurried down Beacon Street in the direction of Cleveland Circle. He had been there a few times when he had gone to school in Boston, taking dates to the theater and jogging around Hammond Pond. Today he jogged in the rain, holding a coat partly over his head.

The crowds grew thicker as he approached the Circle. Stopping to get his bearings, he checked the directions the pastor had written down for him. The priest had told him it was about three or four miles, not far as the crow flies. He could be there in a couple of hours walking at a steady clip. With the rain and darkness coming, though, Josh had his doubts it would be that easy, especially if the cops picked up his trail, which they could do at any time. He had already noticed an increased police presence in the area, but so far no one had noticed him.

He headed southwest about a quarter of a mile until he found the street he was looking for. Then he took the first right after that and followed it for about a half mile. Making a left on Norfolk, he almost immediately hit Route 9. From there he planned to follow the road west until he reached the street leading to the cemetery. At that point, it would be almost due south about two and a half more miles.

As he moved away from the Circle, the crowds thinned out, which might not be a good thing if he was trying to blend in, but he used the dark inclement night to stay out of sight. He walked with long strides, trying to make the best time possible on foot, looking over his shoulder every now and then to make sure he wasn't being followed. His hair was matted to his head. Beads of water dripped off his nose and eyebrows. Luckily the weather was still unseasonably warm, although the rain felt cold enough. He needed to get off the streets. There was still several feet of snow piled on the sides of the road and on people's lawns, but the rain was melting it fast and washing it into the already full gutters and low places. It had been raining hard when he left the church. It was now pouring even more fiercely. If he didn't find shelter soon he'd drown or catch pneumonia.

Stumbling forward almost blindly, following the highway west but staying in the shadows and the backs of the buildings, he pushed his way through a high hedge and found himself bathed in the lights of a large sports club. He stood staring at an acre of empty tennis courts. Several large tent-like structures stood across the field, lit internally like large gray lanterns, obviously indoor facilities. A couple of the courts at the end of this row appeared to be dark. Josh headed for these, through fields of knee deep snow and slush, keeping to the shadows as much as possible.

On reaching the first of the darkened structures, he circled around the building looking for an entrance, trying each of four doors in turn. They were all locked. He tried the next building, after hiding in the shadows to make sure no one was watching. All its doors were locked as well, but Josh spent more time with the last one. It was at the side of the structure facing the highway, which was about thirty yards away, across a snow-covered lawn dotted with large trees. He would be unobserved and unheard in the rain.

Remembering the keys he had used to unlock the handcuffs, more on a whim than the hope any of them would work, he took them out and one by one tried them in the lock. To his surprise one of them, on the second try, seemed to fit, but didn't turn the latch. Leaving it in, he startled jiggling the door's handle back and forth, first trying the key while pulling it outward, then while pushing it in. He then took the card the priest had given him with the address of the shelter and slid it into the door where the latch met the door-jam, jiggling it up and down in the process, while he shook the door back and forth gently. Before long the card slipped between the latch, and the door opened. Josh entered and shut it quietly behind him.

The inside of the huge cavernous space was almost completely dark. Josh stood still and listened. The first thing he became aware of was the warmth and dryness of the place. Just not standing in snow up to his shins and having the rain pelting him like woodchips was enough to make him breathe an audible sigh of relief. As his eyes became adjusted to the half-light, he made a circuit around the perimeter of the court, feeling his way as he went. Locating several long benches, he circled back to his starting point. There he stopped and took off his stolen slicker, and his wet shoes, slacks and socks. On his second circuit around the court he found a water-cooler and a towel dispenser next to it. He wiped his face and dried his feet, slaking his thirst with a long drink of water. Then barely able to keep his eyes open a moment longer, he crawled onto one of the benches, pulled his coat over his shoulders, and using the crook of his arm as a pillow, fell almost instantly to sleep.

Fred Stanley was at a loss when the officer in charge of the dog - a large, mostly black German Sheppard - asked him for a piece of clothing or some personal belonging from the escapee. Not having thought of this eventuality, Stanley had nothing belonging to the fugitive and had to order some of Josh's belongings brought from his house, which was an hour away. By the time they arrived, it was almost nine o'clock and four hours had gone by. Once they got started, the dog had difficulty following the trail due to the hard rain.

Luckily for Josh, Father Peters had not connected the man the police were after with the volunteer he had given directions to, at least not immediately. Josh's story had confused the aging pastor and Stanley's sloppy interrogation methods and haste only made it more difficult for the flustered priest to respond.

"Hello, Father. I'm with the FBI," Stanley had said. "We've tracked a fugitive here wanted for terrorist activities. A phone call was traced to these premises by the fugitive just a few hours ago."

"No one made any calls from this house. I'm the only one that can use this phone."

"Do you have any other phones on the premises?" He read the number.

"That's the public phone in the dining area. It's in the basement of the church. But anyone can use that. We had hundreds of people here today for breakfast and lunch."

"This would have been early, around quarter to seven."

"Well, that's before we open. It would have been my assistant or one of the volunteers. They've all left for the day."

"We'll have to search the premises," Stanley informed him with no preamble. Without asking any further questions; without bothering to get the names of the volunteers; without even showing the priest a warrant or a mug-shot of the prisoner, and over the strenuous objections of the pastor himself; the FBI man had the entire building, including the church – and this just before Father Peters was to start his service - searched. They had found nothing. Now he was waiting in the rain for the suspect's clothes to arrive.

"Here you go," he said handing the articles of clothing to the dog trainer when they finally did appear. "Give the dog a whiff of that. This guy will probably thank us for getting him out of this downpour. He can't have gone far. He's on foot and has no money or wallet."

"I don't know if the dog will be able to follow the scent in this rain," said their trainer. "It'll get washed out pretty quick in this weather, just like footprints."

"Great. I can't use the satellite. I've had to send back the helicopter. And now you tell me the dog won't work."

"Oh, he'll work, especially if your suspect is still around here, but the more time he's had to travel, the harder it's going to be for the dog to pick up his trail."

They started the search in the church, where the dog picked up the scent right away, much to the consternation of the pastor who was in the middle of his service and an old lady sitting in the pew. The Shepherd followed Josh's scent to the back of the building's basement and kitchen area, where he had worked all day. Within another few minutes it had found the bed where Josh had lain for all of ten minutes, and his path out to the front of the building. From there, however, nothing, the scent petered out on the street. The suspect appeared to be heading west.

"Have Riley and Jackson check-out Chestnut Hill," said Stanley through his car radio, while he studied a map on his video console. "I want a couple of cars out to Hammond Pond as well." He looked up at the canine-officer. "Can we get any more dogs out here tonight?"

"I don't know, sir. Most of them are on crowd control in the city. After what happened last night, they're taking every precaution. Tonight promises to be even worse. A lot of people got it into their heads the world's going to end."

"Well, they're certainly reacting in a stupid way. See if you can get a couple more dogs. It's a matter of national security. We've got a terrorist on our hands."

"Yes, sir," said the officer, relieved to be able to get his animal out of the rain for a few moments while he called headquarters.

"Where the hell could this guy be running to?" Stanley asked another field agent, who had brought him a cup of steaming coffee. He hadn't eaten since lunchtime. "Or is he holed up somewhere? How's that house to house coming?"

"Slow," said the other man. "It would help if we had a dog or two for that as well. He could have gone in any direction."

"Yeah," said Stanley, scratching his head. "But most probably he's heading west or southwest out of town." He pointed at the map and the western suburbs of Boston. "I think I'll talk to that priest again."

He went back into the church to find the priest, who was just starting his sermon, again preaching to a full house. The FBI agent stood at the back of the building by the doors waiting for the priest to finish.

"So what if the world is ending tomorrow?" said the preacher. "If God in his wisdom has ordained it, then let it be. Thy Will be done. But I say to you, a true Christian should live his life as if each day is his last, as if the Lord could see fit to take him at anytime. The Lord giveth and the Lord taketh away. Do not take these simple familiar words too lightly, for they point to the true meaning of life. That which is given will be taken away. This is the way of God's perfect creation. All that begins shall end, blessed be to God. Go out and live each second of your life to the full. No matter it will end. That you cannot control. All you can control is how you live each day that you have, the choice you must make each minute between good and evil. So I say unto you, make each moment count. Make each minute mean something. God, in his everlasting mercy has sent his beloved son to redeem us. No matter if the world should end, His word is eternal. Thou that know the son shall know the father and find salvation. Do not worry about what has not yet come or what might be."

Stanley thought the priest was finished when he paused, and looked around the congregation to see their reaction to the preacher's sermon. There were well-to-do families and downtrodden single moms; athletes and bookworms; the mild-mannered and the wild and rude; the well dressed and the slovenly; locals and out-of-towners; the old and the young and everything in between; a weirdly out of the ordinary collection of disparate lives all jumbled together by fear of the future, or the lack of it. So far there wasn't much for Stanley to object to in the priest's sermon and he found himself enjoying it, "Yeah, Father, give them hell," he muttered to himself under his breath. But then the pastor ventured off into apocalyptic dogma and Old Testament rhetoric that put Stanley and much of the congregation to sleep. The FBI man stepped out after twenty-minutes more to have a cigarette, when it appeared the priest wouldn't be stopping any time soon. It was still raining.

"Anything?" he asked his partner, who was just coming up the short, broad steps fronting the building.

"No, not yet. We've checked out Chestnut Hill, the Pond and Cleveland Circle."

"OK, let's get the dog out to the Circle and see if it finds anything. That's a good a place as any to start. Maybe it'll pick up something. I doubt he'd head back into town. He's trying to get home, I figure. I've got people at the toll-booths leading out of town on the Pike, roadblocks on the other highways and roads. His rental house is under surveillance. He can't get far."

After seeing that his orders were being carried out, Stanley went back into the kitchen area to see if there was anything they had missed in his earlier search. Then he waited in the rectory for the priest.

Pastor Peter had seen the rude FBI agent standing at the rear of the church, and had purposely extended his sermon, both to avoid having to talk to the man and to give him a lesson in patience, not that he didn't have a lot of good things to say. The bible was nothing if not full of Old Testament passages about the end of the world. He was offended how the lawman put his priorities before those of God, and certainly didn't like his preemptory manners, or being ordered about. And to bring a dog into his church right before a service and scaring his parishioners half to death, well, he had a good mind to complain to the Bishop.

It had finally dawned on the slow-witted priest that the police were after the man he had let stay in the basement, the one who had volunteered and had come to town to find the gravestone of his dead son, if that's who he really was. It had to be him. He was the only person who could have used the phone at that early hour, and had obviously left in a hurry. The man hadn't seemed like a terrorist, but he certainly didn't seem to be who he said he was either.

The priest was having a mental tug of war over whether he would tell the police about the directions he had given the man. Why would he have wanted directions to a cemetery if not to see his dead boy? What was he going to do, terrorize the deceased? No, if their suspect really was a terrorist, he'd be going to some busy place like the airport or the National Grid. There were crowds everyway, plenty of places to hurt a lot of people. Why go to a quiet, out of the way cemetery? But then one never knew what these types of people were thinking or how their minds worked. It was quite a quandary for the churchman. He didn't know what he was going to do as he made his way from the back of the sacristy to the rectory.

"I tried to tell him you weren't in, Father," said his housekeeper as he entered the building. "But he insisted on waiting and snooping around."

"That's OK, Phyllis," said the priest, handing her his coat. "I'll take care of it."

He went into the small back room he used as an office. The FBI man was standing by the wall, looking at the priest's collections of photographs and mementos from years of working with young people, baseball and basketball teams, young athletes in their running gear, rows of boys and girls in their school uniforms and blazers.

"Can I get you anything?" asked the priest as he entered the room.

"No, thank you. I'm fine, just looking at all your pictures. Working with young people must give you a lot of satisfaction."

"Yes, it's one of the many rewards for doing God's work."

"Hmm, yes. You had a good crowd tonight."

"Yes. It's been like that all week with the holiday season."

"I suspect there's more to it than just the holidays. I wanted to ask you a few more things I didn't get a chance this morning."

"Yes, you were in a bit of a hurry."

"We had just missed our man by minutes. I was hoping to catch him before he did any more damage."

"And what damage is that?" asked the priest, sitting down behind his desk.

"I'm really not at liberty to say," said Stanley sitting down opposite him. "He's stolen some top secret documents to start with. If these fall into the wrong hands it could be very damaging to our national defense. He may also have been involved in a kidnapping and possible murder."

"That does sound serious. And you think he was in our church?"

"We know he was here. There's not only the phone call. Our dogs have tracked him here. He was staying in your back room."

"Oh, you mean the man who came to find his dead son's grave?"

"Is that what he told you?"

"Yes. He showed up late last night during our midnight service. Looked pretty down and out; dirty clothes; unshaved; long, dirty blond hair; tall; down on his luck. He said his boy had died recently and that his ex-wife didn't tell him. He's here to be with his dead son when the end comes."

"That sounds like our man, at least the physical description. The story is obviously a lie. This guy was never married and has no children. Did he say where he was going?"

This was the question the priest had been dreading. He certainly didn't believe the man's story, not now after what the FBI agent had told him. But he wasn't sure if he believed the lawman's account either. He probably would have said the man killed his own mother and eaten babies if it suited his purpose. Father Peters didn't know who to believe. He answered slowly, as if trying to remember.

"We didn't talk for long. I told him he could eat here. He volunteered to help at the soup kitchen. Seemed nice enough. Didn't appear to be running from anyone. He didn't know where his son was buried, wasn't even sure of the town. Just asked if there were any cemeteries in the vicinity."

"And are there?" asked Stanley taking out his notepad and pen.

"Yes, several, some pretty big ones." He started rattling off names. "There's the Holyhood, that's the closest. Then there are several big ones down Hammand Street toward West Roxbury. There're also a couple in Newton."

Father Peters didn't care for the way the FBI man asked his question, with a crisp aggressiveness that seemed to assume complete compliance; the way he slouched in his chair as if sitting up straight would take more effort than his interviewee deserved. He even had the effrontery to light up a cigarette, not even waiting for an answer to, "Do you mind if I…" Whatever they were after this guy for, they would have to find him without the help of Father Peters and his church. After all, for all he knew the world could be ending at noon tomorrow, then none of it would matter. If it turned out otherwise and this person really was a dangerous terrorist, he could always tell them he had given him directions to a specific cemetery.

Stanley jumped up from his seat and rushed for the door, hardly stopping to say thank you, and called in instructions to his team to converge on the cemeteries in the area. In the meantime, the dog had picked up the fugitive's scent again near Cleveland Circle and took off in the direction of Route 9.

"That's it!" yelled Stanley jubilantly. "We've got him."

Chapter 17

Josh woke with a start. Despite the hard bed, he had slept soundly for almost five hours. He woke with the same disorientation he had that morning in his car watching Maria Cavello's apartment, the night her friend was murdered. Since then he had slept in jails, motel rooms, on couches and bunks, even in the back of a police van, sometimes for little more than a few hours at a time. He was almost getting used to it. It had been so long since he'd slept in his own bed - and that only a rented one - that he had almost forgotten what a good night's rest felt like. He hadn't exactly expected to live like a nomad when he signed up for this job, but it had certainly turned out that way. He should be getting combat pay for what he was doing, but he was doing it for nothing, au gratis.

He lay there for some time, trying to think things through, not wanting to move. He was safe and dry for the time being, but for how long? What if the priest had told them where he was going? He could just as well give them directions to the place as he had Josh. Why not? Why would the churchman cover for him, especially with what the FBI was probably telling him? If so, they may already be outside waiting for him. In any case, he'd have a better chance of eluding them in the dark than in broad daylight. That is if the sun showed at all. This thought and the hardness of the wooden bench finally caused him to stir.

He sat up and stretched. Bending over slowly, he put on his clothes, which were partially dry, and his shoes, which were not. Then he got up and found his way around the court again to the drinking fountain, where he drank his fill of cool water before going back to the bench to get his coat. He hadn't eaten since noon the previous day. That would have to do, that and the pudding he had taken with him to the room and gobbled down before lying down.

He let himself out of the tennis court by the same door he had come in and found himself on the side of the tent-like structure facing the highway about thirty yards away. It was still raining hard and still dark, Josh figured sometime after midnight. He pulled the slicker tight around his neck and started out, crossing Route 9 and heading up Hammond, south toward the cemetery.

There was a surprising amount of traffic heading out of town on the highway, but otherwise there were few people about, especially walking in this area. Hammond Street was devoid of cars, but he stayed well off the road and in the shadows, moving along the rear of buildings, through empty alleyways and deserted lots. Soon he came to a cemetery on his right. The priest hadn't mentioned this one, but it was too soon to be the one Josh was looking for. This particular cemetery appeared to be quite busy.

The lights of several vehicles blazed across the gravesites, their beams throwing the tombstones and mausoleums into sharp relief. Josh crouched down low and skirted to the other side of the street. Keeping beneath a stone wall and behind some parked vehicles, he continued to move south, putting distance between him and the police activity.

He wondered what the lights meant. Were they looking for him? Maybe the priest only told them he was going to a cemetery but not which one. Or perhaps it was just a coincidence. He had to assume they were looking for him, although there was enough going on this evening to keep the authorities otherwise busy. Maybe someone was digging up graves, thinking the dead were coming back on the last day. After what he'd seen recently, Josh would have believed people were capable of just about anything right now.

He continued south figuring he had a couple of miles to go and several hours before daylight. He would find someplace close to the meeting point to hide for the rest of the night, someplace where he could observe the situation come morning.

Suddenly, he heard a dog bark behind him and a man yelling. The noise came from much closer than he had expected, being a block from the cemetery, which he had thought he passed unnoticed. Apparently the dog had noticed. Somebody appeared to be on his trail. He started running through the rain.

Passing a large baseball field and what looked like a good-sized school building in the darkness, he kept running until he came to a wooded park, which appeared on his left.

Still hearing the barking of a dog behind him, Josh darted up a path into the woods. The rain continued to come down hard, churning the snow-covered ground into slush-covered mud. The pavement was relatively free of snow, but the path he was on was slippery and thick with mulch that sloshed when he ran through it making his footing precarious. Water had already begun to collect into large, dark pools in the low places. As hard as the going was, he figured he'd have better luck eluding his pursuers - if indeed someone was after him – in the woods than if he stayed on the street. He'd just have to be careful not to lose his bearings.

He tried to keep somewhat parallel to the road, which he managed to do as he moved south through the large park. He could still hear the barking of a dog somewhere behind him, but he had definitely put more distance between him and whoever it was. Suddenly, he stepped from the woods into a wide open area devoid of trees and structures. A broad swath cut through the woods that lined it on both sides, a snow-covered thoroughfare stretching in both directions before him. It took him some time to realize he was on the fairway of a golf course, by the looks of it a straight, wide par-five. He vaguely remembered the priest mentioning it when he had given him the directions. At least he was on the right course, he quipped to himself.

Were they after him? Did the dogs have his scent? Would they find him before daylight or would he be sheltered by the rain? And what would he do tomorrow to elude his pursuers while he pursued the missing Dr. Teller? Josh wondered all these things and more, as he ran down one fairway and across another. He tried to stay on the paths where there was less snow, but his footprints were clearly visible where he had to travel across the greens and fairways. Retracing his steps, he headed off in another direction where he was less likely to leave tracks. He moved in this way, retracing and brushing his steps at times and as needed, until he found a small auxiliary building not far from the main lodge of the country club, which was closed for the season.

His feet were wet and cold, his nose running and red. He had somehow managed to keep ahead of whoever was after him, but they were still coming, closer now by the barking of the persistent canine. Yes, someone was definitely after him, he was sure of it now.

Josh had an idea. Sprinting by the building, which was sitting on posts a few feet above the ground, he ran across the adjoining two fairways to a patch of woods and up a small hill, which looked down on a rotary where roads branched off in several directions. He had left clear tracks. He recognized the spot from the directions the priest had given him, 'take LaGrange Street from the rotary'.

Moving the rest of the way to the road, he left the woods and ran briefly up the street in the direction of a large sports field, which he could just make out in the distance. Then he turned and retraced his steps, being careful to walk in the same foot marks he had made previously, moving backward to make sure his feet were placed in precisely the same spots. By the time he had retraced his steps all the way back to the shed, the search team was almost on him.

Standing in the middle of the tracks near a window of the building, he quickly hoisted himself up onto an old oil drum that stood next to one of the posts. He peered in. It was pitch dark inside. Without pausing, he grabbed a board hanging over the window, and stepping up onto the sill used his arms and his elbows to half-shimmy, half-pull himself onto the flat roof of the structure. Peering down at the white ground below him, he could see his footprints running by in the snow. There was no sign that he had stopped and climbed to the roof. The barrel was clear and smelled strongly of oil, he hoped strong enough to confound the dogs.

He noticed a canvas tarp that had been used to cover a hole in the roof. The opening was too small to crawl through, but the large heavy tarp offered some protection from the elements. Josh hunkered down beneath it and waited for the dawn, or his capture, whichever came first.

It wasn't long before he heard the sound of footsteps.

"Over here," said a voice. "There're tracks. The dog's got the scent."

There was barking and several people ran by. The jingle of their firearms and handcuffs soon disappeared into the distance with the sound of the dog. Josh crouched further under the tarp and held his breath. They soon came back.

Stanley swore at the traffic as they tried to make their way west on Route 9.

"Where are all these damned cars coming from?" he fumed in frustration, as he sat in traffic. "It's two-o'clock in the morning. You'd think it was frigging rush-hour."

"It's New Year's Eve, remember, the big end of the world bash? All the sane people are trying to get out of town."

They had just received news the suspect had been located and were rushing to the spot to help in the search, along with every spare resource he could get his hands on. Unfortunately, those resources were few, with major riots taking place in the city and environs.

"Yeah, and every crook and crackpot in the state is out taking advantage of the situation for mayhem and illicit gain," replied Stanley. "I wish we could get more men."

As on the previous night, gangs of youths and others intent on mischief roamed the streets, while armies of shoplifters roved the strip-malls and department stores, picking up anything unattended and not locked down.

"There are just enough men to go around," the governor had told him. "Let alone assist in a vague, non-critical manhunt. There are no children involved, and the person is unarmed and not considered dangerous. It can wait until the day after the End of Days, can't it?"

He was told he'd have to do the best he could with a scattering of city cops and troopers, along with a few of his own agents."

Washington was having its own problems with riots. Even if the weather had permitted, which it didn't - Logan had been closed for days for all but essential flights – they probably couldn't have given him much help in any case. In spite of this and the weather, however, they had found their man. Now here he was stuck in traffic.

"Stinking traffic!" he swore again, when they had sat in one place for almost five minutes. "This is nuts. The exit's only a quarter of a mile ahead. We'd be there by now if we were walking."

"There must be something blocking things up ahead."

"Don't they see our flashing lights? "

"There's no where to go," observed the driver.

"I'll show you where to go," replied Stanley. "Get out. I'm driving."

"But…"

"Out!"

He unfastened his seatbelt and jumped out of the car, running around the front of the vehicle, much to the surprise of the motorist next to him.

"Come on," he ordered impatiently, as his driver still hadn't gotten out. "Move!"

The other officer reluctantly got out of the car and made his way to the passenger side, while Stanley proceeded to walk up the row of cars in front of them waving his badge and bellowing at the top of his lungs.

"Emergency! Move those cars. Can't you see we've got an emergency? Just because we're not in a black and white doesn't mean you don't have to move those cars over when you see a flashing light."

Then he got in the driver's seat and strapped himself in, telling his passenger to do the same.

Stepping on the gas and leaning on the horn, with the siren blaring and the lights flashing, he hung his head out of the open window and yelled at the motorist to get out of his way. Bullying his way through traffic, he pushed past vehicles by a hair's brush, scraping others when they were too slow to move. Sometimes he drove along the central median strip or far to the right on the shoulder of the road. At times he'd drive right down the middle of the dividing line separating the two lanes. Soon they were at the exit, much to his passenger's relief.

Once on the road that led south the going was easier and they made good time to the park, where there were several patrol cars blocking the entrance.

"What have you got?" he asked the officer in charge, after skidding the car to a stop and jumping out.

"The dogs picked him up back near the cemetery there. He fled through the park and into the golf courses. There are two of them down here. They've tracked him through the woods to the rotary."

"OK, keep an eye out here. He may try to double-back."

He got back in the car and continued down the road.

"I wish we had more men," said his partner, a junior agent fresh from Quantico. "There's a lot of land in there. Maybe come daylight, if this rain let's up, we can bring the helicopter back in."

"Yeah, and get some satellite coverage so the boys in the NSA can be more help," replied Stanley.

"So why do you think this guy is trying to get to a cemetery? Does he really have a dead kid or something?"

"No, according to his bio he's not married and never had kids. The boys in research wouldn't have missed that." He thought a moment and continued. "My contact in the NSA mentioned something about an ad they discovered that appeared to be a coded messages to this missing Teller character, the scientist from the Peeble Telescope project. It said something about meeting at the beloved meadows or something like that. Is there a Meadows-something cemetery around here?" he wondered out loud.

"I don't know, sir, but it'll be easy enough to find out."

The rookie agent switched on their mobile computer unit – an IPOD with a console mounted on the dash and a Wi-Fi antenna mounted on the hood. He was instantly connected to the worldwide web and searching the area on a web-map.

"You kids. What have you got there?" asked Stanley.

"A bird's-eye view of the area on a GPS map. Here we are at the golf course. There's another one right here. There's the rotary. Down here's a cemetery, and another. Hey, look, there's at least three of them, big ones too. The first one's named Meadow Glenn."

"So that's where he's going?"

"Yeah, but why?" persisted the new kid.

"I don't know. The ad also mentioned Teller's name. Said something about Teller for hire or Fortune Teller wanted. Something like that. Maybe he's trying to hook up with this Teller guy."

"Aren't we looking for Teller as well?" said the young agent, logging into the agency database and querying the name.

"Yeah," said Fred Stanley, slightly ahead of his young colleague's train of thought.

"Maybe one will lead us to the other."

"I was thinking the same thing," said the senior agent in charge of the case.

Stopping at the rotary where another group of squad cars ringed off the area, he braked and talked to the trooper in charge, who told him the dog had tracked their man to the rotary and then seemed to head down toward the large sports field on their right. However, they were having trouble picking up the trail from there.

"He could have gone anywhere from here," volunteered the trooper.

They looked at the map on the statie's console.

"He might have gone toward the field here," continued the trooper who knew the neighborhood well. "It might have looked inviting since there are no lights in that direction, but the ground is covered with snow. We'd have seen tracks. There's also a large residential district down on the left. He could be headed toward West Roxbury through that area. Or he could have doubled back. I've sent the dog back to check."

"We know where he's going," said Stanley to the trooper's surprise. "We've got the NSA tracking him. Do you know where Meadow Glenn cemetery is?"

"Sure," said the trooper. "Right down the road here, you can't miss it. Takes up both sides of the street, not more than a half mile away."

"Pull back the dogs. Make it look like you're searching the field and the residential area further on. Then pull your men back to route 9 before daylight. We'll set up a trap for him and the people he's involved with. Make sure he doesn't circle back. If he gets cold feet, I want him trapped between you and the river. Got it?"

"Yes, Sir," replied the trooper almost saluting.

"God, I love these staties," said Stanley. "They're so eager."

"Yeah, especially when they're giving out tickets," observed his younger partner.

Chapter 18

Josh lay beneath the canvas top on the roof of the shed until the sound of the search party was gone and he could stand it no longer. While the weather continued to remain mild and well above freezing, it was little better than lying in a soggy refrigerator as far as Josh was concerned. His feet, especially, were freezing. That's when they returned. They remained for quite awhile, doing everything but enter the building itself. Josh was sure they would find him, but eventually, after peering in every window and trying the door, they finally went away.

While he lay there hiding, he tried to decide what to do. Now that they knew he was here it all seemed so hopeless, and the thought of giving himself up recurred repeatedly during his deliberations. Second on the list of favorite options was to try and get out of there, but other than the directions he had on a small slip of paper, he had no idea where he was or where to go to escape his predicament. He doubted very much if he'd be able to retrace his steps back to Route 9 without being spotted. That left him the dubious alternatives of trying to find his way home through the maze of streets and residential areas, or proceed to the cemetery and try to meet up with Teller on the outside chance he saw the ad and had actually responded. The more he thought it over the longer his odds became, but as he saw it, he really had little choice. None of this would matter if he didn't get out of the cold and dry his feet.

A slim idea began to develop in his frazzled brain, not so much a plan as a desperate attempt to relieve his present discomfort. After the second search party had been gone for some time and no further sounds were heard, Josh crawled out from under the tarp and glanced down from the rooftop. He was at the rear corner of the shed, right above where the dog, after returning, had stopped and whined so pitifully Josh had thought he'd been discovered for sure. The trainer, after shining his flashlight into the dark, empty dwelling, had to pull the dog away from the door beneath where Josh lay, before they both moved off at the orders of another officer, to continue the search further on.

Since they had already searched the shed twice, spending considerable time there, Josh took the chance they wouldn't return, and let himself down onto the stoop to the rear door. He stood on a large, square slab of concrete reached from the ground by four wide stone steps. He tried the handle. The door was locked. The ground had already been stirred up by the dog and his handler, so Josh's footprints would not be noticed. Using the same method he had tried earlier on the indoor tennis court, he managed to jimmy-open the door and let himself in. Hopefully, they wouldn't notice anything if they came back to check yet once again, but part of him didn't care either way.

The inside of the shed was dark, what little light there was hardly penetrating the dirty windows. As he tried to feel his way around, he kept stumbling over things, knocking into tools and equipment strewn about the floor. At least the place was dry, and he hoped free of prying eyes.

Perhaps his trick had worked and they had actually continued down the road after him. Did they know where he was going? There was always the possibility that the priest had told them. Should he abort his mission, he asked himself for the hundredth time. He felt like crawling in a ball and crying. Instead, he rummaged through the darkened building looking for anything that would help him.

One of the first things he found was a bathroom, a simple toilet set up in a corner of the shed with three walls and a curtain, but it had real plumbing. Perhaps it was for the groundskeeper so he didn't have to be seen in public. In any case, it offered well-needed relief. He even found a box of matches on a stand in the makeshift john, next to an astray full of half smoked cigarettes. A half-pack of them sat nearby. He almost lit one up. Instead, he used the matches to take a look around, holding each one high over his head until it went out.

It indeed looked as if someone stayed there, at least during the summer, most probably one of the groundskeepers, for there was also a cot next to a small ice box, which was empty except for a bottle of beer. There was even a wood-burning stove and a pile of wood, though Josh was not quite at ease enough to build a fire. For all he knew, there could still be someone out there just waiting for him to show himself. He did, however, drink the beer.

Besides being filled with rakes and shovels and other implements to till and otherwise maintain the grounds, there were various implements for seeding and watering the greens, including gardening tools and sprinkler systems. There was even a set of golf clubs. In the corner next to the bed were a couple of metal lockers. They were mostly empty but he did find a towel, which he used to wipe his head and dry off, and an old pair of socks, which he immediately exchanged for his wet ones. The dry sox, together with a pair of clean golf slacks he put on, gave him a new lease on life. It was the first time in a week he had changed his clothes. He even found a hat to keep off the rain. All of a sudden there was a glimmer of hope. He found a pair of coveralls. Besides the glimmer of hope, a hint of an idea began to flicker into his mind.

Fred Stanley had stationed men and vehicles around the area, but made sure everyone kept out of sight. Instead of trying to find Josh Banks, they were now trying to lure him in, in the hopes of catching both him and Dr. Teller in the event he responded to the news reporter's secret message. To this effect, he sent most of the uniformed men back to the north along the park to prevent the fugitive from escaping in the event he tried to circle back toward route 9. A few of his men in plain clothes and unmarked cars sat in various places throughout the cemetery, which covered both sides of the road for several acres. To add to the confusion, there were two even larger cemeteries a short distance further down the road. Even though this was the only one with 'Meadow' in its name, there was still a chance the meeting place could have been at one of these.

He grabbed the last Danish from the box and took a sip of coffee. The old donut and cop joke might be a cliché, but he for one was glad the boys in blue always knew where the nearest bakery shop was located. At least the rain had finally let up.

"When it gets light, we'll separate," said Stanley. "Try to look inconspicuous. Hopefully he'll think the search was called off and continue on his mission. He certainly can't go back the way he came. It will look like they're searching the park and the first cemetery."

"Do you think I'll blend in with this suit?" asked the rookie agent.

"Yeah, if they're burying somebody today. Maybe you should stay in the car. I can call you if I need you. I'll be able to see better on foot. What time is it?"

"Almost six. It'll be light in another hour."

"Christ, I don't know if I can keep my eyes open for another hour. I've been up all night."

"Why don't you relax and rest your eyes. I'll keep a lookout until daylight. Nothing's going to happen until then anyway. We'll probably be staked out here all day."

"Yeah, not a bad idea. Let me know as soon as it gets light. Look's like it's finally going to stop raining."

153

"Yep," said his partner, looking up from the computer console. "Supposed to be nice, at least for the first part of day. That is if the world doesn't end." He laughed.

"It'll end for somebody."

With those ominous words, Stanley slouched down in the seat, bunched his jacket up in a ball, placed it and his head against the window and closed his eyes. It wasn't long before he was sleeping. It wasn't long after this that his young apprentice woke him.

"It's getting light," he said, shaking the supervising agent in charge politely.

"What time is it?" Stanley demanded.

"Almost seven. There's a black and white coming."

"Any word on our fugitive?" Stanley asked the officers as they stopped their car to report to the FBI man.

"No, sir. Everyone's hanging back as you ordered. They've got units at the park entrance and along Hammond and the rotary, and back at Route 9. We've also got a couple cars up at the field and one patrolling the residential district bordering the cemetery on the north. We've left everything else open."

"Good, that will leave him a nice wide path right to us. Don't stop like this again. I don't want to be noticed."

"We'll make it look like routine patrols, nothing out of the ordinary, don't worry. They told us to expect big crowds today," said the sergeant through the car window.

"What do you mean?" asked Stanley.

"Headquarters says the newspapers are predicting a lot of people will visit the cemeteries today to be with their loved ones when the world ends. Some even think that the dead will rise again on the last day, so they expect their share of crazies as well."

"Great," said the FBI man, who thought he had seen and heard everything. "Just what we need. Hopefully your patrols will deter the troublemakers."

"Do you want us to throw up a road block?"

Stanley ducked his head back into his car and asked his partner to bring up the map again.

"No, not yet," he said after inspecting a satellite view of the area. "It would tip off our man. No, I want him to think we're falling for his little trick and hunting off in the direction of the sports field and the area beyond. Carry on."

His phone rang as the squad car proceeded on its rounds.

"Stanley here. Oh, hi, Ted. Thanks for returning my call. Get my message? Yeah, we're at the cemetery now. What have you got? Teller's wife? A few years ago? I see, that makes sense. That would be a good place to meet. Yep, yep. Today? Today's the time? Ah, she died on New Year's Day. Makes sense. What about the name, what was it? Yeah, Chic? Do you know who that's supposed to be? No, not yet. Yes, that's a big help. Yep, I'll let you know. No, that's OK. We might even get Teller too if we're lucky. Can you get us a bird? Great. OK, thanks, bye."

Leaning into the car, he said to his partner, "Take the car back behind the hill over there. Stay near the radio. I'm going to take a little look around. Hey, while you're sitting there twiddling your thumbs, see if you can pull up a map of the cemetery and tell me where Teller's wife is buried. She died ten years ago today. This is definitely the spot and today is the time. See if you can find out where the plot is. Give me a call on the cell when you do."

It was just seven-thirty am. The sun was starting to warm up the ground with its glow, making the sky pink. As his partner drove the car back up out of sight, Stanley started walking down the roadway, winding his way deeper into the cemetery. Cars full of people were already beginning to arrive, as if it were the middle of summer and Memorial Day instead of the first day of January.

Chapter 19

Josh felt fatigue creep into his very bones as he rested in the shack at the golf course, sitting in a threadbare easy-boy covered with old clothes and coats. He had only meant to rest his eyes for a few minutes before setting out on his impossible mission to meet Teller, but was fast asleep as soon as he closed them. Because of the relative comfort of the old recliner and his lack of rest he did not wake up until well after daylight, some time around eight or nine by the look of it. He sat up with a start.

Once he realized where he was and what he was in the middle of, his resolve left him, and he was ready to give up and turn himself in. He sat there undecided for some time, oscillating between thoughts of surrender and finding breakfast and a cup of coffee. The more he thought of it, the more he realized that he was in it whether he liked it or not. He'd probably suffer the same punishment whether he gave up now or carried on, so he might as well push on to the end. Who knows, he just might succeed. Stranger things have happened. What he might succeed at, however, eluded him.

He looked out cautiously from each window in turn. The sunlight bounced off what was left of the snow, stinging his tired eyes like beams from a laser. He could see no sign of the search party. They must be long gone by now, he reasoned, as he made his way to the door and opened it warily. He expected to hear the barking of an angry dog and a shout of alarm, but there was nothing. Stepping out into the day, he tried to get his bearings, looking at the directions the priest had given him. The temperature, now unseasonably warm, was already in the fifties. After making sure that there was no one around, he followed his path of the night before.

As he looked out from the patch of woods above the road, he could see rows of residential houses leading gradually up a hill. If he continued south in that direction for about a half mile, according to what the priest wrote down, he would hit the cemetery. There was a large field to his right, beyond the rotary. It might be a possible escape route if this was what he had in mind. He knew from the angle of the sun that this led west, but that was the extent of his knowledge of his surroundings. He'd be wandering in unknown territory.

When he left police custody more than twenty-four hours before, he had been wearing the clothing he was arrested in, the clothes he had worn for the previous five days. This was probably what he was being described as wearing. On the way out of the shack he had exchanged his wet shirt for a gray sweatshirt and the green golf slacks for an old pair of coveralls. Putting on a red baseball cap he had found on a hook by the door, he had felt like a new man. What better disguise for a day at the cemetery than that of a caretaker. Never mind they probably didn't bury many people in January, it wouldn't be unusual to have someone tending the grounds. Hopefully, he wouldn't bump into the real caretakers if there were actually any around.

The disguise might give him a chance to locate the gravesite of Teller's wife without being noticed himself. To make it look good, he took along a rake and a hedge-clipper he had found in the caretaker's cabin, Now, as he looked south across a quiet street, he wondered if he could make it though the blocks of closely packed houses undetected. Giving himself less than a fifty-fifty chance, he started out. There were no police cars in sight. Perhaps they had moved off west to search in the direction he had started for the previous night. Or maybe they were waiting for him at the cemetery.

Staying in the protection of the trees as long as possible, he moved east along the lip of the rise until he was out of sight of the rotary. Then he descended to the street, and crossing it, moved in a southeasterly direction through the blocks of houses. Eventually he hit the road leading to the cemetery, the one written on his directions. He walked fast and with a purpose, as if hurrying to work. He hoped whoever saw him would assume he was doing just that, and he wouldn't look too out of place.

It wasn't long before he reached an industrial park with a wide field that rose up a hill behind it. Beyond that, on another hill, was a large cemetery extending along both sides of the road, its rows of tombstones bathed in the early morning glow of the sun.

As he approached the cemetery, Josh noticed the traffic. There seemed to be a lot more activity than he would have thought for New Year's Day. He might have expected to see this many cars at the shopping mall, but not the cemetery. It wasn't Memorial Day, but it looked like it with all the people flocking to the graveyard. Then he remembered the rumors that the world was going to end at noon and everything made more sense. It was just a continuation of the mass hysteria he had been witnessing these past forty-eight hours - the riots in the streets, the packed-to-the-rafters churches, the end-of-the-world parties. Now this, coming to be with loved ones on your last day on earth. Or maybe they came to see the dead rise again on the Day of Judgment as foretold in the bible, who knew? People did funny things when they were scared. Whatever it was, perhaps he could turn it to his advantage like he had during the riot.

The place was much larger than he imagined and dashed his hopes of being able to find the gravesite easily. He hoped that if the cops were here looking for him, they'd have a tough time picking him out of the crowd.

The sign at the gate at the top of the hill announced that he had found his destination. He gazed southward down the slope of the hill. The gravestones went on as far as he could see in that direction. He went through the gate, the old baseball cap pulled down tight over his forehead, as if shading his eyes from the harsh glare of the sun. As he walked he looked at the stones to the left and right of him for the name Teller.

In addition to the information contained in the rather extensive article about the scientist that Josh had read, there was a provocative picture of him standing by his wife's gravesite after her funeral. Josh tried to visualize the picture again as it appeared that day in the sharp image of the online article, with its angels and curlicues of marble, the name Teller in large, bold letters emblazoned across the top. It was larger than most stones and seemed to be clear of any trees or fences so should be easy to spot from a distance. Of course, if someone else had decoded his ad, he might not be the only one there looking for it. Hopefully his disguise would give him an element of cover and allow him to observe the area without being spotted.

As he walked he noticed carloads of people parked in various places around the cemetery. Some sat in lawn chairs they had brought along for the occasion. Some stood and tended the graves, placing fresh flowers around the sites or picking up debris. Some sat in their cars reading. Some stood on soap-boxes preaching apocalypse. There were whole families, generations of people with the same name as the ones on the stones they stood around. Small children ran among the plots laughing and playing while adults stood with bowed heads. Some knelt alone by a single grave communing privately with their long-lost loved ones. Some talked and carried on as if at a tailgate party. One person even set up a barbeque. Many were evidently not there to see anyone in particular, but thought it a good a place as any to continue partying after the previous evening's festivities. Strangely, there were no police. They were probably out quelling riots and other disturbances.

Josh thought there'd at least be a patrol car or two out looking for him, especially after the events of the night before. Maybe they hadn't been looking for him after all. Maybe they had caught whoever they were looking for. Josh didn't know if he was just being optimistic or delusional, but he clung to the thought as the only glimmer of hope he had.

As he moved through the cemetery Josh stopped periodically in places where there were fewer people and pretended to tend the plots, raking debris and arranging things, as he surveyed the surrounding area. At one point he even took out his hedge-cutters and trimmed some branches from a bush, not only on the lookout for the Teller stone but the FBI as well.

The size of the place was daunting, with walkways crossing back and forth, and car-paths seeming to go on forever, a whole city of the dead. Locating one stone among so many, even a unique one, would be almost impossible. Much of the snow had melted, but there were still large patches of it here and there sparkling in the sunlight, covering the still green grass that showed in spots like a white cloth. There were a large number of trees throughout the grounds and parts of the cemetery were quite wooded, almost like a park. Other areas were set on small knolls and hilltops with picturesque views of the surrounding countryside. Josh headed for one of these clear, high places, one that had a promising looking stone at the top, avoiding the spots where people were congregated.

The particular plot he headed toward appeared to be deserted, but when he got near the top of the knoll he noted a man standing next to a small dump truck. The man stopped what he was doing and looked up at Josh curiously as he approached.

A quick look about told him that this was not the Teller site, but he hoped whoever this was might be able to help him.

"Hi," said Josh, approaching the man with a smile. "You work for the cemetery?"

"Yeah, with the city. Why?"

"I was hired to do some work for a..." he stopped and took out the directions the priest had given him. "Ah, on the grave site of a Mrs. Dorothy Teller. I thought I had directions, but I'm totally lost now. I'll have to go back to where I started an hour ago. I was wondering if you could help me."

"Nah, you'll have to get the plot grid from the parish. Down in West Roxbury a couple of blocks away."

"Ah, it'll be late by the time I go down there, get the information and come back here. That is if they'd even give it to me. I've been out of work for almost a year now, and this was a chance to earn some money around the New Year. Now I'll have to tell my wife and kids I couldn't go to work."

"I'm sorry, pal," said the man with a genuine look of compassion. "There's nothing I can do. I'm just bringing in a load of dirt for the road here. I've got other things to do. It's kind of strange the person who hired you didn't give you more information."

"The whole way he hired me was strange, but I couldn't afford to be too choosy. He said he'd pay me fifteen dollars an hour for six hours of work. He gave me directions, but it was over the phone and he talked very fast. I wrote them down as best I could. He mailed me half the money the next day and told me to be here today. It was all very strange, like he wanted to take care of his beloved's grave but was afraid to do it himself. Anyway, I figured the least I could do was try to keep up my end of the bargain. His instructions were pretty specific as far as what he wanted me to do. He not only wanted me to tend the area but sort of stay by as a witness, you know, to show that this person was being remembered."

"Hmm, that is strange, but there's nothing I can do. What's the name? I mean of the person who hired you?"

"He didn't give me his name. There was none on the envelope the money came in."

"What was the name on the check?"

"He mailed me cash. All he said was the name on the stone, Dorothy Teller."

"Teller!!" exclaimed the workman. "You don't know who that is?"

"No, not really," lied Josh.

"Why, Teller's that famous missing scientist you hear about in the news all the time. He's the one building that telescope there. You talked to him?"

"I don't know," replied Josh, adlibbing madly. "You think it was him? It was just a voice on the phone. He told me to be here today and what he wanted done. That's all. You can speculate all you want. I just want to get the other half of my ninety dollars."

"Well, you should tell the cops or something. Everyone's looking for that guy."

160

"I just might do that," said Josh, "after I get paid. Say, I know. You look like you're all finished here. Could you bring me to the parish office so I can find out where I'm supposed to be?"

The workman thought awhile, but couldn't think of a good excuse to refuse the request, especially since he happened to be headed in that direction anyway.

"Oh, I don't see why not, it being New Year's and all."

They drove back out the road Josh had come in on, then east through a couple of blocks of residential streets to an old parish church, with a large, red brick building behind it.

"Go up the stairs in the back there and knock on the door. That's where the parish offices are. Ask for Father Damian."

"I was wondering," Josh said as he hesitated by the door of the truck. "I need to get back to the cemetery. Would you be willing to wait and take me back? I won't be long."

The man thought again and again couldn't find an excuse to say no. Besides, the world might end in forty minutes. Perhaps the cemetery wasn't a bad place to spend his last minutes on earth. God knows he didn't have any place else to be and no one to be with.

"I'd of thought you'd want to be with your family," he said, looking into Josh's eyes probingly "with the world ending and all."

"I don't believe that. I'm more worried what well happen when it doesn't end. When I have to wake up tomorrow and tell my little boy he doesn't have anything to eat. It's come to that. They're in a shelter back in town. They'll be fine as long as I can get this money."

"Yeah, I'll wait. I'd like to see this famous person's plot anyway. I can tell the boys back at the shop I've seen the Teller woman's grave and talked to someone who's talked to the famous man himself. Maybe you'll end up with your name in the papers."

"I hope not," said Josh, meaning it earnestly.

It wasn't easy getting access to the location of Teller's wife's plot. The suspicious priest wasn't in a hurry to give out such information to a stranger under dubious circumstances. Josh's persistence won out, however, when he finally thought to mention the friendly cleric from the day before. When the parish official called his fellow clergyman across town, he confirmed Josh's story. It helped that the poor, well-meaning churchman was still unsure about just who Josh really was, still believing at some level that he was actually trying to find his dead son's gravesite. Luckily the call was short and Josh's false identities were not discovered.

After obtaining a printout of the location of the Teller plot, he got his new friend to drive him back to the cemetery. In times like these, the working stiffs of the world had to stick together.

"I had the directions completely wrong," Josh confided. "It's on the other side of the road."

"Yeah, your employer isn't making it easy for you."

They turned off the street onto the drive leading up the hill into the other side of the cemetery. This area was also covered with headstones of all shapes and sizes. Before long they stopped along a cluster of graves on the crest of a hill looking south. From where they stood they could see clear to the Charles River. Between them and the river was nothing but gravestones, long, endless lines of them.

"There's a couple more cemeteries down the road," the workman informed him, pointing southward.

"Quite a view," said Josh, impressed. "I never would have found this place. Thanks. Now I can do my work."

"You've got ten minutes," said the man, looking at his watch."

"Why do you think the world's going to end at noon? Don't tell me they've predicted it right down to the time of day." Josh looked up toward the sky, but the bright sun obstructed his vision. If there was a comet coming he couldn't see it.

"I don't know, but they say the four blood-moons at the end of the twelfth year of the 64th cycle in the Mayan calendar, which only occurs twice every twenty-four millenniums, is going to happen today at twelve noon. And there's that scientist out in California who's predicting that meteor's going to hit today. It's too many coincidences. I believe them."

"You sure it wasn't twelve midnight?" asked Josh, humoring the man, who seemed to know a lot about the predictions.

"That's what I get for helping you," said the workman, not amused at being made fun of. "Some people may think the end of the world is something to joke about, but I'm not one of them. I'm damned scared and so are a lot of people. Don't be so smug, mister."

"I'm sorry. I didn't mean to offend you, but I think the best thing is to keep on living. You're going to go anyway, sooner or later, maybe getting hit by a bus on the way home from work. You can't hide from the inevitable. The world ends for thousands of people every day. That's the way of the universe."

"You sound like a skeptic," replied the workingman. "What did you say you used to do?"

"I was a writer," answered Josh, telling the first non-lie of the day. "I wrote for a newspaper, several of them really, but they all went under. I guess I wasn't that good of a writer."

"Well, good luck to you. I hope you get the rest of your money. Good day."

Josh thanked the man and watched him get back in his truck and drive away. Then he waited. To keep up appearances he began working around the area. It just so happened that the place needed attendance. The ground was covered with dead leaves and tree branches, scattered between patches of leftover snow. As he raked and cut and cleared the area, he surveyed his surroundings.

The good news was he had a clear 360-degree view of his surroundings. The bad news was he was sitting like a beacon on top of the hill for all to see. Hopefully, he wouldn't be noticed. It was only noon. There were enough other people about to help him blend in. There was no sign of Teller. Josh was famished and thirsty, but tried to keep busy. At least it wasn't cold. The sun felt good as he worked. It must have been almost sixty degrees by the feel of it.

After two hours of this he became bored and wandered off to another area of the cemetery for a stroll, always keeping the Teller stone in view, which was easy given its exposed vantage point. After two more hours of waiting, during which he had constantly thought of how to get something to eat and a cup of coffee, he sat by the gravestone staring dumbly into space, numb of all feeling or thought. It would soon be dark and Teller had not appeared. Most of the visitors had left for the day. The cemetery was practically deserted except for a few diehards disappointed the world had not ended. Life was still going strong.

Josh was snapped out of his stupor by the sound of someone approaching from behind him on the dirt road. He turned to find a young man in a blue jacket, with a white shirt and black pants, walking toward him.

"Are you here waiting for someone?" the stranger asked as if he too were looking for somebody.

"Yes," replied Josh, momentarily taken off guard but quickly recovering. "I did some work for someone here today. They were supposed to come by and pay me."

"And who would that be for?" asked the man.

Josh looked at him.

"Are you the one who hired me?" he said, almost holding his breath. Then he realized this guy, only in his twenties, was too young to be Teller.

"I could be. Who are you?"

"I'm the person you called and told to come out here and clean up this gravesite," he said, staying in character and pointing to Dorothy Teller's stone. "You paid me forty-five dollars and were going to pay me another forty-five. I've been here since ten. That's six hours."

"You've done a good job. The place looks great. My father will be very pleased," said agent Doherty, playing along with the suspect, his every instinct alerted.

"You're Teller's son?" asked Josh in surprise, not aware the missing scientist had any children and giving himself away. "Is your father here?"

Maybe it was the lack of sleep, or the lack of food, or the stress of being on the run for a week, but Josh was ready to believe anything or anyone at this point. He wanted it to be true so bad he suspended all disbelief.

"Yes," replied the rookie agent, doing his best to think on his feet. He was sure he had come upon the escapee, not believing his story for one minute despite his caretaker's getup. He hadn't been able to locate his senior partner, the agent in charge of the case, but he had to somehow let his boss know he had found their man.

"He's down in the car waiting to meet you. He's got to be very careful you know."

"Thank God I've found you," said Josh, overcome with relief.

"Come on," ordered Doherty. "We've got to hurry."

"Wait a minute," said Josh, regaining his wits. "How do I know you're who you say you are? I didn't know Teller had any kids."

"They didn't," the agent informed him, pointing to the stone and thinking fast. "She died before they had time. I'm from his previous marriage. The one they don't talk about, to his sixteen year old sweetheart when he was fresh out of high school. We were brushed under the rug. He got to go to prestigious colleges on scholarships because of his brains, while my mother cooked for him and washed his clothes like a scullery maid." His professors in criminal psychology back at Quantico would have been proud of his role playing ability and his quick adlibbing. He hoped his ploy had worked.

Josh's frazzled brain was working at the speed of frozen molasses. He couldn't think and was having difficulty coming to grips with the situation. He was having trouble just grasping what the other man was saying.

"He's just down here. Why don't you follow me. If it looks all clear, you can meet him."

"Sure," said Josh, following the young agent as if he no longer had his own volition. "That's what I've waited all day for."

"Oh, he's looking forward to meeting you too," said agent Doherty, hardly able to contain his excitement.

The sky was turning red in the west, a brilliant mixture of violet and orange and yellow and pink that dazzled the eye and reminded one of the beauties of creation. It really could have been the last sunset on earth. It was as if the sun were exploding in colors as it sank beneath horizon, seeming so big and close it would swallow the world, while thick, ominous black clouds were massed in the northeastern sky.

Josh started to hang back, as much out of fatigue as wariness. He was looking around for possible escape routes just in case. He saw none. He didn't notice the young agent calling his partner using his Wi-Fi ear set with his cell phone. Nor did he notice the agent dialing the number on his quick dial list. The call started a chain of events that rippled across the cemetery, as numerous men carried out their marching orders.

Everyone converged on the two men walking slowly down the hill, but Fred Stanley made sure they all stayed out of sight as they formed a cordon around the area to seal it off from escape. Stanley placed himself at the bottom of the dirt drive where Josh could see him standing near a large stone pillar by the entrance of the cemetery, but too far away to be recognized.

Stanley had been at the cemetery since early in the morning with little sleep and nothing to eat except donuts and stale sandwiches. He was about to call it a day, with no sign of their suspect and none of the missing scientist, when he got the call from his errant partner. Doherty had driven off in their car late in the afternoon and hadn't been seen since. Stanley hadn't realized that his phone was off. It must have happened when he had tried to get a few hours sleep. It wasn't until later that he realized it was off and turned it back on. In the meantime, his young protégé had been to the parish church and talked to the priest, who had informed him that someone else had come by only a few hours earlier and asked for the same information. The rookie had rushed back to the cemetery with the news but was unable to contact his boss, so he headed directly to the location of the plot where he found the suspicious workman.

Everything was in place. Stanley could see the two men walking down the slope of the hill among the stones and mausoleums. The nosy newspaper man had threatened to blow everything sky high. He had been caught only to escape, twice. The police had cordoned off the area. Mr. Josh Banks wouldn't escape a third time, even if they hadn't caught Teller.

Suddenly, Stanley noticed something out of place, a bright red 1959 Chevy pickup truck zooming between the tombstones like a dragster from the Indianapolis 500.

"Quick!" yelled the lawman into his radio unit. "All cars, all cars, converge, converge. Red truck in pursuit of suspect. All vehicles converge."

Josh saw the truck at the same time, tearing across a dirt and grass track perpendicular to the one he was on, coming directly at him from the right. What now, he wondered dumbly, as if it was happening to someone else and he was only watching from the sidelines. The man ahead of him turned in alarm on hearing the truck's motor rev-up as it approached. It almost hit him as it turned at the last minute throwing dust and debris up at the surprised FBI agent. Doherty leaped to the side just in time to avoid the back of the truck as it fishtailed around in his direction. Then it drove right up to Josh and screeched to a stop.

"Get in," yelled the driver, a large, dark, burly man with short black hair and a five-o'clock shadow of like-colored stubs. He shouted at Josh as he flung open the passenger door. "We've got no time to lose if you want to get away. I'm the person you've been looking for. Nice to meet you, Chic."

The clouds, which had been massing in the north all afternoon, were now overhead and unleashed a torrent. Josh hesitated, but only for a moment. There was something in the man's voice, something in the look of his eyes, which held Josh's gaze steadily and told him that this was someone he could trust.

"Get in, now," the man urged again. Josh jumped into the truck just as a bullet pinged off the rear bumper and smashed a taillight.

"Look's like they want one of us real bad," said the man, as he jammed his foot down on the pedal of the Classic Chevy pickup.

They skidded up the hill, between gravestones and trees, and down a bumpy incline not made for the speed they were going. Josh held on for dear life as the truck sped toward a clump of trees and what looked like a low but solid stone wall. He held on even tighter, as at the last moment before crashing into the obstacle, the driver veered to the left to follow a small rise in the ground and took it accelerating to fifty. They flew over the stone wall surrounding the cemetery and across the road behind it, sending sparks flying, and landing right in front of a police car that had just sped toward them from further up the street. Without hesitating, the driver of the truck turned the wheel sharply, spinning the vehicle down a steep incline that bordered a large sports complex that reached right down to the river. Josh, hanging on for all he was worth, felt like a bobsledder as they careened onto to a series of broad, flat fields that disappeared into the gathering gloom.

Once on the smoother, level ground of the fields, the driver of the truck slammed his foot even harder on the pedal. They sped across the still snow-covered landscape, which was filled with unseen dips and mounds, bouncing up and down violently. On they went, down a gradual incline, pounding over boundary stakes and low snow drifts, churning up dirt and slush as they raced across the soccer fields and dirt tracks toward the river.

When he wasn't staring out the window in fear for his life, Josh studied the driver. He was a large man with big forearms and broad features. He looked more like someone who worked with their hands than a person consumed with mathematical equations, but it was definitely the same person he had seen in the news photos. He had just found the missing Dr. Benjamin Teller. Or rather, Teller had just found him.

They were on the last of several large playing fields. The faint lines of white painted on the grass to mark the boundaries were barely visible between the mud and wide patches of snow. The truck veered through the field toward the river. The chase vehicles, momentarily stymied as the drivers stopped short of the harrowing incline leading down to the field, circled back to a nearby roadway. They had just entered the field area when Teller skidded to a stop right before a railroad bridge that crossed the river at that point.

"Come on," said the driver, jumping out of the cab. "We only have a few minutes."

"You're not going across that?" asked Josh in dismay.

They were standing on the bank of the Charles River, which was swollen and flowing fast. The bridge itself, normally fourteen feet above the flowing water, was now less than three and offered little in the way of handholds or walkways. The river, normally placid and slow moving was a veritable torrent, muddied with the dirt from its flooded banks, as heavy rains in the north poured more water into it. The other side looked far away, the bridge itself narrow and long. There was nothing between the tracks and the onrushing torrent. One false step would plunge him into a broiling cauldron of swirling death.

"You have no choice," said Teller. "Unless you want to spend the next decade talking to them you'd better get moving." He pointed back to where a dozen police cars came swarming onto the large soccer fields only a few hundred yards away. "We've got to go now. Time is running out. Time to move."

Still Josh hesitated.

Teller looked at his watch calmly. "This bridge will be gone within the next ten minutes."

Then without waiting for Josh to reply, Teller grabbed him by the shoulders and pushed him forward toward the bridge.

"Move!" he yelled.

Josh jumped and started making his way cautiously over the bridge, stepping gingerly on the wide ties. Teller was right behind him.

"Faster," yelled his rescuer.

The man who had just saved him seemed more like a commando than a mild-mannered scientist. The way he drove the truck across the cemetery like a stunt driver, taking chances even a trained professional would have avoided; the size of his arms, more like those of a dock worker than an academic whose life is spent in class rooms; the way he barked orders, like a drill sergeant, and tossed him about physically. All bespoke someone used to being in command.

"You better start moving or we're not going to make it."

It didn't take another shout from Teller, who was running behind him pushing him sharply, to get Josh moving. The look of panic in Teller's eyes said it all. Forgetting completely his fear of the river beneath him, Josh started running full speed across the narrow structure taking rails two and three at a time.

With Teller right behind him, pushing him and telling him to run like his life depended on it, Josh ran across the bridge at full speed and leapt to the bank with Teller right behind him. Not a moment later the structure seemed to rise up in a wave of smoke and flame, as it exploded at their heels. Josh didn't hear the blast at first, but felt it hit him with the concussion of its impact, which ripped his clothing and tore up the turf he was laying on, rolling him on the ground as if down a hill.

Looking back through the black smoke and flaming debris, Josh could see several men scurrying to the opposite shore, while the swollen water swept the charred wood and remains of the track away. There appeared to be one or two bodies in the river amongst the rubble. Josh had never seen anything like it, and stared in disbelief. He would have gotten trapped in the surging chaos of the river, which was flooded with debris, and a twelve foot high wave from the explosion, if Teller hadn't grabbed him by the collar and pulled him to safety.

He lay on the side of a broad hillside dividing the river from the highway, surveying the devastation and breathing hard, half in a state of shock. Further on, at the top of the incline along the highway, motorists had stopped their cars and were staring out at the catastrophe in disbelief. Some were taking pictures with their cell phones. One or two had video cameras.

"Come on," said Teller, helping Josh to his feet. "We've got to get moving. We have a long way to go. Once they recover they'll be after us with a passion."

"You got my message," stammered Josh, following the scientist in a state of disbelief, groggy from shock and lack of rest.

"Yeah, and so did every lawman in the country. But that's OK. I knew they'd be awhile figuring it out. I was a couple steps ahead of them. I've got another vehicle up here a little ways. We've got to move, take advantage of the confusion of the moment if we want to stay ahead of them, and that's what I aim to do. Let's go."

Josh followed without a word as the object of his long quest led him up the side of the highway toward what should have been the setting sun, as the sky lit up with a brilliant blast of lightning and the thunder pealed like the Day of Judgment was at hand.

Chapter 20

Fred Stanley of the FBI, senior agent in charge of the StellarScope affair, stood on the bank of the Charles River and surveyed the scene of destruction. Three men injured in the car chase, one man killed and three more nearly so in the explosion on the bridge, and both fugitives escaped. Fred Stanley was not having a good New Year's Day.

Once all his men were accounted for and the injured taken care of, he issued orders to all available units in the vicinity. Presumably the suspects were on foot, but they were now on the other side of a swollen river. The only way across was several miles west of them. Units were being dispatched to the vicinity, but it would take some time. The devastation caused by the explosion only added to their worries and stretched the available resources so that they were now paper-thin. His only hope was that the fugitives would remain on foot.

The weather had become so bad that he was having trouble just making it back to route 9. A major storm had come in with hail and near hurricane winds, which threatened to put a hold on all their activities. Maybe the end of the world really was coming, thought Stanley, as he peered through a rain-splattered windshield, his wipers working furiously to little avail, trying to keep his car on the road.

"They're probably heading west," observed his junior partner. "90 is right across the river where they got over."

"If that was Teller, he's probably got a car or something on the other side," said Stanley. "He's no fool."

"Who else could it be?" asked Doherty.

"I don't know. Maybe Banks has an accomplice. He had that Peters fellow helping him, and the computer geek we arrested back in New Hampshire. There could be others. There're all kinds of nuts out on the streets these days. That's how we lost him in the first place. Maybe Teller hired someone to rendezvous with Banks. Whoever was driving that truck knew what he was doing, almost professional if you ask me. Whoever it was, I want him."

The thing Stanley dreaded most was informing his superiors that the fugitive had gotten away. Even worse, that Teller may have just slipped through his fingers. It was bad enough they'd had Banks in their net the night before and let him go, on his orders. But the fact that the bigger fish had taken the little fish with him, only added to the senior FBI man's discomfort. He knew too much. If things went wrong he'd be the one to take the fall. However, the rewards would be even greater if he could pull this off.

The same men who had stolen billions from the Peeble Telescope project had also hoodwinked the government into believing the project was something it was not, a potentially powerful weapon, in order to secretly increase funding far beyond the officially approved budget. They had even sucked several people in high government office, including the Secretary of Defense, into participating in the scheme. If any of this got out it would mean a major political scandal for the administration, not to mention ruining the lives of several prominent and influential men. This, of course, could not be allowed to happen, thus the unlimited though covert resources available to the case and himself as agent in charge. Some of this illicit gain had been promised to him if he succeeded in finding Teller and shutting the blabbermouths down. So far he had been exceedingly unsuccessful in his task. Having the bureau's Internal Affairs Department involved in the case had been a sticky problem, but their agent, Tom Hagan, botched it up and put them out of the picture, a big embarrassment better left forgotten.

"I'll see if I can put up some road blocks along the Mass Pike and 128," said Stanley. "My guess is they'll head south and try to get out of the area. I'll have units on 93 and 9 as well, just in case, but we don't have many available. We'll have to do the best we can with what we have."

"Teller had to be within a day's drive of town to respond to the ad in time."

"He could have been in New York, or up in Maine. Christ, he could have flown in from Florida. He could have come from anywhere." Stanley glanced at the map displayed clearly on his partner's console, while he vainly tried to see out the window of his car.

"If it keeps up like this, we could have some major flooding," he observed as he turned his full attention back to the rain-pelted road.

"Yeah," answered his junior partner. "*The* flood!"

Josh and Teller walked along the highway a short distance into a residential area which adjoined it. The Mass Pike and Route 128 were gridlocked with vehicles. People stood by their cars in the downpour scratching their heads and trying to see what was holding up traffic. Through it all the rain came down relentlessly, like it had the previous day only harder, if such a thing was possible. Of course, the explosion and its aftermath had more than a little to do with the traffic jam, as emergency vehicles and the curious rushed to the scene. Most of the stranded drivers, however, knew little about this or the roadblocks that Stanley had managed to throw up on the major thoroughfares. Teller knew exactly what was going on.

Crossing the highway he led Josh into the Wellesley Hills district where he had a second vehicle parked, this one an unassuming gray, late-model Honda. It was a dark night. Despite it being New Year's Day, few buildings had their lights on, as if no one was home, or didn't want to appear to be. Altogether, the flooding, the pouring rain, the doomsday predictions, did not make for a very festive holiday. For Josh, though, it was the most joyous time of his life. Once again he had escaped capture and arrest. Even better, he had found the elusive Doctor Benjamin Teller, the cause of all his troubles.

Using back roads and side streets they made their way westward through the suburbs of Boston, crossing routes 9 and 90 near Morse Pond and Cochituate. From there they moved in a general westerly direction through towns whose names were only vaguely familiar to Josh.

"That explosion was really something," commented Josh as they drove through seemingly deserted back roads and country lanes, between sleepy villages and rain shrouded fields. Occasional houses, all seemingly deserted, dotted the landscape, these for the most part set back from the road and surrounded by trees. "You knew it was coming, the explosion I mean?"

"Yes, of course," his rescuer replied. "I've got something to drink and some junk food in the backseat if you're hungry. By the looks of you, you've been on the road awhile. There're some dry clothes back there as well."

"Thanks," said Josh, still in a minor state of shock. "I'm famished."

He reached back and rummaged through a box Teller had placed in back of the seat containing various candy bars and pastries, pulling back a pack of powdered donuts and a can of soda.

"You've got sugar-donuts. I love these things," he said, like a schoolboy opening his lunchbox on the first day of class. He ate it greedily, chugging the soda, as he pulled off his wet shirt and slipped on a large, warm, dry sweater of Teller's. After a package of crackers filled with peanut butter, he slipped on a pair of dry pants.

"So to answer your question," continued Teller, as he drove through the rain-drenched night, along dark back roads. "Yes, I knew the explosion was coming. I planted it, used a timer mechanism of course, but I'm afraid it was a bit last minute and crude. One can't be too complacent with these things. It was close, but it had to be, with the authorities right behind us like that. I am not without my resources." He said this after seeing the look of perplexity on his new companion's face. "As a matter of fact, I was rather relying on things working out the way they did. Otherwise, we would have been in a bit of a pickle back there." He laughed on saying this, the loud hearty laugh of someone who enjoyed life and adventure.

"Where are we going?" asked Josh.

"You and a lot of people would like to know, no doubt, and you will know soon enough if you answer my questions correctly. So tell me, why are you in such a worry to find me? Who are you working for? What do you know?"

"Wait a minute," said Josh. "I should be the one asking the questions."

"I'm the one who rescued you, remember. I'll ask the questions. You answer them and act reasonably grateful."

"I'm sorry. It must be the strain of the past few days. I haven't gotten much sleep. Thank you for helping me back there."

"They laid a trap for us. They were using you to get to me."

"I know that now. I'm sorry. I stumbled into this whole thing by accident. I figured if I could find you and publish your story, I'd be vindicated and maybe get my job back. You knew it was a trap?"

"Of course, but I do admit, your ad got my interest, especially the way you signed it. I thought you might have been someone else. There aren't many people who know that name. But I also knew if I could decipher your little message than others could, especially given the people involved. We can talk all about that later. Now, suppose you tell me your story and I'll decide whether to take you with me or drop you off by the side of the road."

Josh hesitated for a moment to clear his head and gather his thoughts. He didn't like being talked to like an errant schoolboy, but he supposed he did owe the man an explanation for contacting him in such a manner.

"I was investigating the story of your disappearance and the subsequent fallout for my company, World News Affiliates out of New York. I interviewed one of the employees from StellarScope. She had just been fired, really didn't say much. Nothing would have probably come of it except when I walked her to her car a couple of their security goons tried to accost us in the parking lot. They chased us back to my house and actually had the gall to take us in for questioning. The guy that interviewed me was a real arrogant prick. Said they were just protecting their employee. Protecting her, my ass. They got her to say I took her car and tried to rape her. They arrested me for kidnapping! The company took her kid to make her lie to discredit me. She must have known something about their dealings and they were afraid she would tell me, the stupid bastards."

"Come now, my good man, try to control yourself. There's no call to swear."

"Sorry. Can I have another candy bar?"

"Sure. We'll be at the house soon. We can fix you up something when we get there. In the meantime, take whatever you want back there."

Josh reached over and grabbed a handful of candy bars and snacks, along with another can of soda.

"When the girl who had swiped Maria's kid for them tried to bring him back, along with a satchel full of incriminating papers, they killed her, right in Maria's apartment."

"What did you say her name was?" asked Teller.

"The woman I talked to was Maria Cavello. The woman who was murdered was Ellen. I can't remember her last name."

"Ellen Primrose?" volunteered the scientist.

"Yes, I think so. Yes, that was it."

"I know them. I played softball with Cavello. Nice girl, but rather simple. She probably didn't even know what she had. I worked with the Primrose woman, very efficient secretary, could actually follow some of the discussions. You say they killed her?"

"That's what Maria said."

"Where is Maria now?"

"I don't know," said Josh, remembering her for the first time in days. "We were arrested together by the FBI about a week ago. I was abducted by a group of, well, I'm not exactly sure what they were. I'll have to tell you about it sometime."

"Tell me about it now," Teller demanded, still not satisfied as to his guest's intentions.

"I don't know who they were. When we first were on the run we met this guy named Dan Little-Wolf. He's half Micmac Indian. He had a sled and a team of dogs, if you can believe it, and was able to help us get away during the snow storm. I had tried to upload the StellarScope papers to my agency, the ones the Primrose woman was killed getting, but they somehow traced our message and chased us. We met up with Dan a short time after that. He and a group of his compatriots took me when the FBI was bringing me back to Boston. They don't exactly see eye to eye with those government revenuers. So far I've seen nothing in the papers concerning the information I released. Either they couldn't decode it or someone got to them and is covering it up. There were incriminating notebooks proving massive embezzlement and outright theft of millions of dollars earmarked for your telescope project. There were also a number of internal emails about how you had somehow sabotaged the project."

"Sabotage hell," said Teller. "They're the ones who sabotaged the project with their lies and scheming. I knew they were stealing. Hell, I encouraged them, kept them out of my hair, but I had no idea they were taking so much. It all started to snowball when they conned the Defense Department into believing we had some high-tech weapon up our sleeve. Then the money really started rolling in, billions. It was amazing the amount we had to work with, the wealth of the world. But with the secret funds also came massive government intrusion. Enough of that for now. I've already told you too much. So tell me what happened. Why were you trying to get in touch with me?"

"I'm not sure. Every other avenue was closed to me. Especially after Dan and his gang of anti-government good-old boys broke me out of custody. That's when I tried contacting you. My story had been squelched. I was a fugitive from the law, like you. I guess once a newshound always a newshound. You were the biggest story since Jimmy Hoffa, if you excuse the analogy."

"No offense taken," said Teller, rather pleased.

"I figured if I could find you and maybe get your story it would not only provide me some security but might actually get my job back."

"I take it they laid you off?"

"They dropped me like a piece of rotten meat when the news of my alleged rape of Maria broke. I had this weird idea you might be out near the Quabbin Reservoir, because of these ads for time travel on my friend's web page. He thought that because of your ties with Professor Peeble, they might have something to do with you. It was his idea to put an ad in the Personals to try and contact you. He was the one who came up with the idea of signing it with the name of your old teacher, 'Chic'."

"Smart person, where is he now?"

"He's probably in FBI custody with his half-sister, Maria Cavello."

"So that is what this is all about?" said Teller, sounding a little put out, "an interview!"

"My survival!" Josh yelled back a little louder than he had intended to. "You're in just as much trouble as I am. You're a fugitive. The people after you don't give a damn how smart you think you are. You've ticked off the wrong folks. They'll stop at nothing to shut both of us up. They've already killed two people,"

"Two? You only mentioned the Primrose woman."

"They killed Maria's mother too, when she refused to tell them where we were going. This goes all the way to the Defense Department. Who knows who's looking for you. They had me last night sure as shooting, dogs and men all around. Then just before they're about to nab me, they call the whole search off. One minute you can't move without bumping into a cop, the next there's not a one in sight for miles. Didn't make sense, but they figured out where I was going and set a trap. They were willing to take a chance I might get away to get you. It's you they're after. Like you said, they're just using me to get to you. That's what Dan Little-Wolf told me, but I didn't believe him."

"So you or your friend figured out how to contact me and set up a time and place. Very clever. How'd you get from Amherst to Boston? Not by dog sled I assume."

"No, the FBI picked me up again, along with Dan. Someone informed on us. They were bringing me back to Boston to take me to Washington for questioning. That really made me nervous. I mean, why take me all the way to DC to interrogate me when they could just as easily question me in Boston? Sounded kind of suspicious, like someone in a high position in the government with a stake in the outcome was controlling things, someone with their own agenda. We ended up in the middle of a riot. The mob broke me out of the car when they tipped it over. I got away and made my way to the cemetery where I hoped to meet you. I didn't know where else to go. It was like I was on autopilot. I wasn't sure what I was going to do after that. I wasn't thinking straight at that point."

Josh stopped to catch his breath and take a swig of soda. It was still raining hard. They were on a winding road surrounded on both sides by thick stands of pine interspersed with an occasional house or two. At one of these - a low, gray-shingled, ranch-style dwelling surrounded by trees - Teller pulled into a driveway.

"This is the house. It's safe. We can stay here tonight and go the rest of the way tomorrow. Hopefully, the rain will let up a bit. The water will be high."

"Well, if it's as high as that flooded river today I don't want any part of it."

"No, nothing like that," said Teller, leading Josh to the house across a lawn of snow puddles and wet pine needles.

Inside was plain and unadorned, like the home of a single male academic with little artistic taste. At least it was warm and dry and the kitchen well stocked. Most of the rooms were empty but for the barest of furniture. An old, rustic wood table with four heavy chairs sat in the kitchen. There was a couch and well used recliner and lamp in the living room - no TV. A metal desk and cabinet occupied the den, along with an outdated home computer. A plush leather swivel chair, also in the den, was the only sign of luxury. The bedroom had a single bed with no headstand and an old, battered dresser. The spare room was full of books and papers, and that was pretty much it.

"You look like you need a rest," said the scientist looking at Josh as he ate a plate of breaded baked chicken and mashed potatoes, his favorite as a kid.

"A clean bathroom and a hot shower would be a luxury," he replied. "Then I could sleep for days."

"Well, you've only got a few hours but they'll be comfortable and quiet. We can get you another change of clothes while we're at it."

As Josh finished his meal, he asked a few questions of his own.

"So you knew about the stealing? And you did nothing?"

"Like I said, I knew something was up, but not the full extent of it. I was busy trying to complete the project. As long as I got what I needed, and I did in full, I could care less who pilfered the leftovers. Anyway, it kept them out of my hair. I didn't much care about the money. I worked for practically nothing. I wasn't in it to get rich."

"Is that why you sabotaged the project?" asked Josh, not at all caring that he was biting the hand that was literally feeding him.

"Not all at. I didn't sabotage the project. I built what was intended from the start."

"By who? That's not how I understand it. I don't want to be rude and ungrateful, Doctor, but you owe the public, the tax payers all over

177

the country who've been footing the bill, some kind of explanation. You promised to build a deep space probe, a telescope that could see planets in the vast distances of the galaxy as if they were as close as an orbiting satellite."

"And for what?" answered Teller angrily. "To see if there's intelligent life in the universe? Of course there is, life too numerous to count and intelligent too. It exists wherever there is the slightest set of conditions to support it, and those conditions are everywhere. Look around on any clear night and you will see thousands of millions of twinkling lights, some from distant galaxies millions of light years away, some of from nearby stars, only a few thousand million miles from us, and many of them, more than you might think, have stable planets that could support intelligent life. But we're not ready to encounter intelligent life yet. Look at the human race. Listen to the headlines on any given day. We have a lot to learn before we bother other planets with our probes."

"So you did pervert the project," said Josh, as if vindicated.

"If you want to call it that. Instead of using the telescope to spy on distant planets, I used it to look back in time, to look back at our origins and history, to learn more about ourselves."

"A time machine?" asked Josh in astonishment.

"No, I didn't say go back in time. I said look back in time. But you're tired and we have a good little jaunt ahead of us in the morning. There's plenty of time to explain once we get to the bunker."

"The bunker? What's that?" asked Josh, more perplexed than ever and not a little concerned.

"This house is just a cover, a temporary stop-over. It's just one of several safe houses I've established for just such occasions. You don't think I'd disappear without making adequate arrangements to carry on my work, do you? You may think you were looking for me, but I have been looking for you, my young friend. You see, Joshua, can I call you Joshua?"

"Most of my friends call me Josh."

"Well, I like Joshua, has that good old bible sound to it, and we'll need plenty of bible where we're going. I want you to write my story, Joshua, and the story of my new machine, a window back in time, a lamp to shed light on the past.

Chapter 21

Josh's mind was a jumble of thoughts and images as he made his way to the sparse bedroom. Teller would be sleeping on the couch, which was a pullout, while Josh had a few hours of comfort on the seldom used king-size bed. He could hardly believe the last twelve hours and played it back over and over until he fell asleep, which didn't take long. His host didn't wake him until almost eight hours later, a little before six am. After a simple though filling breakfast of hot oatmeal with honey and hotter coffee, Josh felt like he had a new lease on life, especially when he put on a good fitting pair of heavy jeans and a clean t-shirt and sweater. Then he heard what Teller had in store for them.

"The roads where we're going are washed out, heard it on the weather report this morning. We're going to have to take the canoe. At least the rain's let up."

"Canoe? Where the heck are we going?"

"You'll see when we get there. You want a story don't you, mister newspaper man? The only way you'll get your story is in a canoe. It's in the back."

He looked at his watch.

"We leave now." Getting up, he handed Josh a waterproof poncho and a small satchel filled with supplies. "We have a few hours of travel ahead of us."

Without further ado, he led Josh out the back to the rear of the house, which appeared to border a large pond or swamp. The lake, which was actually a hundred yards behind the house, had now crept up to within ten or fifteen feet of it, through tangles of bare trees and bushy pine. There was a channel through the woods to the small lake itself, which in drier times was a wide path. A canoe sat upside down on the back deck, partially covered with a tarp.

"It look's like it's going to be a nice day. Some kind of heat wave we're having. It's going to be sunny and in the fifties."

"Thanks for the weather report. I'm glad to see the world didn't end."

Teller laughed. "You didn't believe that nonsense did you?"

"No, not really, but I met a lot of people who did. The streets were full of them in Boston. They were rioting, preaching on the street corners, attending end-of-the-world parties and séances at the cemetery. I'd believe anything just about now. What about the comet everyone was worrying about? Where did that go? And the solar flares? I thought that was supposed to destroy the solar system."

"Well, the comet ended up following the Japanese models and was no closer than 100,000,000 miles away from the sun, nowhere near enough to be considered a threat to earth. All the panic was caused by the fact they didn't see it coming and there was some uncertainty because of the lack of models. Christ, I told them when we spotted it, it was no threat. The solar flares are a much more serious issue. There's always the possibility they will kick up. We still know very little about the sun, but the chances are pretty slim right now. Old sol is as stable as ever and will probably be so for another five thousand million years. There was some unusually high solar flare activity these past few months. A few of our satellites and earth based communication stations that don't have adequate shielding may have been affected, but most people here on earth won't notice a thing. It certainly doesn't affect my equipment and it doesn't have anything to do with the unusual weather patterns we're seeing. That's caused by good old global warming. There are a lot of other things that could destroy the earth, including the human race itself. But then every school boy already knows that, though it doesn't seem to make a bit of difference in our response."

"Yeah, and how about the human response to being conned?"

"Now, Joshua, you're being unfair. I'd save my strength for the trip ahead if I were you. You're in the front." He pointed to the canoe, which they had just turned over and dragged to the edge of the creeping lake. "When I tell you to paddle left, you paddle as hard as you can on the left. When I tell you paddle right, you do the same on the right. Got it? Otherwise, you can paddle nice and leisurely on any side you like. I steer, remember that. You just keep us moving forward. We shouldn't have any problems unless we hit some fast moving water, and then we'll have to be alert. Follow my orders and we'll be fine. Ready? Good, then let's go."

They pushed off from the sloping yard and moved between the walls of gray, bare trees, down the wide channel until it opened out onto a small lake, its shoreline obscured by the high water. Teller headed the canoe to the right, along what looked like the normal course of the lake, which was river-like in this direction. To the left the lake opened out into larger bays and adjoining ponds that looked like wide fingers.

Teller guided the canoe smoothly along the swollen shoreline into another small lake, this one narrow and choked with ragged islands of cattails and reeds. Trees crowded the lake-swollen shore. This waterway in turned opened up into another wider lake, which seemed to go on for some time before it narrowed as it approached the road. After paddling a short distance along the shore they came to a flooded boat ramp. Water rushed over the ramp and across what appeared to be another road in a veritable torrent. The sun had risen in a clear blue sky, as if it had nothing to do with the day before.

"Just over this road is a trail leading into the woods," said Teller. "Look's like we'll have to canoe a bit further."

As he said this they rushed past what had once been the river bank, over the road, and down what was now a fast moving river.

"Paddle!" yelled Teller behind him. "On the left, hard!"

Josh did as he was told, as they narrowly missed a tree and a number of large boulders.

"Now, hard on the right, paddle," Teller ordered.

Josh saw another large tree coming toward them as the water-filled path cut to the right. He tried to steer them away, but his efforts were having little effect.

"Paddle!" yelled Teller loudly behind him. The sound made him jump in his seat it was said with such force.

He started paddling furiously, stroking the water with all his might. It was just enough to gain the momentum they needed to get by the obstacle as Teller steered them to the right, and sped them down the swollen stream. Soon they came to a bayou-like area of sunken trees and muddy lagoons, where the scientist guided them to a dry, high bank.

"We're here," he announced. "Time to walk."

Josh stepped out of the canoe onto the sloping land, where he held it steady for his enigmatic guide. After hiding it in the bushes, they shouldered their packs and started on their way into the woods.

"We're lucky the weather broke and it's staying warm," said Teller. "It'll make our hike a lot more agreeable."

"Where are we?" asked Josh, intrigued with the whole setup. They were now walking along a well-tended path between high pines, in what looked like a very old forest.

"This is part of a state park, quite a nice hiking area. It borders the place where we want to go."

"Cool," Josh agreed. "I had no idea there was anything like this around here."

"Oh, there's a lot of land in this area kept from development. The place we're going has been off-limits for years."

"What do you mean, off limits? Is it government land?"

"Used to be. Now it's in a sort of limbo, under various litigations. As a matter of fact, one of the litigants is StellarScope, though I doubt many even know they own it, but that's not our problem."

He led them along the path and over a few dead trees that had fallen across it. At one point, where it veered off to the right like a wide horse trail, Teller stopped and looked up and down the track in both directions.

"Here's where we leave the trail," he said, removing what looked like a living bush from in front of a small path that snaked off to the left. A short time later they came to a fence with barbed wire on the top and signs forbidding entry under the direst of consequences. Some of the signs indicated the area was a wildlife sanctuary, while others notified him it was U.S. Government property.

"This used to be an army base. It was established during the Second World War. Since then, up to a few years ago, it's been used for military research. So the place has been off-limits for decades. Then, about ten or twelve years ago the government sold it, but because of what they did to it over the years, the new owners sued them and tried to get their money back. I guess there was live ammo and everything on the place, all sorts of pollutants and chemical hazards. The EPA doesn't even know what half of the stuff is, since it was all highly classified secret weapons research. There's a defunct Air Force weather station on the facility as well, with a satellite dish."

"How convenient," said Josh, following Teller to a wide gap in the fence, which they darted through, stopping on the other side just at the edge of the trees.

"Well, here's your new home," said Teller, sweeping his arm across a wide arc of land.

They appeared to be at a cross-road, where two country lanes intersected at a right angle. The one passing in front of them continued to the right off into the distance, rising gradually up a large wooded hill, while to the left it curved slowly around a wide bend to disappear into the trees. The other road ran straight ahead through a canopy of high, leafless maples, whose interlocking branches hung over it like a bower as it disappeared into the distance. Ancient telephone poles, long ago bereft of functioning wires, marched along the road. What wires there were hung lifeless to the ground. The whole place looked as if time had passed it by, as if it hadn't changed in fifty years.

"This is the edge of the old base. We'll be going straight ahead right down that road there."

"Nice," said Josh, surveying the landscape. "Kind of like the land time forgot."

"An apt description," said Teller. "That road to the right heads down to the other end of the refuge." He pointed vaguely in that direction. The road disappeared into the early morning mist at a distant hill.

"Even when the Army was here, it was a wildlife refuge as well. Still is. The Fish and Game Department patrols it from time to time, but mostly it's deserted. You don't want to be caught in here, though. You'd be charged with trespassing on federal land. We'll stay on the back trails. We shouldn't meet anyone. The place is surrounded by barbed wire. We got in through the only breach in the fifteen mile perimeter I've been able to find, and I've hidden it well. Anyway, no one patrols where we're going."

He led them a short way up the road leading straight ahead of them, then veered off to the right to follow a wide trail of pine needles and packed snow, which ran parallel to the road but several yards back in the woods.

"This is the old railroad track," said Teller, giving his guest a guided tour as they walked. "They supplied the bunkers by train. You can see the old ties along the path in some places, but the ground is too damp and soggy now to go exploring."

Unlike the day before, the weather was fine, and Josh was enjoying himself, although they had to pass around a few wide puddles and deeper patches of snow, which collected on the path. After walking perhaps a mile up the trail, which was littered with fallen tree branches and covered with dead wet leaves, they stopped for a brief rest. Teller removed a plastic bag from his poncho and pulled out a sandwich.

"We'll stop and eat something here. There are a couple of rocks we can sit on that should be dry. I made chicken salad sandwiches."

"Great," said Josh, taking one and surveying the scene around them. The grassy road they were on continued through the dense woods, while to their right was a wide, broad field, ending in the distance where the land rose to a small rounded hill. The field was ringed by trees of all sizes and descriptions, most bare of leaves this time of year except for a copse of pine on the hillside. "Nice spot."

"Yes, it's absolutely beautiful here in the summer and fall, but nice enough anytime of year." He looked around as he cleared a spot on a few large rocks for them to sit. "The snow and rain's caused a bit of havoc with the trees, a lot of dead wood on the ground. I hope the antenna is all right."

"You've got an antenna?" asked Josh, taking a bite of his sandwich.

"I've got more than that, but you'll see for yourself."

"You don't seem too worried about getting caught."

"Oh, we're entirely safe here. We're among friends now."

"Friends? What do you mean?"

"I mean that we're not alone. The people patrolling this place are my people, as are the ones who help me work the telescope."

"You've got the telescope here! You built it here?"

Teller didn't bother answering but stood up.

"Let's go. Just a short way up the road, then we'll head in to the bunker."

The trail emerged back on a deserted backcountry lane, where they continued a short distance until it made a sharp turn to the right. Again removing a number of fallen branches, Teller revealed yet another path that ran to the left through the woods.

"What I'm about to show you is unprecedented," said Teller, as they continued down the secret trail. "It is one of the greatest discoveries of our time. I want you to describe it and what it will mean to mankind. It's important that you gain an adequate understanding of the machine. I know you minored in math and science in college where you got your degree in journalism, and that you've done several scientific pieces for your agency. Not bad if I may say so, readable at least. I also know that the Pulitzer Prize your colleague, Frank Sullivan, was awarded was as much your work as his, but he got all the credit. Such is life. Happens in my field all the time. So you have good credentials. But you've never covered anything like what I'm about to show you."

"A telescope that looks back in time. Yes, that's some story. I hardly believe it myself."

"And why not? It's perfectly logical. When you look at a star, you're looking at light that was emitted perhaps hundreds or thousands of years ago, and those are the close ones. When you look at the night sky, you're looking back in time, and the further you look, the older the images. The Hubble Telescope looked back thirteen billion years to the beginning of the universe. But some of the closest stars are only a few hundred light years away. Now suppose the opposite is true. If you were on that not so distant star and could magnify the light reflected from the earth, you'd be seeing images a few hundred years old. That's what I've done. We're here. Do you see it?"

"What? See what?" replied Josh, trying to take in all that Teller was saying, while he looked around vaguely for whatever it was his guide was hinting at. All he saw were trees and more trees, and the dirty yellow of the pine and snow that covered the ground, which seemed to rise dimly behind the foliage.

"You're looking right at it, the bunker."

Josh shook his head. He still could see nothing but tree-covered forest. Teller moved a little further down the trail and then followed a glimmer of a path that ran to the right toward the mound of land. As they moved closer, the dim outline of the bunker became clearer, rising in a long, wide hump about twenty-five feet high and forty feet long. Although still hard to distinguish from the ground and surrounding trees, Josh saw it had a concrete frame fronting it, where a massive steel door stood tightly closed. He noticed a small metal chimney at the rear. These were the only things that gave it away as a manmade structure and not a natural mound. Numerous trees grew on it of all sizes and shapes, some quite large, adding to the deception.

"Home sweet home," announced the scientist, walking up the half-dozen stone steps to the concrete platform in front of the bunker and taking out a key.

"There are dozens of these things scattered through the area. They go for miles. Some of them are still filled with live ammo. Others contain more toxic material. My people live in some of the others."

Josh stood in amazement staring at the odd structure. As he studied the building more closely, he noticed electrical cables and vents going into the bottom of the concrete front of the bunker. Teller worked his key into a padlock latched on the door's massive handle. Once the lock was removed, he turned the handled and leaned back, pulling with all his strength. The old rusted hinges creaked loudly, echoing back into the cavernous interior, as the heavy steel door swung slowly open.

At first Josh could not see inside, which was black as night, but gradually his eyes became accustomed to the darkness as light flooded into the room. Soon he was able to distinguish things clearly.

The interior was smaller than he expected given the dimensions of the mound and the massive concrete entrance, but roomy enough for two and comfortable looking. It had a half cylindrical shape, which was to be expected given its outside appearance, and was about twenty feet wide and the same in height, and about thirty-five feet long, with perfectly rounded sides and ceiling.

"You'll get used to the stale air," said Teller, switching on an electric lamp. "I have my own generator and pump, but it hasn't been on for a few days. We'll have fresh air in no time. There's even a stove."

"Neat," replied Josh, taking things in. There were a couple of canvas cots next to the far wall and a table with chairs near the door. Several reading lamps were placed about the room. There were also modern lights strung along the ceiling, which gave the place a warm glow. Teller turned on the air-filter system and shut the door, sealing them in with a loud, echoing clang.

"Yes, it's nice and cozy in here. Now we can talk. I have a lot to show you."

The cold cement floor of the bunker was covered with thick rugs. In the corner near the wood stove with its stovepipe leading up and out the rear of the bunker, was a large desk with several computer screens stacked side by side. Beneath the desk was a red, ornate oriental carpet.

"Let's put on some background music, shall we," suggested Teller, switching on his computer and streaming in some classical station playing an early Ravel piece. "Yes, that will do fine." Teller listened for a moment then turned the volume down. "Can I get you anything, Joshua? Lisa, one of my assistants, will be by in a few hours. She'll fix us up something to eat. How about a drink in the meantime, something alcoholic? Would you like to take notes while I talk?"

"Thanks, Doc. A drink would be great. Do you have any Red Bull?"

"No, what's that?"

"Oh, just an energy drink. How about a Twisted Tea?"

"No, what the hell's that?"

"It's like a wine cooler with ice tea."

186

"No, I don't have anything like that. I have water, beer and Jack Daniel's."

Josh thought for a moment. "I'll have a beer," he said finally.

"And I'll have a Mister Jack and Daniel's with water. All I have is Sammy Adams light, but it'll taste good after what you've been through. That was quite a story."

He handed Josh a cold bottle from a small refrigerator and made himself a drink.

"I think there's a pad and pencil in the desk somewhere, if you want to write some of this down. It probably wouldn't be a bad idea."

"I have a pretty good memory, Doc. I have a feeling I'm going to be hearing it plenty of times. We'll be here awhile, right?"

"Yes, that's right. We've got plenty of time, but not as much as you may think. The resources they have looking for us will be significant, especially after things settle down now that the end-of-the-world scare is over and the weather has cleared. But I hope to go public before they discover us, and you're going to help me."

He opened the top draw of the desk and withdrew a pad of legal paper and a pen, which he threw to Josh.

"Have a seat my friend, and start interviewing me. This is your big chance."

"OK," said Josh, changing gears and getting into his newsman's attitude. Sitting down in one of the chairs at the table, he put on his game face and collected his thoughts.

"Do you have an operational Telescope? Is the Peeble Telescope operational?"

"Those are two questions. The answer to the first is yes, I have an operational telescope not far from here. The answer to the second, if you are referring to the StellarScope version of the thing, is no. Their telescope is missing a key part and some critical software, but all the deep space components, the space-mirrors and telescopes and intelligent servo-mechanisms are in place. I've taken control of these and added the missing and critical pieces. Everything is working as I've designed it, has been since shortly after I disappeared. Of course, I'm the only one who knows this."

"Well, I guess the question everyone is going to want to know, is why? Why did you do this? Why did you say you were going to build a telescope to look for life on other planets, and end up building some kind of camera on the past, or whatever it is you've done?"

"Ah, I see, Joshua, getting right down to the nub are we?" said Teller, sitting back in his comfortable desk chair and taking a sip of his whiskey and water. "That's a good question. I've already answered that when I told you we, the human race, aren't ready to go barging in on other civilizations. Look what we've done to ours. Look what's happened to every primitive culture we find. Why go searching for other beings when we have so much to learn yet?"

"Well, first of all we really might learn something. We might encounter beings with more intelligence than we have who can guide us and teach us, help us evolve to their level. That's a lot better than looking back at human history. We have books and old movies for that."

"Exactly, books and old movies, that's all we know about what we are, what we have been, where we've come from. Many of the deepest questions of science and religion deal with those very subjects. Where did we come from? Why are we here? My old teacher, Henry Thomas, Chic, as you called him, used to say, 'if you look out far enough, you will find yourself.' But they only wanted to look in our own galaxy, not that far at all, although that would have been a good first step."

"So you've found a way to look back in time. I've read, or been told by those who've read more, that your old mentor, Professor Peeble, believed in time travel. That's what discredited him and finally got him fired from his research position, before he too disappeared. Are you in touch with him? Do believe his theory on time travel?"

"Well, Josh, that's a mouthful. Let me see if I can untangle that rather ambiguous set of statements and satisfy you with an answer. Doctor Peeble was discredited by a bunch of academic hacks who half-read and completely misunderstood his statements, which were never written down by him, by the way, but only given in lectures and public talks he gave throughout the world. He was naive and answered truthfully, regardless of the shock some of his statements caused to the uninitiated. But that's the curse of the modern astrophysicist when he tries to turn his rather arcane mathematical theorems and calculations into everyday speech and concepts. Some of the things we talk about are beyond this world, and well beyond the ability of most people to conceive."

"I know what you mean," said Josh, finishing his beer and starting to get into the conversation. "Can I have another one of these?" he asked.

"Sure, my boy, but take it easy with the second one. It'll be awhile till we eat yet and I don't want to get you so tipsy you can't write."

"Thanks," laughed Josh, grabbing another brew.

"What we've done is impossible," continued Teller, seeming to dash all his credibility with one statement. "It just can't be done given the state of modern physics and the theories of general relativity and quantum mechanics. There are just too many problems."

"Well, then, it was nice talking to you. You can explain it all to the judge from here on."

"You sound more like a prosecutor than a news person. I told you, I have a working telescope."

"How, if what you said is true? It's either not possible or it is. Make up your mind."

"I said it wasn't possible with the current state of knowledge. I mean just look at the problem, think about it. Here you have an event on Earth, say something that happened, oh, around 2000 years ago. That's a good round number. Now, according to Einstein's theory about the propagation of light, the quantum of light that burst from that image travel through space at exactly 300,300 km per second, and this light travels at that speed through space forever, as it has from the distant stars and galaxies we can see that are millions of light years away. That's the facts. The other facts are that even at that speed, light takes 2000 years to travel the vast distance of space to get there. Which means to bring that image of earth back from the star would take even longer. Then there's the problem of magnification and diffusion, not to mention diffraction and the actual bending of light by gravity. On top of all this, there's Relativity itself and what it does to our perception of time, especially at the speeds and distances you'd have to theoretically move the light around. You actually need to accelerate it, but that's impossible under General Relativity. So you see, there are a number of insolvable issues. That's what everyone told Peeble and are still saying after all these years. Now with this invention, this telescope, his dream can be fulfilled, at least partially. My teacher has been vindicated."

"So how did you solve all the problems? What do you know that no one else in the world knows?"

"When they came to me with the idea of a deep space telescope to probe the galaxy, they weren't sure what they wanted. I thought it was going to be the next generation super-telescope, something to extend the findings of the giant Hubble project that looked at the very edges of the universe speeding away at 270,000 km a second. That's almost the speed of light, almost eighteen billion light years away, as if such a number means anything. My question to them was, why only probe our galaxy when you're trying to answer the question of where we and all this came from. What was it like at the very first moment of creation? That's the question. And what would you find out anyway? Just the confirmation of one creation theory – I call them myths – or another. No, if you really want to know where we came from, you don't have to look back to the edges of the universe."

"They wanted to look for life on other planets within our galaxy," continued Teller. "But I had different ideas. The latest technology and breakthroughs in astrophysics, especially the study of so called black-holes, had made things which were unimaginable a decade ago, reachable today. There was only one thing standing in the way."

"And what was that?" asked Josh, when Teller stopped and fixed himself a second drink, this one not as strong as the first.

"The math. The quantum gravity field equations. The big hole in the middle of our grand unified theories."

"Which is?" asked Josh again, when Teller stopped and took a long pull of his drink.

"Look at these," he answered, handing Josh several large, eleven-by-eight glossy photographs of grainy images, which appeared overly magnified.

"What are they?" replied Josh, looking at the pictures one by one. "They look like stills of old movies taken from the back of the theater. Who's this supposed to be?"

"We believe that's Napoleon at the gates of Moscow," said Teller, not batting an eyelash. "We think that one there is Genghis Khan, back around 1050 AD."

"I suppose this one is Jesus Christ," said Josh sarcastically, holding up one of a man wearing what appeared to be woolen robes."

"We think it might be. He's in the right vicinity at the correct time. His activity pattern appears to match our historical profile. But we still have a lot to learn, and much experimentation to do."

"You expect me to believe these are actual pictures of events that took place thousands of years back in time?"

"Wait until you see the real thing," said Teller with a gleam in his eye and a smile on his lips.

Josh sat there in disbelief, his pen long ago ceasing to scribble anything on the page. "This is incredible."

"That's nothing, Joshua. I've solved the equations for quantum gravity. Or rather we've re-written them to account for the four forces in the universe in one unified theory, with the field equations and geometry to prove it. That's the really amazing thing. This makes things possible we've not even begun to dream of. And yes, time travel is part of it."

Josh sat there in amazement.

"I could tell you more, but I see you're exhausted. Perhaps we've gone over enough for now. Lisa will be here soon. Why don't you refresh yourself after your journey. There's another change of clothes in that chest there, and something to spend the night in. It gets kind of cozy with three of us in here, so you'd better get anything of a private nature you want to do out of the way. I'll tell you how it all works tonight at the weather station, after we've had a good meal and a few hours sleep. My dear boy, don't look so worried." He laughed and patted Josh on the shoulder when he said this. "Your journey has only just begun."

Chapter 22

A little while later Josh relieved himself in a closet-sized head and washed up in a basin of hot water. After changing into a comfortable pair of loose slacks and a sweatshirt, he sat at the desk looking at the odd photographs of the past while Teller went about some chores. Soon after that someone clanged at the door. It was Teller's assistant.

Lisa was a pretty brunette with brown eyes and a lithe figure. She reminded Josh of his friend, Dan Little-Wolf's sister, but wore her brown hair short and had a tougher look about her, more attitude and cynicism than sweetness and light. She had sharp features, not much softened by her brown eyes, which looked at Josh questioningly as she entered the long, rounded room. Teller made the necessary introductions, explaining that Lisa had been a research assistant of his at the college, who had also done work on the project from time to time. As a matter of fact, as Josh was to soon realize, Teller used a lot of his graduate students on the company's work, using the project as class assignments. a clear breach of corporate policy. This is what allowed him to bypass many of the formal procedures and get things done without the meddling of others. Together with his small cadre of loyal students he had been able to steal the project and set up his own facilities.

The jury was still out as far as Josh was concerned on the scientist's ulterior motives. Whatever they were, there was a good story in it. Teller's lame excuse that the human species wasn't ready to encounter beings from other planets was complete hogwash. Who was Teller to say who was ready for what? Regardless of that, if what the scientist was saying proved true it was a revolutionary concept. Such things had been known to shake the world. How would the world take this revelation?

Despite her polite greeting and friendly smile, Lisa remained aloof and didn't spend much time socializing, but went right to work preparing a meal in the bunker's makeshift kitchen, pulling fresh vegetables from the small fridge, chopping and tossing some of them, while she steamed others on a single electric burner. While she worked, Teller told Josh what was in store for the evening. He couldn't tell, but it must have been around four or five in the afternoon. It felt like dinner time.

"We're going to the station tonight. We'll wait until the moon is up. It's just a short way down the trail. It's an old defunct Air Force weather station. Even though it's no longer used, it still has a lot of the infrastructure intact, even a few satellite hookups, everything but the actual dishes. That was easy enough to remedy and get something up quickly. We've got everything we need right here hidden right under their noses, at least for the time being."

Teller talked as they ate by the light of a small lamp, around the square plastic outdoor dining table. Lisa used chopsticks to eat her salad and mixed vegetables even though she wasn't oriental, while their host explained their backgrounds to each other. Josh was surprised that Teller knew so much about him, and a little shocked by the description of some of Lisa's more colorful escapades with the authorities.

"That was you?" Josh blurted out, after Teller told of one of her more notorious exploits that had made it into the nightly news.

After dinner Teller suggested they get some rest, as they would be working most of the evening.

"Of course, we do much of our work at night. It's much easier to align the stars we need for our observations without our own star blinding us."

Josh was assigned the cot on the left side of the bunker, tucked tight next to its curving wall, while Teller took the one on the right. Much to Josh's consternation Lisa unrolled a sleeping bag and slept on the floor near the desk on the thick Oriental rug.

When Josh protested, she was adamant, insisting she was much more comfortable on the floor and preferred her sleeping bag, thank you. Once Josh lay down and tried to sleep on the lumpy, unforgiving canvas cot, he understood why.

Six hours later, around midnight, they were up and ready. Teller pushed open the heavy steel door and stepped out into a cold wintery night. It had begun to snow.

"I wish it'd make up its mind," complained Josh, perturbed at the sudden change in the weather.

"This is more like it," said Teller, who seemed to enjoy the white stuff. "With the skis it will actually be easier moving about on the trails. It just started. It won't be a problem walking out. We have gear at the station if we need it to get back, but we can stay there just as comfortably. Ready? Let's go."

They headed down a wide path, just dusted with light snow. As they walked, the path grew narrower, the snow imperceptibly higher, until after twenty minutes they were walking on a thin trail a half-inch thick with it. By the time they reached their destination - at the top of a hill, the highest point in the area - it was snowing hard and over their shoes.

The complex was comprised of a structure resembling a short, squat water tower, but with a window-paneled room at the top like an air traffic control tower. Next to it sat a single-story, pale-green concrete office complex. All of it appeared deserted, like it hadn't been used in years. A gaggle of strangely shaped antennas, each about twenty-feet high and barely visible in the half light, rose ghost-like in the night from the top of the tower, while behind the buildings on a slight rise squatted a couple of satellite dishes pointed at the sky. The whole scene looked oddly out of place, the last thing Josh expected to encounter in the middle of the woods.

"Here we are," said Teller stating the obvious. "It snowed a little harder than I expected. It might make things difficult, but nothing we can't handle, right Lisa?" She nodded noncommittally. Josh was starting to think she didn't like him.

They climbed the stairs that circled around the tower to a door at the top, and entered a single room with circular walls, which was forty-five feet above the ground and made up the last twenty feet of the tower. From here they had a good view of the surrounding area, which was completely wooded for several miles in all directions. The inside of the buildings was darkly lit, with the glow of phosphorescent screens and scopes the only illumination. Computers competed with generators and stacks of electrical equipment for the wide ample floor space. A large console with rows of levers and switches covered one side of the large room, with half a dozen flat-paneled TV screens placed in two rows above it. A couple of dozen clocks and meters hung along the opposite wall, all telling time, air pressure and temperatures in various locations around the world. There was nothing that resembled an optical telescope sticking out of the roof, but there were several smaller optical scopes placed on the fenced-in, wide metal grate that circled the room on the outside. These were used to help position the deep space telescopes and mirrors.

Lisa went to work immediately on a panel of computers, generating the calculations they would need to focus the network of telescopes and mirrors, and send the instructions required to position them in space.

"As you probably know," began Teller. "There is a grid of mirrors and telescopes placed throughout the solar system and beyond, which we can point and maneuver any way we like. The intelligent servo-mechanisms at each key sight further compensate for the minute effects of gravity and the curvature of space. As a matter of fact, we use such bending to speed up the process so we can see the images in almost real time instead of waiting hundreds or thousands of years.

The mirrors help focus and magnify the light needed to form the images. The telescopes can be directed at the mirrors or at distant objects, or even the image of another telescope, again magnifying and focusing the pictures we receive at a specific star-point from earth. The grids of stars used are all chosen to provide light and images from the desired timeframe, up to a few hours.

All of this would be useless, however, without the key process needed to speed up the light. We don't actually speed it up, which is impossible, but we can bend the space to such an extent that time is warped, so to speak, taking advantage of what general relativity and quantum theory say."

"Are you talking about worm-holes?" asked Josh, as the idea popped into his head.

"Very astute of you, Joshua. That is precisely what I'm talking about. The very laws of the universe, as we know them, break down in the infinite gravitational field inside a black hole. Our mathematics fails us when faced with these infinities, at least the current equations do, but a quantum theory for gravity can handle it. At the very edge of the black hole, where the Event Horizon, the point where light nor anything else can't escape the gravitational pull, there is an edge of empty space, which is not really empty at all. There the strange laws of quantum uncertainty rule. And if you aim your beam of light close enough and take advantage of these uncertainties, you can bend it and shoot it out beyond the normal cone of light that Relativity demands. The trick is to use the angular momentum of a rotating black hole to hurl the images, accelerating them like a slingshot."

Josh understood none of this, as his expression evidently showed.

"Here, let me show you," offered Teller, reading this expression and determined to overcome it. "How we coming, Lisa?"

"Fine, almost finished," said the comely assistant.

First Teller displayed an image of the earth from Jupiter as it looked with the naked eye, a barely visible white smudge on the screen, forty-six light minutes away. This he then magnified to show a small, round, bluish glob.

"Here is how the Earth looks from Jupiter through a large, earth-based telescope," observed Teller, clicking a control on the computer screen again. Josh could make out the blue of the oceans and the white clouds covering green and brown land. Another click and Josh could make out continents and the outlines of large cities, clear signs of intelligent life.

"Now here's what it looks like with the Peeble Telescope," announced Teller, clicking a few keys on his terminal.

The picture enlarged and Josh was looking down at a wooded area as if a few hundred feet off the ground. He immediately thought he recognized the place.

"We're seeing Earth forty-six minutes ago," said the scientist. "Look, Joshua, do you recognize what you're seeing?"

In the greenish-phosphorescence of the night vision lens, Josh saw three people leave a low bunker-like structure. One of the figures had on a baseball cap and looked immediately familiar. That person was accompanied by a larger man and a woman.

"That's me!" shouted Josh with a flash of realization, shaking his head in disbelief. "That's us leaving the bunker!"

"Oh, by the way, Merry Christmas, Joshua. I know you missed the holiday this year due to circumstances beyond your control. I don't have anything for you, but perhaps this will do."

He clicked a few keys on one of the computer consoles and the TV screens above it sprang to life, some showing magnified images of Earth as seen from deep space, while others displayed visual white noise.

"The whole idea of Christianity originated in a small village called Bethlehem at the head of a long dead sea around 2000 years ago. There is a star called XNA-2A near our edge of the Milky Way approximately 2000 light years away. We've set up our telescope to use it to look back at Earth 2000 years ago, give or take a few days. We can adjust this further to sweep back and forth a couple of centuries in each direction, using slight adjustments that leave the basic configuration in place. Otherwise we'd lose the images. What you're looking at," said Teller clicking a few keys on his keyboard. "Is the equivalent of a satellite view from Earth of that village at the traditional time of the birth of Jesus Christ."

"Christ," exclaimed Josh, as the satellite image of a small desert town sprang into focus on the central screen.

"Exactly," said Teller, smiling at his guest. "We've been monitoring this period for some time, trying to gather evidence for the historical existence of Jesus Christ. So far we haven't found any, although we have found supporting images from a bit later date, but nothing as to a birth. However, recently we have picked up evidence of large migrations at this period that could coincide with Herod's order to the inhabitants of Galilee to return to their birthplaces for a census. We have been looking for signs of massacres or the killings of babies and children."

"I hope you don't find it," said Josh. He looked at the images closely, but could make out little but general outlines of houses and roads running between the hillsides and desert, along the dark blue of a large oblong lake or inland sea. "Is this as close as you can get?"

"Oh, no, you've seen the photos. We can get right down and personal. We've already adjusted the mirrors. It will take a few minutes for them to actually change the picture on the screen though. I said real-time, but that's all relative of course. The farthest images take hours to get. These closer ones only take a few minutes to adjust. Oh, here we go."

Josh looked up to see people passing along the dusty roads, the sand rising in brown clouds as camel trains moved through the desert. The crowds along the date palm-lined streets were considerable, a thriving, bustling oasis village nestled in a sea of sand, with people coming and going from all directions, some on camels and some with mules, but most on foot.

It was a strange sensation. Josh didn't know what to believe, whether he was looking at an elaborate hoax, perhaps images from old moving pictures pieced together to give the semblance of something real. Whatever it was, it sure did look interesting. The more he looked, the more he began to believe the truth of the images.

"This can't be," he said finally, his mind giving up on coming to grips with what he was seeing.

"Oh, but I'm afraid it is, all too real. And we can go back to any period you wish. We've watched the battles of Yorktown and Waterloo, and Nelson at Trafalgar. We've followed Columbus's ships across the Atlantic and the construction of Stonehenge. I've watched Bach conduct his B minor Mass, Genghis Khan lead his Mongol hoards across Asia and most of Europe, and many other things. It's not

197

a movie. It's not a false image. It's the real thing, Joshua. You are looking at the past."

Josh, still not convinced, asked Teller if they could get images from the more recent past.

"Sure, like I said, any time period you like from hundreds of thousands or millions of years ago to events occurring just a few minutes in the past. We can watch the ice age and the dinosaurs just as well as we can look at events of a few years ago. There are stars only a few dozen light years away. We could theoretically watch the birth of the solar system, but we haven't worked out those equations yet. We can also replay images from the sun, the closest star of course, only eight light-minutes away."

"Can you show me something from my past, my childhood?" asked Josh tentatively. Seeing a glimpse of his own private history would cinch the claim as far as he was concerned.

"Of course," replied Teller. "You'd have to tell us the time and place, and it would take a while to set up, but we happen to have a configuration already established for that time period, let's say twenty-years ago."

While Teller went to work with Lisa to set up the demonstration, Josh looked around the building and asked questions about this piece of equipment or that, not understanding much of the explanations Teller deemed to provide.

"So if you can do this, it must not be hard to do what they originally thought it was going to do, study other planets."

"Right again, Joshua, just a few minor readjustments needed to realign all the telescopes and space-mirrors would do the trick. We could do it from here. That comes for free, so to speak. We've done a little of that. Nothing interesting, at least in our galaxy, just dead planets and empty barren waste. We see the same thing when looking at our own solar system. As I told them when they suggested it, there's not much chance of life in our own Galaxy. We may be rather unique as the Milky Way goes, but there are hundreds of billions of galaxies out there, and the odds are that many of them probably have intelligent life. As I've said many times, however, we're not ready."

"Why don't you let mankind determine that? Who are you to decide for the human race? Kind of presumptuous of you, don't you think?"

"There you go again, Joshua, being judgmental. I have the knowledge. It's my invention, my idea. I'm the only one who knows how to do it, so I get to say what it does. That's just the way it is."

"Well, that's a pretty arrogant answer. A lot of people may disagree with you. You're going to have a lot of explaining to do when all this comes out. People just aren't going to believe it, even after they've seen it."

"What do you think the average person would rather see, pictures of old galaxies, faint splashes of light tens of billions of light years away, pictures of barren, lifeless planets, or living pictures from our past?"

"I don't believe any of this," said Josh, objecting to the whole idea.

"Do you believe this?" asked Teller, clicking a few keys on his keyboard and looking up at the central display. "Do you recognize this place?"

Joshua followed his host's gaze up to the display screen and instantly recognized the area.

"Yes, that looks like Burlington, Vermont and the shore of Lake Champlain. That's main street, the town where I grew up There's the high school. Looks like summer with all the leaves on the trees."

"Yes, I've fed in the street name you gave us. We have the exact coordinates. The image should appear soon. Yes, there it is."

Josh found himself staring down at his boyhood home with the field next door and the farm down the road, much as he remembered it. It resembled the image he saw that day he had viewed his address in 'satellite' mode using MapQuest, but this was somehow different. To begin with, these pictures were moving although in slow motion, as though someone had set the replay on the DVD to slow. The picture grew larger until he could recognize his back porch. His breath froze and he tried to swallow. There he was, a small boy in a baseball cap standing in the back yard hitting stones into the empty field.

"That's me!" he yelled, standing up and pointing. "That's me as a kid, hitting stones. That's me," he said again in disbelief. Then as he watched in utter amazement the image of a man appeared on the porch, as if calling him in.

"Dad," Josh blurted, tears rushing to his eyes. "That's my dad!"

It took a while for Josh to recover and stop the flow of tears so he could speak again.

"The past does that sometimes," said Teller. "It can have a powerful effect on someone not used to it. You can see things perhaps best left unseen, but the past can be liberating as well, especially if you have unfinished business left behind."

Josh felt drained, as if he had actually traveled all those light years himself, instead of the light doing all the traveling. He couldn't, however, doubt what his eyes had seen. No one could have faked those images. There were no old movies of Joshua as a boy hitting stones into the field next door.

"That's incredible!" said Josh, when he could finally speak again.

"I told you," replied Teller. "Now you're going to help me tell the world."

Agent Fred Stanley was getting nowhere fast. Now, on top of the flash floods and rain, it had begun snowing again, with no sign of letup in sight. He still had no news on the whereabouts of his two fugitives. They could be anywhere by now.

Obviously, Teller had a car stashed somewhere on the opposite side of the river, and despite the huge traffic jams and road blocks, had eluded capture. Since tracking was out of the question at this point, he had begun using the computer and his own instincts to try and locate them. He found his young partner, with his technical savvy, a good asset.

Before the bad weather had set in, Stanley had obtained access to some additional resources, a spy satellite manned by the NSA and a helicopter from the bureau, as well as a fresh team of field agents from Quantico. So far, though, even with the extra eyes in the sky and feet on the ground, they had turned up nothing.

"What's this here?" Stanley asked his partner, scrutinizing a blank area on his mobile display, with no detail except a vague splash of grey and brown as if the terrain were nothing but bush or desert.

The young rookie studied the display a moment, clicking a few icons to obtain additional information.

"Seems to be a restricted area," he replied finally. "Belongs to the military by the looks of it. They must have it blocked from observation for security reasons."

"I'll have to ask my man in the NSA about it," said Stanley. "See if we can get access. You thinking what I am?"

"Well, it would be a perfect place to hide. No satellites spying on you, at least not casually."

"That's out beyond the 128 ring. I'll see if we can find someone who knows the area to check it out. It wouldn't be difficult for someone to get from Wellesley Hills along 128 where they got away, to this point here. A lot of back roads and small country lanes. I'll get on the phone and check with the State Police out that way. This damned snow's going to foul things up. The bird's already grounded and we probably won't get another clear satellite view until the storm lets up."

"What if they got it wrong?" said his partner.

"What do you mean? Got what wrong?" asked Stanley.

"What if it's not yesterday the world's supposed to end, but today?"

"Oh no, not you too." They both laughed.

Chapter 23

"Too bad you can't get the sound too," said Josh.

"What's that?" asked Lisa, only half listening as she sat working next to him. He had brought her a cup of coffee and joined her at the table.

"I said, too bad you can't get the sound along with the picture. That would really make it interesting."

"This isn't a motion picture, you know," she said, not at all amused. "Sound waves can't travel through a vacuum. There's no way the sound waves could travel through space to a distant star and back like light waves or particles."

"I was only kidding," said Josh, slightly embarrassed at his question. "Can't you take a joke?"

"There's nothing funny about what Doctor Teller is doing. It will change the world."

"That's what I'm afraid of. He said the world wasn't ready for meeting people from other planets. Maybe it's not ready to see the past."

"There will be some who aren't ready for it, but most of mankind will find it beneficial and enlightening. A lot of old myths and prejudices will be wiped away."

"Yeah, along with a lot of people's beliefs and religions."

"The truth will set you free, for those who have the courage to see it."

"If you can see into the past, can you go there as well?" Josh asked tentatively, afraid of making another gaff.

"Ah, that's a good logical question," said Teller joining them. "We've been asking ourselves the same thing, but that's a completely different problem. We're only capturing light that's been traveling through space, as reflected from a distant star of our choosing, so we can see back to almost any period in history and even earlier. That's hard enough and violates some of the known laws of physics as expressed in Relativity, and that only affects light quantum. That only needs to be rectified with a gravitational field theory as I have done. Actually moving matter into the past, like you or I, is out of the reach of science as we know it at the moment, but that's not to say it's impossible. Even affecting something back in time as small as an electron is beyond our capability. It just can't be done.

Of course, if one uses imaginary numbers in one's equations," said Teller. "Then time becomes just another spatial dimension, which you can walk back and forth on just as one can go left or right or up or down in three dimensions. So time travel becomes possible, both forward and backward, at least in the world of imaginary numbers. But you and I, and everything here on earth, live and move in real time, in the world of real numbers, not imaginary numbers where 2 x 2 = 4 and -2 x -2 equals something else entirely. So that method of time travel, the abstract mathematical one, is not open to us either. However, there might be a way."

Teller stopped as if that's all he had to say. Josh was going to ask him to go on, when Lisa interjected.

"The quantum uncertainty principal says that a sub-atomic particle like an electron or photon can be thought of as both a wave and a particle. Because it can be thought of as a wave, it can be thought of as actually being in two places at once. Since it's a wave, it's spread out over space and time. Its position and speed can never be calculated or known precisely but only estimated based on the probabilities computed from all the possible paths it could take from one point to another over time, its wave-function, and because of that, it could be in two places at once."

Josh shook his head, having trouble following their point. Lisa seemed too brainy to be so attractive. It was intimidating.

"If you split a beam of light or a photon, say," continued Teller. "And do something to affect one of the pieces of the photon that flies off in one direction, the other piece, flying off in a different direction will be affected instantaneously, even though it's far enough away where such communication should take some amount of time. The pieces seem to be in direct communication with each other, simultaneously, no matter how far apart they are, faster than the speed of light. How can something move faster than the speed of light? How can one thing, based on probability, be in two places at once? How can a photon be in two different places at once?"

"Are you saying that if you have the light particles you can somehow go back in time?"

"Something like that, but not quite," said Teller. "There is a possibility, a statistical probability let's say, that that burst of light, a quantum of photons, traveling through space at 300,000 km per second, can be split in the infinite gravity of a black hole, or at it's edge actually, and if we can complete the equations, we can figure out how to affect the particles emitted by that light. It might be possible in this way to effect change in past events. Only small changes could be affected in this way and only at the sub-atomic level, but even small changes in events could have immense consequences. The dream of science fiction writers everywhere is a distinct possibility."

What he had already seen was hard enough to get his mind around without this ridiculous twist.

"Don't worry, Joshua," said Teller as if reading his mind. "Don't bother about that for now. Concentrate on the telescope and what it means for humanity, good and bad. Speaking of that, are you all right? Sometimes seeing one's past can be a little disconcerting."

"Yes, I wasn't expecting that. It's not like seeing an old home movie. It was real, as if I were right there, back in time watching myself from, from heaven," Josh exclaimed, not being able to find any more adequate term. "It's a shock."

"Yes, exactly," replied Teller with a sigh. "It's a problem I wish I didn't have to concern myself about, but it has to be dealt with in some way, the human reaction. We've had a few scary episodes with some of my researchers who we've been working with. Watching your mother give birth to you, or seeing a long lost loved one alive again, can be emotionally devastating. We've had some close calls where I thought for sure we'd have to bring in the padded wagons, but everything turned out OK. We have some very good psych majors in our group." He smiled and looked at Lisa, who didn't change her solemn, almost stern expression.

"I'm afraid there will be a lot of hostility to what we're about to do. There are people and groups who will not want it to succeed for one reason or another, especially our own government. They will want to control it and restrict its use to only top-secret military or scientific research purposes. Even though you and I might not see any military use for the telescope, they've been sold a bill of goods that it has something to do with national defense. That will be the end of it. I want my invention to be used by everyone, not just scientist or soldiers, not just Americans. We also need to understand the effect this will have on people and offer some sort of assistance and support."

"I don't know, Doc," said Josh hesitantly. "There might be some good reasons for keeping it out of the hands of the public. Don't we have enough trouble in the world without conjuring up the past? Maybe it belongs to the prerogative of researchers and scientists, like the big telescopes on the mountain tops. You can only get access if you belong to some university and have a PhD."

"I'm surprised at you, Joshua," said Teller, although he had a smile on his lips. "I didn't know you were such an elitist."

"You just got through telling me how it affects some people. Perhaps you should be careful about how it's used and by whom."

"I don't think you understand, Joshua. I want to commercialize the telescope. I want to make it available to every man, woman and child on earth, like Ford did the model T. I want to change the world."

Josh was a little taken aback. He didn't expect this turn in the conversation.

"Don't look so surprised, Joshua. Why do you think I worked for nothing for the past eight years? How do you think I recruit such bright, talented people, for the joy of pure academic research? Come now, Mister Banks, even you couldn't be naïve enough to believe that? It's worth millions, billions!"

"I should have known."

"Yes, and you can be a part of it, in on the ground floor, so to speak. As I've said we need a publicist."

"That's not exactly the kind of work I do."

"Yes, I know, you're an investigative reporter. You expose graft and scandal."

"You'll never get away with it," said Josh indignantly. "It's like trying to steal the space program for your own use. It doesn't belong to you. It belongs to the tax payers who footed the bill."

"You mean the U.S. government? You want the government to control it? Hmm, maybe we had him all wrong, Lisa."

"Look," interjected Lisa. "StellarScope are the ones who stole from the tax payers. You exposed them, or at least tried to. We know all about that. Doctor Teller has promised to return all the money. Once your story's out and the crooks and the government officials on the take are dealt with and out of the way, once the world hears about what we've done, every country on earth will demand to see it and have a piece of it. Who are we to deny the rest of the world what is by all rights theirs, their past as well as ours. Much of what we'll be seeing and studying has taken place on their soil. It belongs to the world, not the stupid American tax payers."

"She's right," continued Teller. "All the money that went into its development during the past ten years, will be returned, all 280 billion of it. That's nothing to the billions to be made licensing the technology and commercializing it. And yes, there will be plenty left over for research. The learning potential is astounding, not only for history, but geology, physics, you name it."

Josh found himself starting to give in. Perhaps they were right after all. As long as they returned the money, who would care, especially when they found out what Teller had really done. Josh had to agree, short of actually finding life on another planet, which according to most astronomers was unlikely in our own galaxy, the Milky Way, what could be more sensational than what Josh had just seen with his own eyes. And while there might be some who would have difficulty with the revelations, most would find them enlightening, astounding, life-changing.

"The storm's really coming in strong," said Lisa, looking at the latest reports on the regional weather bulletin. "A northeaster with sustained winds over fifty miles an hour, almost hurricane strength, and blinding snow. They expect eighteen inches by the time it stops."

"OK," said Teller. "We can't do anything more here tonight with this blizzard bearing down on us. It's probably time to get going."

"It's going to be rough out there," observed Lisa. "We'll need the skis."

"Maybe we should wait until morning," offered Josh.

"It's not far, we'll... What's that?" said Teller sitting up.

Someone was trying to open a side window. Soon there was a noise at the door of the tower.

"Someone's here," announced Teller, stating the obvious.

"Who could it be?" Josh asked in alarm.

Before anyone could respond a man in a light blue, hooded parka walked into the darkened room.

They all stood up in alarm. The man looked right at Josh and started walking toward him. For a moment Josh didn't know who it was, but as soon as the intruder stepped into the light, Josh recognized him.

"Dan!" he cried, moving to meet his friend Dan Little-Wolf.

"Josh, there's no time to talk. We've only got seconds. I'm here with Agent Hagen, the one who first took us in. They know where you are. They'll be here any minute. They've got a large force cordoning off the area, military boys and everything. Tom's been monitoring their calls. We were able to get here first while they're getting organized. That's why two are better than an army sometimes. We can move faster."

Josh barely had time to make introductions when Tom Hagen burst into the room, gun drawn, and ordered everyone out of the building. The urgency on his face was apparent.

"Everyone into the truck!" he shouted. "They're here." He pointed to a large, black Jeep Wrangler parked below. "Hurry!"

The sounds of heavy vehicles could be heard approaching, as the light of their high-beams lit up the snowy darkness like a low flying jumbo-jet.

Josh didn't have time to even grab his coat or utter a surprised gawk, and the five of them were running down the snow-covered metal stairs and jumping into the waiting jeep. The next second they were speeding down an unseen road covered with six-inches of wet snow. The visibility was near zero and the snow was hitting the side windows of the vehicle like someone was throwing it."

"You know a way out of here?" queried Dan, sitting in the driver's seat, while Tom Hagen strapped himself in the seat next to him. The rumble of large motored trucks plowing through the drifts behind them grew louder. The lights of the first truck was just rounding the bend at the top of the hill. Hagen's jeep sped down the road in the opposite direction.

"Yes," said Teller, calmly, as if sitting in a classroom discussing his theories. "If you think your jeep can handle it, we can cut through the woods along the old railroad bed. They won't have any birds up to track us in this weather."

"I wouldn't be too sure of that," said Hagan.

"This thing will handle just about anything you got," said Dan proudly. "I've done some work on it. She's my pride and joy. When I'm not racing dogs, I'm tooling around in this thing."

"Here," said Teller. "We're coming up to it soon. Slow down."

Dan barely tapped the brake, as he turned left off the old road onto a wide trail that led down the sloping side of the hill. Josh turned and looked out the rear window.

"There's someone behind us, an SUV. It's coming fast."

Dan let the Jeep pick up speed as gravity did its job, pulling them faster down the modulating trail. It was like riding a 4000-ton metal sled, as they bounced around like bobsledders on an Olympic course. Josh belatedly thought to put on his seatbelt, but found it more difficult than expected. The Jeep fish-tailed left and right as Dan fought to keep them on the narrow track.

"Here," said Teller. "Up here is where the trail meets the lower road. Keep going straight as it flattens out, straight all the way. There you go."

Dan stepped on the gas as they reached the flat straightaway. The Jeep Wrangler bounced over a slight depression as the trail met the old tarmac, jarring Josh's teeth. On they went.

"Go, go!" yelled Josh, looking back and seeing the chase vehicle right behind them.

The classic 4x4 picked up speed, throwing him back in his seat, and almost spun off the path. Dan recovered quickly and sped them down the road.

"Up here there's a turn-off, but I want you to keep going straight," said Teller. "There's an iron gate a short way further on. You need to get us through it. It's going to be tricky, but I think you'll have room."

"Room for what?" yelled Dan, as they rushed by the turn-off on the right. The ruins of an old stone house were just visible in a snow-covered field off to their right. It was all that remained of a once prosperous farmstead, cut off from the world for the past seventy years.

"There's a space on the right between the gate and a few rocks and trees. I think we can make it."

"What?" yelled Dan.

"Either that or we can all give up and go with your friends," said Teller calmly. "I'm sure they'd be happy to see you."

"Do what he says," ordered Hagen. "We can't let them catch us."

Dan swore under his breath as they came to the cross-roads where the north gate of the restricted area blocked the path.

"There, just to the right," counseled Teller. "Go as if you're going to smash the gate, then duck to the right there. You can just scrape by. They'll never see it in time and will smash into the gate, which is locked and made of steel. I think that'll stop them for awhile."

Dan did as he was told and swerved the jeep to the right at the last moment, just slipping by the metal gatepost and two large boulders planted next to several young trees. Dan cringed and yelled in seeming pain as both sides of his truck scraped between the rocks and gate, throwing up sparks as it did so. As he squeezed through the gap onto the other road running at a ninety-degree angle from the first, they heard the chase vehicle crash head-on into the gate, smashing the front of the SUV with a sickening crunch and knocking the gate open.

"Now what?" yelled Dan, confronted with another gate blocking his path.

"Smash it," replied Teller in his ear. "It's only made of wood. We can lose them in there. There're all sorts of roads back here. Go, smash it!"

With little choice but to continue on the path of destruction he was committed to, Dan hit the second gate squarely, smashing through it, splintering wood and denting the chrome front of his pride and joy. Dan Little-Wolf swore silently as he strove to keep his damaged vehicle, which fish-tailed dangerously to the right and left, on the road.

The snow-covered dirt track descended suddenly down a long hillside before it reached a low gully, then ascended another long incline to the next hilltop. Dan bounced them over a little bridge spanning a small creek and back up the other hill. At least it was a fairly straight stretch. They sped up the road to another highpoint, this one covered with a thick forest of tall pine trees.

"Here they come!" shouted Josh, looking back "They're moving again. "They've just come through the second fence. Now I can't see them any more."

"Here," said Teller again, as if he had a solution to every predicament and had lived back here all his life. "There's a fence all along the road here on our left. See it? There's a gap in it a little way up. If we can just keep out of sight long enough to reach it, we might give them the slip."

Dan pressed his foot gently on the pedal, pushing his vehicle as fast as he dared along the narrow dirt road.

"I don't see them," said Josh. "There, they just reached the top of the first hill."

As he said this, they reached the top of the second rise and bounced over it and down another slope. "They're gone. I can't see them."

"Good," said Teller. "Get us to the bottom of this hill before they get to the rise behind us."

They sped down the snow-covered road, more a ski slope than a track, bouncing dangerously off the ground then skidding in the wet slush when they landed, but somehow Dan held them on the path. Even Teller was gripping the edges of his seat, cringing in fright as they narrowly missed trees and boulders on the sides of the road.

"There, there it is," yelled Teller pointing. "Off to the left. Keep your eye on the fence. See where it ends? That's the gap. Get us through that then keep going. Follow it off to the left where it diverges away from the road. It's our only hope."

"Dan did as directed, keeping one eye on the road ahead, while he watched the gap in the fence approach in his peripheral vision.

"Still no one yet," said Josh, who preferred looking backwards than ahead toward the perilous path they were on.

"Good, now!" yelled Teller.

Dan decelerated just enough to swerve the Jeep off the road and to the left, just missing the fence posts. Letting them coast through a narrow opening, he plowed through a drift and over a small mound onto another track, sending the snow flying as they passed. This trail led roughly parallel to the first before turning gently away and to the left. They were all flung upwards as they flew over a small embankment, but Dan was miraculously able to keep the Jeep under control. They bounced over another mound, then down a gentle slope through an area of widely scattered, old forest trees.

"I think we lost them," observed Josh.

They were barely moving now, as Dan crawled along trying to follow what was left of the trail. "Where's the road?" he asked. All there was to follow was a vague path where the space between the trees appeared to be wider than the surrounding forest.

"Keep on through those trees there and up that rise," advised Teller.

"I hope you know where you're going," said Dan. He was not at all happy with the damage done to his vehicle and didn't relish the prospect of leaving it stranded in the middle of nowhere. Loyalty and friendship was one thing, not to mention a pardon for his crimes, but this was far beyond the call of duty.

Tom Hagan looked around nervously as they drove slowly through the wide-spaced, snow-covered forest. "They'll figure out we've ducked out on them soon enough and circle back. They've probably got more trucks following. Hopefully by the time they do figure it out, our tracks will be mostly covered."

"The way it's coming down," replied Dan, as he peered intently out the vehicle's front windshield, "I don't think we'll have anything to worry about, except that is, getting out of here ourselves."

"There's another auxiliary road up this way a short distance," Teller informed them. "We can get out of here that way."

Now that they had a little breathing space, and appeared to be hidden for the moment in the white protective embrace of the storm,

Josh started to breathe a little easier. As he did, a flood of questions came bubbling to the surface of his mind.

"Where'd you guys come from?" he asked, the events of the past half hour suddenly hitting him all at once. "How did you know what was going to happen? How did you find us? How come you're helping us?" He looked pointedly at the FBI agent, Tom Hagen, when he said this.

"I knew something was up when Agent Stanley tried to take you back to DC. This was a local affair under my jurisdiction. He had no authority and no reason to get involved. Or so I thought. Then I started to put things together. That satchel of documents and papers you had was the key. The more I studied it, the more I began to understand what was going on and who was involved, and what they would do to stop that information from getting out. What you sent to your agency was suppressed by government orders. Those orders came from someone very high up in the Defense Department. The agency's behavior became suspect as well when they authorized Stanley to take over and sent him up here. They've got the whole NSA establishment behind them as well as Defense. If they get their hands on you and Doctor Teller neither of you will ever be heard from again, along with your invention, Doctor, whatever it is. I'm not so much helping you as stopping these pricks from doing more damage, the arrogant bastards. To think they could get away with this on my watch."

Josh was impressed with the lawman's righteous anger. Years of working in Internal Affairs had sharpened Hagan's senses, made him more perceptive to the shadier dealings of his associates in the Bureau. He could tell a cop on the take as easily as a bloodhound smells a fox. However, with just a year and a half to go before retirement, he may have gotten a little sloppy and missed some early cues. He had chalked the whole thing up to the typical arbitrariness of a bureau run by politicians and bureaucrats, but he didn't like being the fall guy, not when he was about to retire. Well, maybe he wouldn't be the only one leaving early.

"Don't get me wrong," he said, looking back at Josh. "When your buddy here took you from my custody, I was so mad I probably would have shot both of you on sight." Josh for one believed him and gulped visibly. "But after talking to your friend Maria and Dan here, I began to realize your predicament and why you were so eager to find Doctor Teller. Once I knew for sure what was going on, I decided to monitor the situation on my own. Dan here has turned out to be a big help. You were lucky to enlist him in your cause."

Josh looked at the intense little man working the clutch and gears to keep them moving in the blizzard. "I think it's more like he enlisted me in his cause."

"Never thought I'd be working with the FBI," said Dan Little-Wolf. "But Tom here's one of the good guys. He's helping the little people."

"On behalf of the little people," said Teller. "I thank you."

"Me too," added Josh. "You guys saved our lives. I don't know how to thank you."

"Just stick with me and collaborate what I say when they haul our asses before the judge," replied Hagan. "Not that this bunch would be so foolish. No, if they catch us it'll probably be a firing squad."

"How did you find us?" asked Josh, still not finished with his interrogation. "I mean, how did you know where we were?"

"Like I said, we were monitoring their calls," Hagen replied. "It helped that Dan here had an inkling where you were headed when you broke out of their trap. That was quite a feat. Was that your doing?" he asked, looking back at Teller.

"You could say I had a hand in it," said the scientist. "But their own stupidity did most of the work for me."

"Well, good job. Dan knew you'd head west, and he knew about the old army research center."

"I was stationed here for a while before I went overseas," Dan informed them, "training. I figured it might be a good place to hide out. It's where I would have gone."

"Dan suggested we head in this direction when news of your escape went out. We monitored Stanley's call to the state police barracks out here, so we knew they were checking the place out, and that they'd probably find you. Luckily, we were closer than they were when they got the confirmation. Someone must have come out here and seen you. We had the advantage of mobility. We knew it would take them a while to organize and come in with force. Dan knew a back way in. We were able to get to you just before they did."

"Thank God," said Josh.

"I think it's just up here," said Teller, leaning forward and peering out the front window between Tom and Dan's shoulders. "We should be coming to the road shortly. There, up that slope."

Dan gunned the engine as they followed the disappearing trail up a steep embankment, spinning snow behind them as they spun up the slope. They smashed through bushes and branches going too fast over the embankment, and left the ground completely as they reached the road, which intersected the trail at a ninety-degree angle. Shooting over the track, they plunged into the high snow bank on the opposite side and crashed down another embankment into the trees and rock at the bottom of a gully. Luckily no one was hurt, but the vehicle was further damaged. Try as he might, Dan could not get it out of the ditch and back on the snow-covered dirt road.

"It's not far. We can walk from here," said Teller, after watching Dan fruitlessly try to get his Jeep out of the gulley for half an hour. "We'll freeze if we stay here."

"What's not far? Where are we?" asked Tom as Dan finally joined them on the snow-packed track. The wind blew unabated, slapping cold, icy particles against their exposed faces.

"There's a regional emergency facility just up the road a bit. I'm not sure if it will be manned or not in the storm."

"Doesn't matter," said Hagen. "I've got full authority here where they're concerned. It will be the perfect base of operations until we can get some help."

Teller led them along the road, between intermittent stands of wood and frozen marshland, until after about twenty minutes, when Josh thought sure he was going to freeze to death, a chain-link fence appeared surrounding a large, empty field. At the end of the field where the ground rose gradually, they could vaguely make out a complex of buildings through the snow.

"This is it," Teller informed them, pointing in the general direction of the fence. "It's up here on the side of the hill. It's an underground facility actually."

They trudged up the road as it rose next to the fence for a few minutes until the shapes of buildings - trailers and large garages where several vehicles, plows, and vans were parked – became visible. Lights were on, but there appeared to be little activity. The parking lot was empty of cars.

After traversing the length of the facility they found themselves at another auxiliary road, which ran perpendicular to the one they were on and fronted the building. They could see what appeared to be a major highway a half-block further up this road, which was plowed and well lit. The entrance to the underground regional emergency center glimmered like a beacon in the storm, a few hundred feet away.

Josh followed as Tom Hagen led the small party toward the light.

Fred Stanley studied the map on his mobile display screen.

"What's this?" he demanded, pointing to a cluster of buildings ending at a cul-de-sac off Route 27.

He couldn't believe their targets had gotten away. Someone must have tipped them off, probably a sentry or tripwire somewhere. He wouldn't put it past this Teller guy to rig up something like that. They had followed the fugitives in a daring chase through woods and fields only to lose them when they crashed into a metal gate. But they couldn't be far.

According to the satellite of the area, the defunct army base and wildlife sanctuary covered several miles of state and federal forest land, surrounded by more state forests and finally routes 27 and 62. Since they had approached from the south, the suspects must have headed for the north side. He immediately ordered his troops to set up road blocks and cordon off the area.

The Sherriff's deputy sitting next to him in the van finally answered after a long delay. "That's the regional government emergency center."

"Is it operational?"

"I don't think so. No one's declared a state of emergency. We're not under attack. The blizzard's supposed to end tomorrow, probably just a skeleton crew and security detail on duty."

Stanley got on the radio and issued a few more orders.

"Yes, Stanley here. Get some men over to the Regional Emergency Center off 27. It's on the other side of the army base. What? On whose authority? Well, we'll see about that."

He slammed the flat of his hand on the dashboard and swore.

"That bastard Hagen has taken over control of the regional center. What the hell is he doing here?"

He thought for a moment then picked up the radio again and started issuing more orders, as if he had been juiced with an extra boost of energy.

"Get every man you have over to the Regional Emergency Center off 27. Yes, all of them, all the troops you can. Make sure they're armed. Get me a tank if you can. Yes, I said a tank. Get me everything you can. We have a war on our hands!"

Chapter 24

"This is wonderful," proclaimed Teller, examining the control console and satellite connections in the underground facility. "We've got satellite hookups to anywhere on earth. I can even link up with the Peeble telescope back at the weather station. This is perfect. We can operate right from here and beam the images to anywhere we want. I thought this place would be ideal when I first saw it, with the array of receivers and satellite dishes they have in back, but I never thought I would gain access to it."

"Well, you have," said Hagan. "Now make the most of it."

"Do you think they'll figure out where we are?" asked Josh nervously.

"Yes, I'd count on it," said the FBI man. "I've got a call out to my own people, but God only knows when they'll get here, or how many there will be."

"It looked like your counterpart had the whole army with him," said Teller.

"Yes, he had a good-size force, big enough to cordon off the whole area. But he'd have a problem trying to break into this place. It was built to withstand such a siege. Unless he's got major fire power we should be OK, as long as the security people here obey my orders. We're fine for the time being. Hopefully that's time enough."

Josh looked doubtful but said nothing.

"What did you tell them?" asked Teller.

"I told them who I was and showed them my orders."

"Those must be some orders," replied Teller, "to get the guy here to go along with you like that."

"They're from the president," announced Hagen matter-of-factly. "I had to go over my boss's head."

Without hesitating he turned to Josh.

"The sooner we start broadcasting the better," he said. "Josh, we'll need you to help us put our message together. We want to expose the guilty, provide the evidence, then explain what Doctor Teller has invented and show them the results. Once it's out, they'll be too busy trying to save their asses to worry about you."

"We're almost ready here. How are you coming with our little story, Joshua?" Teller asked.

"OK, I just want to go over it again then you guys can have a look and let me know what you think."

"Well, hurry up, we don't have much time," said Hagen.

Josh went back to a quiet corner of the large, minimally lit control room and checked his report on the computer. As he did, Dan Little-Wolf joined him with a steaming cup of something.

"You want some tea?" he asked, sitting down in a steel chair next to Josh as he worked at his text.

"No," said Josh. "It'll just make me jittery. I plan to sleep a long time after this."

"So, what did Teller actually do?" asked Dan, curiously. "Did he really make a time machine?"

"Something like that," replied Josh, concentrating on his paper, a little annoyed at the interruption although he couldn't blame Dan for being curious. They hadn't talked since they had been arrested that second time at Dan's sister's house.

"He can look back in time. He can literally use his telescopes to see the past."

"You mean I could watch the battle of the Little Big Horn?" said the descendent of a Micmac chieftain.

"In full living, bloody color. It's amazing. I'm not even sure if the world's ready for it."

"Then why are you agreeing to help publicize it?"

"Because it's the only way to save all of our necks. Otherwise, we'll just look like the bunch of terrorists the government's trying to make us out to be. We have to vindicate Teller to remove the guilt from ourselves. After all, we've broken several laws. Teller's invention and his promise to return all the money will help mitigate things. That along with the fact he's going to make it available to the world."

"Free of charge?"

"Not exactly. We might all become multi-millionaires. You too, if you want to be part of it."

"I don't know," said Dan Little-Wolf, not sure if he liked the idea. There was too much heartbreak and misery in the collective past of his people to want to relive it, even if he could see a great victory or two like that on the banks of the Little Big Horn. "He's not exactly the kind of man I expected."

"What kind of person did you expect?" countered Josh.

"I don't know. Someone with more vision maybe."

"Oh, Teller's got plenty of vision, and it's filled with dollar signs."

"We've got company," announced the man nominally in charge of the facility before Hagen arrived, rushing into the room. "There's a company of soldiers outside demanding immediate entrance. The guards want to know what to do."

"I'll handle it," replied the senior FBI agent, standing up from his seat at the console next to Teller and following the nervous official. "Keep on what you're doing."

"We can preempt the network stations from here," said Teller, excited as a kid in a toy store. "Beam our message to the world whether they want to see it or not."

"Josh, keep working on that draft," Hagen yelled over his shoulder as he left the room. "I want to see what you've got as soon as you've finished." With that he was gone. Dan got up and followed him out a few moments later.

Josh went back to his piece, building the arguments that would vindicate them and support their case against not only corrupt executives at StellarScope, but top officials in the Defense Department as well. With that out of the way, he set about describing Teller's amazing invention.

'Imagine if you could go back to any period of history you wished and watch it as if from a spy satellite in space, with the ability to zoom down and magnify things so you could read license plates and recognize individuals.' He stopped and looked at the page, not sure how to continue. Before he could frame his thoughts, Dan Little-Wolf burst into the room.

"They've got a tank out there! They're threatening to blow us all up."

They all got up, including Teller, and ran to the front entrance of the building. As they reached the top level and the glass-paneled entrance, they could see Tom Hagen with his FBI jacket standing in the blizzard outside talking to another man in a bullet-proof vest. Behind them was a phalanx of armed men in uniform with jeeps and rifles. Directly in front of them facing the entrance was a large tank with its cannon pointed at door. It was easy to hear Hagen's voice raised above the wind.

"I've got jurisdiction here, Fred, and when you find out what's going on, you'll be sorry you got involved in this whole mess."

"You're the one's who's going to be sorry," said Fred Stanley yelling back just as loudly. "Now hand over my prisoners."

"They're under my custody and I'm not handing them over to anyone but the president of the United States."

"I don't know who you think you are, but I've got the head of the Bureau on the phone. He's the one we take orders from, not some bureaucrat in Washington."

"I'll tell the President you said that. Who do you think our boss reports to? Look Fred, it goes all the way to the Secretary. That's why you're involved. You're working for the wrong guys."

"I don't know what you're up to, Hagan, but you're way out of line here. I'm taking over as ordered. I'd advise you one more time to cooperate and hand the prisoners over or I'll have you arrested right along with them."

"On whose authority?" asked Hagen, not giving an inch.

"On my authority!" yelled Stanley, losing his temper.

"You have no authority here. You saw my orders. Stand down, mister, or you'll be implicated in your boss's crimes and the cover-up."

"You're crazy," said Stanley, not at all convinced. "Those papers could have been typed up by anyone. I'll give you five minutes. Then we're coming in."

He turned and walked back to the line of men behind the ominous tank. Hagen did the same, hurrying back into the building. The two security guards and the supervisor looked scared.

"What's going on here?" asked the man in charge of the facility.

"We have a rogue agent," Hagen told him. "He's purposely trying to interfere with the president of the United States in his defense of the country by kidnapping the people in my care. They're needed in Washington for a very important mission. If they don't get there, it could hurt the country. If you and your men want to leave, feel free to do so. We don't want to involve you, but my orders are from the President himself."

The official still didn't appear convinced.

"Would it help if you heard it from the man himself?"

"Yeah," the supervisor replied finally, his security men listening right behind him. "I guess so. If the President says so, but you'd better do something fast. That guy outside, whoever he is, has all the cards."

"I'll give you a number," said Hagen, writing it down on a piece of paper and handing it to the official. "You can call him yourself."

A moment later, after talking to a phalanx of intermediaries, the supervisor heard the familiar voice of the President of the United States on the other end of the highly-secure line.

"Hello, sir," said the nervous supervisor. "This is Paul McMahon from the Regional Defense Center in Maynard, Massachusetts. We have sort of a situation here, sir. No, it's not the storm. That's winding down, sir. I have someone here that wants to talk to you, a Tom Hagen from the FBI. Yes, sir, here he is."

He handed the phone to Tom a little in awe. Tom put the receiver to his ear.

"Yes, sir. Yes, it's me. I have him. Yes, both him and the newspaperman who uncovered the conspiracy. You have the documents? You're having your people go over them now. Good. Yes, it does look pretty incriminating. Yes, sir, I think so, all the way up. Well, sir, that's the problem, they've got their people here now threatening to break in. They've got a tank. Yes, but I'm not sure how long it'll take them to get here and I don't think they have a tank, sir."

He listened a few minutes, looking at the official who looked back with profound interest.

"Yes, sir, that would help immensely. How long do you think? OK, yes, sir. I think we can hold them off for that long. You want to talk to him? Yes, sir, I think we can arrange that." He gave the president his cell number and handed the secure phone back to the impressed official. "Here," said Hagen. "The President wants to talk to you."

As the other man babbled words of agreement and respect, Hagen headed back out to face his nemesis.

"Well, have you decided to surrender?" asked Fred Stanley, cold and hungry and about as tired of this whole affair as a man could get.

"Someone wants to talk to you," announced Hagen, handing his cell phone to the other agent. "Look at the number." At that moment the phone rang. "Answer it."

Fred Stanley reluctantly flipped it open and put it to his ear. "Hello," he said slowly.

He stood there listening for several moments, looking at Hagen the whole time, his eyes narrowing. Then without saying a word or taking his eyes off Hagen, he flipped it closed.

"I don't know what you're trying to pull,' he said. "But I've had about enough of your crap, Hagen."

He tried to grab the other agent by the wrist and pull him forward, but Hagen easily slapped his hand away and moved Stanley backwards with a few well-aimed jabs. For a moment they tussled back and forth in front of the entrance.

"Move in!" yelled Stanley in alarm. "Move in now." The rows of men behind the tank started moving in, their guns raised.

It all happened so fast Hagen barely had time to think. "Don't shoot! Don't shoot!" he called out loudly to the two security men who had accompanied him to the front entrance and had just drawn their guns. He grappled with the other FBI man, grabbing his wrist and locking his arm at the elbow when he tried to draw his service revolver. Hagen had not taken his with him, but was now faced with several dozen men armed with large caliber automatic weapons pointed in his direction, not to mention the tank, which had lowered the barrel of its cannon and leveled it at the glass-paneled entrance. He didn't have time to think, only react.

Parrying his opponent's clumsy attempts to strike and grab him, Hagen used his strength and leverage to twist Stanley around in front of him. Then he jammed his heel into the back of the hapless agent's knee. Stanley's legs buckled, and he found himself kneeling on the ground in front of Hagen facing his own men, Hagen's forearms locked tight across his neck in a classic choke hold. Stanley gasped for breath.

"Stop!" yelled Hagen at the top of his lungs to the oncoming soldiers. "I have orders from the president."

"Get him," gasped Stanley, through the clamp-like hold Hagen had him in. "Shoot him!"

At that moment, when all seemed lost, there was a loud humming sound and the windblown snow seemed to swirl and blow even harder. Suddenly, a giant form loomed out of the darkness as a large military helicopter landed on the snow-covered parking area right in front of them, throwing up walls of blowing whiteness. Even in the swirling snow and darkness, the helicopter's array of hardware - missiles and Gatling guns - was obvious. Everyone stopped dead in their tracks.

For a moment nothing happen. The big bird sat like a giant dragonfly dropped from the sky, its large, slowly spinning rotary blades the only thing moving. The soldiers stood and stared in disbelief, their weapons lowered. The tank crew opened their hatches and popped their heads out to get a better look. Tom Hagen loosened his grip around Fred Stanley's throat and breathed a sigh of relief. Then a voice blared out from a loudspeaker inside the helicopter.

"This is General Blunt from the 31st Division Headquarters. You men are to cease and desist under orders of the President of the United States."

As he said these words, a number of jeeps and troop-carrying trucks turned off the main highway and made a beeline down the auxiliary road toward the standoff.

"You are to hand over your weapons to the relieving force and stand down. Return to your barracks," the voice on the speaker ordered. "Only your commanding officer will be involved in the subsequent court martial, unless there is resistance, in which case you will be tried to the full extent of military justice. And let me add that justice will be swift."

The voice went silent as the relieving forces came on the scene. There was a general feeling of relief as the troops met and men started handing over their weapons as ordered. Hagen turned over his errant associate and went to meet the general as he exited his helicopter.

"Hello, sir. Boy am I glad to see you," said the relieved FBI agent. "A few more minutes and I don't know what would have happened. They didn't seem to want to listen to the President's orders."

"Are you Hagen?" asked the general surveying the agent sternly.

"Yes, sir, Tom Hagen, senior agent in charge."

"Good, I don't know what's going on here, and I don't want to know. I have orders directly from the President of the United States to give you and your associates my full cooperation. I'm to take Agent Stanley into custody, as well as the Colonel in charge of these men, and anyone else who resists. Though thank God, I don't think we're going to see any of that here today."

"We're fine now. Thank you, sir," answered Hagen, "though I would appreciate it if you could post some of your men around the area and keep everyone out. We're going to be attracting some attention in the next few days and weeks, and we don't want to be disturbed."

After rounding up any remaining sheriff's deputies and state police still on the alert for the supposed terrorist, and leaving his own men to cordon off the area, including the weather station where Teller's telescope was set up, the general left Hagen and his small party in charge of the facility with all its assets, and went back to his base.

Josh was sitting in one of the rooms of the spacious underground control center getting ready for some much needed rest. The regional official who had stuck with Hagen despite the overwhelming odds and who now felt empowered after talking with the President, assigned each of them a room and ordered them food. Only Hagen continued to work, making calls and arrangements to carry out the next phase of his orders.

"Boy, that was something the way Tom faced off the whole army and that tank," said Dan Little-Wolf, as he watched Josh change his T-shirt. "It was right out of the movies."

"It was a little too real for me," answered Josh, still not recovered from the ordeal enough to expect to fall asleep. "We were this close to getting blown to smithereens." He pinched his thumb and forefinger so they almost touched.

"Who'd of expected I'd be praising an FBI dude," said Dan, laughing.

Teller walked in at that moment.

"I want to thank both of you for helping us," he said. "Your contributions won't be forgotten. I hope I can count on both of you continuing to work with us."

"I was thinking my work's done here," said Josh, anticipating the Pulitzer Prize he was sure to get for this exclusive story. This time no one else would get the credit. "I'm looking forward to getting to work again. If my old agency won't hire me back, I know a few that will."

"I'm sure," said Teller, visibly disappointed. "But what makes you think it's over, Joshua? This is only the beginning."

Chapter 25

Josh woke up to the hum of an air conditioner and looked sleepily around his expensive downtown Boston hotel suite, compliments of the new Teller-Scope Corporation. Plodding across the plush carpet in his bare feet, he threw open the curtains to a wide picture window and looked out at the skyline of high-rise apartments and offices that made up the quaint port city. Much had happened since that cold January night in New England.

Teller's telescope had been a sensation, totally eclipsing the arrest and subsequent trials of the conspirators uncovered by Joshua and his incriminating material. With the indictments against the defunct StellarScope Company executives came a flood of testimony, mostly accusations and counter-accusations, which uncovered even more illegal activity. The murderers of Maria Cavello's mother and Ellen Primrose were finally brought to justice and sent to prison, where they all died in violent accidents. Some suspected involvement with the mob, but since none of the ex-executives and involved personnel had underworld connections, their deaths were marked up to unfortunate coincidence. Josh, remembering what Maria had said about her Uncle Louie, suspected otherwise.

The scandal in the Defense Department was another matter and would drag on for months into years before finally being resolved to everyone's satisfaction. By that time many in the government would be voted out of office or fall in disgrace, including ultimately the Chief Executive himself, but that was in the future. Now all anyone could talk about was the miraculous Teller Telescope, a tool that allowed man to literally look back in time to almost any period desired. To say it caused a sensation, along with an ocean of controversy, is to put it mildly and Josh found himself right in the middle of it. The whole experience of the past few months was so fantastical that sometimes it felt like the present was just a dream, and only the past and the telescope were real.

In the months since the standoff he had tried several times to leave because of the pressure. Every time he attempted to do so, something pulled him back. He had to admit, the money was good and he was fascinated with the new invention and the possibilities it opened up. It seemed to promise great discoveries in science and history, as well as anthropology and geology, even in philosophy and religion.

Now you could look back and see for yourself how things happened and who did what, replacing speculation, interpretation, and theory with observation and fact. But many were not pleased with what they saw. Many thought the new invention was evil, the work of the devil. Some thought it sowed the seeds of destruction and should be destroyed itself, along with those who invented and promoted it. Then there were the numerous special interest groups who seemed to come out of the woodwork to try to take it as their own. Between all of these and the telescope's armies of supporters, Josh found himself trapped in a never ending battle he felt somehow compelled to make his own.

Already, in the six months since the telescope's unveiling, when Teller himself appeared on a special worldwide TV broadcast from the underground regional facility to reveal what he had done and why, most of the 200 plus billion dollars owed to the U.S. tax payer had been repaid. The broadcast itself would have made Josh, who was the interviewer, a household name and ensured him a lucrative and highly visible anchor position in any network news agency he wanted. That was nothing, however, compared to the huge sums Teller was paying him as a media consultant for the new Teller-Scope Corporation, which the scientist had built on the ashes of the old StellarScope.

Until the telescope was available for commercial use, which had taken several months, huge amounts of funding were needed to pay back the initial 'loan' and keep the project going. This money came from a variety of sources, each financial backer wanting a piece of the action. Some of it came from foreign governments eager to ensure a say in the new invention's use. Some came from private corporations wanting a piece of the potentially large profits. Some came from groups or associations with specific social or philosophical agendas. While Teller held the controlling shares and was chairman of the board, there were several stakeholders who were close behind in power. They had to be accommodated in one way or another. Their representatives sat on the board of directors of the new company, all of them jockeying against each other and Teller for control of the astounding invention.

Of course, there were many in the country that wanted Teller prosecuted for his misuse of taxpayer's funds, even if the money was being paid back, but in the complicated contracts and secret clauses contrived by his original partners and backers, and in all the documents pertaining to the case, there was not one shred of evidence of wrong doing on Teller's part. He had broken no laws, stolen no one's money, and had technically told no lies. He claimed he left because of what he saw going on, after his objections and warnings were ignored by his superiors. He hid out due to fear of just the type of thing the ring-leaders proved themselves capable of. As far as the misuse of government funds, there was strong proof that he had done just the opposite. He had accomplished something that promised to benefit the entire world at no personal gain for himself.

The line of people and institutions waiting to use the telescope and the variety of uses that were being proposed for it were overwhelming. Because the Peeble was really a series of telescopes, which could be independently directed, and the images processed in parallel by Earth-based satellites and computers, it could be made to view many different periods at once and accommodate the high demand planned for it.

Right from the start there had been a vast response from those wanting to see the past. Researchers in history and biology, heads of churches and states, as well as just plain folk, all wanted to see for themselves the wondrous machine that rendered from light-beams after their stupendous journey through space and back, the recognizable images from another time. The telescope was in effect more a series of giant cameras than anything, and as such allowed the possibility of broadcasting these pictures to the world. Already scores of companies had sprouted up to franchise and license the new invention for countless ventures. But not everyone was happy

There were some, and not a few of considerable scientific standing, who thought the very idea of transporting light particles by Teller's methods was preposterous, a downright hoax. Not a few found the quantum gravitation calculations Teller had devised, along with the field equations that supported them, the figment of a mad imagination and refused to accept the whole theory. Many announced in journals and newspapers and scientific papers that what Teller was claiming was impossible. However, no one could deny the images, some of which were extremely powerful.

Lately, Josh felt like he was being followed. Or was he becoming paranoid, the fish-bowl existence of working on such a highly visible project starting to get to him? He couldn't decide. He turned to find he *was* being followed.

"Wild night last night," said Lisa, wearing only his pajama tops. "I thought those talking-heads would never shut-up."

For the past six months Josh had spent considerable time with Teller's research assistant, Lisa Sanders, who now headed operations at Teller-Scope and sat on the board of directors. She also served as

Josh's conduit to Teller who was too busy to explain the basics of the telescope's operation to him, let alone the next stage of his research, which even Lisa didn't know much about. During this time, Josh had grown close to the comely, intelligent PhD student. They had become intimate and were now lovers, much to Josh's eternal gratitude. He had grown tired of meaningless one night stands and lonely holidays. He had craved companionship and Lisa had given it to him, although she seemed totally consumed with her work most of the time.

"I guess Teller's announcement has stirred up a lot of interest," said Josh. "Not every day someone produces a global broadcast televising images from the past, all selected by a worldwide viewing audience. There was enough money floating around in that room last night to fund a hundred telescopes and everybody wants a piece of the action."

"That and a lot of hot air and self-congratulations," replied Lisa. "The way Benjamin droned on about his next new big discovery, you'd think he's already forgotten about this one, which we need to focus on and promote. No one gives a crap about his next big discovery except a few die-hard academics that wouldn't know 'the next big thing' if it bit them in the ass."

"I have to admit I didn't know what he was talking about," confessed Josh. "It was over my head."

"That's the problem. He's over everyone's head. He's gone back on his promise to commercialize the telescope. Now he wants to use it for pure research, to further his next big discovery, as he says. Sometimes I just want to kick him in the butt."

"I thought he was your mentor. I thought you looked up to him."

"I did, when he was working on the telescope and talking about how it was going to change the world. Now he could give two figs for the thing. It's maddening."

"Well, that's a genius for you, always looking at the next horizon, never stopping to rest on his laurels. Anyway, what's wrong with wanting to use it for research instead of just making a buck? I don't know, using it to somehow promote change for the better, as a tool to learn how to live with the earth, how to get along with one another, how to share the wealth and understand ourselves. I liked what he said about doing more study on the psychological effects of the telescope before making it available to the general public."

"Oh, Josh, you're so naïve. I guess that's why I love you, but sometimes you're just as dumb as Benjamin when it comes to doing things. Now's the time to commercialize it, while the demand is so high. Do you know he doesn't even want to do the broadcast now, say's it's premature. After six month of preparation and countless promises, he thinks it's too soon. He hasn't even pursued the patent litigation yet. Says no one could reproduce what he's done in another hundred years. If he can do it, so can someone else. I want research as much as anyone, but we haven't even begun to tap the potential of what we've just unveiled and he's off after the next big thing, which could take decades of work before it's ready for commercialization, if ever. In the meantime, we'll miss the boat. Why give everyone else the benefit of reaping the rewards when we've done all the work? You heard him. There are billions to be made. Now he wants to tie it all up in research, pure research. That's pure bullshit."

Josh liked it better when she didn't talk, when her intense dark eyes and full lips were closed, when she wasn't sprouting some angry agenda or bitter complaint. He wondered whether he could live his life with this woman and kissed her instead.

"Have you had a chance to review the list of requests for the broadcast?" asked Josh. "Quite a hodge-podge, 64,000 requests down to 120. There's bound to be some disappointed people."

"Who cares. In any case, it's not going to matter much with Benjamin calling the shots. He's about to pull the plug on this whole broadcast thing. After all the work I've done setting it up. I could kill him."

"Easy there, girl," said Josh, grabbing her around the waist and pulling her close as he caressed her shoulder with his other hand and kissed her softly on the neck. "Save those thoughts for me. You can kill me tonight."

"No," she cooed. "I couldn't kill you. You're too cute. And you're too good of a cook."

"By the way, why were you so miffed at that Lovejoy guy last night for wanting to include some images of the purported Jesus Christ on the broadcast? His ideas were intriguing. I'm sure a lot of people would be interested in seeing the real Jesus Christ on TV. I'm sure mom would get a thrill out of it."

"Yeah, and a lot of people would be upset as well. You heard what the Pope said. Not to mention the Muslim extremists. No, that's the last thing we want. That is, unless we show the opposite, that Jesus never existed. We need to dispel these superstitious ideas once and for all.

"I wouldn't be in too big a hurry to do away with people's religions, their sense of hope. What else will they have when that's gone?"

"Science of course, that's the answer to our problems."

"Some would say science is the problem."

"Those are the ones we have to disabuse of their superstitions."

"Well, your global broadcast is sure to be provocative. But there's a lot of time. You don't have to dispel all the myths overnight."

"The sooner the better," she replied, then changed the subject as he pulled off his shirt to take a shower. "You were cute last night. I like it when you get a little drunk. You're not such a stiff. You were a tiger in bed."

"I'm always a tiger in bed. Anyway, if you'd let up once in awhile and relax like you did last night, we'd have a lot more wild evenings."

"You know how important this is to me. There aren't many women in the position I am. I want to prove I can do it. I admire Benjamin and what he's doing. He's on the verge of some great discoveries, but that shouldn't keep us from reaping the rewards for what we've done, and I'm talking millions, for you as well as me. But sometimes Ben can be such a jerk. He has such strange views on things and won't listen to anybody."

"It's all beyond me. Say, did you see anyone watching me last night, you know, following me?" he asked suddenly.

"No," she said, a little curious. "Why, you think some woman is after you?"

"No, I just felt like, I don't know, it felt like someone was following me when I left the ceremony."

"I told you, you should have left with me. That's what you get for staying late. It probably *was* some woman. I'm glad you're so oblivious to that type of thing. It's one of the things that attracted me to you. You're not full of yourself."

"Thanks, Lisa. You're pretty down to earth yourself. No one would put up with my ignorance like you have in explaining things. You're very patient."

"That's because I adore you. Now take your shower. I've got to go to work."

"What, today? It's Sunday."

"Yes and tomorrow is the big broadcast. So I've got work to do. Teller's going to announce his new invention. If it's anything like what he said last night, we'll lose most of our audience before he's halfway

229

through. The director has told him he only has thirty-minutes for his introduction, the last ten of which has to be about the telescope. The rest will be narrated by a well-known actor. We've promised not to use his name, but his voice will be instantly recognizable, which will be comforting because what they will be seeing might get some of them pretty excited.

The demand is incredible," she continued, excitedly. "We'll have to add more telescopes and hookups to meet it. We're limited to how many images we can pull down at any given time with the available alignments. We can cover a few dozen periods with the set of configurations we have, and cover a few hundred years with each by maneuvering the space mirrors and scopes around a cluster of stars relatively close together, but changing these requires some time. Because of this we've tried to group the requests around specific periods. It's still difficult though. We've got the geologists and physicists wanting to look way back, to the beginning of life on earth and before, back to the formation of the tectonic plates and the very planets themselves.

"Well, I hope it goes all right," said Josh.

"We'll find out soon enough. But I don't trust Ben. He's already threatened to preempt the broadcast and I, for one, take him at his word. We can't override him if he wants to drone on for three hours. We can't go to commercial. There are no sponsors, although there should have been. We could have made millions on this one broadcast alone, but Ben didn't want one minute of commercials to interrupt the flow of the narrative."

"I don't blame him," replied Josh. "Who wants to switch to an ad while you're watching something that happened hundreds, perhaps thousands of years ago."

"There are ways we could have done it without interrupting the show. We could have tacked them on at the end, or included images on the bottom of the screen, or scrolling messages. There were dozens of ways we could have sold advertising without interrupting the flow of the show, but Benjamin nixed them all."

"Now I see what you're up against, sweetheart. I hate to see you under so much stress. I wish we could just split and go somewhere."

"It will all be worth it if we can just get through it without any trouble."

"What are you going to do?" asked Josh, concerned for his comely bedmate.

230

"Oh, I don't know, but I'll think of something. I usually do. Ben has a tough time saying no to me."

That statement worried Josh even more. He suspected Lisa and Teller may have been lovers at one time. As he showered, he wondered if she would sleep with the man just to get her way.

While Lisa took her turn, Josh went to the computer to check his mail. It was the usual stuff, mostly from the day before, which he hadn't read because he'd left early to go to the kick-off ceremony for Teller's global broadcast. One caught his eye, an urgent note from Tom Hagen.

Tom Hagen was no longer with the FBI, having retired in the wake of the StellerScope scandal. Even though he was the one that cracked the case and brought the culprits to justice, it didn't do his career any good that one of those culprits was the head of the Bureau, his boss, and another was the Secretary of Defense. Teller had made him an offer he couldn't refuse, so now he was head of security at Teller-Scope. Lately, his sole job seemed to be protecting his boss from all the death threats his invention had prompted.

Josh opened the memo, which said nothing except the ex-FBI man wanted to see him about something urgent. He finished changing and ordered eggs-Benedict and pancakes through room service. Then he called Hagen as soon as Lisa left for work, around 8:30, for her twenty-minute drive to the office.

"Hi, Tom, it's Josh. What's up?" he said on hearing the security chief's voice.

"Hi, Josh. I wanted to talk to you. There's been some very disturbing developments on the Internet."

"What, you mean those fringe conspiracy-theory sites talking about the evil telescope and the end of the world?"

"More than fringe sites, Josh. Some of the major Islamic sites have declared that showing any images of the Holy Muhammad, the founder of Islam, would be blasphemy and punishable by death. They're promising a jihad if we show any pictures of their founder. There have been angry demonstrations in all of the major Middle-Eastern countries."

"So what? Salmon Rushdie's still alive, and no one I know has gone on a jihad in awhile."

"This isn't a joke, Josh. There have been threats of violence."

"So what else is new?"

"Did you know Teller is getting five or six death threats a day? There are so many threats against him it's impossible to know which ones to take seriously. And Josh, some of them are against you."

That shut Josh up for a few moments. Tom Hagen continued.

"I want to put a twenty-four hour guard on you. I've already got one on Teller."

"That's out of the question," replied Josh, abhorred by the idea. "My life is already a fish bowl. I need some privacy or I'll go absolutely bonkers."

"Maybe it's a good time to go take a vacation, go home, chill out for awhile."

"What, now, when Teller's about to announce the biggest thing since electricity?"

"That's right, and it's big enough it doesn't need you or me. I'm thinking of getting out myself, but I can't discuss it over the phone. You want to meet for lunch?"

They made arrangements to meet later in the day.

Before meeting Hagen, Josh headed over to the Teller Center, where the inventor was doing some advanced research. Already focused on the next phase of his discoveries, he had left the entire telescope venture to Lisa, that and a good deal more.

After winning a rather lengthy verbal tussle with the security guard, who insisted the Director could not be disturbed, Josh rapped the inside of Teller's door and let himself into his office. He found the scientist working in front of a cluster of large computer screens, all connected to an array of processors, which allowed him to view several images from the telescope simultaneously, while performing prodigious calculations on his new equations.

Teller sat facing him, totally absorbed in the images on the screens.

"Sorry to disturb you, Doc."

The scientist looked up with a startled expression, as if he had been caught pleasuring himself. His eyes were red-rimmed and glassy, as if he hadn't slept or was high on drugs.

"Oh, hi, Joshua," he said, recovering quickly. "I didn't hear you come in."

"Sorry, Doc, didn't mean to startle you."

"You'll have to excuse me," began Teller. "I've been working hard on my theorems." He glanced at the screen, then started switching off the various images, one by one, staring longingly at the last one before it too was shut off. Josh just got a glimpse of a wispy-haired young

232

woman with a willowy figure and a far-away look in her eyes, in the arms of a large, dark-haired man with a full beard.

"I know you've been busy," said Josh. "I wouldn't bother you except the broadcast is tomorrow and I need to finalize some things."

"No, not at all. You are never a bother. You're always welcome. I've always got time to talk to you, Joshua. After what you've done, it's the least I can do. None of this would be possible without you."

"Thank you, Doc. I appreciate it. It's just that I haven't had a chance to talk to you with all the hubbub and everything. I wanted you to take a look at the introductory piece I wrote for you for the broadcast before it's finalized. I wanted to make sure it covers everything you wanted. There may be some controversial topics among the final lists of requests and I wanted to make sure we're ready. Of course, I know you want to talk a bit about your newest discoveries, so I tried to keep it short, but there's a lot to cover."

"I'm sure everything will be fine, my boy. You and Lisa are doing a fine job. I think you two are good for each other. Do you like her?"

Josh wasn't ready for the question and didn't know what to say for a moment. Teller continued.

"She wasn't sure about it either at first, but I think she's taken a liking to you, as I knew she would."

"What are you talking about?" asked Josh, one of his buttons having been inadvertently pushed by Teller's casual comment. "What do you mean, she wasn't sure about it? You two been discussing me?"

"Now don't take offense, my boy. I was just nudging things along. She's not the easiest girl to get to know."

"So you encouraged her? I didn't know you were such a matchmaker."

Josh didn't know whether to be grateful or take offense. He didn't like being manipulated, and wondered to just want extent the scientist was involved in his current love life. He made a mental note to ask Lisa about it.

"Don't tell her I told you."

"Don't worry," Josh lied. Then he changed the subject. "Everything seems ready for the big broadcast."

Teller seemed to ponder Josh's light words as if they were a weighty mathematical proof.

"I wonder if things are moving too fast," he said finally. "I wonder if we should postpone the broadcast and ..."

"Postpone the broadcast?" interrupted Josh. "Now, after all the hard work and money everyone has put in. You can't do that. Your board of directors wouldn't stand for it."

"I own controlling interests in the company. In any case, Joshua, these are things far beyond your purview. I have no intentions of canceling the broadcast, but I do intend to control what we put on. I won't be dictated to by the agendas of a few special interest groups."

"Those special interest groups, as you call them, paid your debts, or should I say paid for the money you stole."

"Joshua, you're getting all worked up over nothing. Did you look at the list of requests? Some of my colleagues in the fields of anthropology and history want to rewrite all the text books. Those in geology and astronomy want to go back to the formation of the continents and the very Earth itself. Then we've got a majority, millions, who want to go back to their childhood or some event in their insignificant family history. It's crazy. It has to be controlled. We just can't throw the thing out there for sale to the highest bidders just to make a profit."

"But you said…"

"I know what I said, Joshua, but I was wrong. What's happening, what's become of my invention, is just crazy. It has to stop."

"Maybe you're right," said Josh, seeing an opening for something he wanted to say.

"Tom told me he's getting numerous death threats a day against you. Perhaps it is a good idea to lay low right now. I'm not saying to cancel the broadcast, but you don't have to appear before a live audience at the auditorium. We could tape your address or have the actor read it."

"Now, Joshua, you know that's impossible. I have an announcement to make of the greatest importance. It eclipses the telescope like the computer eclipsed the adding machine, although what I'm proposing can't be done without the Peeble."

"Well, you don't have to give the talk before a live audience. We'll tape it from here."

"Now what would be the fun of that? How would I answer people's questions?"

"I don't know. Tom said one of the Mullahs in Mecca has put a price on your head. That sounds pretty damned serious to me."

"It's not them I'm worried about," replied Teller. "There are more sinister things out there than the Mullah."

"That just goes to prove my point. Every crackpot with an axe to grind is out gunning for you. It just isn't safe."

"Now you want to run my security too? Josh, I didn't know you were such a control freak. Let Tom do his job and worry about that."

Josh gave up any further attempt to change Teller's mind. He had little hope Lisa's broadcast would go smoothly. In way that surprised him, he found he didn't care.

On his way to the restaurant to meet Tom Hagen, Josh tried to phone Lisa, but she was busy and didn't answer his call. He left a message.

He met the ex-FBI agent in one of the more exclusive Boston clubs where politicians rubbed elbows with local celebrities from the town's sports franchises. Hagen was seated at a table large enough for six and invited Josh to join him when he noticed him standing by the door being totally ignored by the hostess.

"Some place," observed Josh sitting down. "I'm impressed. I didn't think you FBI guys had this much class."

"Don't get smart with me, newsboy," laughed Hagen. "It's good to see you. Been awhile."

"Yeah, I guess everyone's been kind of busy."

"How's it coming, the broadcast I mean?"

"Good, everything's on target for Monday after the board meeting."

"Yeah, the security headaches are keeping everyone on their toes, but I think we can handle it."

"I'm sure you can," agreed Josh, remembering how the ex-agent had handled himself in front of the regional center, facing a tank and a hundred armed men. He ordered a drink from the waiter who seemed to disapprove of Josh, who had neglected to wear a tie.

"So, can I put a man on you?"

"I don't think that would look too good. Lisa might get jealous."

"You know what I mean. I want to put a detail on both of you. Now you're going public, you're going to need twenty-four hour protection." He showed Josh the threatening blogs and articles posted on the Internet.

"Nice," said Josh reading a few of them and suddenly losing his appetite. "I saw Teller a little while ago."

"Oh yeah? How did he seem to you?" asked the security man.

"Ok, a little tired maybe, pre-occupied with his work, I suppose. From what Lisa tells me it's nothing less than changing the past. Why?"

"Nothing, just heard some things. Probably just rumors, that Teller's been acting sort of strange, spending a lot of time on the telescope, monopolizing it. Won't let them change the settings. It's hard to pin down though, because when I ask the people in charge they say everything's fine. It's just cafeteria talk, from secretaries and mailroom clerks, but persistent just the same. We've got to follow up everything we hear."

"He looked preoccupied," repeated Josh, remembering how Teller appeared when he first entered the lab. "He's got a lot on his mind. He was looking at images from the telescope when I walked in. Something from his past I think. I wonder if that was..."

"What?" asked Hagen as Josh went quiet and the drinks came.

"Nothing, just thinking out loud. I think I was followed last night."

"What, from the party? I told you to report anything suspicious like that."

"It was just a feeling. I didn't' see anybody. I really didn't think of it until this morning. Lisa left the party early with Teller. I stayed and entertained the guests until closing, at which point I decided to walk the short distance back to the hotel. It was just down the street. But I had the distinct feeling I was being followed."

"But you didn't see anyone?"

"No."

"Then it was probably your imagination, but don't do that again. I'm putting a detail on you starting tonight. I'll give you the call number. They'll be stationed right outside the hotel. I'll put a man on your floor as well, and somebody in the lobby, see if I can get them in as part of the staff."

"Great," said Josh, not at all pleased.

"It's amazing he's gotten away with it," observed the ex-agent out of the blue.

"What?" replied Josh.

"I mean was able to keep control of the whole thing after what he did."

"You mean Teller? Well, you're the one who helped get him pardoned. It didn't hurt that he gave back all the money and is the only one who understands how the thing works. I don't think they had many alternatives."

"I don't know. Bigger fish than he went down. Look what happened to the Secretary of Defense."

"They were involved in the graft and political scandal. No one's electing Teller for office."

"Still, it just seems funny he got away scot free and gets to keep all the rights. You'd think they would have imposed some sort of steering committee on him or something."

"There's the board of directors. There'll be some powerful people and organizations sitting at that table tomorrow, and they'll have a lot of say in what he does. The problem is he holds most of the cards. He'll threaten to can the whole thing if he doesn't get his way. He did it once. He could do it again."

"Someone should call his bluff."

"Well, it's too late now," said Josh, with a slight feeling of misgiving.

Later that evening Josh confronted Lisa with what had been on his mind since his meeting with Teller earlier that day. He had been waiting for her since five and had still not eaten at seven-thirty when she came in. He had wanted to approach the subject casually as they ate dinner together downstairs in the four-star hotel dining room, but he started off abruptly as soon as she came in, frustrated and angry at being stood-up.

"Where have you been?" he asked, not even waiting for her to put her bag down. "Why didn't you call? I don't mind you being late, but it's Sunday night. We were supposed to have dinner together, remember?"

"Cut the crap, Josh, I don't need this right now. You know perfectly well where I've been and what I've been doing, and you know how important it is. We'll have plenty of Sunday nights together. I had to finish getting everything ready for tomorrow's broadcast. You know how important this is to me. I'd of thought you'd be more understanding. Let's get room service, I'm bushed."

Josh didn't give her an inch, but pulled the noose tighter around his neck.

"Did Teller tell you to go out with me?"

"What?" she replied, surprised at the question. "Who told you that?"

"Ah, so you don't deny it then?"

"He may have suggested I date you, so what?"

She was tired and irritable, and didn't have time to deal with his stupid questions. She should have been a little more careful.

"Does Teller always tell you who to go out with or am I just special?"

"Josh, what's wrong with you? You're being childish. Are you trying to pick a fight with me? What's the big deal?"

"I don't like being manipulated. It's nice of Teller to give me his hand-me-downs."

"Hey, screw you, Josh. It's not like that at all."

"Why's Teller playing matchmaker? What's he to you that he should tell you who to date? What's he, your father?"

"In a way, yes, he is like a father to me. My own father practically ignored me all my life after divorcing my mother, didn't even send me a card at Christmas or my birthday. I was pretty bitter about life in general until I met Benjamin. He changed all that, gave me a reason to go on living."

"That's nice. I bet he gave you a lot more than that. Is he a good lover?"

"Josh, don't be like that. That was a long time ago. A lot has changed since then. Anyway, it's not him you have to worry about."

She hadn't meant to end it like this. She preferred more subtle methods of breaking a relationship. But she had grown weary of the dull little newspaperman with the quaint ideas and square wardrobe. While she had enjoyed their times in bed together, especially the previous evening, he was an embarrassment to be seen with in public, and being seen in public had become her whole life.

"What do you mean?" stammered Josh, already hurt before the first shot was fired.

"This isn't working. You can keep the room. I'm leaving."

"What?" Josh blurted out, bewildered and wounded. "Why? What's wrong? I thought things were going great."

"I don't have time to talk about it. I've got more important things to think about than you, Josh Banks, mister reporter man. Let's just say I've put up with my last night of being embarrassed by you in polite, intelligent society."

"You can say what you want about me, but I'm going to have the last laugh. Good luck with Teller tomorrow."

"I'm not worried about old Benjamin. If he thinks he can stand in our way he's in for a big surprise."

"What's that supposed to mean?" asked Josh. "What are you up to? You know the board can't fight him on this."

She was tired and had said too much already, but once she unburdened her soul she seemed unable to stop.

"It's all over. It's all taken care of. Don't worry about it."

"What are you talking about?"

"Nothing. It's board business. It doesn't concern you."

With that, she picked up her bag and left the room.

"I've already eaten," she said on her way out the door. "I won't be back."

"What about my press release?" Josh shouted after her. He thought he heard her say she had already had one of her staff writers do it and they wouldn't be needing him any longer.

Unbeknown even to Teller, Lisa long ago had her own agenda and she was far from alone. Lisa, who sat on the board, represented the majority view. When it became obvious that Teller was going to preempt the broadcast for his own ends, negating everything they had been working for, including recouping the billions of dollars in bailout money, she had taken measures into her own hands.

Josh was stunned. If he had heard her right, he had just been dumped and fired all at the same time. He wondered if this meant she wasn't going to be sleeping with him any longer.

He was surprised at how quickly his only real relationship since college had disintegrated before his eyes. It seemed everything in his life was falling apart, just when things were coming together. The large, expensive hotel suite began to close in around him. Soon the room was stifling and he could hardly breathe. Despite the damp wet night, he rushed out of the building.

He felt like he'd been used. The sense of loss engulfed him and made him feel empty inside. Despite his pain, Lisa's words echoed in his ears. What could she have meant? Were she and the board up to something? Were they planning on locking Teller in his apartment? Or something worse, like making him disappear again, this time for keeps? Josh wondered all these things and more as he walked the damp streets of the city. He considered calling Hagan, but the ex-FBI man had enough to worry about without Josh's vague concerns. After all, what did he have to go on? Nothing but the half-heard words from a woman as she told him he was no longer needed.

Though he loathed the thought of returning to his cold, empty hotel room, with nowhere else to go, he ended up back there near midnight. He finally dozed off in front of the TV around three AM, a man caught in the present, unwilling to relive the past, afraid to look into the future.

Chapter 26

The next morning Josh slept late and spent most of the day in bed trying to decide whether to attend the board meeting later that afternoon or hand in his resignation that morning. About noon he got a call from Tom Hagen who was still worried about death threats against Teller.

"Hey Josh, I was hoping to get in touch with you. My counter-intelligence team picked up some hard evidence of a plot to blow up the Teller-Scope building. Several people were involved. Luckily we discovered it early enough to notify city and federal authorities. They rounded up and arrested several suspects in early morning raids but I'm concerned we may have missed a few. They could be planning to continue the plot, which was scheduled for early this week, possibly today."

"It's that organized? I'd figure one lone crazy with a handgun or maybe a sniper but not something like this."

"You'd be surprised. Teller has some very powerful and dangerous enemies."

"Why do I always feel so lousy after talking to you?"

'You have no one to blame but yourself. Is Lisa there with you?"

"No, we had a fight. Apparently I've been set up."

"What do you mean?"

"Oh, never mind. It's personal. She did say something funny though, before she left and fired me."

"No. She can't do that."

"You know Teller was putting the brakes on the commercialization of the telescope, which has gotten completely out of hand with Lisa and the board's management. He's threatened to cancel or postpone the broadcast. I asked her what she was going to do. She said it was all taken care of. Not to worry."

"What did she mean by that?"

"I don't know. I was wondering the same thing."

"Great. It's bad enough I've got every crazy and fringe group in the world wanting to kill him, now his own people want to do him in?"

"I didn't say that. They probably just want to keep him from attending the event and giving his talk. You weren't there the other night. All people wanted to hear about was the telescope, but all he would talk about is this new discovery of his, something about changing things in the past. The world's not even come to grips with his last discovery and he's off on this new thing. And it's so arcane. He's not even talking about things on a normal, human level, but at the sub-atomic level, with particles and sub-particles. It must drive some on the board crazy. Especially those who want to get their money back. There's a lot at stake."

"I'm getting too old for this," said the ex-FBI man. "I'll tell the men assigned to Teller to be on alert. Maybe it wouldn't be a bad idea to cancel the broadcast. Doctor Teller in front of a live audience is the last thing I need right now."

"You and me both. I'm sure Lisa and the board would agree with us, probably for the wrong reasons. But none of us have the legal authority to stop him."

"It's not the legal ways of stopping him I'm worried about," said the security man.

"In I way I agree with Lisa. It's a shame to spoil all their work and keep this incredible thing from the public. In any case, the cat's out of the bag. The world's been told. They expect to see this broadcast. I don't think the stockholders or board members or anyone involved could live with the uproar that would result if the thing's canceled. Especially not Teller, not after what he did to build the thing in the first place. People would be justly and royally peeved. All the security in the world couldn't help him then."

"Does Doctor Teller realize that?"

"Of course, but he thinks what he's about to tell them is worth the risk. He believes it's even more earth-shaking than the telescope, though it won't be seen that way by a disappointed public. He could preempt everything talking about theorems and equations that no one but a handful of listeners would understand. I wrote up a nice tight twenty minute summary of it that Lisa helped me with. But even she doesn't truly understand it and I doubt he'll use my text. He hasn't even looked at it."

"What if they could find him mentally incompetent and unfit to carry on as CEO of the company? Could they keep him from talking then?"

"Yeah, but not from being chairman of the board and controlling owner. He could just pull the plug on the whole thing and everyone would lose."

"OK, Josh. I've got terrorists to track down. I'll double security on Teller. Let me know if you hear anything in the meantime, and tell Lisa to call me."

"Yeah, OK, sure. Take care, Tom, and thanks for everything."

Josh sat staring vacantly at the TV wondering about the events of the past year. Things had happened so fast. One minute everything was normal, the next he was caught in the most bizarre chain of events imaginable, chased by the police, wanted for murder, promoting a machine that looked back in time. It was all too incredible. He wanted his life back. He wanted things to be normal again, but knew things would never be the same after what the world was about to see in full living color. He was concerned about everyone involved, especially about Teller, who had become, like for Lisa, a father figure to him. He decided the best thing to do was accompany him to the broadcast and the preceding board meeting, and be by his friend's side.

He rushed back to Teller's apartment building and penthouse, but the scientist had already left. On his way out of the parking garage after getting his car, Josh thought he recognized Lisa's red BMW and slowed down to say hi, hoping perhaps to smooth things over. He still wasn't sure what had happened. It was Lisa all right, but she was talking to a man hanging halfway in the car through the opened driver's side window. Josh slouched down and sped out of the garage. As he looked back he could see the man's white cowboy boots. It looked like they were kissing. Suddenly, the words she had spoken before leaving made sense. Now he could see just who it was he should have been worried about.

The board meeting was being held on the top floor of the Teller-Scope building where the live broadcast would also take place a few hours later. Josh hoped he wouldn't be too late. For what, he wasn't quite sure.

The traffic was light on Storrow Drive, although it was still overcast and drizzling, the weather damp and humid, the result of a high-pressure trough just offshore. He made his way to the Teller-Scope headquarters, an imposing new structure on the green-belt and a twenty minute drive from his hotel, wondering vaguely how close the terrorists actually came to blowing up the building. From what Tom Hagen said, not very, since they were rounded up from their beds in the early morning hours. He wondered if there were members of the cell still out there.

As he approached the company's main building, he could see the large glass and steel structure with its tall radio tower standing on the roof, already a major landmark in the city. The security guards checked his badge even though they had seen him every day for the past six months. Going into the nearest elevator, he pressed the button for the top floor where the executive suites were located, and made his way to the boardroom. Opening the double doors, he entered the room. The board meeting had already begun.

The large interior had a stunning view of the city below. Teller and Lisa were there, sitting at a long, oak-paneled table, along with the other members of the board. The meeting was well underway.

Facing the room, at the head of the table, was a tall man with short blond hair who stood with his arms folded. The twelve other board members sat along each side in plush leather chairs. Josh had apparently interrupted Simeon Lovejoy's arguments. Josh found a chair against the wall and sat down.

Things had long ago stopped being fun at the quarterly board meetings. Teller, who should have been the nominal leader as Chairman, usually let Lisa do his talking for him and was content to let the lesser stakeholders fight among themselves, a tactic he had used with his original StellarScope partners to ill effect.

The bickering and power-struggles made Josh regret his participation, and was totally disheartening to one who saw so much promise for mankind in the new invention.

"That's very interesting, Simeon," said Teller when Lovejoy was finished. Josh had caught something about using the broadcast to focus on proving the existence of Jesus Christ, but little else of the suave European's discourse. "We have already considered this issue. There will be ample time to discuss these things. For now we have to focus on less controversial subjects."

"What could be more important than proving for millions that their faith and the Word of the eternal Jesus Christ is founded on the truth."

"We could just as easily disprove such notions and end this superstitious nonsense once and for all," interjected Lisa, Lovejoy's prime nemesis on the board. The two had been over this subject a hundred times and did much to disrupt any peaceful moments the board might otherwise have enjoyed. Teller said as much and sat silent for a moment.

Everyone waited for the great scientist to continue. Teller looked around the room.

"I've solved the final equation for a multi-dimensional gravitational string-field as it relates to photons that split in an infinite gravitational field. I can affect that photon back along its orthogonal amplitude and change its history. I can literally go back and change things in the past. If we can see it, we can change it. Of course, I'm talking at the subatomic level, but that's just a technicality. It's just a matter of time before we can change the past."

Teller eyes seemed glazed, his breathing shallow. He hardly looked at the people sitting around the table as he spoke, in rapid sentences that Josh had trouble following.

"It's all in the equations," he said finally. "It's all in the equations."

"Thank you, Benjamin," said Simeon, smiling at the scientist and perturbed at having his most important proposal dismissed so casually.

Josh looked at Lisa, who also seemed annoyed with her ex-lover, as if his great new discovery was just another obstacle in her path to riches and glory, totally beside the point, irrelevant as was Teller himself. The great scientist seemed not to notice.

"I've spent years building these equations and more decades solving them, but once understood, the secrets of the universe stand revealed," he informed them.

"Can you tell us what all this means," asked the Chinese representative.

Teller took a deep breath and continued.

"Simply put, I have discovered how to step back in time and effect matter at the sub-atomic level. This same approach, given sufficient time and funding, could lead to man's dream of actually affecting change in the past. For instance, it would be possible to save a person's life if you knew how they died. Say for instance, by preventing them from taking that drive or plane trip, or any number of other things that have led to so many needless tragedies. Deaths that could easily have been prevented if one had a little foreknowledge.

"Of course, there's nothing we can do about old age," he continued, "but even that might be conquered someday with my discoveries. It will be a new world, where lives that were lost and once ruined can be saved and renewed by science. Imagine, loved ones saved! We can correct God's mistakes, rectify all the senseless tragedy."

Josh was having trouble following Teller's rapid ramblings, not so much because he couldn't understand the words as he was having difficulty getting his mind around the ideas themselves. Finally, Lovejoy burst out, interrupting Teller's monologue.

"You're not actually saying you can prevent people from dying by going back into the past are you?" He was so agitated and frustrated he could hardly contain himself. "That would open up a Pandora's Box, not to mention cause some rather bizarre situations. Who's to say the opposite wouldn't happen? What's to keep someone from going back in time and killing someone else's ancestor? You could wipe out a whole branch of a family tree like that." The tall blond snapped his fingers. "You're trying to play God!" As he heard these words, Josh found himself agreeing.

"I didn't say go back in time. In any case, there is no God, don't you see?" said Teller, leaning forward and speaking forcefully. "How could God let all these horrible things happen? How could God take one's loved-ones with a stupid, senseless accident or sickness? God is a superstition. People will be free of these superstitions, free to embrace the truth now being exposed by science. We will explain everything. Infinity is within our grasp. We are the new Gods."

Teller's eyes blazed as he said this. He leaned forward over the table, the veins in his neck and temples throbbing and pulsing. He seemed like a man possessed.

Finally, Simeon spoke again.

"Thank you, Mister Teller. See ladies and Gentlemen, why it is so important to put control of these powerful technologies firmly in the hands of responsible representatives from the European community."

"Now see here," said the U.S. representative, on the board in response to the huge sums borrowed initially from the American taxpayer. However, due to the scandal it was someone from the State Department and not Defense. "If anyone's going to control this thing, it's the United States government. We paid for the damned thing."

"That is no longer the case," said Quin Je Pin, the Chinese board member. "Since then we have paid back this loan in full and then some. That is why we have this board meeting here today. There should be no talk of takeovers or a single country or group having control of this tool. But it seems our most honorable doctor has been working too hard. Perhaps we should postpone this meeting for another time."

Simeon, however, would not be denied.

"I know I speak for everyone on the board when I say that Doctor Teller is our most renowned member and is held in the highest esteem by everyone present. No one can deny his contribution. None of us would be here without him. But the stakes are too high to leave things to chance. Doctor Teller's condition is quite delicate and it is evident to all who know him that the strain of his recent work and administrative duties as Chairman have grown too burdensome for him. For his own welfare and health, several of us agree that now is the time for him to step down and take a less active role as director of the company, to concentrate solely on his scientific work."

Before Josh even had time to register his surprise, Pin and the U.S. representative, Bigsley, seconded the motion. All of the other members, except Lisa, voted along with them. Teller was out. Someone must have done some early and successful behind the scenes lobbying. Now that he seemed to have the board on his side, Lovejoy went on.

"The first order of business then is to elect a new chairman. It's obvious we need someone who can represent the widest possible group of interests, as well as the largest stakeholder."

"And who would that be?" asked Lisa, obvious taken by surprise by Lovejoy's sudden maneuver, but like a boxer dazed by a blow not wanting to show it.

"Why me of course, and the European community I represent," said Simeon. "This invention is a very powerful tool that can change man's destiny for good or ill. It is our duty to make sure this change is for the good. It is time for God's justice to rule in the world. The light of the Holy Ghost will shine on the world through the lens of the telescope, and the truly Living Jesus Christ will lead the way for the glory of God."

"Now just a minute," said Bigsley, the assistant Secretary of State. "If anyone has a right to chair this committee, it's Miss Sanders. She's done most to realize the financial potential of the project and has worked the closest with Doctor Teller. She's the only one here with the credentials to take over."

Things were happening so fast Josh was having trouble catching up.

"You can't do this!" yelled Teller, getting to his feet. "I'm in charge here. You can't, you don't have the, how dare you!" he finally stammered, too flustered for the moment to speak. The others ignored him, intent on making their own points in the ever more heated discussion.

The Chinese representative surprisingly sided with Simeon Lovejoy, more out of antipathy to a U.S. dominated board than any affinity with the Christian League's agenda, which he had just opposed. Several of the lesser board members sided with the U.S. Secretary and lobbied for Lisa's election as chairman.

"How could you," said Teller again, this time addressing his remark to Lisa directly.

"It's not me," she said in defense. "It's your own fault, you and your stupid equations, trying to bring back your dead wife. She's gone," she yelled. "She's gone."

"No!" shouted Teller, seeming to recover himself. "You're gone, all of you."

Suddenly, Teller's security detail arrived and stationed themselves around the room. They were all armed. Josh breathed a sigh of relief.

Teller continued as if nothing had happened.

"Together you all own 48.5% of Teller-Scope. I own the other 51.5%. That was the deal. If you want to get a bunch of doctors to come in here and prove me incompetent go right ahead. I can get a dozen more to say I'm perfectly sane. In the meantime, the broadcast will go on as I say, when I say. I'm going to announce my latest discovery and explain it to the world." He looked over at Josh. "I'm sorry, my boy, but I'm not going to use your prepared text. I know you and Lisa worked hard on it, but I can say it best and it will take more than the twenty-minutes you've allotted me. Don't worry, we'll devote some time to the telescope everyone's so fascinated with, but I want to use that interest to fuel my newest discoveries. What good is looking back at the past if you can't change it? I've found a way of potentially doing that."

Several on board stood up to object, but Teller waved them down. "Sit down gentlemen, and ladies. "You've all been outvoted, and because of your attempted takeover, you can all consider yourselves dismissed. Your services are no longer needed. Now I have a broadcast to give."

As usual, despite his apparent nervous condition, he had been one step ahead of his adversaries and had his men in the room at just the right moment. Once again victorious, he strode back and forth in front of the wide picture window looking out over the Boston skyline.

"The telescope will be used to further work on the Particle-Time Affector. The present invention will be used to reach back and look at the past. The next one will reach back and change it for the benefit of mankind."

As Teller spoke, rambling on about how his quantum gravitational theories would change the concept of time itself, another one of his security detail entered the room and spoke quietly with one of the other men. After conferring for a short time, three of them hurriedly left, leaving the new man and one other.

Things seemed to be in control again, but Josh wondered what the activity with the guards was about. He hoped it didn't have anything to do with the recent terrorist activity. Teller was finishing his harangue and was about to leave for the broadcast. Josh was surprised at Lisa's silence. She seemed to be taking the whole thing in stride, which wasn't like her. Then he noticed something.

The latest security guard picked up something on his head-set and after talking on the unit briefly, went over to the remaining guard and whispered something in his ear. It wasn't this that attracted Josh's attention, however. The new agent had on white cowboy boots.

Josh sat to attention. The second security man then left as the newcomer with the white boots started walking toward the front of the room where Teller stood being congratulated by those in the board who still thought they had a chance of holding their jobs. Lisa and Simeon Lovejoy weren't among them. Josh thought the man was going over to protect his charge from any potential hostile action by a disgruntled board member, but the way he was staring at Teller, with a look of such utter hatred and hostile intent, made Josh start up in alarm.

It all seemed to be happening in slow motion, though things were moving fast. He tried to yell a warning, but all that came out was a croak of anguish. It was enough to attract attention, however. Teller looked up in his direction. Josh ran toward him yelling a warning. Still in seeming slow motion, the security guard with the white cowboy boots pulled back his blazer and whipped out an oversized 45-automatic, which he fired five times point blank into Teller's chest. The force of the bullets threw the scientist back off his feet into the plate glass window, shattering it and sending him flying through it into space.

Josh was standing near Teller when the man, who was not far from them, fired the gun. The shock of seeing Teller being killed right in front of him and the noise of the concussive blasts, which almost deafened him, sent Josh reeling. He didn't recollect much of what happened after that, but had a vague recollection of someone running back into the room to shoot it out with the assassin, hitting and wounding several other board members in the process. Josh fled the scene through a back door that led to a stairwell, which he bolted down headlong, not stopping until he reached the bottom.

The same vague sense of uneasiness that had prompted Tom Hagen to forgo sleep all the previous night while the terrorists were being rounded up, prompted him to get in his car and drive to the Teller-Scope building. The sense of unease built to a climax as he got closer to the city's new landmark. He began to ponder the possibility that some of the terrorists may have slipped through the net to carry out the planned bombing, or that the group they had recently arrested was only a clever decoy, while the real terrorists carrying out the attack lay hidden. However, the agents in charge had assured him this was a very unlikely possibility. He tried calling Josh as he drove, but there was no answer. He gave up after almost crashing into a lamppost while redialing the number.

As he pulled his car into a no-parking zone in front of the Teller-Scope offices and got out, he noticed what appeared to be a crowd of people standing in front of the building, as if someone had pulled a fire alarm. As he approached the crowd one of his men, wearing a purple blazer with his security badge dangling from the jacket pocket, approached him.

"Sir, we have a situation," the man said as he came up to Hagen. Hagen's apprehension raised a notch and his heart-rate started to increase accordingly. "Someone has fallen from the tenth floor. They've been shot."

Hagen's heart skipped a beat. He followed the other man rapidly toward the knot of people. He wondered who it could be and tried to steel himself, but despite years on the job – admittedly in Internal Affairs – he had never grown used to the sight of death, especially death from a couple hundred feet up.

His breathing became rapid as he saw the crumpled form lying inert and sprawled on the pavement face up. It became shallow and difficult as he got closer and recognized who it was, and saw the five large bullet holes in his chest. There was a pool of blood, like an oozing halo, around the victim's head.

"Oh, Jesus," he said. "It's Teller." He swore again, in spite of the number of women standing around him looking at the body. At that moment, Josh grabbed him by the elbow.

"You can't help him, Tom," said Josh, coming up behind him. "He's been assassinated. One of your guys with a .45. He went flying out the window. They killed the assassin. It all happened so fast I'm almost not sure what I saw, but he was gunned down as sure as I'm standing here. There was a gunfight, although I was mostly ducking. Bullets were flying everywhere. Lovejoy and the board were trying to take over the company but he was one step ahead of them. That's when your extra security detail got here."

"That wasn't my detail. Teller had his own men there. I guess he knew what they were going to try and called my team off. He was the boss, you know. I was trying to call and tell you."

"Well, whoever it was got to him," replied Josh, as they moved away from the scene back toward the security chief's car. "I suspect Lisa."

"What do you mean?" asked the agent, looking back and forth between Josh and the gathering crowd in front of the Teller-Scope building. The First Response teams were just arriving. "You can't be serious."

"I'm dead serious," said Josh looking around nervously. "The guy who shot Doctor Teller was on his security team. At least the other men knew him. He came during the meeting and soon after three of the others left. Then the other guard left. Everything was set up from the inside. If you look at the assassin's feet you'll see white cowboy boots. That's something you don't see very often, white alligator cowboy boots, the same boots I saw sticking out of Lisa's car while the rest of him was leaning in kissing her. I saw him when I stopped to pick up Teller. He'd left, but Lisa was there with this cowboy. She must have assured him everything would turn out OK, that he would somehow get away, but like everybody else she's had anything to do with she double-crossed him as well. And why not, no sense leaving incriminating evidence around, but I know it was her. She set the whole thing up."

Hagan focused on Josh for the moment.

"Wait a minute, Josh. Those are pretty serious accusations. You should have snapped a picture with your phone or something. Why would Lisa do something like that? You said yourself you're not sure what you saw. Maybe you're mistaken."

"You should have seen it, Tom. The whole board was against him. They voted him out and were ready to put him into a mental institution but his men came in just in the nick of time and he had the last laugh. I guess Lisa infiltrated one of her boys into the group. If I know Teller, he probably had her set up his private security detail for him."

"He never did trust my men," said Hagen ruefully.

"We've got to stop them," urged Josh.

"Let me go up and see what's going on. You stay here and out of sight."

He left Josh near his car and headed up to investigate the scene of the crime.

He came back a short time later with a perplexed look on his face.

"It's like a Kafka novel up there. The police are already on the scene and have apparently solved the case. They have a motive. It seems this guy was acting alone. He was a suspect in a homicide that took place last summer. He must have been planning this thing for a very long time and somehow got on Teller's private security squad. They searched his computer and found several files having to do with the telescope. Most of them are saved articles that focus on the telescope's potential for solving crimes. If you could look back say a few months or a year, and see what really happened to some murder victim, you might eliminate a good deal of crime overnight. They believe this guy was afraid they would use the telescope to go back and see that he killed his business associate. He figured if he murdered Teller, the only one who really knew how to use the thing, it would then be useless and he'd be safe from prosecution."

"That's ridiculous," replied Josh. "That's what Lisa and her gang want us to believe. She's behind it I tell you. She set it up and concocted the cock-and-bull story. How do you suppose they got all that information so quick? It didn't happen more than ten or fifteen minutes ago and they've already got this guy's life story. Not even the FBI works that fast, let alone Boston Homicide. We've got to stop them. This telescope has driven them all out of their minds. They're all trying to take it over and use it for their own gains."

At this point Josh was sounding a little crazy himself, but then again what he was saying made sense. There was a lot at stake.

"OK, take it easy. You're probably in a state of shock. That must have been quite traumatic."

"I'll say. It's the worst thing I've ever seen. Poor Benjamin. That great genius, that great man, oh, my God. This is terrible."

"Easy, Josh. It's OK. There's nothing you or I could have done. It was bound to happen. You say the guy you saw with Lisa had white leather cowboy boots?"

"Yes," said Josh staring back. "I just remembered something else. As I was trying to warn Teller and he looked up and saw the guy coming at him with the gun, and saw I was going to try and jump in the way. He held me back and said something. I wasn't sure what at the time, because the gun went off at that moment, but now I know what he said. 'Destroy it. For God's sake destroy it'. I think he wanted me to pull the plug."

"What do you mean, pull the plug?" asked Hagen.

"When I first met Doctor Teller and he took me to his hideaway, he mentioned his failsafe device. In the early days of the project, he had anticipated a hostile takeover attempt, much like what just happened. In the event he lost control of the telescope he had planted small explosive devices in all the controllers and servo-mechanisms sent out into space. This switch was set to detonate all of these bombs. It was his way of erasing it all in case it fell into the wrong hands. It's in his bunker."

Hagen said nothing for several minutes.

"Josh, do you know what you're saying?" he said finally. "I can't let you do that, let alone be part of it. "

"It's what he wanted," Josh assured him. "He told me where it was and that I might have to do it someday. I think he realized the whole thing was a mistake. That we humans weren't meant to look back at the past like that."

Tom Hagen was about to object again, when two security guards from the company approached them.

"Excuse me, sir. He'll have to come with us."

"What do you mean, he'll have to come with you?" said Hagan, a little annoyed at their preemptive manner. "I'm talking to the man. What do you want with him?"

"He's wanted for questioning by the police," said one of the guards. "They're saying someone may have paid this guy to kill the Doctor, and it could have been this individual. We need to take him with us."

"You aren't taking him anywhere. Do you remember who I am? You both report to me. I'll handle the police."

"Sir, Miss Sanders and the board are our bosses now, and that includes you."

"Lisa," snorted Hagen. "Who died and made her God?"

The two men looked back at the scene beneath the Teller-Scope building where they could see the dead body of Benjamin Teller being wheeled away on a gurney.

"Who said that I was involved?" asked Josh, shocked at the accusations. "He was assassinated. The board is involved or someone on it. They had just voted him out of his position and tried to take over his company, for God's sake. It had nothing to do with me. Who in hell told you I paid to have my friend killed?"

"Everyone," said the guard.

Josh couldn't think, his mind was so cramped with anger and fear. He could only look at Tom Hagen with a pained, pleading expression.

"Josh is with me. The police can question him when I'm through. You're both dismissed."

The men stood where they were, uncertain what to do next.

"We were told to bring Mister Banks back with us. You can come back with him if you want, but we aren't going without him."

"You boys want to go a round with me?" Hagen said ominously, his voice full of venom, his eyes narrowed. "Get out of here!" he bellowed.

Both men turned on their heels and left.

"Something weird's going on," said Josh.

"You're telling me," said the security chief. "Since when do we take orders from Lisa Sanders? Where did you say you wanted to go?"

Chapter 27

"They're all crazy," said Josh, for the twelfth time, as he and Tom Hagen drove west up Route 2. The bizarre scene of the boardroom played out in his mind like a deranged soap opera, each character adding another plot-turning twist to an already unreal situation. He wondered how he could have gotten mixed up in all this. Then he remembered how it happened, how the slow chain of events and happenstances overwhelmed him before he had a chance to realize what was occurring.

Suddenly Josh was overtaken by a feeling of self-pity, as he was washed by a wave of sadness that almost made him want to cry. The tendency he'd had as a youth to feel sorry for himself had never really left him. Now he was bathed in it like a cold sweat. The worst of it was the constant realization that he had been used. That when he finally thought he had found someone to share his life with, it had turned out to be a lie. How could he have been so deceived? For all he knew, the whole thing was one big lie. We're all being manipulated, he thought.

Teller had been playing God, Lisa the Anti-Christ, while each member of the board was trying to use the past and the technology of the future for their own ends, whatever the cost. Well, no one would be using it for anything if Josh had anything to say about it.

"You know how to get there?" he asked Hagen who was driving.

"Yeah, I think so. We can get off at 62 in Concord and head south."

"Is everything still intact?"

"As far as I know. Teller wanted it kept as he left it. They were going to turn it into a museum."

"Anything for a buck," observed Hagen.

Hagen took the exit at Route 62 and headed through back roads and country lanes in the direction of Sudbury. As they approached the center of the quaint New England town - four roads meeting at an intersection with large white buildings on each corner - they saw a State Police car sitting at the light.

When Hagen made a right and headed west, the Statie's lights blinked on and started flashing. The ex-FBI man slammed his foot on the pedal and sped down the road. Cars swerved out of his way as he navigated the twenty-five mile per hour lane going fifty-five. Instead of turning at the junction toward the Regional Emergency Center, where several cars were halted at a stop sign, he continued straight down the road they were on. Gaining speed, they saw the state police car, its siren blaring and its lights flashing, giving chase behind them.

"There's another entrance to the place down here," announced Hagen, as he raced the car up the small narrow road, whizzing past numerous vehicles, far exceeding the speed limit and violating every traffic law in the book. "We want the South entrance. It's closer to the bunker."

Just then a helicopter flew into view, low and right over the road.

"Crap," exclaimed Hagen. "That's going to make things difficult."

"What are we going to do now?" asked Josh.

"I don't know, but they sure must want you bad."

"We need to throw them off. We'll never make it like this."

"What do you have in mind?" Hagen asked, barely negotiating a sharp turn in the road and then another.

"Keep going when we reach the entrance. Don't stop. A short way past the reservoir, there's a sharp right where the road goes along the lake. It's easy to miss. The Staties might go right by it. It goes under the trees for some distance. That's where Teller and I went in the first time. There's a hidden trail. We might be able throw them off. I'll jump out and you keep going. By the time they figure out I'm not with you, if they ever do, I'll have done what I need to do."

"Sounds good, just let me know when it's coming up."

The road twisted and turned at this point, making several sharp S-curves, as it ran past a large reservoir.

'Ready, here it comes. Slow down. You're going too fast."

Tom Hagen almost didn't see it, as the side road appeared immediately after a sharp left turn that rose over a slight hill. The police car was less than thirty yards behind them, but hidden by the curves and rise of the land. Tom slammed on the brakes and jammed the wheel to the right, skidding the car expertly around the corner and down the side road.

"They teach us that at the academy," he bragged.

"I don't see anyone behind us," observed Josh. "They must have driven past the turn-off."

"It won't take them long to figure out what happened and circle back."

The helicopter, which had veered off because of the high tension wires and tall trees at this point in the road, could be heard somewhere overhead, but could not be seen through the intervening branches of the thickly-leaved trees.

"Just up here," said Josh, "where the lake comes up to the road, there. Slow down. Here, stop!"

Hagen slammed on the brakes and the car skidded to a halt. Without saying a word, Josh jumped out and quickly disappeared through a clump of trees. Hagen gunned the engine and sped on down the road.

Jogging along a trail into the woods, Josh was soon hidden in thick pines, well out of sight of the road, moving along the same trail he and Teller had walked along that New Year's Day. It seemed much longer than six months ago. Even after that short time span, Josh hoped he'd remember how to get to Teller's bunker.

Following the trail, he soon found the spot where the side path, hidden by a large overgrown bush, split off from the main track. He followed this and soon came to the barbed-wire fence, which he followed until he came to the spot where a gaping hole allowed easy access to the old military research area. There he stood for a moment trying to get his bearings. A deserted road ran to his left and right, along the twelve-foot high fence. A tarmac lane led straight ahead through a bower of trees fringed by old telephone poles, their wires hanging in disarray.

Josh wished he had brought something to drink, as he started moving down the road ahead of him. He soon reached the old railroad bed and followed it into the forest to his right. Soon after that he reached the bunker. Much to his dismay, a large padlock had been placed on the metal latch of the big steel door.

In the early days, while Teller was setting up his clandestine operations, even before he had decided to leave the Peeble project, he had anticipated the possible necessity of destroying it all. Accordingly, he had enabled the destruction of the whole thing from his bunker. He would destroy the telescope if they tried to take it away from him. Connected via an underground cable from the bunker to the defunct weather station where it would transmit the signal that would begin the destructive process, the little red button lay concealed under his ornate oriental rug. Once pressed, it would cause, one by one, each telescope, mirror, and servo-mechanism throughout the galaxy to be destroyed, all 132,000 of them. All Josh had to do was get inside the bunker. As he examined the lock his hopes of doing so diminished rapidly. He wished Tom was here. At least he could have shot the damned lock off.

"Get away from there," a voice said from behind him.

Josh whirled in alarm. There facing him was Lisa Sanders. She had a gun in her hand.

"Lisa! What are you doing? Are you mad?"

"Get away from the door, Josh. I'm not going to let you destroy the telescope and all we've done. I'll kill you first. Now move."

Josh stood where he was, not so much out of obstinacy as the fact that there was nowhere for him to go. He was standing at the top of the concrete platform in front of the door. She was at the bottom of the stone steps leading up. The only place for him to go was down the steps toward her, and Josh had no intention of doing that, not when she was standing there pointing a gun at him.

"Lisa, have you gone crazy? The door's locked. I can't get in. Anyway, I don't know what you're talking about. I'm here to get Benjamin's papers. You're acting crazy. Now please, put down that gun and tell me what's going on."

"You know damned well what's going on. Neither you nor anyone else is going to steal the telescope from me. Now that Benjamin is gone, it's mine, not Simeon's, not the Chinese, not our government's. It's mine."

"Sure, Lisa, anything you say, just put down the gun. Do you have a key?"

She stood there for a moment, but did not turn the barrel of the weapon from Josh's midsection.

"Don't patronize me," she said. "You're lying and I know it. I know what you're up to, you sniveling little coward. You want to destroy the greatest discovery since Relativity. You're not going to deny me what is by all rights mine. Neither you or Simeon or anyone is going to take it away from me. You're one of those who want to perpetuate the old myths and superstitions. You're afraid of what we may find. Maybe you're afraid of what we'll find in your past. Is that the problem, Mister Joshua Banks?"

"Oh, come off it, Lisa. You're nothing but a crass opportunist. You think looking back at the past is the secret to happiness? I've got news for you, there's nothing in the past but a long history of mistakes and regrets. If I thought we'd really learn anything I'd say go ahead, but it's just the opposite. You're all so intent on using the technology to further your own views or stuff your pockets, or lord it over those with less power. It makes me sick. Shoot me if you want. I'm so stinking tired of this whole mess I don't care anymore, but I'm not the only one who knows about the failsafe device. Sooner or later someone's going to put an end to this whole thing and the sooner the better."

"Josh, you can't hold back progress. You can't turn back the clock. It's like trying to plug a dike with your thumb, it just can't be done. The momentum for progress is just too strong. That's why I'm fighting Simeon and others on the board who want to use it to brainwash people. We only want to use the telescope for what it was originally intended, pure scientific research. The whole board is behind me."

"What about Simeon? Is that why you're here all alone? Simeon's taken over hasn't he? That's why you're flying solo. You're out and he's in. You're trying to preempt him from the bunker, just like Teller did when he went into business for himself."

"Work with me, Josh. Let's work together to beat them. You can't possibly believe in all the hogwash Lovejoy was sprouting. Can you believe him? He's trying to create a whole new world order, with him at the helm. We're looking into his background. He's not who he says he is, that's for sure."

"Who are these *we* you keep talking about? Speaking of backgrounds, exactly who are you working for?"

"Scientists, like Teller and people like you, who are tired of all the lies and superstitions. People who want to see the telescope available to the world, not hidden away in some research facility. People who want to see it used for socially beneficial things."

"You're all the same, as far as I'm concerned. You're talking out of both sides of your pretty mouth. I don't believe a word you say. You're just in it for the buck. Who do you think you're kidding? You've perverted the very science you claim as the savior of mankind, perverted it for your own gains. We should be looking forward not backward, outward at the stars and new worlds, not at the past, at what has been."

"I'm not arguing with you any more. Come down from there."

"Why did you tell them I paid to have Teller murdered? Why are you trying to frame me? I saw you with that cowboy, you know."

"Framing you was Simeon's idea. He was afraid you would spread misleading and damaging reports about the take-over and perhaps ruin his plans for the second coming. And what are you talking about? What cowboy? I had nothing to do with Benjamin's murderer. The police want us all for questioning. I'm not going to let that conniving bastard, Simeon, get away with this."

"Then join me in destroying this thing, so that he and those like him won't get their hands on it."

"No, never. I'll kill you first," she said, raising the gun to aim it at his head.

Josh feared he may have said too much when he saw the crazed look in her eye.

"Hold it," said the voice of Tom Hagen, somewhere behind and to the right of Lisa. A moment later the ex-FBI man stepped from behind a large pine tree. He was holding his own gun and had it pointed at Lisa. "Put the gun down, Lisa. Nice and easy. I don't want to shoot you, but you wouldn't be the first female I've shot, so don't get any ideas."

Lisa hesitated for a brief moment then put down the gun.

"You can't let him destroy it," she said, pleading her case to the new arrival.

"Simeon's agents are right behind me," he said, picking up Lisa's gun. "He's taken control of the company and has the police working on his side. There's an all-points bulletin out on all three of us. They don't know where we are, but it won't be long before they figure it out. Where'd you get this?" he asked Lisa, looking at the rather large .44 he had just confiscated.

"It was Ben's. I took it from his apartment when I came out here looking for Josh. I knew he was coming here."

"How'd you get away from the helicopter?" Josh asked Tom, not a little curious.

"I happened to know where there was another way in a mile or two up the road from the spot you jumped off. There's a small bridge where the road curves and narrows quite a bit. I made it look like I missed the turn and drove off the bridge into the river. Then I headed back a few yards and went through a fenced-off dirt road that leads into the restricted area a couple miles up the trail from here. Dan and I used it when we came to warn you that last time. I wasn't sure I'd find the bunker. Luckily, I remembered the track that cuts through the woods near this spot."

"You got here just in time," said Josh. "Were you really going to shoot me?" he asked looking at Lisa.

She stared straight ahead and said nothing.

"Do you have a key?" Hagen asked her.

She didn't answer, but shook her head slightly in the negative. With that Hagen shot the lock clean in two.

"Shall we?" he asked, straining to pull the massive, creaking steel door open. The stale air hit them like a solid wall of noxious fumes. "Whew, we'll need to turn on the blowers. This thing's been shut up for quite awhile."

Lisa coughed as she entered the darkened space.

"Do you know where it is?" Hagen asked Josh.

"Sort of, I've never actually seen it though. There's a cable coming in under the door. Here it is. The button's at the other end of this." He pointed to a thin vanilla cable snaking along the rounded wall. He was about to follow it under the oriental carpet Teller had placed beneath the desk when Lisa suddenly sprang toward Hagen who was looking where Josh was pointing.

Grabbing a chair as she attacked, with one swift motion she brought it down sharply on the security chief's head, knocking him out almost instantly. Without hesitating, while Josh was still frozen in shock, she tackled him like a linebacker blitzing the quarterback. Josh was on his back with Lisa on top of him pummeling him with fists and elbows, trying to claw his eyes out. He was surprised at her strength and ferocity, and momentarily defenseless. Then, with a swift fit of strength, he spun her to the side and threw her off. She was on him again, however, as he staggered to his feet. Leaping on his back, she wrapped her arms around his neck. Choking off his air, she then bit him on the shoulder as he tried to fight her off. He was about to go down, when several men with weapons raised rushed into the bunker. One of them grabbed Lisa and pulled her off Josh, who was almost out of air. Falling to his knees on the floor, he could see Tom Hagen just coming to and trying to rise. Lisa was still struggling with the trooper who held her, as a second officer went to help him.

"Arrest them all," said Simeon Lovejoy walking into the dark, rounded cement structure like it was a holding cell and he was the head jailer. "They're all guilty of attempted sabotage and terrorism. They should have all been arrested a long time ago."

These words made Lisa go even more berserk. Hagen started to object and questioned their authority, but he was no longer in the Bureau and had no authority there himself. With everyone's attention occupied, Josh found himself sitting on the floor next to the wall on Teller's expensive red Oriental carpet. While everyone's attention was focused elsewhere, he casually felt the rug beneath him until he found what he was looking for.

"Get them out of here," Simeon demanded, amidst Lisa's yells and Hagen's oaths. As one of the troopers came toward Josh to help him to his feet, he quickly flipped over the carpet to expose the concrete floor and the thin wire running along the base of the wall to a small black plastic case. On the case was a red button.

"No!" yelled Lisa and Simeon simultaneously, as Josh pressed his thumb to the button as hard as he could, and kept clicking it until three troopers jumped him and tore it out of his hands. Something hard hit the back of his skull and everything went black. That was all he remembered.

Chapter 28

Josh didn't remember much of that day when he pushed the button that destroyed the most expensive deep space telescope ever built, ending the dreams of millions and the promises of the next century in this one. He did, however, remember all too well the six week court case and his six year sentence in a minimum security federal prison for destruction of government property and trespassing in a restricted area. Not to mention sabotaging an international treasure. Out in three due to good behavior and the heavy lobbying by many influential friends and supporters, one of whom was Tom Hagen, ex-FBI agent and once head of security for Teller-Scope, Josh was being released today.

Much had been uncovered during the trial, much of it to the detriment of those on the board of the now defunct company who had tried to discredit Teller and take over his work. When it was discovered that the Vatican was behind the maneuvering of their agent Simeon Lovejoy, the scandal was huge and made the pedophile priest affair seem tame in comparison. The financial impact of the latter was not nearly as severe as the losses the church suffered this time. However, they did benefit from substantial evidence accumulated by Simeon for the existence of the historical Jesus Christ and the discredit of those scientists who had tried to conceal or cover up this evidence.

While Simeon and the board were guilty of much, it was Lisa alone who turned out to be responsible for Teller's murder. The motive had been the oldest in the book, jealousy and greed.

Josh was met on his release by Dan Little-Wolf, who had helped him escape in the blizzard with his dog team. With him, much to Josh's surprise was Maria Cavello.

"How's it feel to be a free man?" asked Dan, who greeted him with a smile and a handshake. "Tom would have come, but his kid's graduating from college today. He's in DC. He sends his best."

"Hi, Dan. Nice of you to come. I guess I don't feel too bad for a man with no job and a prison record, with little prospects and a bleak future."

"I wouldn't say that," replied Dan. "You've got a great story to write and a lot of friends. I'd say you were pretty well off."

"Hi, Maria," said Josh, sliding next to her in Dan's pickup. "How's everything?"

"Good. I guess I can't complain after all that happened."

"I hope you didn't come all this way just to see me sprung from jail. What brings you out here?"

"When Dan phoned and told me you were getting out today and he was coming to pick you up, I just had to come. I wanted to see you. I'm sorry I got you in so much trouble. I never had a chance to thank you for helping us. You just got spirited away that day and I never saw you again."

"Yeah, a lot has happened. It's real nice to see you."

She smiled at him shyly. He looked at her again and decided then and there she really was his type after all."

"How's Robby?"

"Good," she said, smiling even wider.

She didn't move away when his arm touched hers and their knees came together accidentally, as Josh got settled in the seat beside her.

"Where would you like to go?" asked Dan. "How about a nice home-cooked meal?"

"That would be great," said Josh. "Have you heard anything about the telescope? Are they going to try and rebuild it?"

"No, you pretty much put an end to that. Without Teller, no one's been able to duplicate the necessary equations. You know he never wrote any of it down. The only thing we have are his lecture notes and public talks. It's all lost."

"What about Lisa," Josh asked. "She must have known a lot."

"No, she knew how to operate it, but that's all. I understand she was really clueless. Anyway, she might as well be a leper. She's completely discredited. She'll be away for a very long time, in any case."

"You should be proud of yourself, Josh," said Maria, who supported his actions, as did her brother, Jeremy, who now lived with her and was helping support the child "It wasn't right what they were doing. We should be looking forward, not back, out to the stars, not back at Earth's past. I'm glad you destroyed it."

"Me too," said Dan. "There's nothing in our past I want to see, just broken promises and misery, although I would have liked to have seen some of the Little Big Horn in the summer of 1876."

"I don't know," said Josh. "I keep telling myself I did the right thing, but sometimes I wonder. It's like I killed the greatest living thing on the planet when it was only a baby. Who knows what would have become of it, what would have happened if it lived, if Teller had lived for that matter? He would have changed the world."

"Yeah, but for better or worse?" asked Maria.

"They say there was one scope that wasn't destroyed," Dan informed him, as if the news had no import.

"What?" exclaimed Josh. "There's still a piece of it working?"

"Well, it's only a rumor, nothing substantial. No one's been able to prove anything, you know, just one of those conspiracy theories you're always complaining about. They're saying one portion of the telescope wasn't destroyed and was still beaming back images from some distant star system. The explosives detonated all right, but it didn't destroy the scope, it only knocked it out of alignment. Instead of looking back at Earth, it was looking at and magnifying light from another planet. They say it looked so much like Earth, it took them awhile to notice. It has less water and larger ice-caps. They say it has two moons. They're also saying it has intelligent life, cities and highways and everything."

Josh looked up at the stars just starting to form in the young night sky and thought of the vast distances of space, and how it was a mirror reflecting back our dreams and thoughts. He realized at that moment that every event, everything that had transpired on this planet from its first days three billion years before, through the ages to the present, including his own childhood, all those images, born of light, will never die and never grow old, as light itself never dies or ages, but like the ripples in a pond keep flowing, forever outward. At some point in space, at some point in time, they will always be out there somewhere. And he knew that if he went far enough, he'd find himself.

The End

To my dearest wife, for her devotion and understanding, her tender heart and loving support. If ever a wife lived up to her vows, it's my Kathleen. To her I dedicate this book with love.

www.ingramcontent.com/pod-product-compliance
Lightning Source LLC
Chambersburg PA
CBHW070336260626
47160CB00003B/1059